Waking Dreams:

The Torment of Colin Pierce

By JD Kaplan

Mom & Dad,

This would never have happened without you,

Joel

Copyright © 2013
All rights reserved by the Author.

This novel is entirely a work of fiction. The people contained within these pages live and breathe only there—and perhaps on the Dreamside.

The author can be reached via email at jaydel@gmail.com, and found at http://www.thedreamside.com.

Cover design by Emily Kaplan.

This novel uses the Gandhi Serif font, which was created by LIBRERIAS GANDHI S.A. DE C.V., and freely distributed at http://www.fontsquirrel.com.

Acknowledgements

I've been extremely lucky. I've had help from many talented and insightful people. Forgive me if I forget someone.

Thanks to Alison Wise and Jeff Cross, both extremely talented writers, for giving me wonderful comments and criticism.

Thanks to Esther Kaplan for reading the evolving manuscript in so many versions. Her technical and artistic insights were invaluable.

Finally, thanks to my wife Emily. Without her feedback, support and inspiration, this story remains locked in my brain.

For my wife Emily and our two children, Theo and Riley. My own Dreams made real.

Part 1: Dreamer

Crash

Colin stood at the tail end of the cabin next to the tiny bathroom closets decorated with vacancy lights and stern warnings from various government agencies that no smoking related activities would be tolerated. The interior of the McDonnell-Douglas MD-80 stretched out before him, a long cylindrical tunnel, baggage compartments snugged into the graceful curve of the top of the cabin, and chairs in tight rows all the way to the front like soldiers in formation. The cabin was cool and clean, and smelled of the oppressive freshness of canned air. And it was quiet and still. Too quiet and still. There was no uncomfortable feeling of pressure, no sense of motion, and no throbbing noise of the engines. Nothing to interrupt the absolute silences that filled the empty space.

Colin had no idea how he'd gotten there.

The airplane was completely empty of passengers or flight crew. He decided to take a seat but as he raised his foot to step forward, people appeared in the seats, the wave of their sudden materialization rippling away from him toward the front of the plane. At the same time the muted roar of the engines bloomed into a white wall of noise and his head was surrounded by the thick pressure of high altitude, almost painful in its suddenness.

The flowing wave of passengers appearing in their seats gave it away; he was dreaming. That realization eased the tension that had grown in the pit of his stomach. He wondered if he had a seat and began to search, walking slowly up the aisle, occasionally putting his hands on the backs of seats to keep his balance when the plane shuddered and shimmied slightly with the motion of flight. When he was about halfway to the curtain that separated first class from the rest of the passengers, he saw a single empty seat on the aisle of the right side, and a woman and child sat in the other two seats. It was the only open seat he saw so it must be his. As he got closer he recognized the back of the woman's head.

Slowing down he peeked around at the front of her face. Yes, he was right—it was Marianne. Another clue that he was dreaming—she wasn't supposed to be on this airplane either. Not yet. They were both supposed to be at home sleeping in their own bed.

The dream was so realistic that he might not have recognized it for a dream. Everything felt so natural and complete, with no blurry edges hiding the parts of the dream that didn't matter. Even the sudden appearance of the passengers, the noise and the cabin pressure hadn't bothered him. But even though he knew this wasn't real, he still felt nervous and scared for his girls. He never liked when they travelled without him—he was always afraid something would happen to them. That would just ruin him.

Colin sat down beside her and studied her, unable to look away. As always he was captured by her beauty—the soft brown flow of her hair pulled back in a tight, practical pony tail, revealing the graceful curve of her neck. She must have felt the weight of his stare because she glanced over at him. Her hazel eyes were sharp and intelligent with a promise of warmth and laughter. She arched an eyebrow at him in surprise.

"Colin," she said. "What are you doing here?" He had no good answer for that.

"I think I'm dreaming, Mari," he said. "Are you dreaming, too?"

"No," she said and leaned in for a quick kiss. As always the soft touch of her lips warmed him. "We're going to visit my parents. You know that." She gave him an admonishing smile that quickly gave way to a small frown that knit her brow. "Why are you sleeping in the middle of the day? You're not sick are you?" Her strange acceptance of his presence only reinforced his conviction that he was asleep and dreaming.

That was Mari through and through—ever grounded and strong. Add in her intelligence and snarky sense of humor and Colin had found her irresistible from the moment they first met. Her strength was an inspiration to him. Nothing daunted Marianne. Any trouble or difficulties that arose she faced squarely and efficiently. She referred to the unplanned surprises that life offered up as opportunities. Colin liked to tease her about that. If one of the kids spilled something, he'd smile and ask if this was another opportunity. She usually laughed along with him and then told him deadpan that it was going to be an opportunity to kick his butt if he didn't watch his step.

"I thought you were leaving Friday, Mari?"

"It is Friday, Col. Are you okay?"

"Sure, sure." He forced a smile but inside apprehension roiled in his gut. That was how dreams worked, wasn't it? Knowing it was a dream didn't stop the flood of emotion brought on by the situation he found himself in.

He looked beyond Marianne and saw Emma in the window seat. She was wearing a little flowered sundress with a T-shirt underneath it. She stared out the window while kicking her feet slightly, the merry click-clack of her flip flops smacking her heels barely carrying over the noise of the airplane.

She was their younger daughter. He'd always wanted children, and had dreamed of having boys that he could roughhouse with, play catch, go to all their sporting events. But instead of sons, he got daughters.

Emma was vivacious, strong-willed, and playful—a little sprite moving through their lives breaking things, testing them and most of all showing them all how to live life to its fullest. She was a smaller, younger version of Marianne.

As if she felt his eyes on her, she looked over, saw him and her eyes lit up.

"Daddy! I'm flying on an airplane."

"I know, sweetie." This time his smile was warm—not forced at all. "Do you like it?"

"Yes, it's really cool." She leaned toward him and stage whispered. "But Buddy is very scared." She held up her little stuffed animal unicorn.

"Why is he scared?"

"Oh, he's scared of lots of things," she answered. "He is scared of aliens and monsters. I tried to tell him there're no monsters or aliens on the plane, but he is scared anyway. Knowing doesn't always help."

"Well, maybe if you just hug him he'll feel better."

"That's what I'm doing."

"Is it working?"

"Oh, so far, so good." She favored Colin with a quick smile and then turned to stare out the window. Colin glanced across the aisle, past an older man and found Sidney in the window seat, staring out the window. He could only see the back of her head, but his heart warmed as he watched.

She was her father's daughter—a chip off the old block, Marianne liked to say, usually with a wry smile and a shake of the head. Sidney, at eleven years of age was tall and willowy, with dark brown hair and fair skin. Her eyes were steel gray, which lent her expression an intensity that was belied by the dazzling smile she fixed on Colin all the time.

She was quiet and thoughtful—always wrapped up in her mind. Her fantastic imagination ran at full speed. When she'd been a couple of years younger, she'd had the tendency to embellish stories, turning the most trivial of events into sweeping epic tales full of dragons, fairies and princesses. Colin and Marianne used to amuse themselves trying to identify the exact moment in the story where fact gave way to fiction. It wasn't easy. She might start out talking about a spelling test at school and end up talking about a beautiful heroine defeating an evil dragon and rescuing the handsome yet helpless prince, but the transition was not as clear as one might think. Where some parents might stifle that imagination and try to drag her back to reality, Colin and Marianne encouraged her to grow and explore the wild creativity of her mind. They both considered it the greatest of gifts.

Sidney, and later Emma, had showed Colin he didn't need sons after all. At 33 years of age he was married to a wonderful woman, had two intelligent and precocious daughters, and was experiencing the first successes of his chosen profession. He'd always wanted to be an author and in the last few years had been able to quit his job and devote himself to his writing full time. Two books published and another in the works. Life was on track.

It was like a dream, and a small part of him wondered how long that could last.

Finally he looked back at Marianne.

"Well, this is a good dream, at any rate," Colin said and felt rather than saw her smile. Stranger than finding himself in the airplane was that she so readily accepted his assertion that he was dreaming. It made no sense at all. She was so practical and logical that she tended not to buy into more fantastic ideas. To her, monsters, vampires and ghosts were just fun bits of fiction. The idea that they just might be real struck her as completely ridiculous. If he really thought about those things, Colin would also have to admit it was unlikely they existed, but at a gut level he was much readier to accept the strange and bizarre.

The plane interrupted his thoughts with a sudden lurch and shudder before settling down again. His heart popped up into his throat and then back down leaving him breathless. Marianne squeezed his hand once. He glanced at her and she gave him a little smile. He'd never really liked flying. Intellectually he knew that the odds of a crash were so remote that it shouldn't even worry him. But fear wasn't a rational emotion, of course.

He looked beyond Marianne and saw Emma looking back with wide eyes, and then a smile to match.

"That was a big bump!"

"Yes, it was, honey." He managed a laugh even as the butterflies in his stomach turned into the first hints of outright fear.

She hugged the stuffed animal tight again. "There, there, Buddy. It was just a bump. Everything is fine."

There was a click and a noisy burst of static over the intercom.

"Ladies and gentlemen, as you can tell, we're headed into some rough weather and will experience some turbulence..." The captain's voice was cut off as the plane lurched again. This time there was nothing slight about the dip and shake—the world dropped out from under them. Colin waited for the plunge to stop and the plane to stabilize again, but instead the nose of the plane fell further and other passengers cried out and gasped. The engines shrieked—a high whining sound—and Colin swallowed hard against a rush of nausea. He looked over at Marianne. She wore a mask of grim determination—not a hint of fear. She had pulled Emma close and squeezed Colin's hand again, this time harder.

"Colin," she spoke loud enough to be heard over the noises of the cabin. "Go sit with Sidney." She gestured past him with her chin and he turned to see Sidney gripping the arms of her seat. The elderly man that sat beside her looked at Colin with surprise on his face and then just faded away, leaving the seat empty. Sidney glanced across at Colin and the terror evident on her face was heartrending.

"Daddy? I'm scared."

Colin pushed himself up and fought the growing force of gravity enough to slide across the aisle to sit beside her. He reached over and took one her hands and she gripped his tightly.

"It's okay, Hon." Somehow he managed to force a soothing quality into his voice despite the roiling fear in his gut. He wasn't afraid for himself as much as he was for his three girls. "It's just turbulence. It will be over in a few moments." The white noise of the airplane had turned into something louder and more desperate, the whine of the engines becoming a high pitched, desperate wailing. Around the cabin other passengers were yelling and screaming as the angle of descent increased.

Colin glanced back across the aisle at Emma and Mari. The girl looked stricken and clung to her mother tightly. Colin couldn't hear what Mari was saying but he knew her voice would be calm and soothing. He could see that Emma was not reassured and as she squeezed closer to her mother the first tears slid down her face. Colin wondered how Mari could be so calm and collected. She turned to look at him and her face had gone white, her eyes wide with her own fear. She reached across the aisle and took Colin's hand, squeezing hard.

"We're crashing," she mouthed at him, her eyes filled with certainty. He shook his head.

"No, we'll be fine. They'll pull out of this any minute now." But he knew she could hear the lie in his voice, even over the chaos of the cabin.

"No, Colin. We're going down. This is what happens next." She spoke with a surety that was chilling. "I love you, but you need to wake up. Before it's too late. The girls will need you. Take them with you." That completely confused him—take them where? And through his confusion came despair and he shook his head.

"No." He gasped and clutched at the armrest on the aisle side harder. "I won't leave you. I can't leave you." The idea was worse than dying.

"You must, Colin. Wake up now." Her voice took on a hint of iron and she fixed him with her best stern glare. The airplane was nosed down at such an angle that it seemed he was looking down a shaft, with the cockpit door at the bottom. With a sharp jolt the plane bucked and lurched sideways, buffeted by the sheer violence and speed of their descent. What an inadequate word turbulence was, he thought.

Abruptly a metallic ripping sound rent the air and painful pressure squeezed his eardrums. Wind rushed past him, blinding and deafening him, tearing at his hair and clothes, stinging his eyes. Where their window should be a gaping hole opened out into cold air, revealing a jagged stretch of metal where the wing had been. The pressure of their insane descent had ripped it loose entirely, pulling off a section of the fuselage. He couldn't do anything but stare in shock at the expanse of blue sky. Something smashed into the back of his seat, jarring him and he looked up in time to see a man sucked out the hole and into the sky. Then there was another violent shake and then a loud cracking sound and the deep blue rushed at him. Time seemed to stretch out and in the long moment that it took for the seats to rebound off the side of the hole, tearing away more metal, Colin realized what was happening. As his hand was torn away from Marianne he screamed inarticulately.

As he and Sidney were sucked out into the sky, still belted in firmly to their seats, Colin smashed into the side of the jagged hole and blacked out for a moment. When his vision cleared they were already far from the plane. Around him the noise of the rushing air was almost soothing compared to the stark terror of the airplane. The stink of sweat and fear that had appeared in the cabin moments after the first bucking of the plane was replaced by the fresh clean air of the high altitudes.

He never had a chance to look back and see Marianne and Emma. They were just gone.

The icy cold of the air seemed to cut through him to his bones and he held on tightly to Sidney's hand as she shrieked and clung to his arm. With his other hand he gripped the armrest thinking inanely that everything would be okay if they could stay in their seats. They spun in the air with the ground, sky and the shuddering bulk of the airplane twisting past them. Their descent was so wild that he wasn't even looking at the plane when he heard a crashing boom, and a huge hand swatted them violently to the side, taking them out of their spin and briefly slowing their descent. Colin craned his head and saw that the plane had simply exploded in midair and now flaming chunks shot away from the hot core of the explosion, leaving dark trailers of smoke. Metal and other things arced away from the explosion like fireworks blooming a huge smoking flower.

His stomach flipped and he swallowed hard to keep from vomiting.

Dreaming, he thought incoherently. *Wake up.* A thought tried to push through his panic and fear. It niggled at the back of his mind, slipping out of his grasp when he tried to bring it to the front. Something about waking up. A dream.

Then it clicked into place.

A dream. If this is a dream, can Sidney wake up, too?

Maybe that was what Mari had meant. Desperation turned him to face Sidney, shouting over the wind so that she could hear him.

"Sid, you've got to wake up." He didn't know for sure if she heard him but she looked at him with terror etched onto her face and abruptly faded away, leaving Colin staring at her empty seat. He wondered if she had woken up—if his idea had been right. Something seemed to click in his mind, some huge idea that he couldn't touch or see. But the world screaming and rushing around him tore it away from him before he could wrap his mind around it.

Rage filled his mind and he fought his helplessness and searched wildly for something he could do to change all of this. But there was nothing. He was losing everything. Everything. With that realization his rage fled and he was left with despair and resignation. He relaxed in the seat and closed his eyes, trying to focus only on the fact that Sidney was safe. He hoped she was safe.

Suddenly, over the deafening wind, Colin heard Mari's voice, clear as a bell. "Wake up, Colin. Sidney will need you." He opened his eyes and looked around wildly but there was no sign of her at all. He knew she was right, so he closed his eyes and concentrated on waking up. Nothing happened.

Then as his frustration began to rise, he felt a hand take his and he opened his eyes and looked at Sidney's seat again. Instead of Sidney a young woman sat, looking at him intently and cupping his hand in hers. She wasn't even belted in but sat easily on the seat as if the wind and cold couldn't touch her. In a heartbeat the wind and cold disappeared and they were falling silently through the air. If not for the ground rushing up to meet them they might have been hanging in midair for all the sensory input that remained—even the ground was so far below them that it was impossible to measure it approaching.

"Colin Pierce, it is time for you to wake up," she said and her voice was clear and bright. She was short and thin, wispy almost. Her hair was a choppy mess that managed to look haphazard and stylish at the same time. Her eyes were a startling grayish blue, irises ringed by a darker circle of gray and she didn't look scared or worried at all. He couldn't tell how old she was but she seemed younger than he'd originally thought—maybe only a few years older than Sidney. The girl gave him a soft, sad smile, reached up and put her free hand on his face.

He looked down involuntarily. They were over farmland and below them was a large farm house. They were so close that he could make out the car and tractors around the house and barn. The girl pulled his eyes back to her face and stared at him intently. As the ground hurtled up at them silently, the sound of her voice chased him awake. "Wake up now, Colin Pierce. You have much work to do."

Her words chased him out of the dream.

※

He woke up screaming, bathed in sweat, and his sheets were slick and wet against his skin. He lurched upright and out of bed and fumbled for the lamp on his nightstand, but missed and knocked it off, sending it crashing to the floor. There was a quick blue flash as the bulb popped.

"Shit, shit, shit." The words poured out of him as he tried to contain his panic. He remembered the dream in agonizing detail. "Just a dream," he muttered. He sat back down on the edge of the bed and put his head in his hands for a moment and took several deep breaths. "Just a dream."

"Colin?" Mari sounded muzzy with sleep but concern reached through. "What's wrong?" He glanced back at her and saw that she had pushed herself up onto her elbows and was looking at him. For a long moment he drank in the sight of her alive and half asleep. A thrill of relief pulsed through him and he gasped at the intensity of the feeling. She reached out and put a warm hand on the bare skin of his back. "A nightmare?"

"Yes," His heart hammered in his chest in a churning race to nowhere in particular. "Just a dream, Mari. Go back to bed."

Liar, a voice in the back of his mind said and unbidden the dream rushed back at him, the details screaming, burning and searing through him as if a fire raged in his body. He felt sick to his stomach and ran toward the bathroom, but tripped and staggered into the doorway. He barely made it to the toilet before emptying his stomach violently. After heaving a few times he slumped to the floor and put his cheek on the cool tiles. The layer of sweat on his body turned cold right away and he began to shiver.

"Colin, Honey," Colin glanced up from where he sprawled and found Mari watching him, concern and worry on her face. His heart leapt into his throat again as he remembered the explosion—the end of her life in his nightmare. Standing before him she brought back his earlier sense of relief. The voice in his mind chanted over and over *they're all right, they're alright*.

He pushed himself awkwardly to his feet and rushed out the door. Mari stood out of the way as he strode—almost ran—down the hall to look into the girls' room. Each was asleep and quiet, faces relaxed with the calm of deep sleep.

They're alive. Safe.

"What's wrong, Col?" Mari had followed him down the hall. "It was that lasagna wasn't it? I hope it hadn't been in the fridge too long." He didn't want to tell her it wasn't the lasagna but as he considered it, he realized it might just have been. Perhaps the dream had been triggered by his nausea. At the moment he couldn't say which had come first.

He turned away from the girl's doorway and found her staring at him. Her hair was tousled and her eyes bleary from sleep but she was still the most beautiful woman he had ever seen. He slid to sit against the wall and forced a smile up at her.

"I don't know. It'll pass though."

"Can I get you anything? Your shirt is soaked. You must be freezing. Let's get you a fresh shirt and back into bed."

"Not yet, the cold feels good. You go back to bed and I'll be in when I'm sure I'm not going to be sick again."

She stared at him, studying his face. A small frown creased her forehead. He didn't want her out of his sight, but he really needed to just sprawl on the floor and not think.

"Okay." He heard the reluctance in her voice. "Call me if you need anything."

"I will."

She turned and walked back into their bedroom leaving Colin to try to push the dream away, trying not to remember, not to relive it again. He concentrated on physical things: the texture of the carpet under his legs, the smell of his own vomit, and the quality of the moonlight filtering in through the window to bathe the floor around him.

Eventually he stood and walked back into the bathroom. He ached all over as he moved and that pain triggered something, some nagging thought that hung just out of reach. He studied his face in the mirror. In the darkness he could make out his shape reflected back but not much in the way of detail. He reached for the light switch, but hesitated. As long as the light was off he didn't have to face what he already knew to be true. Tiredly he pulled his t-shirt off, steeled himself and flipped the lights on.

The light overpowered his senses and he squinted to protect his eyes. But then he began to see again and stared into the mirror at himself. His heart sank as he saw that his upper torso and arms were covered with fresh bruises. Every excruciating detail of the crash came back to him and the flood of sensations was almost as powerful as the emotions that clawed at him from the inside.

Suddenly, something clicked in his mind—a door unlocking and swinging wide open—and for the first time in sixteen years he remembered another nightmare. One just as real and terrifying. It had been about the two girls who'd lived across the street when he was a child. The entire nightmare came rushing back to him. It was as if there had been this empty space in his mind that he hadn't even known was there until that moment—in defense of itself his brain had carefully built highways that skirted the memories. The horrible dream. The smoke and flames. The searing, burning pain. And worst of all, the death of the Jenks twins. He'd managed to forget all of it—memories so horrible that his brain folded them up and buried them deeply in his subconscious as if the nightmare had never happened.

Until now.

Burn

Colin was fifteen years old. He wouldn't know it was a dream until later—at the moment the world was vivid and tightly bound to a sense of realism that he'd never experienced in a dream. Usually his dreams were flights of fancy or fear, and rarely constrained by the laws of the waking world. Often the dreams changed course in the middle and his mind was able to rewrite what came before so that the new course made sense. It was never perfect though. A blurred series of disjointed moments still lingered and his dreaming mind did its best to ignore them—messy artifacts of the rewriting of the dream.

In those dreams nothing was static or logical—usually Colin could tell that he was dreaming. He might still be wrapped up in the flow of the dream and the emotions it evoked, but in the back of his mind he knew that he would wake soon enough and all that had seemed logical would reveal its strangeness. Tiny drops of logic stretched along a thin thread of nonsense. The sense of the dream would linger throughout the day, details fading until only the emotions remained and then finally those too would disappear.

But this dream was different. He was sure he was really in the Jenks house. Really in the corner of the twins' bedroom. But his certainty confused him. He'd never been there before. The twins were in second grade that year—far younger than Colin. But even though he'd never been in this room, or this house, he saw the girls' bedroom in such detail that he was certain that was what that room really looked like. It made no sense.

Immediately he could tell so much about the twins. A pair of twin beds bracketed a window that looked down over the front yard. Each side of the room was filled with identical furniture. Bedside tables, dressers, even the lamps were the same—shaped like small trees with fairies revolving slowly around the tree trunk, flowers opening and closing in a slow dance—doomed to circle endlessly as long as the power and mechanisms held out.

At least until they burn. The thought came to him unbidden.

The only real difference between the two sides of the room spoke volumes about the girls. One side was neat and well organized, everything in its right place. The other side looked like a train wreck. Colin could better relate to that side—his own room was usually a chaotic mess. Something about this sole difference made the twins seem more...real.

Snugged in their beds, the Jenks' twins slept peacefully. Colin stepped forward from the dark corner until he stood between them, moving without volition as if his course were already mapped out, the placement of his footsteps already decided. As he watched the twins slumber and dream their dreams, he felt uncomfortable—he had no idea how he'd gotten here, but knew he shouldn't be watching these girls sleep. It was an invasion of their privacy that brought him to a halt, reluctant to move any closer.

He tried to back up, to leave the room and return to his own bed in his own house, but found he was frozen in place. Something was incomplete—like there was more he was supposed to see. Something had brought him to this room, and he wouldn't be allowed to leave until he witnessed whatever was going to happen. He was struck by the sense of being two different people at once. One caught up in the flow of an emerging story and the other a casual observer—one in the dream, the other watching.

Then he smelled smoke, just a slight acrid tingle in his nose, bringing him the urge to sneeze. It wasn't an unpleasant smell, but it didn't belong here—more of an intruder than Colin. That first hint of worry broke whatever held him rooted in place and he turned around and saw fingers of smoke curling under the door, questing along the wood and reaching for the ceiling. For a moment he couldn't figure out what was happening. His mind refused to process what he saw.

He knew what was happening, and that knowledge changed his nervous anxiety to the first stab of fear. And that fear burned through him edging closer and closer to outright panic, but he fought to get himself under control. Quickly a memory blew through him, hot and dry. He'd been in grade school when a firefighter had come to visit the class. He had spoken for an hour on the dangers of a house fire and what to do in the unlikely event that the students found themselves in one. The idea that most people sleep right through their death was terrifying—that they suffocated on the smoke before the first flames even reached them. Through this awful memory, Colin knew there was something he needed to do.

Stop drop and roll. Don't play with matches. Check the door? Check the door, that's it.

He crossed the room to the door and reached out gingerly and tested it. It was like touching a hot pan on the stovetop. He snatched his hand back, and licked his finger tips to ease the stinging pain. The brief flash of pain helped his thoughts settle and begin to move quickly.

If it's hot, don't open it. What next? He searched for what to do as the smoke curled up from under the door. He wracked his brain until it came to him. *Stop the smoke. Seal the door. Find another way out.*

He turned and grabbed some of the clothes that lay on the floor of Kimmy's side of the room and started shoving them into the crack at the bottom. He crammed the clothes in, using his now tender fingertips to bunch more of the cloth in and cut off the flow of smoke. For a quick moment he was relieved to see the smoke stop. But before he could even start to consider what to do next the smoke was back—thicker than before. The clothes became tinder, began to smolder, then burn, sending flames up to eat at the bottom of the door.

Wet. The clothes need to be wet.

But it was too late. The smoke was filling the room at a fast pace, turning the softly decorated room into a deathtrap.

Behind him the twins stirred in their beds and he turned to look at them. They were sitting up in their beds, drowsy and confused. Sleepy expressions turned to surprise as they saw Colin standing there, and then fear as they saw the fire eating toward the ceiling and smoke piling in, creating a layer of dark grey at the top of the room, almost like a cloudy day. The wallpaper began to brown and peel from the wall where the merry fairy procession ringing the top of the room caught fire and turned into ash and smoke. As the smoke thickened, it pressed down toward the floor. Already the upper third of the room was filled with dirty grey smoke and the flames on the walls made the smoke flicker in the half light.

"Mommy?" one of the twins said, and Colin turned to see the fear etched in both girls' faces. A part of him knew fear would be the last expression on their faces.

No more smiling. No more laughing. Fear. That look of utter terror mobilized him again and he reached out and pulled them to their feet off the beds.

"Lie down on the floor," he said, giving each of them a shirt from the floor. "Breathe through this. Hurry." The twins did as he said. Kristie was crying hard and Kimmy put her arms around her, comforting her even as she faced her own fear. Colin was impressed with her strength and he managed to shove his fear down.

I'm their only hope. I've got to do something. Find another way out.

The heat from the door drove him back further and he looked around in desperation. As his eyes swept past the window he had an idea. It wasn't a particularly good idea, he knew, but it was the best he could come up with on such short notice. The bedroom was on the second story and a jump would probably hurt them badly, maybe break bones. He'd never broken anything, but he was sure that was much better than a fiery death.

Colin crawled across the bed to grab one of the lamps and hefted it in his hand once, testing its weight. He took a blanket off one of the beds and wrapped it around the lamp. Turning back to the window, he sought leverage to slam the weighted blanket through the glass so that they could crawl out and jump down to the lawn. But it was too late—flames licked at the outside of the house, covering the bottom third of the window and flowing upward. His heart fell as the last possible avenue of escape vanished in a fiery holocaust. Hungry fire ate through the sill and the bottom pane of glass sagged, melting right in the frame before sliding out to land on the floor with a thick thud. Where the glass landed the floor burst into flames and flames rushed in through the window. The rush of heat pushed him back and he fell backwards into a tangled heap on the floor, right on top of the twins.

The fire was moving too fast now, and help couldn't possibly come in time. Then, over the roar of the fire a strange sound came to him—he could swear it was the fluttering, flapping of wings. It was as if the volume of the destruction around them was muted long enough for the sounds to reach his ears. Or maybe the sound of the wings was just more important. He glanced around in time to see a dark shape land on the headboard of the opposite bed. He peered through the smoke, but couldn't see any details.

The heat and smoke combined to make the air heavy and thick, difficult to breathe. The noise of the fire was loud and hungry as it chewed its way across the floor toward them. He stared into the smoke and flame, sure he heard a loud cawing sound and then the dark shape took to the air, flew into the flame and was gone, leaving them to die.

"Daddy!" He thought that was Kristie. The girls held on to each other, sobbing.

"Shh," Colin reached out pulled them to him and they both wrapped their arms around him, clinging to him tightly. The feel of them in his arms wasn't comforting, but the idea that he had to protect them gave him a sense of purpose and helped to push his fear back enough so that he could act. He put his back to the flames and tried to shield the girls from the fire as it crept toward them like some demon monster. "It's okay. Everything is going to be all right." But it was a lie. There was no way out—they were going to die. Nothing would ever be all right again.

He tried to shield them with his own body in the vain hope that they might survive long enough to be rescued. It was a defining moment for Colin. He didn't have time to think of his bravery as he put his body in between the twins and the fiery beast prowling toward them, crackling and roaring as it came.

Then it was upon them. Flames licked hungrily across his skin, burning away his hair, leaving behind searing pain and a foul stench. Screams broke from his mouth as the fire bit into his flesh, killing him slowly and underneath him the twins began to shriek in pain as well.

In that moment his bravery was completely gone, burned away by the fire, leaving him only with the ravening beast of his panic and pain. But it was far too late to change his mind. He choked on smoke but unconsciousness wouldn't come—the pain kept him awake and suffering. Within moments his only desire was to die so that the pain would end.

Rational thought fled and he woke in his own bed screaming.

His door burst open and his mother and father stood in the doorway, eyes still filled with sleep. Light from the hallway cut across the room, but Colin was wrapped in shadows.

"What's wrong, Colin?" His bed sagged slightly as his mother sat on the edge. Colin couldn't force words through his frantic sobs, and she tried to gather him into her arms. Sudden and searing pain burned along his skin where she touched him and he writhed and shrieked and tried to push her away, each movement another lash of excruciating pain. She released him and pulled back, but even though she no longer touched him, the searing pain increased in a terrible crescendo. Another ragged scream tore from his throat. His mother drew back enough to study him closely.

"Oh shit," Her voice was a ragged hiss.

"Rita..." his father started, but she cut him off.

"Charlie, get the lights," When he didn't move fast enough she shot him an angry look. "Now!"

When the lights flooded on and drove the shadows away from Colin, her face went white and she stared at him. He looked down and saw his arms covered in ugly red burns, the skin itself seared away in places and blistered and bubbled in others. As he got a good look at the burns, the pain flared higher as if it had been waiting to surprise him. He gritted his teeth in agony and tried not to move as the pain just grew and grew.

Then blessedly he passed out.

※

When he woke later the pain was a dull throb. He was in a hospital—the cloying antiseptic smell of the place was unmistakable. As the room came into focus, he saw his parents sitting nearby.

"Ow," he mumbled. Immediately they both came to their feet and to his side.

"Colin, honey." His mother reached him first.

"Mom." He felt something on his face, slightly itchy. He started to reach up to touch it but a tug of pain stopped his arm. He gingerly lowered his hand.

"Don't move, hon. Are you all right?" Immediately chagrin flew across her face. "Stupid question. How's the pain?"

A slight frown wrinkled his brow as he considered the question. The pain was coming back slowly but nowhere near the screaming, blinding agony from before.

"Not good. But better."

"They've got you on strong pain medicine. I imagine you're feeling fairly loopy too?"

"Tired. Stiff. What's on my face?"

She reached across and pushed the call button that hung near his hand. "Bandages." Her face was bleak but she visibly steeled herself. "The doctor wants to take a look at your burns, honey. They're trying to decide if they're going to do surgery." She'd never been one to hide the truth and he appreciated that.

The idea of surgery put a shock of fear through him.

"How bad is it?" He was covered to his neck in a light white sheet and couldn't see his body. Neither of his parents seemed to want to answer.

His father broke the brief silence. "Colin, how'd you get those burns?" Colin didn't know what to say. The truth sounded so strange and unbelievable that he couldn't bring himself to say it out loud. Instead he just shrugged. His father grimaced but before he could go on, Colin's mother interrupted him.

"Let's worry about that later. Right now I think it's best to just let him relax and work on getting better." She reached out and tousled Colin's hair.

"Where's Deck?" Colin asked. He wanted his brother there. Despite their difference in age they were close. They often played together with Legos, Matchbox cars and tiny plastic soldiers—creating large cities on the kitchen counters until Mom chased them out.

"He's downstairs with Grandma—they won't let him in until…" She stopped talking and looked worried. Colin wanted to ask her "until what?" but at that moment the door opened and a man and woman came in.

"Hello, Colin," the man spoke. His voice was confident and friendly. Immediately Colin felt worried. "I'm Doctor Heath and this is Jeanne." He smiled in that way that doctors and nurses do when something is wrong but they don't want you to know it. Everything's fine. Really.

"Hi."

"Let's get a look at you and see what we can do to get you on the road to recovery." He nodded to the nurse. "Let's look at the face first." She approached the bed, pulled out a small set of scissors and smiled at him.

"This might hurt a little." The nurse's voice was a mixture of business like and warm that only a health professional could carry off. "If it's too bad, let us know, okay?"

"Okay."

She reached out and slipped the scissors under an edge of the bandage, being careful not to touch his skin or pull the bandage too tight. She snipped through it and began to pull the bandages off, carefully removing the tape that held them together. Colin was surprised that it didn't hurt much. He told them and she gave him a quick smile, murmuring about how brave he was. After a few minutes she pulled the last of the bandages off his face. She looked puzzled. "Doctor?" He looked just as puzzled, frowned and looked down at the chart he held.

"This can't be right," he muttered.

Colin's mother pressed forward to see. "Oh, my God. What happened?"

"What is it?" Fear twisted Colin's gut.

"Oh, not a bad thing." She reached out to smooth his hair. "The burns on your face are...nearly gone. Healed."

"Let's look at his arms," Dr. Heath's voice was businesslike and the nurse began to cut away the bandages and it was the same thing; apart from a few blisters it just looked like bad sunburn. They looked shocked and over the next hour other doctors came in, photos of his injuries when he was admitted were passed around. No one understood what had happened. No one could offer a plausible explanation. Someone suggested that it was some sort of miracle. Others called it a medical oddity that needed to be studied. Colin's parents put an end to that idea firmly and quickly.

When they left the hospital the next morning even his sunburn had faded away.

※

Two days later the Jenks twins died when their house burned down. Their parents had been out for dinner and a movie, and returned home to find their home and dreams a pile of charred ashes.

The papers said the fire was caused by an electrical short in the living room. The babysitter had made it out with minor burns and smoke inhalation—she'd tried to get up to save the twins but the fire moved too quickly. The papers also said that the twins likely suffocated while sleeping and never regained consciousness. Colin really hoped they hadn't been awake—burning alive and full of terror like in his dream. He felt sick to his stomach whenever he thought about it.

Eventually, in a stunning example of the power of the mind to protect itself, the incident faded and after a while he forgot the entire thing, pushing it into some locked room in the depths of memory.

※

In the aftermath of the violent rediscovery of these memories long hidden, feeling like a burned out shell, he stood, brushed his teeth to get rid of the taste of bile and staggered back to bed. Mari had fallen back asleep, her face calm and blank—wearing the peaceful innocence of children and sleepers.

Finally, as the walls in his memory crumbled, revealing the horrific dream, he was confronted with the fear he'd felt as a young man—had his dream been some kind of prediction or foretelling? Prophecy? He wanted to wake Mari and tell her about the dreams—tell her not to get on that plane. Beg if he had to, but he knew she'd think he was crazy. And he had to admit to himself that the whole thing did sound crazy. After wrestling with the urge he decided to just sleep on it and see what it felt like by the light of day. It would keep until morning.

Coincidence. Just coincidence. Just dreams.

But he knew he wasn't going to sleep.

Sidney

As it turned out, he was wrong. He fell asleep after all—the stress of the dream, the memories and his physical reaction drained him and he'd dropped off right away. But even then he slept restlessly, constantly shifting and fighting dark, exhausting half dreams that plagued him until dawn.

Sunlight and seeing Mari roll over and smile at him drove much of his fear away, replacing it with doubt. By day the dreams seemed small and nowhere as important or real as they had at night. He decided not to mention it. The last thing she needed before getting on an airplane was to hear his horrific dream of a plane crash.

She pushed up onto her elbows and looked over at him through the strands of her hair.

"Feeling better?" Her warm smile was edged with concern.

"Yes, much better."

"Good. Maybe it wasn't the lasagna after all." She leaned over and gave him a quick kiss and then smiled. "You don't taste bad. Must have brushed your teeth." She kissed him again, lingering this time, and he closed his eyes to the soft warmth of her lips. When she pushed away finally she swung her legs off the bed and sat up. "Better get those girls up and off to school. I've got a lot to do before Friday." She glanced back at him. "Are you sure you're going to be all right here without us? I mean, you remember how to cook? Dress yourself? All the hard stuff?" Briefly he considered telling her that he wouldn't be all right at all.

Instead he forced a laugh. "I'll try to survive." The memory of the dreams was already becoming less distinct—fogged over with the passing of time. He wasn't losing any of the details, but they seemed to have retreated from the realm of prophecy into fancy, where dreams belong.

She stood and walked out of the room. He heard her pushing doors open and waking the girls. He strained to hear their quiet replies and the sounds of the household soothed him further.

Abruptly he remembered the bruises he'd had on his arms and chest and he sat up to examine himself. But he found no bruises, no marks at all and he sighed with relief. He must have imagined it—the tricks a mind will play on itself in the middle of the night and under great stress. He shook his head, feeling slightly foolish and got out of bed to start the day.

He began to believe everything was going to be all right.

✳

The next night he had the dream again. It played out exactly as it had the first time with the exception that he knew how the dream ended. He was trapped in it like a fly in glue, repeating the same words, doing the same things, but this time with a terrible awareness that they were hurtling five hundred miles an hour toward death and destruction at thirty-five thousand feet. As he and Sidney plummeted through the cold air still belted to their seats, he waited frantically for the moment that he told her to wake up and she disappeared. And when the strange young girl appeared in her place and chased him awake, he was screaming and thrashing.

"Colin!" Sleep still muddied Mari's voice. "Wake up, Colin, you're having a nightmare."

He sat straight up in the bed and stared wildly around the room, trying to convince himself that it had been only a dream. He avoided looking at himself. He really didn't want to see any bruises or cuts. As it was he struggled to convince himself it was just a dream.

He panted and felt cold sweat sliding down his chest and back, making his T-shirt cling to him.

"It's okay, honey," Mari said. Her voice was pitched low and soft, the sleep gone from her voice as she tried to calm him.

"Shit." His voice was rough and raw. "God damn it."

Mari reached over and clicked on her bedside lamp and even the soft 60 watt bulb turned the room into an almost unbearable brightness. He squinted and put his face in his hands. He felt Mari rub his shoulders, kneading his muscles gently. Then she froze.

"Col, you're bleeding." She reached up and touched his scalp carefully. He winced and drew away slightly. "Let's go get this cleaned up." The initial sound of worry in her voice settled back into a more soothing sound as she helped him up and led him into the bathroom. He was shaking as she turned on the lights. Sure enough his arms were covered with bruises and there was a thin line of blood creeping down the side of his face.

For a long moment they both stared at his reflection in the mirror. He felt like he wanted to throw up and swallowed down the urge. He sensed Mari shake herself beside him.

"You must have hit your head on the headboard. You were really thrashing. I was pretty sure you were going to hit or kick me," a hint of humor softened her voice. "That was some nightmare."

Colin nodded speechlessly.

"Hey, it was just a dream, Col." She pulled first aid supplies out of the cabinet and began to treat his wound.

"I know," he said through his hands. "It was just so real."

"Was it the same dream as last night?"

He nodded.

"Tell me." It wasn't a request and he felt a strong compulsion to tell her about it, but he didn't. Instead he just sat there with his hands over his face and his eyes closed against the light.

"Colin. Tell me your dream. Talking about it will make it less real."

She was right. In the act of talking about a dream the brain realizes that there are so many disconnected things, so many illogical turns of events that it couldn't possibly be real. That discovery in itself would drive any lingering fear away.

But he wasn't sure it would work with this dream. He'd spent a lot of time walking through it yesterday and there were no rough edges. No inexplicable change of location. No completely unrealistic people and creatures. Nothing unbelievable to focus on. Even if he'd been originally surprised at how easily Mari had accepted his appearance in the dream, he knew that everything else could have really happened. And a secret part of his mind believed that it would happen.

That was what finally drove him to tell her.

"I dreamed we were on an airplane heading to your parents' house..." Already he was beginning to feel ridiculous and knew that telling her this awful dream would serve no purpose apart from making her nervous about flying. But if there was the slightest chance that he could talk her out of going—somehow change his dream—it was worth it. "The plane crashed."

For a moment Mari didn't reply.

"Oh, lovely." There was a slight prickle in her voice. "Okay, maybe you shouldn't have told me this one." There was a slight hint of annoyance in her voice—softened by obvious affection and concern.

"I know. But when I woke up I remembered something from when I was a kid." He told her all about the dreams he'd had about the twins, and how real it had felt. He couldn't bring himself to tell her about the burns and nicks—he wasn't sure he believed it himself anymore. And he told her about the dream he'd had last night. She listened as he went through the details and when he was done she took a deep breath before speaking.

"Colin." She spoke slowly, as if weighing her words carefully. "I know you're rattled by this. But this dream you had about the fire—surely that was just coincidence? And one coincidence doesn't mean you're some kind of psychic fortune teller." She paused and he started to reply. She cut him off. "I know you're worried and scared. It was a horrible nightmare. But we've been planning this trip for months and everyone will be disappointed if we don't go." She frowned for a second and then her face brightened. "And besides. You were on the plane with us, right? You're not even going with us."

He'd known she'd respond this way. He had been praying for a little more of that strange acceptance she'd shown on the plane.

Why are you sleeping in the middle of the day? You're not sick are you?

"Maybe you could take a train," Before the words were fully out he knew that wasn't going to fly. So to speak.

"Colin. Honey. I'm not taking the train. Can you imagine being stuck on a train for that long with either of your children? The plane is trial enough, but at least it's only a few hours." He had to agree with that. His brain ran and churned over the entire thing. He wanted to ask her to take a different flight. But would that save them? Or would he be persuading her to take the doomed flight? The entire thing made his head swim. And quite honestly as the immediacy of the dream began to recede he was feeling a bit foolish.

"Yeah, you're right, I'm sorry. You must think I'm stupid. I shouldn't have even told you about it. It's just my brain and neuroses plotting against my sanity."

She laughed—a lovely, soothing sound.

"Stupid is one thing you're not." The humor in her voice helped him relax. "Anyway, if we stay home you won't have time to meet with some mystery woman."

"Yeah, that's it exactly." His answering laugh sounded shaky. As they moved into playful teasing his heart felt lighter. "I was planning on picking up one of the checkout girls down at Jewel this weekend."

"Grocery store jailbait, Colin? I was expecting better than that. If you're going to cheat on me it had better be with a severely hot, legal young thing. No pimply high school chicks, you hear me?"

"Oh, she's not pimply, Mari. And she's not in high school, either."

"Bastard." She laughed again—a burst of cheerful sound. "I expect her to be gone by the time we get home, you understand me?"

"Okay, okay." He grinned at her and the sick dread and fear that the dream had left in its wake was finally driven completely away.

"Good."

"I love you, Mari."

"I love you too, Dave. Oh, crap. I mean Colin. I love you Colin."

❃

"Dad."

"Sid." Colin was sitting at the computer in his basement office, staring at the screen. Mari and Emma had left only a short while ago to catch their flight and in the aftermath of their departure the dream had snuck back into his mind. It was difficult to focus on the writing. Because of his growing frustration layered uneasily over the worried churning in his gut, he was more than glad to take a break from staring at the small dust motes clinging tenaciously to the screen of his laptop. He looked up and saw she was standing in the doorway with her hands on her hips.

"Wanna play chess, Daddy?" Something about her expression tugged at Colin—he had a hard time resisting his girls so he pushed the keyboard away and sat back. He wasn't getting anything done anyway.

"Sure, honey," he stood and crossed to the door, making an effort to shake off his worries. "Although I don't seem to be much of a challenge these days..."

"Oh, but who cares about winning. It's just about the playing, right?" He'd taught her that when she was very young —it was no fun playing Candyland with a four year old who could not handle losing. He got tired of throwing games to avoid the resulting temper tantrums. It wasn't that he minded losing—it had just gotten harder to fool her with his cheating to lose. And it was his parental responsibility to teach her how to handle winning and losing gracefully.

He chose to teach her chess. It was more accurate to say that he passed along his limited knowledge of the game—just enough to play. He figured he would win more at first due to the complexity of the game. Things had gone according to plan until last year when Sidney tired of losing and read a book on chess. She devoured the book in record time and her game improved immediately. Within weeks she was the better player by a long shot. Ironically, now that she could absolutely annihilate him in chess, she wasn't hung up on winning. He couldn't remember the last time he'd won.

"Easy for you to say," he answered. "I appreciate the gracious manner in which you dominate me in chess."

She laughed and stuck out her tongue.

"Well, if you'd put any effort into learning how to play you'd win more often. Heck you'd probably beat me every time." She walked out of his office without a backward glance.

"Yeah, right." He stood up and followed her out into the play room. He'd finished the basement when they had first moved into the house and had created a large playroom outside his office so that he could be near enough to watch them, but not so close that he couldn't concentrate. His office itself was spacious and full of his many toys and tools of his trade—mostly oriented around his imagination and obsession with science fiction and fantasy. One thing that he and Marianne had decided was important was that his office had to have a large, wide doorway but no door, so his girls could get to him whenever they wanted. The girls fed his creativity and imagination, so the lack of a door was a good thing for everyone. Sure, the interruptions made it hard to concentrate sometimes but overall the easy access they had to him was worth it.

Marianne decorated the playroom in primary colors when Sidney was in diapers. She believed bright colors stimulate the mind and Colin figured she was probably right. As the girls got older she often talked about redecorating the room, but it was one of those projects that always got shoved aside. The room was long and narrow and it was with lined with shelves that held the vast collection of toys that the girls had accumulated. The floor was covered by a well padded yet thin carpet—easy to clean yet less painful to fall on—and plenty of small chairs, throw pillows and blankets.

In the middle of the floor Sidney had set up the chess board; she sat on the white side. Colin groaned as he lowered himself to the floor and tried to find a comfortable position. The creaking sound his knees made was vaguely depressing.

I'm getting old. Well past my prime.

That made him sad and then admitted that it was a silly thought to have at his age. He had to cringe at the thought of how he'd react to being forty, then fifty and beyond. He wondered if there was a red sports car and one or more midlife crises in his future.

"Oh, Dad." Sidney rolled her eyes. "You'd think you were an old man or something."

"Sometimes I feel that way. Especially in the knees."

Sidney made her first move and they were off. The rest of the game would be an exercise in delaying the inevitable and watching his doom take shape. It was gratifying to watch her work. He'd felt for a long time that Sidney was likely the smartest person in the house. Both he and Marianne were intelligent, educated people that came from long lines of intellectual stock, but Sidney was decidedly an improvement on the breed. Where Colin studied his moves deliberately, she moved quickly and decisively. He loved that she was so smart. Eventually she'd be teaching him things—he could already feel the beginnings of that subtle shift in roles.

Emma was also smart, but hers was a different kind of smart—intuitive and mercurial. She often understood things without really being able to describe how she'd arrived at her conclusions. Colin wondered if her teachers might have issues with her lightning quick and often inexplicable arrival at the correct answers—they expected students to show their work but much of that work was synaptic reflex for Emma.

We'll cross that bridge when we get to it.

He loved playing with his girls. Something about the way they looked at him with complete trust made his heart sing. So taking some time away from work to play chess with Sidney was no trial or tribulation. On the contrary, he thought of it as a way of coming up for air and recharging his batteries. They played without speaking for a while and from the start she forced the shape and direction of the game, with Colin blindly reacting to her moves.

"Dad, what time will Mom and Emma be home?"

Inwardly he winced and closed his eyes for a brief moment to get his emotions under control.

Just a dream.

"Late tonight. Probably after you've gone to sleep."

He finally found a move—he suspected it wasn't a good one, but then none of his options looked encouraging at this stage in the game, a stage that began moments after he took his first move.

"I wish we'd gone with them. I haven't seen Grandma and Grandpa since last summer. I miss them."

Colin was so relieved that she'd stayed home.

If the worst happens at least I won't lose her, too...

He immediately cut off that line of thought as a wave of crushing guilt passed through him. He took a sharp breath and shook it off.

"You'd have missed too much school, Sid."

"I know." Her voice held a hint of exasperation as she made her move. Colin sighed as it became clear how poor his last move had been. He thought for a moment that he should read up on the game, if only to give Sidney more of a challenge.

"There's so much to learn. You don't want to miss out on that, do you?" He picked up one of his knights and rolled it around with his fingers while he studied the board.

"Oh, Dad, we've learned a lot already. I can always catch up. Besides, I know everything already." Colin glanced up to see an impish grin on her face and he laughed.

"There's always more to learn, Sid," Colin said. He put the knight down finally, committing to his move. He carefully watched Sidney's eyes, trying to gauge if he'd messed up. She arched an eyebrow and looked up at him.

"Are you still learning things at your ripe old age?" She was still grinning, and he snorted.

"Oh, yes. Every day I learn new things. You never stop learning. Right now I'm learning humility."

"I'm glad I could contribute to your education."

"You go to school for two reasons," he continued, ignoring her jibe. "The first one is to learn things. That's the easy part. The second reason is to learn how to learn things on your own. That's the harder part. Many people never learn that lesson. But if you do learn it, you'll enjoy your entire life so much more."

"Sometimes school gets kind of boring." Marianne really disliked it when Sidney called school boring, but Colin knew it was a sign that her mind was strong—she needed a faster pace of learning to keep her attention. Soon enough she'd be able to start taking some higher level classes out at the community college. Until then it would be up to Marianne and him to keep her on track.

"It won't always be boring, Sid."

She glanced down at the board again. Colin shook his head. The end was near.

"You're super smart. What you do with your smarts is what matters."

Sidney reached out and moved her queen and looked up at him with a dazzling smile.

"Check."

Yeah, just like that.

※

After their chess game he'd given up on writing and instead sat in front of the television watching CNN. He had the phone on the coffee table in front of him and as the morning wore on his mood slowly deteriorated. The cycle of stories seemed to repeat endlessly and each time he dreaded seeing a new story inserted.

Sometime in the late afternoon he received a brief reprieve. Mari called from Phoenix to let him know they were making their connection and that the first flight had gone by without incident. Hearing her voice chased away the darkness that had settled over him.

But it was only a reprieve. Shortly before six in the evening the story broke. An airplane had crashed in New Mexico—only about twenty miles from Tucumcari. They had no details about what flight it was, or even what airline yet, but Colin's heart was already blackening and dying.

One thought kept ripping through his brain, tearing and hurting more each time.

They almost made it.

Goodbye

"No." All the color fled Sidney's face and she gripped the arms of the chair until her fingers and knuckles went white. "No."

Colin didn't know what to say to her. Telling her about the accident was the hardest thing he'd ever done.

"It can't be true," Sidney whispered. Colin felt his breath shorten and his heart pound with the first hints of panic as he watched the tears welling up in her. He hadn't cried yet and seeing her grief come on so fast made him feel...broken. "They're gone?"

He just nodded. The tears started to leak down her cheeks and the tension in her body increased, as if she wanted to jump up and run. All Colin felt was deadness as if his capacity for emotion had been sucked out of him completely.

Abruptly her face flushed and she leaned forward.

"You're lying. They wouldn't..."

He reached out for her, to take her into his arms and hold her. He wanted to offer her comfort. Take away her pain. It made him sick to see the hurt and loss on her face. But she quickly stood up and avoided his arms. Hugging herself she staggered away from the chair, away from him. "This is your fault. You shouldn't have let them go on that plane." Her words cut him to the quick—because they were truer than she'd ever know. Sidney was looking around frantically like a cornered animal searching for a way to escape. Colin rose to his feet and stepped toward her, one hand raised.

"Honey." He pitched his voice low and soothing.

She backed away a step and glared at him. "Stay away from me. Don't touch me." She turned her back on him and then, finally, she ran.

Feeling a wave of exhaustion Colin watched her leave. He knew he should go after her but he couldn't. After a few minutes sat down again and slumped into the couch, turned on the TV and zoned out.

✹

The doorbell jarred Colin out of his stupor. Marianne and Emma had only been dead for twenty-four hours, and Sidney hadn't come out of her room since locking herself in. Colin knew he should be comforting her. Holding her so she could cry on his shoulder, but he was unable to even walk that direction. He couldn't face the accusation in her eyes. Instead he sat on the couch and waited for his parents to come take care of her.

The doorbell rang again and he pushed himself to his feet and walked to the door. When he pulled it open his mother came straight in and pulled him into a tight embrace. She put a hand up on his head and stroked his head. Colin realized he'd been hoping for some emotional release at this moment, but there was nothing. Only emptiness.

"Oh, baby," she said. "I'm so sorry."

After a few moments he pulled away and looked at her face. Her eyes were red from crying but her features were sympathetic and determined at the same time. Behind her his father came in.

"Son," Charlie reached out to put a hand on Colin's shoulder.

"Charlie."

"How are you holding up?" His father grimaced and raised a hand. "Stupid question, sorry. Is there anything I can do?"

"No, not that I can think of right now. I...I don't know what to do. I've been watching TV. Well, sorta watching. The Sox won." He always talked about sports with Charlie—it was safe ground. Sure enough his father gave him a smile and quipped.

"The Right Sox."

"Yep." In a world that had spun out of control at least some things remained the same.

His mother released him and held him away with her hands on his shoulders and peered into his face. She studied him closely and he wanted to turn so she couldn't see the emptiness on his face.

He tried to put a smile on his face. "Thanks for coming so quickly."

"Of course, what else would we do?"

"Sidney is in her room." Colin's voice broke slightly. "She won't come out. Won't let me in. I can hear her crying but otherwise she doesn't answer at all."

For a moment his mother looked at him blankly.

"I thought she went with them?"

"No. We decided a few days ago that she shouldn't miss a week of school. So she stayed here with me."

Thank God.

"That is a blessing." Her face cleared up and the expression of joy on her face that they hadn't lost his entire family filled him with a burning anger, and then a deep shame. It wasn't her he was angry at. It was himself—he'd had the same thought already.

"You look tired, honey. Why don't you get some sleep? I'll go see Sidney." She started to turn away but Colin reached out and touched her shoulder.

"Mom," he started and then stopped.

"What is it, dear?"

He was quiet for a few moments, staring at the wall beyond her, collecting his thoughts. Then he sighed once and spoke.

"I dreamt it."

"Dreamt what?"

"The crash. The whole thing. And..."

Her face has gone pale and she stared at him, waiting for him to go on.

"And when I woke up, I was bruised and injured. And I remembered the twins."

"Oh, God, Colin."

"There's more...I told her about the dreams. I tried to talk her out of going." Not hard enough, he berated himself and felt a wash of nausea pass over him. "I couldn't change her mind. I..."

Before he could say anything more she cut him off. Her voice was rough and low.

"Shh, don't say it. Don't even think it. It was an accident." She pulled him into her embrace again. "It was just a dream." Colin could tell she didn't believe it either. In the aftermath of that dream of the fire, when he'd gotten home from the hospital she'd asked him about the dream. He told her everything and was surprised that she had believed him—something he'd never expected from an adult. She'd told him it wasn't his fault. Told him that he shouldn't tell anyone about it—people were scared of things they didn't understand. And for a while she'd checked with him regularly, asking if he'd had any more dreams. But over time she'd stopped asking him and they'd both forgotten. Or at least he had forgotten.

"It wasn't just a dream, Mom. It was the end of my life."

"Don't you talk like that, Colin Pierce. Your life is not over. You have a beautiful daughter in the other room that needs her father. Now you go lie down and sleep. Feel what you feel. Charlie and I will take care of things while you deal with this. But eventually you're going to have to be there for Sidney." She sighed and studied his face for a moment. "Go sleep, honey."

"Okay." He wasn't sure he'd be able to sleep, but he could use a change of venue. Staring at the ceiling might be just as good as staring at the television. Maybe not. He started to walk toward the bedroom, but paused and turned back to his mother. "Did you know the airline thought Sid was on the plane? They said that she checked in and boarded the plane with Mari and Emma. They want to send a representative out to verify that she's alive."

"Colin, she's asleep in the other room. Who cares what they think. Just get some sleep."

He went to his bedroom, closed the door and pulled the blinds. He walked to the bed he'd shared with Marianne, but couldn't sit down. It would smell like her. He'd never be able to sleep there again. He went to the closet and pulled out a comforter and sheet, took his pillow and threw it all on the floor in the corner. Slowly he sat down, pulled off his shoes and socks, stretched out and put his head on the pillow and closed his eyes.

He was struck with the unreality of everything. He just couldn't believe they were really gone. Gone forever. That thought pierced his mental haze, knifing to the center of him and he gave a quick gasp and pushed it back, unconsciously pulling the blankness over himself again like a shroud.

❈

Marianne stood before him and he drank her in with his eyes. He knew he was dreaming, and he didn't care. In a moment he resolved he'd never wake from this dream. He would live here forever.

"Mari."

"Colin." Her voice was rich and carried a sadness that was almost tangible. "I'm so sorry."

"Everyone keeps saying that."

She just nodded and her eyes were bright with tears. She walked to him and put her arms around him. The feel of her was so strong, so solid. He buried his face in her hair and finally the tears came. His body shook and convulsed as great heaving sobs escaped. For a long time she just held him until finally he couldn't cry anymore. It felt as if he'd cried for days and days.

"Oh, Mari," he keep the hitch out of his voice. "What am I going to do? I'm nothing without you." He felt as though something had broken inside him—some essential part of him dying and fading away in the aftermath of release.

"Shh." She stroked his hair. "You will survive. You will find happiness elsewhere. You will be whole again. I promise."

"No. No, I won't. My life is over."

She pushed him back and frowned at him.

"That's stupid, Colin. Sidney needs you. She needs her father more than ever."

She was right, he had to admit. He was being selfish. He should be in her room holding her and hugging her. Helping her through her grief. But knowing wasn't enough. It never was, was it?

"You can't stay here." Her voice dropped to a whisper. "You know that. You must return to your life." Sadness moved across her face again. "I shouldn't have come to you. But I had to see you one more time. To make sure you will take care of Sidney."

Then something broke in him. In a heartbeat all his sadness flowed away and was replaced by calm. It wasn't the calm of peace—it was the calm of emptiness. Nothingness. He felt as if he was breaking apart, the shattered bits of him drifting away in different directions, but he just didn't care anymore.

"Colin. You have to wake up. Go to Sidney." She reached up and put her finger on his lips gently. "I love you, Colin Pierce."

He looked down and nodded.

"I love you, too."

Then her features started to fade away and she shrank in his arms. He tried in vain to hold onto her but she was already gone. He woke into the quiet darkness of his room and stared at the ceiling feeling cold and dead inside.

✺

Colin eased open the door to Sidney's room and slipped inside. She was asleep and his mother sat on a chair at the edge of the bed, asleep herself. But when Colin entered she opened her eyes and looked over at him. He saw relief flash across her face as she stood and smiled. She didn't show sympathy or pity this time, but the sadness was still there. He was glad—sympathy and pity were like salt on a wound.

She walked toward the door and squeezed his shoulder as she passed him. The door closed, leaving Colin alone with Sidney. He didn't move as he watched her sleep. Her face was peaceful, but her eyes were red from crying.

While he watched, her eyes opened.

"Daddy," she whispered. "Is God mad at me?"

"What?" he asked in shock.

"Does God hate me?" She looked afraid. He went to sit on the edge of her bed and took her hand. He knew he had to be careful in how he handled this conversation. He felt all the parts of his brain click into focus as he studied her face and considered her question. He believed in God, and while he didn't feel close to him at this point, he didn't want to take any solace she might get from faith away from her. She might need it as she grew up. He knew that faith was a good thing to have—it had helped him get through the rough spots in his life. Until now.

"Of course he loves you, Sid. You're wonderful; how could he hate you?"

"Well, if he loved me he wouldn't have taken Mom and Emma from us." The guilt in her voice was heartrending and in a flash of insight he understood—she thought it had been her fault. That was the last thing he'd expected from her.

"Oh, Sid. It wasn't your fault, honey. It was no one's fault. Life is just unfair sometimes." The words felt empty as soon as they fell off his lips. Life is unfair. As if that made anything better.

"I miss them so much, Daddy." Fresh tears slid down her cheeks and Colin gathered her into his arms.

"I miss them too, Sid," he whispered as her tears broke into full on crying and buried her face into his shoulder. He just held her and rocked her gently until the storm had passed, leaving her face and his shoulder wet. "We have to believe they went somewhere wonderful, Sid. They're watching us right now, loving us and waiting for us. We'll see them again someday, I promise."

He realized how completely he had been failing her. She needed him, needed his love and support and he'd spent his time wallowing in his loss and self pity. Marianne was completely right. The sheer selfishness of his behavior shocked him, adding another level to his already massive load of guilt. A stab of shame broke through the numbness that covered him like a thick wool blanket—protected him from the raw elements of pain and loss. He held Sidney close, stroking her hair and he silently vowed to do better by her.

※

During the weeks that followed, Colin found it harder and harder to picture Mari's face, to remember the sound of her voice. Already specific memories were becoming foggier than they had been. He was scared that he was losing the only part of his wife he still had. He wasn't having the same issue with Emma—her face shone in his memory whenever he closed his eyes and thought about her. But Marianne was rapidly becoming a remote concept.

He agonized over details of Mari that he was losing. He found himself sitting in their closet looking at her clothes, her other things—her scent was strong still and brought things back to him briefly before they faded again. Looking at pictures of her had the same effect. He knew his reaction wasn't a normal one and it scared him.

But even his fear had a hard time touching him in the cold, dead place where his heart had been.

Time Goes On

It was four years after the accident—a sunny day in early summer. Sidney loved the heat, but Colin preferred cold weather. He loved dressing up in extra shirts and a heavy parka, wrapping a scarf around his throat and lower face. The sheer anonymity of the winter was soothing to him. But this early in the warmer season it was still cool and comfortable in the early mornings.

When Rita and Charlie had talked him into moving back to Leith to be near them, it hadn't been a hard choice to make—Sidney needed family as much as he did. Leith was a midsize town that perched on an edge of the suburban sprawl of Tayport. Only a half hour's train ride away the center of Tayport was relatively young and urban. Tayport itself had burst out of the northwestern edge of the Chicago suburban sprawl on a wave of tech industry in the late 90s. Cheaper than Chicago but still near enough to O'Hare to be convenient, many small startups had moved there. The METRA line ran right into the heart of Tayport and linked it with Chicago like a pulsing artery moving between lungs and heart.

Deck and his long time girlfriend Susan had a place a few miles away from the condominium Colin and Sidney moved into. Between the weekly dinners at his Mom and Dad's house and the random visits by Deck and Susan, Colin and Sidney were taken care of well. Sometimes it was a balm, other times a chore.

Colin and Sidney's third floor condo was in a rejuvenated part of downtown Leith. While Leith was not a large town—just over thirty-three thousand people—the changes to the old downtown area had been specifically designed to give the area a slightly metropolitan feel. There were a few streets of brownstones, a couple of apartment buildings and a few parks in the area. The entire downtown was geared toward shopping and tourism rather than industry and big business.

The condo itself was more than Colin felt they needed, but it was inexpensive, located in a great place, and in great shape. There was a master bedroom, and three other bedrooms. They used one as a study and the spare as a guest room. The only people who had come to stay were Marianne's parents. That had been an uncomfortable visit. Colin couldn't help harboring a sense of guilt—as if he'd betrayed their trust. The idea festered and grew and it became harder and harder to meet their eyes. He could have sworn he saw accusation in their eyes—he was pretty sure he was imagining it, but that didn't ease the guilt. They spent most of their time with Sidney and Colin was grateful for that.

But this morning Sidney was running late—school started in a short while, and she had just appeared at the breakfast table. At this rate, she'd miss the bus and Colin would end up driving her. That was okay with him—he'd just go on down to the local coffee shop and try to do some work; knock down the wall that had come up between himself and his words.

He enjoyed sitting in the large plush chairs and working on his writing in his Moleskine notebook. He took his laptop everywhere in the hope that something would break down his writer's block. He had really been struggling with his writing since the accident. He'd managed to churn out the last book in his trilogy—it had been mostly done before the accident anyway. His agent and publisher were relieved. He'd gotten a seven-book deal and since then had been struggling with writer's block. He'd long ago gotten past the panic and neurosis over this. His agent was ramping up the pressure to produce a new novel.

"Dad, can I have money for a hot lunch today?" Sidney plopped down in a chair with a bowl of cereal. Colin looked up from his notebook and smiled.

"Sure, honey." He pulled out his wallet. He had a few bills in there and found a ten and handed it to her. "I want the change, okay?" He knew there wouldn't be any change—there never was. But he didn't mind.

"Okay, Dad. Thanks!" They settled into a peaceful quiet and Colin sank back into his notebook again. This was one thing that hadn't eluded him since the accident—he and Sidney were completely comfortable to be around each other and not fill the space with chatter. They were able to share a companionable silence.

After a while Sidney peered at him over the top of the newspaper.

"So what are you up to today?"

Colin looked up from his notebook again. He didn't mind the interruption. So far this morning he'd managed zero words and about half a page of doodles.

"I was thinking I'd go down and get a cup of coffee. Do a little writing. Then I have some cleaning up to do around here. And a few errands." That was the full extent of Colin's plans and in all honesty he likely wouldn't even do much beyond the coffee.

"You should go do something interesting—change your routine." Colin stifled a sigh—he knew where this was going. She had been trying for the last few months to get him to get out of his rut. She'd even resorted to telling him he needed to date again. The mere thought filled him with tension. But he didn't show her any of that—he just nodded.

"Maybe I will, Sid. I could go over to Mom and Dad's place and swim, or something."

"I was thinking of something more...social..."

Of course she was.

"I guess I could go down to the bookstore for a while."

"Dad. That's not what I meant." Her voice sharpened in exasperation.

"Well, what did you have in mind?"

"You should go see if Kate wants to go get coffee with you. She's really awesome, you know."

He did know. Kate lived across the street and a few doors down. She was Colin's age and a single mother. Not by choice—her husband Mark had left her several years ago. Colin didn't know why, but he suspected sheer stupidity. There were so many things about her that were ideal: she was intelligent, pretty, energetic, and had a great sense of humor—all things Colin always appreciated. Under different circumstances he might have pursued her. But he couldn't imagine being in those circumstances any time soon.

"She is awesome, yes."

"And beautiful," Sidney prompted.

"And beautiful," he agreed dutifully.

"More than that. Funny and smart, too." Sid gave up any pretense of casualness and was selling it hard.

"I'm sure she is, honey. But I'm not ready."

"Not ready for what, Dad? Dating? Talking to people? Girls?"

He laughed. "Yeah, that whole thing."

She snorted at him. "You're going to have to deal with 'that whole thing', Dad. I'm not living here forever and someone will have to take care of you."

"What makes you think I'm letting you move out ever?"

She stuck her tongue out at him and cleared her bowl from the table. "You just try to stop me, old man." She grabbed her backpack and came over to give him a quick kiss on the cheek. "Seriously, Dad. We both miss them, but you've got to have a life too." He was always amazed at how mature she was for her age. Barely fifteen and already giving out sound advice. He knew she was right, but he wasn't ready. He didn't know if he'd ever be ready.

"Okay, sweetheart. You have a good day."

"You too, Dad." She stopped in the act of moving away and turned a glare on him. "And don't think we're done with this subject."

"Scoot. If you hurry you might still catch the bus." He gave her a little push toward the door.

She rolled her eyes and left. The room was quieter and sadder once she was gone and for some time Colin stared at the door.

A Pretty Penny

Colin shrugged himself into motion and packed up the tools of his trade: a laptop that was rushing headlong toward obsolescence, the Moleskine, a handful of pencils, index cards, post-it notes and a highlighter. It seemed the longer his writer's block lingered, the more "tools" he acquired. For a while he'd prayed to the gods of organization to save him. Not that he'd actually gotten very organized. He just acquired the supplies and carried them around. Currently he was focused on capturing his every random creative idea. That wasn't working much. He ended up with pages of paper full of doodles: arrows, squiggly lines, and various shapes—all showing what a horrible artist he would have made. He often considered leaving all that crap home. It was harder to doodle on the computer.

Some mornings he would stop at his parents' house and spend sit sipping coffee with his mother. She was more subtle than Sidney and it was easier to ignore the hints and pushes. Today he decided to get right to the writing—maybe this would be the day he broke out of his funk.

※

Colin had his laptop open and his weapons spread around the small table—he spent a while placing them correctly in relationship to each other. He wasn't obsessive really, but it was a way of postponing the inevitable frustration of fighting to get words out. It was an empty ritual. When he had everything arranged he shoved it all out of the way and dropped the notepad directly in front of him and opened to the last page of doodles. Maybe he should start leaving the other tools at home. Pencil, paper and perhaps laptop were all he really needed. Eraser he supposed. The rest was pointless.

At least then all of this other junk wouldn't interfere with my budding career as a crappy artist.

He looked down at the talentless sketches and doodles that filled the page.

Café Cordova was his coffee place of choice; built to be comfortable—a home away from home that served really great coffee. The walls were decorated with art and photos by local artists including black and white macro photography, close ups of a cow's nostrils and farm equipment shot from odd angles. Several large plants, comfortable chairs and couches were arranged haphazardly around a long, low-slung coffee table. Another handful of tables was scattered around the store. A shelf with books, newspapers and magazines rounded out the café's homey feel.

The café was large and had high ceilings with exposed water pipes, heating ducts, wiring conduits, and beams running around chaotically. The front and one side wall were composed entirely of floor-to-ceiling windows, and in the corner they formed the roasting equipment sprawled—a mishmash of complicated machinery that consumed raw coffee and delivered the roast version into big buckets. Large burlap sacks containing the raw coffee lay on the floor along the bottom of the front windows. The counter was on the other wall, a sweeping curve with all the equipment and knick knacks that were standard to a coffee shop: the espresso machine, coffee grinders and various fresh pastries and healthy sandwiches.

Sometimes he'd go to one of the more conventional coffee places like Starbucks or Caribou, but he always started here. He'd spend a couple of hours here and then move on, wandering like a desert nomad in search of the next oasis. He felt uncomfortable spending too much time in one place—like he was wearing out his welcome. Of course, he felt uncomfortable these days when he was trying to break his block.

Rhetorical constipation.

He wrote the words down between a carefully rendered spiral and a series of tiny boxes with dots in them.

He glanced up from his notebook and there was a young woman standing in front of him, a hint of a smile tugging at the corners of her mouth. She looked like she was in her mid twenties, tops. She had an elfin quality—petite face, expressive lips, large brown eyes and spiky medium length jet black hair. Her skin was pale and flawless. She was on the short side of medium height—he'd guess somewhere around 5'6" or so—and lithe yet at the same time shapely. Female but not girly. She wore black leather pants, big combat boots and a black top with spaghetti straps and that revealed her midriff. Her belly button was pierced. As was his habit, Colin immediately began speculating on her back story, trying to understand her. This was what he did with people.

She looked self assured and energetic, and stood with one hand on her hip, her weight on the same leg. In her other hand she held a cup with small tendrils of steam wisping up from the little hole in the plastic lid. She just stared down at Colin with that little smile.

"Hi," he said. He almost asked her if she wanted something but stopped himself, thinking it was a rude thing to say.

"Hi." Her voice was cheerful and she arched an eyebrow at him as if waiting for something. For a few moments he struggled to figure out what he was supposed to do next. Usually he was good with silences and quiet, but this was unnerving. He had no idea what to say so he just offered up his hand.

"I'm Colin."

"Penelope," she answered. Her grip was firm and she held his hand a few long moments before letting it drop. "You can call me Penny." She never broke eye contact with him and he started to expect her to tap her foot. She didn't though. Just kept watching him, waiting again, unflappable.

"Would you like to sit?" He gestured at the table. She beamed at him and plopped down in the chair across from him.

"I thought you'd never ask."

He had to grin at that.

"Sorry, I'm a bit slow on the uptake. Not especially good with people these days." The minute the words were out he wished he could take it back. He hated his tendency to bare his emotions to complete strangers.

"It's okay. I'm probably good enough for the both of us." It wasn't cocky or arrogant; she just said it matter-of-factly. She took a sip of her coffee and stared at him with a small smile playing around the corners of her mouth. After a few moments the lack of conversation started to unnerve Colin a little bit.

"So do I know you from somewhere, Penny?"

"Oh, no." She shook her head once then frowned thoughtfully. "At least not yet. Well, now you do. You know me from the coffee shop." She broke into a bright smile that exploded outward from her mouth to take over her whole face. Colin knew people who smiled with their mouths only—his father for example. He knew some who smiled with their mouth and eyes. But he wasn't sure he'd ever seen someone smile this completely. It was really something to see and he caught himself staring. "And later you'll know me as your neighbor."

That surprised him.

"My neighbor?"

"Yes. You're Sidney's father, aren't you?"

He nodded.

"I thought so. You look like her."

"That makes sense." He managed to suppress a grimace at his not so stellar conversational skills.

"I moved in next door to you this weekend. Sidney helped me drag a few of my things inside. She's a sweet girl." All of this was a surprise to Colin. He hadn't known anyone had moved into the building. Each floor had a pair of large condos and the other one on his and Sidney's floor had been empty for almost a year. Sidney hadn't said a word to him about a new neighbor.

"Wow, I didn't have any idea anyone had moved in."

"It wasn't just anyone. It was me." She grinned at him and he could help but laugh—her good humor was infectious. Though it was a rusty laugh, it still felt good.

"Well, welcome to the neighborhood. It will be nice to have someone next door again."

She nodded and then looked past his laptop to the notebook.

"So you're an artist?" she asked carefully.

"No." Confusion. "Why do you ask?" She gestured at his notepad where he'd filled the page with doodles. "Oh, no, I'm a writer."

"Well that's a relief, Colin." She laughed and then she furrowed her brow. "You don't write art books do you? I'm not entirely sure you've got the gift for drawing."

"No, I couldn't draw my way out of a paper bag."

"So what do you write?"

"Contemporary fantasy. No vampires, dragons or dwarves though."

"I like that. Have you been published?" She leaned forward a bit.

"Yes, I've got three novels and a handful of stories out there."

She just looked at him and waited. So he told her the titles.

"So you're famous, huh?" She sat back.

"Famous?" He broke into laughter. "Somehow I don't think so."

"You've got the whole I'm an author card to play when you meet girls! That's pretty cool."

"Hm, I've never thought of it like that."

"Well, you should, Colin. I bet it would impress the ladies, big time." She paused and then got a wistful look in her eyes. "I wish I could write."

"Anyone can write, Penny." He often talked about this with people. Or he had before the accident.

"Not me. I'm much better expressing myself out loud. I don't know how to write."

Colin made a quick connection and before he could stop himself he spoke again. "Oh, you mean you never learned?"

"No, that's not what I mean at all." She shook her head. "I just wouldn't know where to begin. I've tried before but it always comes out awful."

He shook his head. "Writing is a sharing of self. It doesn't have to be good or bad. It just is." He caught himself slipping into his usual spiel on writing and stopped himself.

"That's a very...generous attitude," she said and then shrugged. "Well, anyway, I've not really had time for it. I've been learning other things. There's only so much room in the brain for new things at any given time. I don't want to explode messily." She grinned.

"Other things?" he asked.

"Yes, you know, magic, woodcraft, tree talking. I had to learn the languages of the forest." He wondered if she were making fun of him but quickly dismissed the idea. Then he wondered if she was serious. He wasn't sure about that, but he discovered that a part of him hoped she was.

"Magic."

"Oh yes, I learned a lot about it." Her eyes seemed to twinkle with excitement and she leaned toward him slightly. "You know; the whole thing. It was necessary. I have only a small magic of my own, but it's important to know about these sorts of things where I come from."

"Where do you come from?"

"Oh, somewhere rather far away." She glanced away for a moment evasively. He decided to just let it go. Lord knows he had his own secrets and things he wasn't comfortable talking about. "At any rate, I think I'd like to know how to write better. I mean, there have to be some rules and best practices and such, right? If I knew what those were, I'd be able to decide which ones I could ignore."

"Well, I'd be glad to help you with that—if you'd like, of course."

"Oh that would be lovely. And convenient! What with us being neighbors and all." He found himself smiling at her. He had the feeling that not smiling at her would take some effort.

"Sure. Once you get settled in, just let me know and we can get started."

"Oh, yes, I will!" Colin thought she really meant it. This girl didn't seem like the sort of person to say things simply out of social nicety.

"So you met Sid. I hope she behaved herself?"

"She's a dream," she said with a smile.

Then she reached across and put her hand on his gently. He was surprised at the contact and had to suppress the urge to pull away. "I've got to go. My stuff won't unpack itself. At least not all of it." She gave him a little wink. "But I will see you again, Colin Pierce." She pulled her hand back and stood up.

He felt an intense moment of déjà vu when she said his name like that—as if she'd said it to him before. But he knew that was silly.

"I hope so." He found he meant it.

"I promise! I'll be over to borrow some sugar at some point, I'm sure," She gave him a little wave and then turned and headed for the door. He saw that she had tattoos on her shoulders—a stylized sun on one shoulder and the moon on the other. The reds, oranges and yellows of the sun were bright —almost startling—and the shades of gray and lavender of the moon were beautiful and mystical. But it was the tattoo of a crow in flight at the base of her spine, just above her belt that caught his eye. The bird was so black that it had a bluish sheen to it and the eye of the bird seemed to follow him as Penny walked away. Then she was out the door and gone.

He shook his head and smiled to himself. He glanced down at the notepad in front of him, the page of doodles staring up at him accusingly. He reached down and flipped over to a fresh page, picked up his pencil and started to write. The words came slowly at first but then it was like a dam broke, thoughts spilling over. It wasn't much—just a brief description of Penny, but it felt like actual writing. Maybe this had been the moment he needed. He really hoped so.

Family Dinner

Colin was sitting on the front stoop when Sidney got home from school. The building they lived in was in good shape and had been designed to look like a large brownstone that you might find in the city. It was a dark reddish brown brick, with the floors separated by a small line of white block that jutted out a few inches from the wall. The windows were large and stretched from the top to bottom of the floor they were on, and were framed by more of the white stone. The stoop was wide and led up to a pair of ornate wooden doors. On the right side of the doors was a set of intercom buttons, with each condo numbered. Colin loved to sit out and watch the life of the neighborhood as it flowed and danced around him. People coming and going, from one unknown place to another as he sat trying to imagine what was going on in their lives. Where they came from, what they were like—the whole nine yards.

Sidney finally arrived, holding a couple of textbooks against her chest in the crook of an arm, and her backpack slung loosely over the other shoulder. She was wearing blue jeans and a short sleeve shirt with a light jacket over it. She plopped down on the steps next to him.

"Hi, Dad." She shot him a sunny smile. He knew his own was a dim reflection, and he reached a hand out to her. She took it and he wrapped hers in his.

"Hi, Sid. How was school?"

"Oh, you know; it was school."

"Did you learn anything new today?" He started off their afternoon ritual.

"Yes, I did."

"What did you learn?"

"I learned how to count in binary." She beamed at him. He blinked.

"Count in binary?"

"Yup, wanna hear?" She sat down on the stoop next to him and started counting. "Zero. One. One, zero. One, one..." That's right about where she lost Colin.

"So what is that good for?"

"It's how computers think. It's the language they talk in..."

"It's too bad they can't just talk in English."

She gave him a little shove and laughed. They lapsed into silence. After a little bit, Colin spoke again.

"Ah, so I met a friend of yours, today at the coffee shop." She cocked her head and looked at him sideways.

"Who?"

"Penny. Our new neighbor. You didn't tell me we had a new neighbor."

"Oh, yeah, she's really cool, isn't she? Did you see her bellybutton ring? Or the crow tattoo? I wonder why she picked a crow."

"I saw them. Yes, they are cool. I'm not sure about the crow. It means many different things in many different cultures."

"I want to get my bellybutton pierced." The words poured out in a rush. "And I want a tattoo, too!"

"I bet that would hurt, huh?"

"Yes, I imagine so, but it would so be worth it."

Colin rolled his eyes. "I think you're probably a little young for piercings and tattoos, Sid."

"Aw, Dad."

He heard the teasing quality of her voice. "We can talk about it again when you turn thirty."

"Very funny." Then she became serious. "She's really pretty, isn't she?"

"Yes, she's very pretty, Sid." He could almost see the wheels turning in her head.

"Maybe we should ask her over to dinner sometime," she said. "You know, because she's new in the neighborhood and all. It would be the neighborly thing to do."

"Yes, that would be very neighborly."

"So then we can invite her over?" She looked excited.

Colin hesitated. This was where he'd normally say that he didn't think it was a good idea, or that he was really busy, or that he expected the world to end before that would happen. But this time he caught himself actually considering it. "It would be neighborly," he repeated under his breath.

"Nothing tricky, Dad. I'll be there, so it wouldn't be a date or anything."

Colin snorted.

"Oh, as long as it's not a date, then it's fine with me. Besides. She's kind of young for me."

"I couldn't really tell how old she was." Sidney's voice dropped and she gazed off thoughtfully. "Sometimes she seems my age and then other times she seems much older."

"I noticed that."

They both fell into a brief silence until Sidney punched him lightly in the arm and stood up.

"Awesome! I'll go invite her over. Is tonight all right?"

"Tonight's not so good—we're going to see Grandma and Grandpa for dinner." He was unexpectedly relieved to have plans. Now that he had agreed to have Penny over for dinner he felt nervous about the idea. The idea of someone new and interesting in their home—in their life—was daunting.

"Oh. Well, then maybe tomorrow?"

"Why don't you give her a few days to settle in, Sid? And do your homework before we go to dinner, okay?" He really didn't have to remind her of that. She was a great student. But it made him feel more parental to say it and she humored him.

"Okay, but I'm going to invite Penny before we go." She ran up the rest of the stoop and into the building, leaving Colin sitting alone again, but smiling. He'd been doing a lot of that today. Maybe having Penny over for dinner wasn't a bad idea.

"Hello there, Sidney!" Charlie said as he opened the door. He was the only relative that called her by her full name. "Come on in!" He pulled her inside and swept her up in bear hug, leaving her feet to dangle a few inches above the floor. She gasped and laughed. Colin watched them. Despite the tension between Colin and his father, the old man doted on her. Everyone got along with Sidney.

"Hi, Charlie!" She had to wait until her grandfather put her down and she could breathe again.

"Hello, Col." Charlie swung and offered Colin he hand as the smile on his face faded into something more reserved.

"Dad." Charlie's hand was huge and wrapped around his as if he were a child still. He was a large man: tall, strong and fit. Not an ounce of fat on his body and even at the age of 61 he looked like he was in his early forties.

"Come on in. Deck and Susan are here." Just as Colin and Deck's parents were waiting anxiously for Colin to move on, they were also waiting for Deck to pop the question. Make an honest woman out of Susan, as Charlie put it. Colin and Deck had been close before the accident, but they'd drifted apart simply due to the isolation Colin wrapped himself in.

Sidney skipped off to find Rita, leaving Charlie and Colin standing slightly awkwardly at the door. For the last couple of years tension had been growing between them. Charlie had made it clear that it was time for Colin to stop wallowing in his self-pity and get on with his life. That's how he'd described it. Concern had slowly transformed into frustration and impatience until finally they had taken to simply avoiding each other. "How've you been, Colin?" Charlie asked as he turned and headed deeper into the house.

"Fine, Dad." Colin spoke to his father's back. "Yourself?"

"Good enough, good enough. Your brother will be glad to see you've come out of your cave."

"I imagine that's true." Colin ignored the subtext.

They entered the kitchen where Sidney was hugging Susan, her eyes bright with youthful exuberance. It lightened Colin's heart to see her so happy. He made his way over to the kitchen table where Deck and his mother sat.

"Hey there, Col," Deck stood up and pulled Colin into a rough bear hug. Over his shoulder Colin smiled at Susan.

"Hi, Deck. Susan, you look lovely, as usual." She gave him a fond smirk.

"Flatterer. It's good to see you, Col."

"So when are we going out to grab a beer, Col?" Deck asked as he released Colin. "It's been too long."

"Well, any time you want." This was the way every conversation they'd had over the last few years had started.

"I'm going to take you up on that one of these days." They shared the unspoken knowledge that he would wait for Colin to make the first move. Deck never pushed but at the same time always made it clear he was there.

"Drink, Colin?" Their mother stood with her arms folded and a tiny half smile on her face as she watched her sons.

"Sure, Mom. Beer sounds good. I'll get it." Before the words had left his mouth, Charlie put an opened bottle in his hand. "Thanks, Dad." He took a long drink of the Fosters; it was cold and bracing going down. He pulled up a chair next to Deck and set his beer down in front of him. He sat back and nursed his beer while listening to the sounds of his family all around him. Deck regaled them all with stories, most of which weren't true. Susan, of course, called him on it whenever she could—both of the brothers had managed to hook up with practical, well-grounded women. Probably an unconscious desire for balance. But Deck was shameless and had everyone laughing.

Colin found that tonight there was something soothing about being surrounded by his family. For the longest time he'd found it oppressive. Invariably the conversation would turn to his life and everyone had an opinion about what he should do. He understood their concern but he wasn't ready for it. For the most part he made himself come for Sid's sake. Tonight felt different though. He closed his eyes and could feel them around him, wrapping him in love. Briefly he had the overwhelming sense that a huge weight was lifted from his shoulders.

Suddenly Sidney stood up and bounced on the balls of her feet, excitement shining on her face.

"Oh, I almost forgot! Guess what, Grandma. We have a new neighbor!"

"Good." Rita nodded. "Never liked the idea of you two so isolated over there. Tell me about this neighbor."

"Yeah, it's a girl. Her name is Penny. She's really awesome."

"Single?" Charlie asked and Colin rolled his eyes.

"Yes," Sidney went on. "And she's pretty, too. Dad said I could invite her over to dinner." He couldn't miss the meaningful glances that shot around the room.

"Really." Deck looked at Colin speculatively. "Dinner, huh?"

"Yes, dinner. I met her in the coffee shop. She came up to me and introduced herself. I have no idea how she knew who I was. Very pleasant though. Interesting."

"Another take-charge woman," Rita said. "You've always been into that type." Colin caught the hopeful look in her eye. Just seeing the expression on her face made him feel tense. Under pressure.

"She has tattoos! And her bellybutton is pierced! She's so cool," Sidney said. Charlie and Rita both raised eyebrows.

"So that's what you meant by interesting." Deck's eyes crinkled in the beginnings of a smile. "She doesn't sound like your usual type, Colin,"

"I don't know that I have a type anymore," Colin muttered. But he realized that he did like the girl—not in a romantic sense. There was something familiar about her. Comfortable. He hoped that he and Sid would see more of her.

"You don't need a type, Dad. You need a girlfriend." Sidney's resolute assertion brought laughter and she exchanged a knowing look with Susan.

"So do you like her, Col?" Susan asked.

"She's kind of young."

"Dad, you don't know enough women to start eliminating them just because they're young." Sidney glared at him severely. "Anyway we don't really know how old she is. Sometimes she seems old and wise. Other times, more like my age."

"So what's for dinner, Mom?" Colin asked, not so subtly changing the topic. Everyone laughed.

"You're not getting off the hook that easily." Rita smirked at him "Tell us more about this girl."

Colin sighed.

"She's a bit odd, but in a good way. Very outgoing and exuberant. Kind of like someone else we know." Colin shot Sidney a glance, and she snickered back at him. "I suspect that's why I enjoyed talking to her so much."

"You should see her, Grandma. She's got a great smile. Her skin is pale white and her hair is jet black, short and spiky. She looks like a really beautiful vampire!"

"Wow, Colin," Susan said. "I had no idea you were into vampires."

"She doesn't look like a vampire." Colin rolled his eyes again. "She's something…brighter. Sunnier. Mostly she's interesting." He stopped himself and shook his head. "Okay, enough about Penny. What's for dinner?"

This time his Mom relented and allowed him to change the subject.

※

"How's the writing?" Deck and Colin sat in the living room after dinner. "Still stuck?" Deck sat on the couch with Sidney next to him, leaning on his shoulder. Susan sat on the other side of her. Rita and Colin sat on the other couch that ran perpendicular to the larger couch, and Charlie was sprawled out in his recliner. Rita referred to the chair as his throne.

"Yeah." Colin felt as if he were being interrogated.

And they haven't really gotten started.

"Still stuck. Although I did manage to get something down this morning at the coffee shop. Nothing major or even any good, but it was nice to put words to paper for a change."

"Good. I'm glad to hear it." Deck looked pleased. "I've been waiting for the next book for far too long now."

"That's what my agent says."

"Hey, I don't want to read it," Deck said. "I just need something to hold the door open." This was an old joke and Colin gave him the obligatory laugh. "Seriously though, I'm glad to hear you're making some progress."

"Me, too." Colin shrugged, though he wasn't sure he'd really call it progress quite yet. "So how's life been treating you guys?"

"I can't complain." Deck shrugged. "Definitely not seeing enough of my brother, but other than that pretty good."

"How about you, Susan?"

"I've been good, Col. Got a new grant, so I'm in heaven pretty much." Susan was an anthropologist at the university. "I'm going to be working on a new book on the impact of computer technology on social communication and storytelling."

"That sounds interesting. I'm into that whole storytelling thing." He smiled wryly and Susan laughed.

"Yeah. I was hoping to pick your brain sometime."

"Of course, tell me about this book."

Susan launched into an explanation and Deck rolled his eyes.

"Now you've done it."

Without pausing Susan leaned over and gave him a solid elbow in the arm. Sidney snickered while Deck pretended to be injured. Colin was suddenly struck by how similar Susan and Mari were. Had been. Whatever.

He felt relaxed as the conversation flowed around him. He couldn't remember the last time he'd felt so relaxed in his parents' house. It reminded him of old times. He had a sudden clear picture of Marianne sitting on the large couch next to Deck teasing him mercilessly, and he felt a lump in his throat.

A wave of bleak sadness washed through him and he closed his eyes while he rode it out. When he opened his eyes his mother had a hint of a frown on her face, but as their eyes met she smiled at him. He returned the smile with a little shrug.

After a while Colin looked up and saw that Sidney had fallen asleep between Susan and Deck on the couch with her head resting on Deck's shoulder, and he glanced up at the clock over the mantle. Going on 10pm. He'd lost track of time, and he sat up straighter on the couch.

"Well," he said. "I suppose we should be going. Sidney has school in the morning." He pushed himself up from the couch.

"It was good to see you, Col," Rita said, and the others echoed her.

"You, too." He hugged everyone but Charlie briefly—Charlie offered the same firm handshake he always did. Colin walked over to where Sidney slept and gently woke her. She looked about blearily and then reached up to take Colin's hand. He helped her stand up and they made their way to the door. When they got there she turned back.

"Goodnight everyone," she said and gave the tired version of her bright smile as she was passed around for hugs. When they were done she pushed out the door into the night and Colin started to follow, but Charlie stepped forward and put a big hand on his shoulder.

"It was good to see you, son." Colin was mildly surprised by the cautious warmth in his voice.

"You too, Dad." He studied his father for a moment before he turned and followed Sidney out into the dark.

When they arrived home, and Sidney had staggered to her bedroom, Colin sat down at the dining room table for a while, just thinking. His mind wandered between his family, Penny and some story ideas that were percolating at the edge of his brain. It was a good feeling. As if he was stretching muscles he'd not used in a while. It wasn't simple or easy, but the pathways were still there. Shortly before midnight he was struck with a strange feeling. It was familiar but at first he couldn't identify it. It wasn't strong—just the faintest whisper, but he liked the way it felt.

After a few minutes he realized what it was: optimism. He decided not to focus on it anymore—he had this tendency to over-think things. Instead he'd just enjoy it. He made his way upstairs and went to bed.

※

Colin woke up standing on a dusty road. His first thought was that he was sleepwalking, but he'd never seen any road like this one. So he found himself standing in the dust, confused and tired. He glanced around, swinging his eyes along the horizon. The sky was dark with no residual daylight, and he could hear the soothing nighttime noises: crickets chirping, the rustling play of wind through grass and leaves, and a hundred other small sounds.

The road stretched away in both directions, running out to meet the horizon—a paved ribbon. The moon hung just above the horizon at one end of the road, a huge white disk, impossibly tall and the other direction was cloaked in a distant darkness. On one side of the road a line of trees stood sentry like a great wall and on the other side of the wall a flat plain rolled away into soft, rolling foothills. Beyond the foothills mountains jutted into the sky, impossibly tall and he hoped that the moon travelled along the road rather than try to cross the line of peaks because it would undoubtedly get stuck otherwise. In the distance he heard the mournful howl of a wolf calling out its loneliness to the night. Colin waited but no voice answered.

The night air was clear and fresh, blowing in off the mountain foothills and across the plains and he stared off into the distance, letting the slight breeze wrap him. He turned his attention to the tree line and it had spread out and darkened into the beginnings of a deep, dark woods. Sheltered from the light of the moon, fireflies danced under the canopy of leaves, tiny pinpoints of light bursting out and then fading away just as fast. He sighed and realized he could just stay here all night listening to the sounds, watching the sights but he also knew, somehow, that he was supposed to move on. But where? A part of him wanted to walk out to the foothills and climb up into the mountains but that wasn't right either.

He decided he'd just follow the road, but couldn't decide which direction. As he gazed down the road, trying to decide, he heard a sound from behind, faintly carrying in the wind. It sounded like the rhythmic beat of a horse moving at an easy canter.

He turned and stared down the road but could see nothing. The darkness at the far end of the road seemed to thicken and grow as he struggled to pick out sight of anything in that direction.

Suddenly Colin had a strong sense of displacement and vertigo. When it passed he stood in a lush glade, surrounded by green bushes and plants, wildly colored flowers and the tallest trees he'd ever seen. The trunks were so wide that you could hide a car on the other side of one of them and never see it. It reminded him of a childhood visit to Big Sur to see the monstrously huge redwoods. He remembered one in particular with a tunnel through it wide and tall enough to drive a car.

He looked up the full height of one of the trees and the trunks and leaves seemed to go on forever. Above the clearing of the glade the night sky was bright with stars. Millions of them. He felt slightly dizzy again looked back down to regain his sense of balance. It was the same feeling he got when he stood next to a skyscraper down in the city and looked up the building's sheer wall—as if the world he stood on had disappeared and all that existed was the towering giant in front of him.

He looked around at the rest of the clearing. There was a small path of stones that split the glade into three sections, and at the center there was a stone bench. He started to walk toward it, studying the plants and flowers around him as he went. Before he reached it, a musical and soothing voice broke through the silence of the glade.

"It is beautiful, is it not?"

Colin turned toward the voice and saw a tall, striking woman standing near the trees on one side of the glade. She was willowy, with white hair and pale skin, and she wore a long flowing white dress. The dress itself seemed to reflect the starlight, glowing softly. She began to walk toward him slowly, graceful and elegant.

"Where are we?" Colin asked, unable to take his eyes off of the woman.

"You are beyond the Wall." Her voice carried across the glade borne on the slight breeze that cooled the night air.

"What wall?"

"The wall between the worlds. The Wall of Sleep." She stopped a few yards from Colin and smiled at him affectionately. There was something familiar about her and the strange otherness of her brought Penny to mind. "The wall that separates your world from the Dreamside." When she was approaching across the glade, she'd appeared to be at least as tall as Colin, if not taller, but now that she was just out of reach, he saw that she was almost a head shorter than he was.

"The Dreamside?" He realized he sounded slightly daft and grimaced. She must have sensed his consternation because she laughed lightly and the sound was sweet and soft, like a gentle breeze moving through wind chimes.

"It is all right, Coilín." Her lips quirked around a smile. She spoke to him using the name Rita called him, drawing him back to an earlier time in his life. No one but his mother ever called him that but he found it strangely comforting from this woman. "It is always unsettling to come here fully. Most people bring only the smallest part of their mind here when they dream. You, however, are able to come here fully—your body and mind are entirely here on the Dreamside." She reached out a hand to him and without thinking he reached and took it. Her skin was cool and soft, and he felt a slight charge of energy where their skin touched. "That is why I come to you, Coilín, my child. Because you are dreaming here so completely, you can alter dreams beyond just your own. I realize this doesn't mean anything to you now, but when you need to understand, you will." Her words were confusing and after contemplating them for a long moment he shoved them aside and focused on what was before him—what he could touch, smell and feel.

"So where is this wall?" He glanced around. The woman laughed melodiously and gave his hand a little squeeze.

"I am the Wall, Coilín."

"You don't look much like a wall."

"I can manifest in many ways. You might say that I am a concept rather than a physical wall. I felt that this form would be easier for you to accept. Not to mention it's hard to carry on a conversation as a brick wall." She smiled playfully.

"Good point."

Then her smile melted away to worry—her exquisite beauty marred slightly by a frown. It was an uncomfortable expression, as if she didn't wear it often.

"An evil has come to the Dreamside. It is newborn and full of rage... Already it assails me, seeking to break through into your world. I..." A brief hint of fear flashed across her features, looking horribly out of place on her face. "I need your help."

"What can I do?"

"I need you to stop this evil. I need you to help me repair the damage it is already doing." She paused briefly and looked past him into the distance, her eyes unfocused. "If it manages to break through, then all the nightmares and dreams will be free to move into the waking world."

"So how am I going to stop this thing?"

"That I cannot tell you. I can tell you how to start though. You will find two companions; one that you already know and another that I have sent to you. They will help you in your task —you must find the places in the Dreamside where the evil attacks me. There you must find a way to drive it away and repair the damage." She pulled him closer slowly until they were a foot apart, and she looked up at him. He involuntarily breathed deeply, pulling her scent in. She smelled sweet—

wildflowers, vanilla and something else. "I cannot tell you any more other than that it is very dangerous to be in the Dreamside as you are. If you are hurt here that hurt will follow you back to the waking world. You will recover from those injuries quickly enough, but if you die here..." she trailed off with a graceful shrug. "Some things cannot be healed."

"Why me? I mean, I'm just a guy..."

"No." She spoke slowly as if choosing her words carefully. "You are not just anything. You are the strongest Dreamer I have seen in ages—if not ever. If you cannot help me, then I don't know who else can." She let go of his hand and took his face in both of her hands. He looked down at her impossibly beautiful face and felt as if he were falling into her eyes. "You have been here awake before this. At least two times I have seen you here. That is how I knew that you were special."

Abruptly she dropped her hands and cocked her head as if listening. Her brow furrowed into a small frown and she looked at Colin again.

"You must sleep now, Coilín. It is too dangerous for you here tonight. I fear you have come to the attention of the enemy." She reached up and touched him at the temple with cool fingers. Immediately he felt a wave of tiredness sweep through him. "Sleep, child, and watch for the dream I have sent to aid you." She stood up on tip toe and brushed her lips on his ever so softly, a chaste kiss, and he fell away into darkness again.

✺

The next morning Colin woke with the feathery feel of lips on his. When he closed his eyes he could see the woman before him, beautiful and pure, glowing in the starlight. He had felt warm and safe with her. But now that he was awake he only felt scared—she'd referred to two previous dreams and he had a feeling he knew just which dreams she meant.

Coffee with Kate

It was Saturday, so Colin slept in and woke slowly to the smell of waffles, sausage and coffee. Over the last few years Sidney had taken to making breakfast for them on the weekends. He'd never asked her to cook, but it had become another ritual in their lives. It smelled heavenly. He rolled out of bed and made his way downstairs. She had set the table, and all of the necessary accessories to waffles were arranged in the middle of the table. There was the little pitcher of heated syrup, a shaker with powdered sugar in it, and various jellies and jams. And of course she'd gone out and gotten the newspaper.

Colin walked in and sat down. He sighed and sat back with a big smile.

"Wow, waffles for me? What did I do to deserve this?" Pretending it was an unusual thing was another part of the ritual. She smiled and dropped a waffle on his plate, still hot from the iron.

"You didn't do anything, Dad." After a beat she continued. "But I was hoping maybe if I fed you, you'd actually do something today. You know, get out and see the world."

"I don't know, sweetheart. I might just be too full after I gorge myself on this. Plus, the world is a large and scary place." He tried to make it a joke but it fell flat and Sidney frowned at him. She sat down in her own seat, but held her tongue.

"Thanks, Sid."

"Sure." They fell into silence. Colin watched her for a moment but she didn't look up from her food. He hated these moments of tension—infrequent though they were. Sidney had been very patient with him but lately he could sense her growing frustration with him. He understood how she felt but he couldn't just flick a switch and be...different. As he watched her eat he felt the pressure of the silence grow and he searched for something to say to ease the tension.

Before he could speak, the doorbell broke through the oppressive quiet.

"I'll get that." Sidney bounced up out of her seat and almost ran out to the living room. Colin heard the door open with a soft gasp as the weather seal broke. He figured it was his mother. She sometimes stopped by on the weekends, especially early in the morning, but Colin had gotten in the habit of letting Sidney get the door.

He set down the newspaper that he hadn't even managed to read. It was just as well, he figured. Everything in it was decidedly depressing—the world wasn't a kind place these days. It seemed that every story was about catastrophic accidents, violence and vitriolic anger and hostility.

The sound of Sidney returning brought his eyes up. He could hear that someone was with her. He looked up from the paper as Sidney came into the kitchen with Kate in tow.

Kate Stimson had full lips under a small nose and slightly almond shaped hazel eyes. Her eyes and mouth were framed by smile lines—not the wrinkles of age, but laughter and happiness. Otherwise her skin was smooth. There was a smattering of freckles across the bridge of her nose that Colin immediately liked. Her hair was light with a slight hint of red and cut short so that it hung an inch or so below the line of her jaw. As far as he could see, she didn't have an ounce of fat on her, but still had supple curves. Colin had known rationally that she was a good looking woman, but he suddenly was surprised to discover that she wasn't just good looking—she was beautiful.

"Good morning, Colin." She looked slightly nervous—her eyes darted around the room. So Sidney had set this unexpected visit up. He suddenly wanted to set Kate at ease and stood quickly, rattling the newspaper into a somewhat folded shape.

"Hello, Kate." He gestured at an empty chair at the table. He resisted the urge to glare at Sidney. *Meddler.* "Have a seat. Can I get you some coffee?"

"Oh, thanks, but I can't stay. In fact, I came over to see if you wanted to go get a cup of coffee downtown with me." The words came out in a bit of a rush and she blushed slightly. This was the last thing he'd expected. "I have to get out of the house and thought maybe you could use the break too," she continued, racing to the end of her explanation as if she wanted to get it out before Colin could object.

This was the last thing he'd expected and surprise made him pause a moment. "Well, Sidney made breakfast already. I think it'd be rude of me to not eat any of it. But I bet we have enough for another if you'd like to join us."

"Oh, Dad," Sidney said. "It'll keep. Just go. Get out of the house." She shot him a pointed glance.

"Yeah, okay." He hid his natural reluctance from both of them. It probably would do him some good. "I'd like that." He glanced at Sidney in mute appeal. "Sid? You want to go with us?"

"Oh, no, Dad." She tried to hide a relieved smile rather unsuccessfully. "I've got some things I want to do this morning. It will be nice to have you out of my hair."

"I wouldn't want to bug you," he said with a quick laugh. He could see Sidney trying not to look smug, and he turned back to face Kate. "Well, it looks like it's just you and me. Shall we go?"

"Sure!" Kate's smile blossomed, shedding the nervousness. He really liked the way the tiny lines around her eyes and mouth crinkled up, and her eyes seemed to twinkle.

As they made their way to the door, Colin was surprised at his own nervous excitement.

☀

At the coffee shop Colin nursed a white chocolate mocha and Kate had a cappuccino. They sat at a small round table that brought them closer together than he'd expected. It was cozy.

"I'm glad you came," Kate said. She seemed to have regained her composure and didn't seem nervous at all.

"I'm glad too." He found that it was true—not just a social nicety. "It's good to get out and talk to someone that's not a member of my family."

Kate laughed.

"Well, I woke up today and realized I was tired of being alone in the house all day. I was hoping maybe you felt the same way. It's been a long time since I really hung out with anyone." She shrugged slightly. "I figure that of all the people I know, you might best understand how I feel."

"Yes, I imagine that I do." He studied her face while she took a quick sip of her drink. She was probably the most beautiful woman that lived within his sphere of acquaintances, but it was the obvious intelligence in her eyes that drew him in right then.

"Not to imply that Mark leaving me compares in any way to..." She paused a moment, realizing that she was wandering onto a painful topic and he could see her trying to find some way to get back onto safer ground. So he took mercy on her.

"The accident?"

"Yes, the accident." She looked relieved, and gave him an apologetic smile.

"Well, I wouldn't ever compare those sorts of things. We both ended up alone and the why and how of it is irrelevant. It's the alone part that sucks." He paused thoughtfully. "A few days ago I wouldn't really have said being alone was bad at all. Funny how things shift in such a short time."

"Well, I wouldn't say that four years is a short time."

"Yes, you're probably right," he said with a laugh, but felt a brief stab of guilt as Sidney came to mind.

She cocked her head slightly and her brow furrowed a bit. "So what changed?"

"I met someone." He immediately realized the implication of that statement and backpedalled. "I mean, not met someone like that. Met someone as in talked. A very interesting girl—a neighbor of ours. She just seems so fresh. It was hard not to be pulled in."

"You must mean Penny."

"You've met her?"

"No, but Sid mentioned her."

"I..." he started. "I'm glad you've been spending time with Sid. Thank you. I've not been the best parent." He flushed slightly as again his mouth betrayed him by saying the first thing that came to mind.

Kate nodded and smiled. "She's been good for me. She is so mature for her age. Insightful. I find myself jealous of you sometimes." She laughed easily. "And she helps me out sometimes—comes over often and plays with the boys." Kate's sons were five and six years old. Colin imagined that they were a handful.

They fell into a comfortable conversation about Sidney and Colin was surprised at how well Kate knew his daughter—understood her.

He had known Sidney spent some time with Kate. She went over to visit frequently, but it was clear that she had a deeper relationship with Kate than he'd realized. He felt a brief moment of anxiety at how far out of touch he was with Sidney's life even though he lived with her, but pushed it aside.

The fact that she was spending time with Kate and the boys was interesting—maybe even predictable. Tying this wrinkle in with Sidney's recent pushing for him to get on with his life he had a suspicion about what direction her plans was taking. Little schemer, he thought, hiding a smile. He understood though. Kate was easy to get along with—a calming influence. It was no wonder Sidney had taken to her.

Colin and Kate continued talking and after a while he realized he was enjoying himself. They didn't venture back into anything too serious, but instead kept it light. It turned out that she also had a great sense of humor and he was surprised to find he was actually keeping track of her good points. So far he hadn't found any bad points.

Colin could feel someone standing at the table beside them and he looked up. Penny was standing there, her hands on her hips and a big smile on her face.

"Hi!" she said brightly. She turned to Kate and extended her hand. "I'm Penny. You must be Kate. Sid has told me so much about you." Somehow this didn't surprise Colin. Kate shook her hand.

"Hi, Penny." Kate took Penny's hand. "It's good to meet you. I keep meaning to come over and welcome you to the neighborhood. So welcome to the neighborhood." She shook her hand once before releasing it.

"Thank you." Penny's quick laugh chimed around the café. She turned to Colin. "Hiya, Colin. It's great to see you again!"

"Hi, Penny." he replied. Penny arched an eyebrow at him for a moment then rolled her eyes and threw up her hands.

"You're supposed to invite me to sit, silly." She didn't wait, pulled out the chair and plopped down in it.

"Oh, geeze, sorry. I'm horrible at these social niceties. Out of practice."

"I understand." She patted him on the shoulder before turning to Kate. She reached out and put a hand on her arm and looked at her curiously. "So tell me about yourself, Kate. I want to know everything. Start with the important things. What's your favorite coffee drink?"

Penny interrogated Kate for a little while and Colin just watched with amusement. At first Kate seemed flustered by the seemingly random questions that Penny shot at her machine gun fast. But after a few minutes she settled down and seemed to enjoy the conversation—she started asking Penny questions as well. By the time they were done trading answers to questions that didn't seem important, they were leaning toward each other. Kate looked relaxed and happy, and Colin noticed that she seemed younger and more alive when she was talking to Penny. He wondered if he looked the same way when he had spoken to the girl the other day.

Suddenly Penny smiled and stood up.

"Well, I've got to go. Things to see, people to do. You know how it is." She reached out and touched Colin on the shoulder lightly and briefly. Something about that moment of contact made him feel more awake and energetic. "Now you two don't be strangers. And enjoy your caffeinated beverages." She grinned, turned and left as quickly as she'd appeared.

Kate shook her head in wonder.

"Wow, she's a ball of energy, isn't she? And so different. I like her."

"Yes, I do too. I imagine it would be hard not to like her."

"I agree."

Colin glanced up and met Kate's eyes and for a brief second he caught her with a slightly anxious look on her face. But before he could puzzle out what it meant, it dropped off her face and she smiled again.

"You know what?" Kate asked him. "We should take the kids and do something fun. Maybe a movie. Or take a train into the city. We could go to the zoo..." She trailed off and looked mildly embarrassed. "I'm being pushy, aren't I? I'm sorry." She looked away from him.

"No, I'd like that," Colin answered automatically and was surprised to realize it was really true—he would like to see Kate again.

"I'm just a little out of practice with this..." Kate said with a helpless shrug.

"God, I know just what you mean." Colin tried to give her a reassuring smile, but he wasn't really sure if he hit the mark. She nodded and they both lapsed into quiet and focused on their drinks for a few minutes. Colin snuck a quick glance at her. He was relieved that she was nervous—he didn't want to be the only one who felt...rusty. If he was going to get back in the habit of being a social animal again, it would be good to do it with someone on equal footing. Quickly and without his even recognizing it, they fell into a comfortable pattern and his nervousness fell away.

Later at home it occurred to him that he hadn't compared her to Marianne the entire time they sat together. Maybe he *should* spend more time with Kate. He just didn't know if he was ready yet.

Fight or Flight

"So, how was coffee? Tell me everything! Did you have fun?" Sidney had been waiting for him on the front stoop and didn't even bother with niceties before pouncing.

The sun hadn't begun to overheat the day yet and a light breeze caressed his skin. It was one of those perfect days that you sometimes got at the extreme ends of summer. There were some kids playing up the street and the happy sounds they made floated on that breeze. Colin felt more relaxed than he had in years but tried not to think about it too much. He didn't want to chase the good feeling away. Some things just don't bear scrutiny.

"Yes. We had a good time. I think she was just as nervous and out of practice as me."

"Good. Are you going to ask her out?"

Colin laughed and shook his head.

"Well, I hadn't really thought it through that far," he lied. "It was great, but really I've got a lot of work to do..."

"Oh, Dad." Sidney threw up her hands. "You're hopeless."

"Oh, Sid," he mimicked. She just shook her head. Before she could continue he changed the subject. "So what do you have planned today? Anything fun?" She glared a moment before relenting.

"I want to go to the library. Penny is going to meet me there. Oh and I told Kate I'd stop by and play with the boys a while this afternoon."

"I hadn't realized how much time you have been spending with Kate."

"Yeah. She's been in bad shape for a while. So I go over and spell her for a while and play with the boys. Sometimes we just have lemonade and talk. She's really a sweet person. Plus, the boys are so cute."

"You're a good person, Sid." After a pause he spoke again. "Well, let me know when you're ready and I'll give you a lift to the library. I wouldn't mind poking around there a bit."

"As long as you pretend not to know me." Softened the words with a grin. "I don't want my friends to see me hanging out with my Dad. How embarrassing would that be?"

"You know, Sid, sometimes I have a hard time remembering that you're only fifteen. And then you go and say something like that."

She laughed but didn't respond. He'd been more than half serious. She'd had to grow up faster than most kids her age. It was a testament to her own strength that her eyes were bright —rarely filled with pain. Guilt swept through him. He hated that the accident, and probably his own reaction to it had taken away so much of her childhood.

The door swung open behind them and a cheerful voice rang out.

"Well, look at what I found," Penny said brightly. Sidney jumped to her feet and hugged Penny enthusiastically. Penny returned her hug and grinned over the girl's shoulder at Colin. "What are you up to? Lock yourselves out? Watching the birds? This is an odd place for it. I wouldn't have thought that there would be many of the really pretty songbirds out here." She glanced up at the sky and her radiant smile slipped slightly and a frown furrowed her brow. "Probably see a few crows and ravens. Maybe a rook or two. Or are they extinct?" Her voice had dropped to a mutter. Then the smile was back and she pulled back from Sid, holding her by her shoulders and inspecting her carefully.

"Good morning, Penny," Sidney said. "Dad said I could invite you over for dinner. Will you come?"

Penny raised an eyebrow and glanced over at Colin.

"Got your little girl doing your dirty work?"

Colin grinned.

"Yeah, she's much more outgoing than I am. I might as well take advantage of it."

Penny gave Sidney a little kiss on the forehead and let her go. Then she bounced down the steps and spun around to face them.

"I would be delighted to dine with the two of you." She gave a quick curtsy. "On which evening shall I call upon you?"

Sidney visibly stifled a laugh and then stood up straighter. "Would the day after tomorrow be convenient for you, my Lady?" Colin rolled his eyes with a short laugh.

"I will have to consult my calendar, but I believe that would be most acceptable, my Lady." They curtsied at each other again and laughed. Dropping the charade, Penny relaxed into a more casual stance. "So are we going to a restaurant or dining in?"

"Let's eat in," Colin said. "Sidney and I can cook when threatened by starvation."

"And if that doesn't go so well we can always order out," Sidney said.

"How does mac n' cheese sound?" Colin deadpanned.

"Oh, mac n' cheese!" Penny enthused. "My favorite!"

"I was kidding, Penny. We'll make something nice, I promise."

"Mac n' cheese is nice, silly. Especially if you put some hot dog slices in it!"

"Well, we'll expect you around 5?"

"Perfect! I can't wait." She turned to Sidney. "Library time?" They declined his offer of a ride and left, waving goodbye at Colin as they went. Colin watched Penny go and was struck by the young woman's almost ethereal beauty, and the confident way she carried herself. But it was her energy and upbeat attitude that really drew him. For a brief moment he compared her to Kate, but the comparison didn't work.

Apples and oranges, he realized. He just didn't think of Penny in that way. She felt more like family for some reason.

That night, after he drifted off to sleep, Colin found himself standing at the edge of the glade again. The otherworldly beauty of the place sank into him, soothing and calm. The lush greenery and radiant colors of the flowers, the mesmerizing sound of birdsong and the soft breeze rustling in the plant life around him. It tasted of home to him. Not his own home but rather the more abstract concept of home. Somewhere that he belonged, a refuge and a place where he could feel safe.

He took a step forward into the clearing and the grass was cool and spongy. He glanced down and saw that he was dressed in the clothes he slept in: boxers and a T-shirt. He felt a little strange being half dressed, but the comfort of the place overrode that immediately. He had a suspicion he'd feel right at home no matter what he was wearing.

Colin glanced around, searching for the Wall. Last time he'd dreamed of this place, she'd been the center of the glade—the heart of it. She must have brought him here, he thought, but he wasn't really sure—he had no clue how any of this worked. Could he come here by himself? He had a strong desire to see the Wall again.

He took another step forward and suddenly there was a strange flicker in his perceptions. It was similar to the disorientation that came from abruptly changing temperatures—coming into an air conditioned house on a scalding hot summer day. That moment where the mind tries to catch up with the unexpected change. When his perception cleared he found he was standing on the dark and gloomy road. It most definitely did not feel like home—nothing like the glade—more like the two places were opposite sides of the same coin. Darkness seemed to flow out of the thick stand of trees almost as if it were a thinking thing, crossing the road and sliding toward the mountains. Tendrils of shadow slid across the pavement, questing and probing as the darkness moved off the shoulder and into the tall grasses that lined that side of the road. Colin felt a strong urge to back away from the creeping shadows, but he found he couldn't move.

Then he heard the clatter of hooves on pavement in the distance. He peered into the darkness, past the shadows creeping across the road, and far away he could barely make out a shape where the road met horizon. There was something odd about the cadence of the hoof beats but he couldn't put his finger on it. While he stood there frozen, listening to the sound and straining to see the shape heading toward him he felt a wisp of apprehension move across his mind. He wanted to leave this place. He wanted to be able to move his feet.

Then he realized what sounded wrong. It wasn't the crashing triplets of a horse at full gallop. There was a different rhythm. As if there were too many legs involved. Maybe it was two horses, he thought.

The pounding of the hooves became slightly louder and Colin could see occasional tiny flashes in the distance. He stared into the darkness trying to see any details of whatever was coming down the road. There was something wrong with what he saw. It was too wide. It had to be two horses.

His apprehension was slowly changing to feelings of dread as he finally started to see some detail. Whatever it was that was approaching him like a train was not a pair of horses. It wasn't even one horse. Then over the hooves he could hear a strange huffing, growling sound that echoed the cadence of the hooves, and his feet seemed to come unglued. He staggered backwards and sat down hard and began to scrabble backwards.

The creature was huge and black as night, an inky darkness that seemed to absorb the light around it. It ran on six legs and had no arms. In fact, where its face should have been was simply a featureless blackness, shining wet and blank. The fundamental wrongness of the creature assailed Colin's senses and his dread burst into terror and despair in the moment. His mind stretched into a galloping panic and he rolled over, pushed to his feet and broke into a lurching sprint. As soon as he wasn't looking at the beast anymore the details began to fade, leaving utter despair to weave around his still growing panic.

He ran as hard as he could. Already his breath was coming in ragged gasps and the muscles of his legs were burning, but still he ran as hard as he could, leaning into the motion, pumping his arms. The only thing keeping him from screaming was the struggle to breathe. Under his feet the pavement flew by at an unbelievable speed. His stride stretched out and ate the ground, trees rushing past and for the briefest moment he thought he would get away.

But behind him the hoof beats were getting louder—almost a deafening drumming that pounded at his senses like fireworks, made his chest thump. His heart fell and the quick glimmer of hope disappeared. He wasn't going to outrun this thing. Not a chance.

Abruptly his foot caught on a pothole and he pitched forward, sprawling toward the ground. As he hit the pavement and rolled a few times, losing his momentum and then catching himself painfully with his palms, he heard a voice in his ear.

"Coilín you should not be here, it is too dangerous." It was the soft melodic voice of the woman from the glade—the Wall. "Wake up now, and do not forget the dream I sent. You must find her before it is too late."

Colin rolled to a stop on his back, scrapes on his knees and shoulders, and tried to push himself up. The huffing growls of the monster had turned to an angry, grating rasp like metal grinding against metal. Colin felt as though he was sinking into molasses, his movements slow and weak.

"Wake now, Coilín." The sound of his given name snapped through him, carrying some tiny measure of power and strength. His thoughts cleared ever so slightly and he stopped trying to stand and curled into a fetal position, making his body as small as possible. Instead of worrying about flight, he struggled to wake up, repeating in his head that this was just a dream. Behind him the growling of the beast escalated into an angry, full throated roar of frustration and then Colin was in his bed again, sweating and charged with adrenaline. He panted heavily and shook. It took him several moments to convince himself that he was awake again, but when he did relief rose like a cooling breeze leaving him shaking.

He pushed up onto his elbows and stared around the room, drinking in the familiar sights, his things. Just seeing his room helped him to slow his breathing and the pounding of his heart. He tried to tell himself the dream had been just another nightmare, but it was impossible to even believe that anymore. Too many strange dreams. Too much truth in them. It was as if something clicked into place and he believed in the reality of his dreams. Now if he could just understand them.

Then he felt the first stings of pain on his palms and looked down to see his skin had been scraped raw. But it didn't surprise him—all of this felt familiar. Hell, he would have been more surprised if his hands hadn't been bloodied.

He got out of bed and walked to the bathroom, discovering other small cuts and hurts as he moved. It took him a while to tend to his injuries and after he got them cleaned up and bandaged he returned to bed. His sheets were wet with sweat and smelled of panic so he grabbed a throw and sat in the recliner that slouched in the corner of his room, close to the windows. He slid one of the curtains back enough to let the light of the moon into the room. For a few long moments he searched the street and yard below but saw nothing out of place.

Finally he settled back and closed his eyes. It took him a long time to fall back to sleep, but when he did, he had no more dreams.

Beastly

The next day Colin woke early and went down to the kitchen to try to write. He pushed last night's dream out of his mind and focused on other things instead, but it was hard to shake the emotions that he'd woken with. The fear, the panic, the despair—they were too much to ignore. So instead he allowed the dream to flow back through his mind and wrote about it, tried to put what he'd seen and felt into words. But while the feelings were still hanging around, what he'd seen was fading fast. He couldn't really visualize the beast that had chased him. It was like a hole in his memory that was slowly widening, expanding as it ate away his memories of the dream.

Around midmorning he closed up his laptop and sat back. He'd managed to capture the feelings in a few pages and that helped him to push away the bad feelings a bit. It had been so long since he'd been able to do any writing. And what he'd put down actually felt good. Not his best work, but still solid and smooth, and it went a long way to easing his mind—bringing him emotionally back into the waking world again fully. And then to his surprise he was able to work on the new novel. It started out slow but as he wrote he picked up speed and found a groove.

When he finally put down the pencil, he had a strong desire—no, a *need*—to go see Deck. He stood quickly, following the impulse before it could fade, and called up the stairs.

"Sid, I'm going over to see Deck. I should be back in a while." She appeared at the top of the stairs.

"Really?"

"Yes, really."

"Wow. Well, good. Tell him I said hi. Susan, too." She had a bemused look on her face and gave him a wave. Then he was out the door.

He pulled into his brother's driveway, parked and started to get out. Before he had a second foot on the ground, Deck appeared at the front door. An expression of shock quickly gave way to a wide smile and he walked out to meet Colin.

"Well, what the heck is this? Did you have much trouble finding the place?"

"Very funny, Deck." Colin rolled his eyes.

"Come on in, Col." His brother stepped back to let Colin in. "I was just making some lunch. Hungry?"

"Yeah, I could eat."

"And a beer, how about a beer?"

"It's not even noon, Deck," Colin smiled wryly.

"And your point is?"

"No point. Just saying."

"So do you want the beer or not?"

"Sure, I'll have one." Colin followed him into the kitchen and leaned on the counter, elbows resting on the cool granite while Deck got a pair of beers out of the fridge.

"Here. Open these while I get started on lunch." He went over and picked up the phone and dialed while Colin rooted around in a drawer for a bottle opener. He found one and the soft snap and hiss of the caps coming off followed.

"Hi, I need to have a pizza delivered," Deck said into the phone. Colin laughed.

"Making lunch, huh?"

Deck grinned at him then continued talking.

"Large thin crust. Onions, garlic, sausage and banana peppers." There was a pause. "That's right. I should have a credit card on file." Another pause. "Three-two-five-one. Great, we'll be here." He hung up and smiled at Colin. "I'm a freaking gourmet, what can I say?"

Colin handed him one of the beers and raised his up.

"To seven pages of actual writing," he said.

"Seven whole pages? Wow!"

"That's seven more than I've been managing lately."

"Hey, that's great, Col." Deck clicked his bottle against Colin's. "The novel?"

Colin shook his head slightly. "Just a few exercises—a little bit about the main character. Helps me learn who she is. I did flesh out some plot ideas too, though."

"Excellent. It's about time. Any idea what's changed?" Deck sat on a barstool.

"Not really. I've always had this feeling that it would just take some important moment to get me back on track. The nearest I can figure it was when I spoke to Penny at the coffee shop."

"It sounds like this girl is having quite an effect on you." Colin could tell he was trying to sound neutral.

"She is, but it's not like that. I can't be sure but sometimes she seems like she's Sidney's age. Other times older than the rest of the world," He paused, considering. "She's slightly otherworldly...and there's something familiar about her. Like we have met before." He shook his head slightly. "Whatever it is, she seems to have loosened something in my brain. The words are coming slow but sure. Knock on wood."

Deck rapped his knuckles on his own head softly with a nod and then gestured at Colin's hands with his beer bottles.

"So what's with the bandages?"

"Oh," Colin shrugged. "I fell on the pavement and scratched up my palms. No big deal." He suddenly realized he wanted to tell Deck the entire thing, but he held back.

They both settled into silence and drank their beers. They'd always been able to be quiet around each other without any pressure to speak. Small talk was completely optional. Colin figured this was one of the things that made them so close. Apart from the obvious familial bond.

"So I know you didn't come over here to subject yourself to more meddling," Deck said after a few minutes. "What's on your mind?" He raised an eyebrow.

"Well, I did have something I wanted to talk to you about. It's kind of strange, and honestly I feel a bit embarrassed," Colin said. Deck laughed.

"Well, I'd promise not to give you shit about it, but hey, I'm not sure I could keep that promise." He grinned wryly and Colin chuckled. Then Deck became slightly more serious, but the sardonic smile remained on his face. "So what is it?"

"Well," Colin started and then paused. "I've been having these really strange dreams lately." As soon as he said that Deck's smile dropped. After the accident Colin had told him all about the dreams he'd had. Deck hadn't made fun of him or anything but Colin could tell he didn't really buy it. Maybe it wasn't really conscious disbelief so much as that he couldn't handle the implication of the dreams and instead chose to think of the whole thing as Post Traumatic Stress Disorder or something like it.

"Dreams, huh?" He waited quietly for Colin to go on.

"They feel very real. I can't begin to explain it. It's like they're really happening."

"And what happens in them?"

"Well, so far they've taken place in two different places for the most part. One place feels safe and wonderful. The other place is dark and threatening." Colin went on to describe the road and the glade. And then he told Deck about the mysterious woman and the things she'd said. "So I imagine you think it's just my overactive imagination, huh?" Finally he told him about the strange creature.

"Well," Deck hedged. "I don't want to discount what you're feeling. That would be not so good. But a part of me wonders if perhaps this is a side effect of the writing coming back. Your imagination drives your writing, right?"

Colin nodded. "Could be. But..." He'd never shared his dreams about the fire and the plane crash before and felt nervous. He'd only ever told Rita and Mari but it was clear he couldn't make Deck understand without sharing those bits of history with him. So he did.

"Do you remember when we were young and I was taken to the emergency room?"

"Yes, the burns that healed so fast. How could I ever forget that?"

I did, Colin almost said, but instead continued.

"Well, I had a dream that night about the twins dying in a fire," he said reluctantly and then steeled himself and forced himself to tell Deck everything.

"Jesus, Col. That's awful. No wonder you've been such a mess for so long...' He cut himself off and Colin couldn't help but smile at the expression of chagrin on his face.

"No, it's true. I'm a mess. I know you don't believe me. You should ask Rita about the dreams sometime. She can tell you her side of the story. The injuries were real both times and they healed within several hours. It's hard to think about these latest ones outside the context of those previous dreams. The have the same feeling. Right on the edge of being real, very little of the surreal flow and change that normal dreams have." He paused for a moment and then held up his hands. "This happened in the dream. When I said I fell on the pavement, it was the road in my dream."

"Really?" Deck looked surprised. "Show them to me."

Colin started pulling the bandages off his left hand. When the bandage came off he wasn't remotely surprised to see that the flesh of his palm was unmarked.

"I promise you it was torn up." He peeled back the bandage on his right hand and found the same thing. He looked up at Deck and saw that his brother didn't wear the skeptical expression Colin had expected, but was staring at the bandages in Colin's hands. Deck reached over slowly and took one of the bandages and spread it out flat. There was a smear of dried blood on the center of it. Colin felt a quick flash of relief. "This same thing happened when I was burned as a child. The burns were awful and the next morning they were mostly gone, no scarring or anything. The doctors wanted to study me, but Rita wasn't having any."

"That's freaky." Deck stared at the blood on the bandage.

"Yeah. That's one way of putting it. Part of me thinks these dreams are...real, for lack of a better word. The rest thinks I'm going crazy."

"Well, let's assume for a moment that these are more than your run of the mill dreams, and that this woman is real. Put aside the possibility that you just need to be institutionalized." He grinned at Colin, who rolled his eyes. "Assuming that what she told you is true, what and where is this 'dream' you're supposed to find?"

"No idea." Colin sighed.

"What about this evil...thing? Any idea what that might be?"

"Again, no idea."

Deck was quiet for a minute or two.

"Well, it seems to me that you need to have another dream before you can really do anything about it."

"Yeah, I guess so. But I'm not really looking forward to that."

"I hear you." Deck stood up and got second beers for both of them. "I don't really know what to tell you, Col. But promise me you'll let me know if you figure it all out, yes?"

"Sure."

"Hey," Deck spoke after a moment's silence. "What if what you're doing is dreaming your next novel? You should capture all this on paper if you can. If it turns out to be nothing, at least it's a starting point for a great story, right?"

"Not a bad idea. Maybe I could just go ahead and dream that it becomes a bestseller before I burn through my savings and have to get a real job." They both knew that wasn't really a problem; Marianne had organized their finances so carefully that Colin could easily pick things up. Marianne had always prepared for the worst. He'd always thought she was being excessively pessimistic. None of that changed the fact that he had begun to feel desperate to become productive with his writing again. He hoped yesterday's few paragraphs were the first baby steps on the road toward that goal.

"Why not just cut to the chase and dream a huge paycheck," Deck said and they both laughed.

The doorbell interrupted and Deck stood.

"Ah, there's lunch." Deck went to get the pizza, leaving Colin alone with his thoughts. Colin wondered if he was overreacting. Maybe the dreams were just dreams. It was more than possible that his imagination, which was kicking back into gear after its long hiatus, was simply working overtime. He'd read about psychosomatic injuries. He was almost able to convince himself but he just couldn't dispel the realness of the dreams. He shook his head, right back where he'd started.

"Let's eat." Deck came back into the kitchen and dropped the pizza on the counter, pulled back the lid and grabbed a piece. "Dig in. Everything makes more sense on a full stomach."

Colin reached for a slice of pizza. He suspected that no matter how many times he turned the dream over in his head it wouldn't make any more sense. But he had to figure out if they were real, if the woman was real and what she said true. One thing was clear—Deck was right. He was going to have to dream of her again. Even so, he'd really prefer that the dreams stopped completely. Who wouldn't?

But somehow he knew that wasn't going to happen.

※

That night, summoned by his acceptance of the possibility that his dreams were real, Colin woke up standing along the road again. The trees on the side radiated a sense of malevolence that was daunting. Rows of all gnarled old men frozen in the act of reaching for him, some skeletal and bare and some covered in brown dead leaves.

On the other side of the road, the plain was swathed in a blanket of foul smoke that hid the mountains he'd seen there on his last visit. From the smoke he could hear the muted cries of unidentifiable creatures. Each sound set his nerves on edge

—almost like running a fingernail down a chalkboard. He shuddered.

The faint sound of hooves came down the road to him again and he turned to face the direction they were coming from but could see nothing. Interspersed between the crashes of hooves on pavement he thought he could hear another sound—it sounded like the slap of sneakers on the pavement. He squinted and peered into the darkness, trying to make out anything at all. Then suddenly a figure appeared at the edge of the gloom, fading into view slowly before bursting from the murk. It was a woman, short and slight.

With a start he realized it was Penny. She ran up to Colin and stopped, barely breathing hard.

"Colin!" She wore a version of her bright smile but there was a hint of nervousness in her eyes. Almost fear, strange and out of place on her face. "What are you doing here? You are so totally here." She grabbed his hand and started to tug him along the direction she'd been heading. "Never mind. We really have to get out of here. It's coming for us. It's really huge and scary and has ugly tusks and sharp fangs. And it stinks. God, it smells awful. Like it's been feasting on week old corpses and hasn't brushed its teeth in forever." She kept dragging Colin along, and he fell into a loping run beside her, the two of them gaining speed. She glanced back at him with a quick grin that didn't quite hide her trepidation. "I don't suppose you brought a toothbrush the thing could use? No? Well, I suppose that would be odd. Why would you be carrying a toothbrush in your dreams along a road to nowhere?"

"Penny," Colin gasped between heavy breaths as he ran alongside her. "What are you doing here?"

"Me? I live here, silly. Well, not here on this road. But somewhere not too far from here." She frowned once as if confused. "I mean, I used to live here, but now I live next to you and Sidney." She smiled and shrugged—an oddly graceful motion even though she was running full speed down a dark road. "Sometimes I am drawn back to this world when I sleep, just like anyone else." She turned to face forward again. "Of course, I'd prefer not to visit nightmares."

For a moment Colin believed her—that she was the real Penny and she was in his dream. But that was silly. Surely his subconscious had simply inserted someone familiar in his dream, so he was dreaming of Penny. He wondered why he'd chosen her—he barely knew her. Sure he liked her, but enough to dream about her? But why not Sidney? Or even Kate? Maybe it was because Penny was so different from anyone he'd met before. Otherworldly. And she was fresh and shiny in his mind.

"At any rate, I was wandering in another dream and was pulled into this place and got lost. I never get lost on the Dreamside." He saw her frown. "It is quite a bothersome feeling, getting lost."

Colin marveled at how she was keeping up a steady flow of conversation as they ran from whatever monster pursued them. He could hardly catch his breath enough to talk and she was chattering away like they were sitting on the stoop shooting the breeze.

Behind them, the clatter of hooves got louder and faster as the beast gained on them. Colin risked a glance back and as in the last dream saw sparks flying from the pavement where its hooves came down.

"It's getting closer," he said between heaving breaths.

"Run faster."

"Good plan." He laced his voice with sarcasm.

"I thought so, too." Penny put on another burst of speed. Colin was already running as fast as he could and he was still losing ground. He wasn't going to outrun the beast, but maybe he could slow it down enough for Penny to get away. He choked back the terror and steeled himself for a moment before coming to an abrupt halt. He tripped and lost his balance for a moment on the rough pavement but recovered and slid to a halt.

"Go, Penny, keep running."

"No, Colin, don't stop." She yelled back at him but it was too late.

"Go!" he shouted and spun quickly to face the beast and his heart leapt into his throat. Now that he wasn't running and he could see it, he wished he'd not stopped. Its stench brought dread and its sound, fear, but it was the sight of it that burned despair through him. His emotions churned and mixed into a miasma of hopeless terror.

It was roughly ten feet tall, black as night and smelled foul. The odor seemed to move ahead of the beast, spreading like some great vulgar wave. It was just as bad as Penny had said, leaving a pasty feeling in his nose and mouth and making his stomach turn. The stink of sewage, rot, bile and sulfur swam around him, but there was something else beyond those odors: evil. There wasn't any other way to describe it.

As it drew closer the rumbling, growling sound became more feral. Out of control. A rasping cough followed by a deep roar that was filled with rage, hatred and hunger.

The beast seemed to be cloaked in inky blackness, making it hard to see any real details. It leached light and color from around it, and the darkness pulsed obscenely. It swirled and churned, revealing parts of the beast—but Colin couldn't understand what he was seeing. Whereas the last time he'd seen it, it had run on six long, powerful legs, it now had only four: two arms and two legs. It had hooves at the ends of its arms, and used them to propel itself down the road at a frightening clip. Finally as it neared him, the darkness peeled back, revealing a gaping mouth filled with rows of sharp triangular teeth and a long, forked tongue. The monster slavered and drooled as it reared back up on two legs and covered the last yards running like a man. One of its front hooves changed, sliding and melting into a huge clawed hand. As it rode Colin down, it drew the hand back and slapped Colin away, claws tearing long scratches across his arm and chest.

As Colin flew off the road into the dry, harsh grasses that lined it, the beast's hand changed back into a hoof and it fell back into a four—hoofed gallop, a huge burst of speed sending it surging after Penny. Colin slid to a halt, with his face pressed into the grass. His entire left side was a molten river of pain. Blood ran in a pulsing flow and his mangled arm hung uselessly at his side. He managed to push himself to his knees and turned tiredly to see if Penny had gotten away.

He looked just in time to see the beast leap in the air, all four of its hooves melting into great clawed hands, and come down squarely on Penny's back driving her to the ground. Its momentum carried it past her and it skidded to a halt. Spinning on a dime it gathered itself to leap on her where she was trying to push herself to her feet.

"Wake up, Colin," she screamed. "Wake up!" Then she was gone.

Panting and bleeding on his knees, he had no idea how to wake himself up. He doubted pinching himself would really do the trick given how much pain he was already in. He glanced down at his torn and bleeding arm and had an idea. Before he could think twice, he jammed his fingers into the huge tear on his arm.

The pain was excruciating and he woke up screaming in his bed, his arm covered in blood, already soaking into his bed. As the pain grew increasingly intense, his mind finally gave out and he slipped into blackness.

This time there were no dreams.

Dreamer and Dream

Colin swam in darkness, peaceful and quiet. He didn't try to move, just drifted in the comforting weightlessness as if floating in a warm dark sea. He didn't ever want to leave this place. As soon as he had the thought, he regretted it. His left arm began to feel warm, and then first hints of achiness everywhere else gradually surfaced. The darkness began to fade into a bleak light and the warmth in his arm turned to heat and kept getting hotter, until it became a searing, throbbing pain and he opened his eyes and stifled a scream.

"Oh, crap." His voice was hoarse as he sat up, every ginger movement jarred his arm and sent jolts of red hot pain lancing up his arm to his shoulder and into his neck. He gasped and just sat there for a moment. Once the pain had at least stopped intensifying, he took a deep breath and then looked at his arm. Skin hung in ribbons across his bicep, and the muscle underneath was exposed and torn. Blood ran down his arm in a slow pulse, mirroring the rhythm of his heartbeat and its dark wetness spread on the sheets beneath him. The pain flared angrily, shooting pulses of agony up into his neck again. He gagged once as he looked around wildly, searching for something he could use to stop the bleeding.

He grabbed one of the pillows and shook it with his good arm, gritting his teeth against the pain, until the pillow fell out, leaving him holding the pillowcase. Before he lost his nerve he draped the cloth over his bicep, gathered both ends of the cloth and yanked and twisted it tight.

The pain tripled again and he gasped and the world started to go dark, but he didn't let go of the pillow case. Through the fog of agony he heard a ragged scream and it dawned on him that he was making the noise and with a conscious effort he managed to choke off the sound. He forced himself to look at his arm and saw that blood was already soaking through, turning the cloth a wet, frightening red color. He twisted it again and again until it was tight on the arm. He didn't know if this would stop the blood loss, but it would at least slow it down.

Once the pain settled back to its previous unbearable level, he pushed himself to his feet and looked around for a phone. He couldn't find it and so he staggered to the bedroom door, wrenched the handle and flung it open. He lurched forward and braced himself on the far wall. The room began to spin and he forced himself to move before he couldn't stay standing.

"Sid," he called out, but his voice was rough and weak. "Sid, help me." He kept moving down the hall toward her bedroom and when he finally got to it, he slumped against it and banged his good arm on it once. "Sid." He tried to grasp the handle, but the pain was rising again and he missed. The room spun and his vision spotted and he began to fall.

Before he hit the floor, sight and sound faded as he fell into unconsciousness again.

※

Colin woke and opened his eyes to see Penny above him. Her eyes were large and tranquil, and the confusion he felt didn't fade so much as it just became less important. He cast his mind back, trying to remember what had happened and why she was here. It all came flooding back to him: the road, the beast attacking him and Penny, and the dire injuries he'd sustained when the beast had clawed him. Rather than clarifying what was going on, the memories only confused him further.

"Penny." His voice was a tired rasp.

"Colin." There were hints of strain in her eyes and face but her smile still contained the bright warmth that it usually did.

"Penny, what are you doing in the hospital?"

"Hospital? Is that what you call this? I would have thought you'd call it Sidney's bedroom. But if you want to call it the hospital, who am I to argue with you? It would be rude to argue with you in this shape." She rambled on, her voice low and soothing as she gently lifted his injured arm. It was carefully wrapped in bandages and she pulled off the small strips of tape that held it all together. Deftly she started unwrapping the bandages, until they all lay in a heap beside her. While she worked she looked up at his face and her mouth curved at the corners playfully. "Besides—it's no fun winning an argument with someone who has almost bled out."

"We're at home?" He couldn't understand why he wasn't in the hospital. Fear gripped him as the thought crossed his mind that he might be dreaming still. Or dead.

"You're awake for real, Colin. And alive."

"What are you, a mind reader?"

"Nope. Just a face reader. It was that deer-caught-in-headlights look that gave you away."

Colin tried to get a look at his arm. He had to raise his head up slightly from the pillow. His jaw dropped. The ugly tears and gashes he'd seen before passing out were scars. Granted they were ugly, red scars, but they looked like they'd had days of healing. He tried to lift it slightly and there was very little pain. It had a dull ache and the skin and muscle felt tight, but the screaming agony was gone.

"Colin, close your mouth before something flies in there and calls it home." Penny grinned at him. From behind her, he heard a nervous snicker.

"Sid?"

"Yes, Dad," Sidney peeked over Penny's shoulder. "Right here." Despite the laughter, he could see the worry in her eyes. Worry barely on this side of panic. He tried to smile reassuringly at her, but wasn't certain it ended up looking anything like a smile, so he gave it up. He glanced back to Penny.

"How long have I been out?"

"An hour and a half."

"I wish I knew how I heal so fast after these damned reams."

"Magic, Dad." Sidney grinned at him. He raised an eyebrow at Penny, and she shrugged.

"Magic," Penny echoed guilelessly. He let it go for the time being and let his head sink into the pillow again.

"Why aren't we in a hospital?"

"Sidney came and got me instead. I figured I could fix you up as well as any hospital but without all those pesky questions and inconvenient answers that would come with them."

"I didn't know what to do, Dad." Colin heard a hint of guilt in Sidney's voice. "I mean, I knew I should have called 911, but I knew they'd take forever to get here, and you were in really bad shape, and Penny just came to mind." She looked down, and Colin wanted to reassure her but before he could say anything, Penny spoke.

"You did the right thing, Sid." She fixed Colin with a meaningful stare.

Colin nodded. "Yes, you did great, Sid. Fantastic." Although her choice flew in the face of any logic he could summon, something told him it had been the right thing to do. Then he remembered the woman in the glade telling him that he could indeed die of his injuries in the dreams if he was hurt badly enough. "You saved my life. You both saved my life. Thank you."

Unexpectedly Sidney burst into tears. Colin reached out his good arm and she poured around Penny and into his grasp. He pulled her to him and she buried her face in his neck.

"Shh, it's all right, Sid. Nothing to worry about here," he spoke softly into her hair. "Everything's fine now." Penny stood. She shot Colin a meaningful glance and slipped out of the room, leaving him to comfort Sidney.

For a while she clung to him tightly and cried. He stroked her hair and made soft noises.

"I thought you were dead, Dad," Sidney mumbled into his shoulder once the tears had slowed. "I thought I was going to be all alone."

"I know, honey. But I'm not dead. I'm right here. I'll be around for a long time embarrassing you in front of your friends and putting the fear of God into your boyfriends. I'm not leaving you." He felt a laugh escape her into his shoulder. He rubbed her on the back and just held her for a little while. Eventually she pushed back and wiped her eyes, looking chagrinned.

"Crying like a baby," she muttered. She looked at his arm. "It really was magic, Dad. You should have seen it." He'd never thought of it as magic when he'd recovered from his dream injuries before, yet the idea didn't seem quite so farfetched. It surprised him that he was actually willing to believe something so completely impossible.

Penny reentered the room with a bucket of clean water and came to stand beside them.

"Okay, Sid." She set the bucket down. "Let me get back in there. I'm almost done." Sidney stood up and backed out of the way, reluctantly letting go of Colin's hand.

"Sid, can you give Penny and me a moment please? Maybe you could grab me a clean shirt?"

"Sure, Dad." He could tell it was the last thing she wanted to do but she didn't argue.

"Thanks, Hon."

As she left she glanced back one last time as if to assure herself that he was all right. Once she was gone Colin turned his eyes back to Penny. She looked at him with wry amusement.

"Penny," he started slowly. "I have to tell you how this happened."

"Okay." She nodded at him. She settled back and her face fell into seriousness. It looked slightly out of place, as if it were an emotion she'd had to carefully train her face to express. He remembered in his dream how even in the face of deadly peril she'd retained her good humor and bright smile. He felt warm affection for the young woman. And gratitude, of course.

"I had a dream. A horrible dream. You were in it." He watched her eyes for a moment but she betrayed no surprise.

"A girl doesn't like to hear the words horrible dream in conjunction with her own name, Colin," she admonished but there was a glint of amusement in her eyes. But then she became serious again. "Tell me about your dream."

"You're going to think I'm crazy." He studied her face.

"Where I come from dreams are taken very seriously," Penny assured him. "Especially horrible ones."

So he began to tell her his dream. When he got to the part about the monster that had chased them, she interrupted.

"Murkshifter."

"What?"

"The thing in the dream was a Murkshifter. Awful beasts. Smelly, mean and they can change their shape at will. They can't hide the smell though—that's how you can tell them apart from what they're pretending to be. Most of them don't even bother trying to mimic because of it. They just rely on overwhelming fear to put you at their mercy."

"It did smell nasty. How did you know what type of monster it was?"

"Because I was there, Colin." Her face was solemn and her eyes intent. "And next time I tell you to run, please run. Everyone loves a hero, but the Dreamside needs you alive. More than it needs me, to be honest."

Colin looked at her blankly.

"Colin, the Wall sent me to aid you." She leaned forward. "I am the dream she spoke of..."

Dream Revealed

"You're the dream?" He knew the confusion was obvious on his face. "But you're a person."

"I'm a dream and a person. I came from the Dreamside to find and help you."

"A dream *and* a person," he echoed, clearly bewildered. "How does *that* work?"

"Well, let me tell you of the Dreamside." She paused and he could tell she was collecting her thoughts. "The Dreamside is what we call the dreaming side of the Wall of Sleep. That is the place where people have their dreams. And just as the waking world has day and night, the Dreamside has darkness and light, but the darkness stems from the nightmares of sleepers and the light from their more...upbeat dreams." She paused thoughtfully.

"The world of dreams is defined by what people dream so it's fairly unstable and fluid in shape and form. Think of it as a huge patchwork tapestry—each different bit of cloth is a dream. Places, things and people come into existence because a sleeper dreams them up. The vast majority of dreamers only visit the Dreamside with a very small part of their mind. So the things they dream about only exist for the duration of their dreams. But occasionally people dream harder, and more of their mind is in the dream. When the sleeper dreams harder, what he dreams about gains a permanence of its own—it lives beyond the dream of the sleeper and becomes a lasting part of the tapestry. Thus the dreams are always in flux—changing place, coming into existence and disappearing again from the ever changing pattern of the Dreamside."

"But sometimes there comes a dreamer who dreams with the whole of his—or her—mind in the dream. Usually a dream this strong is brought on by some excitement or trauma. Fear. Or sometimes because of madness or anger. This type of dream can unintentionally lend power to their dreams. And sometimes those dreams and nightmares not only come to be permanent, but powerful and can even visit the waking world, but only in a limited fashion. Some people think of these dreams as ghosts."

"Ghosts?" Colin repeated "I thought ghosts were supposed to be dead people who haunt the world for some reason…"

"I don't know if that ever happens. That's beyond my knowledge. But I can say that the ghosts I know are just dreams and nightmares that have taken on such life and power that they can briefly manifest in the waking world. They can only appear there—they can't touch anything or otherwise affect the waking world. It's more like being able to see the fish in an aquarium through the glass. But that's been happening since the beginning, so it's nothing to worry about." Penny stopped and looked up at Colin gravely.

"The final type of dreamer dreams so intensely that not only his mind comes into the dream, but his physical body comes as well—he is no longer in his bed. If anyone looked for the dreamer that dreams in this way they would not find them in the waking world. This sort of dreamer can create dreams and nightmares so powerful, so real, so alive that they can travel anywhere in the Dreamside, through anyone's dreams. Under the right circumstances these creations can come to the waking world for a short time. It's not unheard of for nightmares of this type to actually take up their lives in the waking world exclusively. Adolf Hitler, Torquemada, Marilyn Monroe and Mother Theresa are just a few. Did you know that William Shakespeare was dreamed by Christopher Marlowe? Try putting that on your blog." She grinned briefly. "At any rate, dreamers with the power to create such dreams are extremely rare."

"The problem now is that such a nightmare has been dreamed into existence. It has not attempted to leave the Dreamside as of yet. It wants so much more than just its own freedom. We believe it has figured out how to damage and possibly destroy the Wall itself. The Wall's job is to keep these dreams and nightmares from entering the waking world fully—they can visit for a time but not stay. If the Wall comes down all of the dreams and nightmares in the Dreamside—even minor, usually transient ones—will be free to flood into the waking world. This nightmare is not satisfied with being able to enter the waking world—it wants to pour the stuff of dreams back among the sleepers awake."

"This will be bad for two reasons: first, nightmares in general are monsters—evil and dangerous. Imagine the pain and suffering they would bring. Second, and possibly more frightening, is that people would no longer be able to dream—there would be no place for their dreams to exist. The sleepers need their dreams and nightmares. Without them, they will slowly go mad and become dangerous and destructive. They'll become nightmares themselves in a sense. Add in that the waking world is already a dangerous and disturbing place and I don't think humanity would survive long." She cocked her head slightly and looked at Colin. His head was swimming and he just looked back at her blankly. He knew he must look bewildered and lost. "If I'd known that sleepers were so interesting in the waking world, I would have come to visit a long time ago."

"So I'm one of those sleepers." It was a hard thought for him to wrap his head around. "In one of my dreams that woman—the Wall—said that I was in the dream entirely."

"Yes."

"How did you get here? I thought dreams couldn't come into this world."

She stared at him for a few moments and then spoke carefully.

"The one who dreamed me up is extremely powerful. I was given more...life than other dreams."

"Who dreamed you?"

"That's a very personal question, Colin." Penny laughed lightly. "Sort of like asking a woman how old she is."

"Oh, sorry." So much he didn't know. Penny waved his apology off but for some reason averted her eyes. The expression on her face confused Colin, but he let it go and asked another question. "So that beast in that dream...is that the nightmare we have to stop?"

"No," she shook her head. "The beast is a creation. A tool that the nightmare sends out to do its dirty work. We call that a Murkshifter. It was created from the raw stuff that gives birth to all nightmares. The fact that this nightmare can create others is one of the things that make it so formidable. This has not happened since the first men lived in caves and huddled around fires, fearing the dark."

Colin thought about this for a while, and Penny waited patiently. "This is all so hard to believe. To wrap my head around. How can any of this be real?"

"Look inside yourself, Colin. Search your feelings. Underneath the doubt you know this is all real, don't you."

The dreams he'd had, both as a child and lately, were not things he could ignore. He'd woken up hurt in almost all cases. Even though he'd healed quickly, he knew the injuries had been real. Unless he was still dreaming even now, of course.

"You're not dreaming now. That's the first thing anyone would think. And before you get to it, you're not crazy either."

He tried one last time to deny the memories, deny what Penny was saying and deny the surety deep in his mind that everything she said was real, but he couldn't pull it off. So he shrugged the denial aside and just accepted what she was saying. "Okay then. When I spoke to the Wall, she told me that we had to find and repair...her in a few different places. How do we do that?"

"We'll have to enter the dream again."

"Enter the dream." *In for a penny, in for a pound, I suppose.* He stifled a quick laugh. Then something else occurred to him. "Repairing the Wall seems like a stopgap measure. What's to stop this nightmare from just damaging it again somewhere else?"

Penny raised an eyebrow but didn't speak.

"We've got to stop this nightmare, don't we?" Colin asked and Penny nodded. "How exactly are we going to do that?"

"I don't really know."

"You don't know?"

"Nope." Her voice was cheerful, optimistic and Colin found it reassuring. "That part we have to figure out. I only know that you and I are going to have to do the dirty work. You and I can affect the two worlds, changing them as needed. My abilities are slight though—given to me by the one who created me. This ability to affect the worlds is what Sidney thinks of as magic. Because I'm not of this world, I can affect it in ways that people who live here cannot. You have the same ability in my world. That's why we have to work together."

"And you have no idea how to do this?" She shook her head once and he rolled his eyes. "We're so screwed."

Penny laughed again and the sound rang through the room warmly. Colin immediately felt a little better. Her laughter was able to change his mood and he wondered briefly if this was more of her magic.

"We are not screwed, Colin. Anything worth doing takes some effort. It wouldn't be much of a quest if we knew everything at the start."

Colin grumbled a bit, but was able to smile back at her in return.

"The first thing we need to do is get Sidney to show us the way."

"Sid? How is she going to show us the way?"

"Well, she'll have to tell you that. It's not my story to tell. But now that I've found you, I have this suspicion she will play a big part in our quest."

"I don't like that idea. I don't want her hurt. I couldn't bear to lose her. She's all I have in the world."

"I know, but we need her help. If the nightmare succeeds, the two worlds can be destroyed. Too much rides on this."

"I don't like it."

"I understand."

Eventually he shrugged in resignation.

"Well, it sounds like we have our work cut out for us. So what next?"

"We have to wait for Sidney to tell us what to do."

"And how will she know?"

"She'll learn in her dreams, of course."

Part 2: Dream

Swing

Sidney was fast asleep, dreaming of Emma. Sidney was eleven again—her age when her little sister had died—and they were in the park on the swings. It was a gorgeous day. The sun was bright overhead, shining in the azure expanse of the cloudless sky. It was ideal early summer weather; somewhere between warm and cool, a slight breeze and birdsong floating around them.

Sidney glanced over at Emma with a bittersweet smile. This was a dream she had frequently and when it was over Emma would still be dead. Even though it hurt, Sidney had learned to enjoy it while it lasted. She suspected that she would always hurt—you just didn't get over losing your mother and sister. She could only hope it would get easier. In the beginning it was awful. She cried often—usually at the worst time, like in school or while out in public. Food was tasteless and the world looked gray and dead. Little things set her off and she hated it—the pitying looks people gave her were humiliating. Even thinking sucked—everything reminded her of Mom and Emma.

The dreams were never exactly the same. Sometimes she and Emma didn't even talk. They just played together quietly, or watched the world around them. Sometimes they talked like the kids they had been when Emma had died. Other times she would bring a problem to Emma and her sister would listen patiently and then give her advice on how to deal with whatever was bothering her. It felt weird to get advice from her dead younger sister, but it was usually sound advice. She assumed it was her own subconscious, of course. At those moments, even though Emma had been three years her junior at the time of the accident, the sisters were the same age.

The swings creaked, sometimes breaking into a shrill squeak, and Sidney concentrated on kicking her feet up and then pulling them back, over and over. At the top of the swing —that brief moment of free-fall where she was weightless—she felt like she was taking flight, that she'd never come down. A giggle escaped her and she heard Emma's answering laugh—a happy, relaxed sound. They were swinging in sync, nearly a mirror image of each other. The back and forth motion created a soft breeze that first blew into her face than her back and the rhythm of the motion back and forth, almost tidal, was soothing.

She glanced at Emma again and they exchanged that secret smile they'd shared ever since Emma had been able to smile.

When Emma had been four months old—a tiny, noisy, smelly little thing—Sidney had been watching her sleep, captivated by her peaceful little face. This was how Sidney liked her best—all Emma did was eat, sleep and soil her diapers with a solid dose of screaming to round out the experience for everyone.

That day while Sidney watched, Emma had opened her eyes, yawned widely and focused her eyes on Sidney. For a moment their eyes met and then a huge smile broke across Emma's face. Sidney had returned that smile and they'd just grinned foolishly at each other. Sidney put her finger into Emma's little hand and they'd sat that way for a while. Emma cooed and made soft baby noises while gripping Sidney's finger tightly—as though she would never let go. Sidney stared in wonder and fell in love with her sister. Until the day that Emma died they'd been the best of friends despite their age difference.

In the dream they just swung and Sidney mulled over that memory, but eventually Emma broke the silence.

"How's Daddy?" she asked and her voice shifted to a more serious, mature cadence. When Sidney started to emerge from the dark, Dad was still a mess—he slept too much, watched television blankly, and spent most of his time in front of his computer. Eventually Dad came out of his funk enough to realize he had abandoned Sidney to herself and started spending more time with her—became more responsive. It wasn't much of an emergence and she understood it was only the first step on a long road to recovery—for both of them. But something had changed lately.

"You know, he's actually doing a bit better," Sidney answered. "He went out for coffee with Kate. I was surprised."

"Really?" Emma asked with real excitement in her voice. "It's about time!"

"I know, right?"

"I like Kate," Emma continued. "She's good for him. Does she like him?"

It was hard not to like Kate. Kate waited a for a few months to pass after the accident before she first invited Sidney to come over and visit, slowly tugging Sidney into her orbit at exactly the right time. She took Sidney to the library, to see movies and often recruited her to babysit her two boys. Sometimes when Sidney would show up to babysit, Kate would tell her that her plans had fallen through and they'd sit and eat popcorn and watch a movie.

"I think so. It wasn't hard to persuade her to ask him for coffee despite how gun shy she is herself."

"That Mark was such a bastard." The word sounded strange coming from Emma's small, young mouth.

It was true—Kate's husband, Mark, was a bastard. He was kind of smarmy, always touching other women—including Sidney. Nothing overt, just a hand on the shoulder or elbow. Really creepy. Sidney decided right away that Kate could do better.

Then one day Kate stopped showing up or calling. Sidney heard from friends at school that Mark had moved out. That moment was the turning point for Sidney. She realized Kate needed her as much as she'd needed Kate—the tables had turned. She started going to visit Kate and the boys without any invitation—she'd entertain the boys and let Kate deal with her own pain. Kate always seemed pleased—relieved even—to see her.

Over time she learned that Mark had been sleeping around. A lot. With many women. It made Sidney furious but at the same time excited. She began to daydream about her dad and Kate becoming friends, and then maybe more. It was hard not to pin her hopes on the woman. She started talking about her a lot to Colin, telling him how beautiful and good she was, and how he should go visit her. Dad smiled his sad broken smile at her but never did anything about it.

"No doubt," Sidney replied. "And stupid."

Emma nodded but didn't speak and they settled into a thoughtful silence. Sidney felt her mind drawn to Penny and as if reading her mind Emma spoke again.

"So tell me about the new girl."

"Penny," Sidney said. "She's cool. She's almost magical. She smiles and the room brightens. I think she's the one that is helping Dad."

When Penny had skipped into their lives she had assaulted them with a burst of energy and vitality. Sidney couldn't pin an age on Penny. Her eyes were wise and there was something knowing in them like she was on the verge of sharing some important secret, but her ready smile and infectious laughter made her seem younger. And the things she said! Sometimes it seemed she came from some magical world that Sidney would never understand. Other times Sidney felt an intense connection to the girl. It was as if they had known one another forever instead of just the handful of days since they'd met. In those few days, Penny had already danced through Sidney and Colin's lives, changing everything in small ways. Maybe the girl would play an important role in saving her father. Oh, it wasn't going to be a romantic type of thing—Sidney just couldn't see any romance between Penny and Colin. But the girl had the spark of energy that he had been avoiding for four years. The day he'd met Penny, Colin shared a real smile with Sidney for the first time in years. Not a blinding smile, but unforced and pure.

Penny's appearance had proved to have other positive effects on him, as well. Penny had brought something critical back to Colin and now it was up to Sidney to make it grow. She had put the wheels in motion and persuaded Kate to come ask Dad out for coffee, and it had worked! Sidney knew that if she'd tried it the day before, Colin would have shut down, eased into the distant politeness that would have pushed Kate away. When Kate showed up at the door, Sidney panicked briefly—what if Colin rejected Kate? But he hadn't.

"How so?"

"Her energy is infectious and not even Dad could resist for long."

"So do you think he'll ask her out?"

"No," Sidney said. "It's not that kind of thing."

"Why not?" Emma asked.

"She's young. Maybe. It's hard to tell. She's a force of nature—I can't see her tied to one person. It's like she belongs to all of us. Sometimes she seems like she comes from somewhere else and is just visiting. Other times it's as if she's always been with us."

"Weird."

"Sometimes it's like she's not even from our world. Like she came from a completely different place. I don't know how to explain it." She smiled over at Emma. "Plus, there's something almost sis—" She cut herself off before she finished the word, blushed and glanced over at Emma unhappily.

"Sisterly?" Emma finished for her with an easy smile.

"Yeah, I'm sorry."

"Don't be sorry, Sid. I'm happy. I wish I could meet her."

"I wish you could too, Em." After a few moments of quiet she continued, "Anyway. I'm betting on Kate—if Dad can get it together. I'm pretty sure she likes him."

"She sounds great."

"She is."

"I was beginning to think Dad wasn't going to come around," Emma said after a pause.

"Me, too. But he's got a long way to go."

Emma laughed—a soft giggle—and Sidney glanced over at her.

"What's so funny?"

"Us. Coconspirators, plotting and planning out his life."

"Yes, and our evil plans are coming to fruition!" They shared a laugh. It felt so good.

The squeak and creak of the swings mingled with birdsong for a while. The combination of the sweet with sharp and insistent blended into something soothing and pleasant—the way harmony and melody mix to form music. Then Emma suddenly spoke.

"Sidney." Something in the tone of Emma's voice made Sidney glance over at her sister, and she saw that Emma's face had gone pale and she wore a fearful expression. "Daddy's in trouble. You have to wake up now and help him." She had her head cocked as if listening to something only she could hear.

"What's wrong?" Panic swept through her.

"She says he's hurt and he needs help." Emma looked like she was going to cry. "Please, wake up and help him. She says to get Penny. Remember that. Get Penny. Hurry."

Before she could ask who this she was, Sidney woke up in her bed.

At Her Door

Sidney heard a soft thump against her door followed by Dad's voice. She couldn't make out the words and then there was a thud as if something heavy had fallen to the floor. She jumped from bed and rushed to open the door. He was lying sprawled at the foot of her door, with a trail of blood behind him. One of his arms was wrapped in a red sheet. She stared at it a moment before her heart lurched and she realized it wasn't a red sheet; it was a white sheet and it was soaked though with blood. Panic stabbed through her, burning along her nerves. This couldn't be happening. She'd already lost too much. She whimpered, and the sound broke her paralysis. She knelt down and touched him hesitantly.

"Dad? Can you hear me?" He didn't respond and her panic rose even higher, threatening to consume her. She knew she had to fight it if she was going to save him. She thought wildly for a second and then remembered Emma's words. Get Penny.

"I'll be right back, Dad" Her voice broke. She stood up again and jumped over him and ran to the front door and burst out into the hall.

The building was oriented around a large rectangular atrium with a large chandelier hanging down from the ceiling. Skylights encircled the chandelier and an old but sturdy staircase spiraled around the outside of the atrium, rising with stately grandeur from floor to floor. Ornately carved wooden banisters swept up along the staircase and a dark red runner of carpet ran up the middle of the steps. Sidney's condo was on the opposite side of the atrium from Penny's—east and west—and there was an elevator on the north end.

Without bothering to close the door behind her, she ran across to Penny's door and rang the doorbell. She couldn't hear the bell, so she banged on the door. Within moments the door opened and Penny stood in the doorway.

"Sidney!" Penny was fully dressed and wide awake. That surprised Sidney slightly—it was the middle of the night after all. "I was just coming to see you..." That threw Sidney off track for the briefest moment. It was the middle of the night. Why would she be coming to visit? She pushed that aside.

"Penny, it's Dad," Sidney said with a quick gasping sob. "Come help please."

"I know, Sid." She took Sidney's hand, moved past her and pulled her along. "That's why I was coming to see you."

"How?" She trailed along behind the other girl.

"Let's just say I had a dream."

Colin was still where Sidney had left him, bleeding heavily, a small pool of blood spreading out underneath him. Penny dropped down beside him and began to inspect his arm. Now that Penny was here, Sidney started to cry silently—tears leaking down her cheeks as Penny start working on Colin.

"I need clean water, warm, and towels. Hurry, okay, sweetie? Quickly, Sid," Penny said over her shoulder.

"Okay," Sidney ran downstairs and found a large plastic bowl and began running the hot water in the sink to get it warm. Tears flowed down her face and her breath hitched but she forced herself to concentrate on the task at hand. Keep moving, she told herself. It took her a couple of minutes to locate the things Penny had requested. She set the water down and watched as the girl gingerly unwound the red sheet from Colin's arm.

"Get one of those towels wet," Penny ordered calmly. She bent down and put her face close to Colin's arm. She had her eyes closed and she was whispering softly to herself, but Sidney couldn't make out what she was saying. Penny reached back without looking and Sidney put a damp towel into her hand.

Penny used the towel to clean the area around a jagged tear in Colin's skin. Sidney focused on the towel instead of Colin's torn, bloody flesh. It was a pretty flowered dishtowel that her mother had gotten before she and Colin had even thought about children and neither Sidney nor Colin could handle seeing it. The flood of memories around that small little thing was simply too painful to endure. Sometimes, right after her sister and mother died, the house seemed filled with these little emotional land mines just waiting to explode into waves of grief—items that always brought Emma and Mom to Sidney's mind. It hadn't taken long for those things to find themselves unceremoniously hidden away in the nearest small place.

The wave of pain forced her eyes away and her eyes found Colin's wound again. The feelings of terror and nausea pushed her eyes away from that as well and she felt caught between the two images and finally settled back onto the towel—the lesser of two painful sights. It was strange to see the pretty towel, a small bit of history and memory, soaking up Colin's blood now.

"One moment, Sid." Penny took her hands and placed both of them over Dad's injury and began whispering again. Sidney looked down at the woman's hands and saw that they were covered in his blood, and heard Colin groan softly. After a few minutes of this she sat back up and gave Sidney a tired smile. "Okay, let me have that. Do you have bandages here?"

Sidney nodded.

"And some hydrogen peroxide or alcohol." Penny glanced back and caught Sidney's eyes. "He's going to be fine, Sid—just needs to rest. I'll clean and bandage him up and then we can try to get him into bed. Now get me bandages and something to disinfect this with." Sidney nodded again and a single relieved sob escaped her. She got to her feet and ran off to find the first aid kit her mom had assembled so many years ago.

When she came back, Penny had most of the blood off of Dad's arm. Sidney could not see the injury and she tried to get a better look. She caught a glimpse of three ugly gashes, but they weren't bleeding anymore, in fact they were already scabbed over and well on their way to turning into scars. Penny reached back without turning around.

"Good, give me those, Sid."

"How..." Penny interrupted her with a soft hushing sound.

"Magic, of course." Sidney couldn't decide if Penny was serious or teasing her. "Go get him a shirt. Short sleeves." Sidney put the first aid kit into her hand and turned to leave. "Oh, and Sid, can you get some water for him to drink? And some snacks. Something healthy if you can. Do you have any granola?" When Sidney nodded she continued. "Bring some of that, too, please."

"Why granola?"

"I'm starving. Using magic is draining—and healing magic is the hardest." Penny shot her a quick grin. "Luckily he has powerful magic of his own. His Kung Fu is very strong," she quipped. "I just had to get him started."

"Okay." Dad had magic? Sidney decided not to question her about that. Not yet, anyway. "Be right back." She ran and got a shirt and then down the stairs to the kitchen where she got a bottle of water and a box of saltines. Whenever she'd been sick as a kid, her mom always gave her saltines, so Sidney figured they must be a safe bet. She also grabbed the box of granola.

When she got back upstairs, Penny already had her dad's arm wrapped in clean white bandages and resting on a towel. She was cutting his T-shirt off with gentle efficiency and his chest was rising and lowering slowly. His color already looked better and Sidney let out a sigh of relief. In that exact moment she decided that she loved Penny. Tears leaked out of her eyes again.

Penny knelt on the floor beside him, slowly mopping up the blood around him with a towel. After each wide sweep across the floor she wrung it out over the water bucket. Sidney watched for a moment, surprised by the amount of blood on her dad, the floor and now Penny. It was gruesome, but more than that she couldn't believe that there was that much blood in a person. Or that he was still alive without it all. She shook herself and put the food, water and shirt down on a clean spot.

"There."

"Thank you, Penny," she whispered so that her voice wouldn't crack embarrassingly.

Penny looked up at her and saw her tears. She reached her arms up to Sidney and pulled her into a gentle embrace. Sidney put her arms around her and cried until the tears stopped and she just felt tired.

"Easy, Sid," she crooned softly. "It's okay now." She rocked slightly and Sidney clung to her, slumped in exhaustion and shaking still.

"You said earlier that you fixed his arm with magic. Was it really magic?"

Penny gave a little laugh and squeezed Sidney, but she didn't answer the question. Instead she asked her own question. "How did you find him?"

Sidney didn't want to answer; she was afraid that Penny would think she was nuts. Of course, Penny had just told her a few times that she'd used magic to heal Dad. It didn't seem such a stretch to trust Penny.

"Emma told me he was in trouble." She knew how completely silly it sounded.

"Emma your sister?"

Sidney just nodded against her shoulder. "Were you dreaming?"

"Yes." Sidney waited for the inevitable disbelief and rationalizations, but instead Penny only waited for her to continue.

"She told me to get you." Sidney spoke into the cloth of Penny's shirt. She didn't want to look up—for some reason disbelief and doubt would hurt more from Penny.

"She's a smart girl then. This could have ended very badly otherwise." With a start Sidney realized Penny wasn't going to tell her she was being silly and she pushed back to study her face. She watched Penny's expression carefully but realized that the girl actually believed her. She experienced a moment of the purest relief and joy. She tightened her arms around Penny.

"Thank you."

"For what?"

"For believing me."

"Why wouldn't I believe you, Sid?" Penny sounded truly mystified. "You've never given me any reason to doubt your word. Perhaps it's naïve but I always give people the benefit of the doubt." She glanced at Sidney with a soft expression. "Especially you."

"Especially me?"

Penny just nodded.

"But she told me in a dream. Most adults would think I was...I don't know. Crazy?"

"Well, I'm not an adult and you are not crazy," she patted Sidney on the back and then pushed her back a bit to look into her face. "Plus, I've seen some really strange and amazing things in dreams. I could tell you some great dreams sometime." She smiled and Sidney smiled back reflexively. "Okay, let's get him into this clean shirt before he wakes up. You'll have to help me lift him. I'm stronger than I look, but he's a lot bigger than both of us." Her smile turned into a grin as they both got up. "Oof. He's a handful, isn't he?"

They managed, just barely, to get Colin into Sidney's bed—it was the closest one. Sidney sat behind him and supported his weight while Penny struggled to put his T-shirt on him. They both eased him back and put the food and water onto the table next to the bed. For a moment Penny sat on the edge of the bed and then she reached out to caress his cheek softly—a gentle comforting touch, almost motherly.

"There you go," she murmured softly. "Just rest, Col." Sidney was slightly surprised at the tenderness in the girl's voice. "Sleeping bags?" Sidney looked blankly for a moment before realizing Penny was talking to her. "So we can sleep in here. I think we should be nearby when he wakes up."

"Oh. Yes, we have some."

"Great." Penny looked exhausted. "I'm going to go clean up. I love Colin but I really don't want this much of his blood on me." She held up her arms and smiled wryly. Hearing the girl say she loved Dad sounded completely natural. *Of course she loves him*, Sidney thought. "You should change your clothes too, Sid. I think I got some of him on you." Sidney glanced down and saw that indeed she had smears of blood on her. Strangely it didn't upset her.

"Okay." Sidney pointed at her dresser. "Feel free to grab some clothes."

"Thanks."

A short time later, Sidney returned with a pair of sleeping bags, some blankets and pillows. Penny had emerged from the bathroom wearing a long blue sleeping shirt from Sidney's dresser, and a pair of boxers. Now that she was wearing Sidney's clothes, it was surprising how similar the two of them looked—apart from the tattoos most of which were hidden under Penny's shirt.

Penny looked tired and after helping Sidney spread out the sleeping bags and blankets, she flopped down on the makeshift nest. She patted the floor next to her.

"Bed, Sid. Now," she put a commanding sound in her voice and Sidney immediately lay down on her back beside her. She wanted to sleep, but found herself staring at the ceiling. As tired as she was sleep wouldn't come. Eventually she glanced over at Penny and saw that her eyes were open as well. As if she'd felt Sidney's eyes on her, Penny turned to glance at her and gave her a warm smile.

"Can't sleep?"

"No. I'm tired, but can't fall asleep."

"Yeah, me too."

They lapsed into quiet again. The darkness in the room was eased by the nightlight in the hallway, and the sound of Sidney's wall clock ticking was a metronome that she tried to let lull her into sleep, but it was no use.

"Penny?"

"Yes?" Penny didn't sound any closer to sleep than she was.

"Would you tell me some of those dreams you mentioned?" There was a moment of silence.

"Sure. Let me think of a good one. I don't want to tell you a nightmare. That would be counterproductive." She gave a quick laugh. After a moment Penny put an arm around her shoulders and Sidney snuggled in closer. "Okay, here's one. Some of the best—and worst—dreams and stories are about the Good Neighbors. This one is about an old woman who could turn herself into a hare..."

Penny's voice was soothing and low and the story she told was captivating and magical but nonetheless Sidney was asleep before it ended.

※

Sidney sat in the kitchen nursing her coffee and trying to force herself to be patient. Her dad had been awake only a little while, and she really wanted to be near him, but he'd asked her to give him a few minutes to talk with Penny.

He'd tried to be more subtle than that—he asked her to start some coffee. She hadn't wanted to leave him, but she'd done as he asked. After the coffee was done she poured herself some, loaded it up with sugar and sipped it while she waited for them to be done talking. But soon she began to lose her battle with her rising impatience. Already she had begun to feel panic rising in her again. She really needed to see Dad again and reassure herself that he was alive and all right.

Finally she stood up and walked back to her room. She pushed the door open and was immediately relieved to see him sitting up talking calmly with Penny. They both glanced up and Sidney felt a bit guilty. She hated feeling guilty and straightened her back.

"I'm sorry." She couldn't keep a hint of defiance out of her voice. "I couldn't stand it any longer. I tried, but I couldn't." Dad and Penny both looked at her with matching startled expressions on their faces. Then at the same time Penny broke into her blinding smile and Dad's eyes softened and he held out his arms. Sidney crossed to him at what she felt was a reasonably calm rate and then flung herself into his arms when she was in range. She didn't cry this time, but she pressed her face into his shirt—relaxing into the warmth and smell of him. She loved that smell—a bit stale and still holding the odor of sleep. And there was a hint of an odd metallic tang, but he still smelled like home.

"Sid, don't be sorry. *I'm* sorry. We went on longer than I'd thought." Penny reached over and tousled Sidney's hair affectionately. Usually this was a gesture that she'd draw away from—she was a big girl now and it seemed like something you did to a little kid. Right now it was wonderful—condescension was something that seemed beyond Penny.

"I smell coffee," the girl said. "Did you make enough for everyone?"

Sidney nodded tiredly but didn't pull away from Dad.

"Great!" Penny left and Sidney could hear the soft patter of footsteps down the stairs.

"Are you okay, Dad?"

"Yep, just fine." She searched for a lie in his voice but heard none.

"What happened to you? How'd you get hurt?"

He sighed but didn't speak and Sidney pushed back from him to look up into his face. He looked tired and confused. He smiled slightly at her but she could see the gears turning in his head and he looked across the room, eyes losing focus as he thought. She just waited until he was ready to talk. A minute or so later he looked back at her and she saw decision and determination come to his face.

"It's hard to explain. I don't know that you'll believe me. Honestly, I'm not sure I do." He paused again and took a deep breath.

"Try me, Dad." She didn't bother reminding him of all the strange, almost unbelievable things that had happened in the last few hours. She sat back so that they were facing each other and put her hands on her lap as he started to speak.

"It all started when I was your age." He quietly and thoroughly told her about his dreams starting with the fire, then the accident and finally tonight's dream. As he spoke, Sidney suddenly understood why it was so hard for him to get past the tragedy—he felt guilty, as if it had been his fault. As if he could have done something more to stop it. She didn't know how to react to that. The lightning realization woke a small part of her pain again and she felt angry; he should have done more. Her mother and sister might still be alive. Even as she thought it, she knew that it was horribly unfair. Mom would never have agreed to any of the things that might have changed the outcome. She was too practical, too grounded in the real world to believe that Dad's dream might be real in any way. She'd have been willing to humor him to some extent, but that was all.

But the larger part of her felt heartrending anguish and sympathy for him. She wanted to hug him and tell him it was all right, but instead she let him tell his story. She knew that sometimes the unburdening itself was cathartic. She wanted nothing more than for his pain and guilt to go away.

While he talked his eyes wandered the room, anywhere but at her and when he finally finished he looked back to her with a mixture of apprehension and relief. She suppressed the question she really wanted to ask: why had he only saved her? Why not Emma and Mom, too? Instead she reached over and took his hand.

"It's a lot to swallow, I know, Sid." He squeezed her hand. "I wouldn't blame you if you thought I was crazy, but I have the scars to show for it." He raised his arm slightly.

"Of course I believe you, Dad. Why wouldn't I believe you? I saw how Penny managed to heal you. And..." She paused a moment and then pursed her lips in determination before going on. "...I found you last night because Emma told me you were in danger. In a dream." His eyes widened.

"Oh, no, you're having them, too?" His voice was soft and sad. "How long?"

"I've been dreaming about Emma a lot in the last few months. At first it was incredibly sad, but then it became... good. We play together, just like we did when we were younger. She loved to swing, so mostly we swing. She asks about you often."

"What does she ask?"

"Mostly she's worried about you. Just like I am. Just like all of us are, Dad. But it feels so real that I guess I started to think of her as real. I mean, I didn't stop and think that. It was more like the way I felt about the dreams changed. Then last night..." She smiled at him. "Last night I knew she was real. She told me you were hurt and that I needed to wake up." She fixed him with a stare. "She told me to get Penny."

"Wow. This just gets stranger and stranger."

"Yeah."

"Well, it's a good thing you came and got me." Penny stood in the doorway. Sidney hadn't heard her return. "I'm pretty sure you wouldn't have made it to the hospital in time, Colin. You lost a lot of blood. All the magic in the world could never bring someone back from death." Penny walked over and put a cup of steaming coffee in Colin's hands. "Your own ability to heal so fast might not have been able to deal with wounds so serious."

For a while they just sat there quietly sipping their coffee. Sidney was beginning to feel really tired. She'd slept a little next to Penny last night, but not for long, and the emotional impact of the night was catching up with her. She started to nod off and Colin stood up and made her get into her bed.

"Sleep, Sid." The fondness in his voice soothed her. "I'm alright. I'll be here when you wake up." He guided her over to her bed, and pulled back the covers for her. She didn't bother getting into pajamas, but stretched out in her T-shirt and jeans. She was already falling asleep as she felt him pull off her socks and pull the covers up onto her. She snuggled down comfortably and realized the bed smelled like him—like home. That along with the warmth of the sheets chased her into sleep.

The Message

She found herself swinging again beside Emma and they both were giggling. Emma had managed to time her swing so that they were at opposite ends of the arc, and they touched hands as they passed in the air. Gradually Sidney slowed her swing until they came into synchronicity again. They moved through the arc of the swing quietly for a while; the only sounds the creak and whine of the chains of their swings. Eventually Emma broke the quiet.

"Good job, Sid. I was so worried. You saved him."

"Only because you warned me." She glanced at Emma. "How did you know?"

Emma frowned slightly in thought.

"She told me."

"Who?"

"I don't know," Emma spoke slowly. "She's a woman that I see sometimes. She's really pretty and always wears white. She shines like an angel." Something about the description reminded Sidney of something Dad had told her and she nodded slowly. Then she steeled herself and asked the hard question.

"So...are you really Emma? Or are you a figment of my imagination?"

Emma laughed but it was an uncertain sound.

"Sidney, I don't know what I am. I only know that I love you, and I'm so happy we get to play together still. Maybe I'm just a dream. I don't know what a dream feels like. I feel like your sister."

"Are you here when I'm not dreaming?"

"Yes."

"What do you do?"

Emma shrugged. "Just whatever. Normal things."

Sidney swung for a while, considering this before she finally spoke again.

"Where do you live? Here in the park?"

"I live everywhere, I guess. I only come to the park when you are here."

"Do you live with..." Sidney couldn't finish the thought.

"No," Emma's was sad. "I've not seen Mom." She shrugged. "Sometimes I live with the woman that glows. Other times I'm alone. Still other times...well, this world is full of possibilities. More than I would have believed."

After a long moment's silence, Sidney spoke again. "I'm glad you're here. More than glad."

"Me, too."

Suddenly Emma slowed her swing and when it was going slow enough she jumped off the swing and landed on her feet, her sandals sending up little sprays of sand. She tipped forward a bit but wind-milled her arms twice to catch her balance. She turned to face Sidney, her eyes bright, and motioned to her.

"Come on, Sid." She held out her hand. Sidney slowed her swing as well and jumped off in the same fashion, landing next to Emma and taking her hand. Emma started to walk swinging their arms side by side. "I have a message for you to give to Daddy and Penny."

"A message? What kind of message?"

"Go to the city. She will send you a sign."

"The city? What does that mean?" Sidney asked.

"I don't know. She also said they would understand."

Sidney nodded. "The angel again?"

"Yes." She smiled widely. "She glows, Sid. So beautiful and nice, too. She makes me think of Mom." She glanced quickly at Sidney. "Not like she is Mom, but like she is a mother—full of love and warmth."

"That sounds like a woman Dad dreamed about. He's been having odd dreams for a long time, evidently."

"She said that she'd talked to Daddy before, but something is keeping her out of his dreams now. She sounded worried." Emma turned and took Sidney's other hand. "I have to go, Sid. It's time for you to wake up."

"Why?"

"I don't know. I just know you have to wake up now. But don't worry—we'll get to play again. I'll be here waiting for you, okay?"

Sidney pulled her sister into a hug and squeezed her tightly before letting go.

"Love you, Em."

"Love you, too, Sid."

Sidney closed her eyes and woke up in her room. She felt peaceful and refreshed, but most of all she felt happy.

※

It was still early when she hurried downstairs to find Colin already at the table reading the newspaper. The kitchen was filled with the smell of coffee freshly brewed and she drew in a deep breath, savoring the odor. Heavenly. After a moment she crossed the kitchen and patted her father on the shoulder as she passed him. She could see that the injuries on his arm had faded to soft, smooth scar tissue, but the redness and puckering was gone.

"Morning, Dad." She poured coffee into a mug.

"Morning, Sid. Aren't you a bit young to be drinking coffee?"

She could hear the teasing smile in his voice without looking at him.

"Nah." He chuckled and let it go.

She pulled out a chair and sat down heavily.

"Penny go home?"

"Yep."

"I had another dream about Emma."

Colin put down the newspaper and looked at her.

"Yeah? What did she have to say?" She saw a quick touch of pain in his eyes. She wanted to reach out to him, but it was gone before she could move. It struck her how strange it was to be talking about her sister like she was alive but just away rather than dead.

"We mostly just talked about sister things. But she gave me a message for you. Said it was from some glowing woman."

Colin looked surprised.

"What was the message?"

"The city. And that you should look for a sign from her."

"The city?" Colin looked mystified.

"Yeah, just the city. Any idea what it means?"

"No, none at all." He frowned in thought and then spoke again. "Maybe we should talk to Penny."

"Oh, yeah, I almost forgot. She said the message was for you and Penny."

"Well, then," He stood up. "Penny it is."

※

Something about Penny's condo struck Sidney as odd, and at first she couldn't put her finger on it. The layout was identical to their own place. Immediately inside the front door was a large open area. The kitchen was separated from the rest of the space by the counter that ran along two sides, opening into the living room and also a breakfast area and large pantry. Dark cherry hardwood floors were made warmer with two large area rugs, and these rugs naturally broke up the remaining space into two rooms. Normally one would have been a dining room and the other a living room, but the only thing really distinguishing them was the flooring—carpet on one side and hardwood on the other.

Of course, that was the odd thing, Sidney realized. There wasn't much in the way of personal belongings. It would have made more sense if there'd been still packed boxes all over the place. But other than the few furnishings and personal items the apartment was largely empty.

A futon, a dresser and a flat panel TV emphasized the emptiness of the living room and dining room. The family room and the large morning room were completely barren. The kitchen, the only exception, was fully furnished with the latest appliances and such. There were several stacks of books in one corner of the dining room and a small radio/CD player on top of the dresser.

But in spite of everything, the apartment radiated a warm, comfortable feeling. It was a home, not a hotel. She figured that was probably because it was Penny who lived here— anyone else and it would look stark and depressing.

Sidney glanced down the hall that led to the bedrooms and briefly wondered if Penny had ever even been down there.

"Not staying long?" Dad asked Penny with a little smile. She looked confused.

"Why do you say that?"

He gestured around the rooms. "You don't have much furniture here."

"You don't have much of anything, Penny." Sidney spoke in a soft voice.

Penny cocked her head and then glanced around the rooms. "Hm, am I supposed to have more stuff than this? I guess I have been planning to get a bookshelf and a barstool, but really I can't think of anything else I would need." She shrugged at them and smiled brightly. "Any more things and I'd start to feel decadent and spoiled."

"Makes me wonder what you've got in the bedrooms." She gestured with a quick nod of the head down the hallway.

"Empty so far. I've been keeping the doors closed and pretending they aren't there for now." Penny looked mildly embarrassed. "I bet it would be nice to get a bed or something in case I have a guest staying here. Not everyone likes to sleep on a futon. Although I can't imagine why you wouldn't like sleeping on a futon. It's like camping out really comfortably. And inside. No bugs." She cocked her head down to consider the futon. "I suppose it's not really camping without the bugs. I take it back." She looked back up at Sidney and Colin with a bright smile. "So what can I do for you two? Want some coffee? Tea? Breakfast? I make a mean omelet." She started to walk to the kitchen.

"Actually, we have something we need to talk with you about," Colin said. Something in his voice made Penny stop and turn around. She studied his face briefly and then walked back over to them. Penny sat down on the floor in front of them, gracefully dropping into a cross-legged sitting position, and she pointed at the futon.

"Sit," she ordered. They sat. She didn't say anything but merely waited for Colin or Sidney to start talking. With a quick glance at Colin Sidney began to tell Penny everything. Given the events of the night before, she wasn't worried at all that Penny wouldn't believe her and when she was done, she looked at the other girl closely.

"The city, huh?" Penny cocked her head questioningly. "Well, that settles it. We're going to the city! Oh! Can we take the train? I've always wanted to ride a train."

"You've never ridden a train?" Sidney was surprised.

"Well, I have on the Dreamside, but they're always different and you know, a bit off kilter. I've always wanted to know what a real train is like."

"Off kilter?" Dad asked.

"Yes, off kilter," Penny repeated. "Strange. Like sometimes the train flies or is full of pirates or maybe even zombies. People dream the trains, you know. People dream everything on the Dreamside."

"That must be...chaotic," he said.

"Oh yes, very chaotic. It's wonderful. But it leaves you wondering what the real things are like."

"Uh, what's the dream side?" Sidney felt as though her head was spinning.

Dad and Penny both looked at her and then at each other.

"You'd better explain it," he said with a sardonic smile. "I'm still trying to wrap my head around it.

"Okay." Penny looked at Sidney. "The Dreamside is where you dream things. It's the mirror of the waking world. When you have a dream, a part of you visits the Dreamside." She went on to explain in more detail and Sidney just listened. She imagined she must look dumbstruck—she certainly felt mesmerized.

"So how do you know all this?" She asked when Penny finally finished.

"It's where I was born and grew up."

Sidney felt as though the ground had fallen out from under her feet. "That means that you are..."

"A dream." Penny was calm, and then her face broke into a sunny smile. "As opposed to being dreamy. Which I am as well, of course."

Dad chuckled softly, earning himself a quick glare from Penny. He held his hands up in surrender. Penny held the glare for a beat and then looked back to Sidney.

"Any of this making sense?"

Sidney nodded.

"Sure. Strangely enough it all makes sense." She recalled the comfortable reality of her dreams of Emma and many things fell into place. Emma was a dream as well and Sidney wondered if she were real enough to live outside the dreams. The idea made her heart beat faster but she put the thought aside firmly and concentrated on the more immediate issues at hand. "Which city?"

"What?" Penny asked.

"Tayport or Chicago? Technically it could be Rockford, I guess, too"

"Well, Tayport is closer," Colin said. "Let's go there first."

"Good!" With that Penny stood up and pulled Sidney to her feet. Dad stood as well and then without any warning, the young woman spun on her heel and headed for the front door. "Let's go! Don't want to keep the city waiting, do we?"

"Now?" Dad asked in surprise.

"Why not? There's no time like the present."

"Uh, I don't know...It's just that..."

"Oh, you're one of those people who has to plan everything out, aren't you?" Penny asked with one eyebrow raised. Sidney laughed.

"No, definitely not," Dad said in a slightly defensive tone.

"Yes," Sidney said at the same time. He sighed and smiled sheepishly.

"Okay, so here's the plan." Penny leaned closer to them conspiratorially. "In about..." She pretended to consult a non-existent watch. "...ten seconds, we're all going to stand up, go out and catch the train into Tayport. How's that sound?"

Dad rolled his eyes and stood up. "Okay, Okay."

Tayport

Penny clearly loved her first ride on a real train—her childlike glee made Sidney smile. She and Dad watched as Penny tried out all the seats that were empty. She talked to other passengers. She chatted up the conductor. It was amazing to watch how she quickly bridged the gaps that separated the commuters into tiny islands of isolation. Within moments she had each one smiling warmly as if they were old and dear friends. She was positively infectious.

When they arrived at the station, Penny clapped her hands and bounced on her toes. Dad and Sidney trailed behind her side by side, and she spun back to face them.

"That was wonderful," she gushed. "Let's do it again. The city will still be here when we get back. So many interesting people."

Dad laughed. "Don't worry; we'll ride it back home after we're done here."

"Spoilsport." Penny sighed and then slipped between them, took their hands and started walking, practically dragging them behind her. Sidney couldn't help absorbing Penny's enthusiasm and she glanced over at Colin and saw it in his face too.

When they reached the revolving doors that led from the platform to the station itself, Penny went around several times while Colin and Sidney watched. Finally Penny emerged from the doors, breathless and happy.

"I think I need one of those at home. Such fun!" She laughed.

"I imagine you'd have to widen your front doorway significantly."

"Oh, I wouldn't use it for a front door; I'd just put it inside the house—maybe the living room."

"But you don't have any doorways that large inside either," Sidney said with a grin.

"Doors don't always have to have doorways to lead somewhere interesting. I once lived near this huge mahogany door carved with ornate leaves and flowers around the lintel and jambs. It just stood on the side of the road and when I opened it one there was nothing inside by star filled sky. It was tempting, so tempting, but I resisted the urge to cross the sill. It's dangerous to go through such a door without knowing what is really on the other side."

The station was nominally two stories tall open in the center to a huge cavernous atrium. Each level was at least twice as tall as normal and the space above the top floor was so tall that a third floor would fit. Shops marched in a stately procession around the outside of each floor and at the highest point in the atrium sunlight streamed in warmly through huge panes of glass. The shops ranged from the obligatory Hudson newsstand to expensive restaurants. The sounds of crowds coming and going were vibrant and exciting. In the background the voice of the person making departure and arrival announcements was rhythmic and almost unintelligible over the other sounds. It sounded like Gregorian chants with a hint of hip hop.

"This place is magical." Awe saturated Penny's voice, and Sidney had to agree. It was strange how something that should have been so mundane was instead a place where journeys started, ended and sometimes merely paused, a waypoint toward some other destination. All of those implied changes seemed filled with stories and possibilities. Sidney would have loved to have had the time to sit and simply watch the travelers go by, imagining their stories. Magic was right, she thought.

"I've always loved taking the train into the city," Dad said.

"Me too," Sidney murmured.

"Well, here we are. Now what? I mean, I never thought about it. We got on the train and now we're here. What now?" As he spoke, they all slowed to a halt.

"We have to find a sign." Penny looked thoughtful. "Any ideas where to look?"

Sidney knew that Penny didn't mean the multitude of signs that filled the station. The girl meant some kind of hint, something more mysterious than words and pictures on a board or wall. Sidney shrugged and shook her head. "Nope, not me."

Dad shrugged.

"Let's just walk for a while and see the sights," Penny said. "Things have a way of being found when they need to be found."

Dad nodded. "Sounds good. Which direction?"

Penny shrugged and looked at Sidney. "You choose, Sid. You're our guide."

"Okay." Sidney wasn't sure she wanted to be the guide but she nodded and headed for the doors that led out of the station.

※

The breeze was stiff and cool, racing between the buildings as if trying to scour the streets clean. Sidney looked around, trying to figure out where to go next.

Downtown Tayport—a modern city, spawned by the tech industry—was a hive of activity. A steady stream of people flowed down the sidewalk in both directions. Their progress toward their destinations was like an intricate dance, the moves as well-known as if instinctive—faster pedestrians winding and twisting around obstacles, slower ones creating eddies and occasionally briefly blocking the flow.

Most of the cars on the street were taxis, a crazy patchwork of colors moving far too fast in an intricate dance. The wind collected the sounds of the city and rolled them up into a strange and dissonant symphony. Horns, whistles, street corner musicians, voices, vehicles and the occasional plaintive siren layered together—the lush music of the city.

As she glanced around, an advertising kiosk on the nearby corner caught Sidney's eye. It was a large cylinder with advertisements rotating slowly behind a Plexiglas cover—at that moment the one facing her was a picture of the Springbok Museum of Modern Art. Sidney had been to the museum once before and the memory of that day was a good one—a trip into the city with Mom and Dad and Emma. When she thought about it, it was one of the last outings they'd taken as a family before the accident. She and Emma had spent most of the time giggling and happy. Sometimes laughing at some of the stranger modern pieces. Oh, they both loved many of the paintings. Particularly the impressionists and the cubists— Sidney liked Kandinsky the best, while Emma liked Monet. But there were a lot of things on display that failed to impress. And the special exhibits had been very odd. Photography of knives from the civil war period placed in odd settings. An extensive collection of paintings of evil circus clowns. Mom and Dad had to shush the girls several times under the pressure of the offended stares of other patrons. But Sidney and Emma had been able to tell that their parents were as amused as they were. So called High Art and a sense of humor didn't always go together well, Dad had explained later.

After being led around a while they had grown bored and their parents had taken them to the nearby Kramer Children's Museum. Sidney had assumed it was for younger children, but once there, she and Emma had a great time. It was an incredible memory and for a long moment she stood still basking in the remembered glow of that day.

As she stood watching the advertisement creep around the kiosk, a black bird landed on top of the kiosk in a noisy flutter of wings. It spent a quick moment settling itself and then turned bright eyes in Sidney's direction and she had the strangest feeling that it was looking at her in particular. The bird cawed once loudly, a sound somehow both plaintive and demanding at the same time, and pecked at the top of the kiosk. Sidney thought it was a crow—a strange bird to see in the city. Didn't crows need corn fields to raid and scarecrows to sit on? She pushed the question aside and turned her attention back on the problem at hand: where to go next.

"Well." Dad broke through her thoughts. "Which way, Sid?"

She furrowed her brow in concentration, licked her finger and held it up as if testing the wind, and then pointed.

"That-away."

So they walked slowly, taking in the sights and watching for any hint of where to go next. Periodically Sidney would take a turn decisively like she was heading somewhere specific. Dad and Penny walked a step behind her and Penny swung her gaze back and forth, studying the city, oohing and aahing appreciatively. She pointed to things occasionally and described the differences between what was there and what was in the dream versions of Tayport. It was entertaining to say the least—Sidney saw the city through Penny's eyes—fresh, as if for the first time.

Penny pointed at the Regal Tower, which was a tall building tapered from its wide, square base as it rose above the surrounding buildings stretching to reach the sky. The top of the building ended abruptly in a sloping plane as if it had been cut off with a giant blade swung at a slightly downward angle. Every surface was covered in highly reflective glass, a giant mirrored obelisk thrust into the blue of the sky.

"Oh, look at that one. Wouldn't it be fun to sled off that?" Penny clasped her hands in a gesture of frank appreciation.

"Only if you could fly, or had a parachute." The idea made Sidney's hands break out into a sweat and butterflies to flutter in her gut. While they studied the building, an airliner flew low overhead, aiming for the airport hunkered down just outside the city. Because they were sheltered in the arms of the downtown buildings, the sound and sight of the plane came suddenly and was gone just as quickly. The only view of the plane they got was its reflection on the side of the building as it appeared to shoot up off the ground like a rocket heading to space.

As they wandered into the busy center of the city, the sparse skyscrapers thickened into a forest of buildings that seemed to tower over the crowds below—silent witnesses of the chaos and life below. It must have been close to lunchtime because the streets were full of people hurrying wherever they were going. On the heels of that thought, Sidney's stomach growled.

The sidewalks were wide and the flow of people threatened to carry Sidney off. She fell back and took her father's hand. He squeezed it once and smiled at her. She was surprised to find that the city was beautiful. She'd always found it exciting and vibrant, but never thought of it as beautiful. It wasn't a natural, earthy sort of beauty—it was visually striking for its towering planes and gaps. The sun shone off the windows, occasionally sending bright fingers of light at her. The busy, hurried crowds themselves moved as if they were the lifeblood of a huge body, bringing life and health to each part of the city. That was it, she thought to herself. It was alive, and that life itself was amazing. She'd never thought of a city like that before—it had always seemed to represent man's progress and technology to her. Grimy, cold and even often dangerous. But this was complex and wonderful.

They stopped often so that Penny could gush, pointing out some wonder that Sidney would have otherwise missed or taken for granted. During one of these stops, she glanced up at a street sign and there was a large black bird perched precariously staring at her. It cocked its head and studied her with its shiny black eyes, and something about its stare suggested ancient intelligence. Not a threatening look—it was familiar and knowing. Sidney watched the bird as it cawed raucously and launched itself away.

Sidney continued to wind through the maze of skyscrapers that made up the downtown district. The midday sun peeked down between the buildings, creating bright spots and shaded areas. At each corner, the walk signs flashed their various signals and the crowds halted and moved under their command. The blaring of horns and the pell-mell rush of cabs all contributed to the chaos. Finally she came to a halt in front of a mom and pop pizza joint.

"Here we are!"

"Our quest is for the perfect slice of pizza." Sidney loved the sound of laughter in her Dad's voice as he spoke.

"I'm starving." Sidney tried to sound grumpy but failed miserably.

"Fair enough," he said. "I could use a bite too."

"It's a long and tiring journey we have undertaken. We must not weaken ourselves by failing to meet the needs of our bodies," Penny intoned solemnly but then spoiled the effect with a snicker. Dad held the door open and gestured to Sidney and Penny.

"After you."

The inside of the restaurant was brightly lit with a handful of linoleum-topped square tables in bright primary colors. Each table was worn looking and surrounded by matching vinyl-covered chairs, most of which had small tears on the cushions. The walls were painted a soft, faded yellow and covered with various signs, ranging from beer ads to sports heroes and cars. The mishmash of décor was like the layering of generation on generation—one family's history recorded in layers of pizza grease and linoleum. A radio in the kitchen blared out classic rock tunes and the warm air smelled of tomato sauce. Sidney instantly loved it.

A young man worked the counter, his hair carefully arranged to look haphazard and a few poorly inked tattoos peeked from beneath the sleeves of his T-shirt. As the doorbell chimed he looked up, his face a studied mask of boredom and even a hint of surliness. But as their eyes met she saw a shy smile break across his face briefly before he settled back into his expression of disinterest.

"Getcha something?"

Sidney studied the menu above his head then gave him a mirror version of his tiny smile. His face lit up and for a quick moment Sidney felt powerful and in control, like royalty bestowing the slightest sign of behavior.

Ha. Queen Sidney the Foolish.

Sidney was surprised at how easily the three of them agreed on toppings for their pizza. There was no argument—they each suggested a topping or two and the others nodded. She wasn't sure she'd ever seen a pizza order made so painlessly.

They all sat down at one of the empty tables. It was a dirty sky blue, but there were spots where the original bright royal blue had refused to fade side by side with rings of discoloration where drinks had sat too long. The legs were slightly different lengths causing the table to wobble back and forth when Sidney put a bit of weight on it. There were initials and pithy sayings scratched into the surface, a living history of the highlights of its career as a table. Sidney sat down and ran her fingers over some of the carvings, tracing out words. Penny, of course, began to speak—off and running again.

"Boy, the city is so exciting. So many people going here and there. So determined, so busy. I bet if we went up in a building and looked down long enough we could see a pattern to the way they flow and move." She didn't seem to take a breath and Sidney squashed the urge to grin. "Everything has a pattern; it's just a matter of seeing it. Figuring it out."

"Yeah, you're right. I never really thought of it that way." Dad was instantly drawn into the conversation. "But I bet it's based on the physicality of the streets. The curbs, the buildings, the signs. Newspaper boxes. Where the doors are. That stuff."

"Yeah, I think so. The pattern is in the place. The people just expose the pattern so that we can see it. I think it's beautiful."

"I wonder..." Sidney joined the conversation. "Do you think that maybe what we should be doing is letting the streets and the crowds take us where we are supposed to go? Instead of choosing, just let the pattern take us where it will?"

"Oh, that's an interesting idea," Penny said. "Let's try it. After lunch."

After a while the boy delivered a huge pizza to their table. Sidney took a slice—oversized and piled high with fresh toppings. She bit into it and sighed happily. It was hot, the cheese gooey and the extra thin crust had been cooked to the perfect stage of crispiness so that it was almost like a soft cracker. Penny echoed her sigh.

Sidney was caught up in the pure magic of the moment. It was one of those sparkling points in time that would be frozen in her memory for the rest of her life. Full of excellent pizza, relaxing in wonderful company...she wanted to stay there and enjoy the warmth of the moment.

✺

Too soon it was time to go.

"I think our quest for excellent pizza is complete," Penny said and Dad laughed.

They stepped outside on the bright sunlit street and Sidney took a moment to get her bearings. Across the street, mounted on the wall was another advertisement for the Springbok Museum of Modern Art. It was a picture of a few paintings with a couple holding hands and staring at them. Come spend time looking at art with the beautiful people. At the bottom of the sign was a scrolling LED sign, red letters moving smoothly across the length of it—a description of the special exhibits. While she looked at the sign a crow flapped in and landed smoothly. It shifted around and settled so that it was facing Sidney. It cocked its head slightly as if studying her. Sidney watched the words slide across the sign. The information about the different special exhibits was punctuated periodically by the museum's current slogan: "SMOMA: Come see us. Now." But her eyes were drawn back to the crow. Hadn't Dad mentioned a black bird when he described his dreams?

"Dad, do crows live in the city?"

"I don't know, Sid. I always think of them as country birds. Sitting on a power line, eyeballing the nearest corn field. That sort of thing."

"That's what I was thinking."

"Why do you ask?"

She pointed at the bird sitting on top of the sign, and as she did it cawed, the sound carrying easily to her ears.

"Huh." He turned to Penny. "Crows in the city?"

She shrugged. "On the Dreamside anything is possible. It's sometimes hard for me to remember there are rules here," Penny responded. While they all watched another pair of crows flew in and landed beside the first. Then there was a chaotic fluttering sound and four more joined the others. Seven sets of bright, beady eyes regarded them.

"A seven crow murder," Dad murmured.

"What?" Sidney turned to look at him.

"A group of crows is called a murder." His voice was quiet and he looked distracted. "I wrote a story a long time ago called The Seven Crow Murder. Never got published though.

"A battery of barracudas," Penny said in a rush. "A convocation of eagles!" Colin smiled absently.

"I think we've found our sign."

"I agree," Penny said. "On the Dreamside crows are harbingers. Tricksters and guides. They can be good or bad depending on how they feel at the moment. They are one of the few creatures that can move easily between the two worlds."

"Well, it's the museum then?" Sidney looked at them and both nodded.

The First Portal

The museum was an odd building. It was a strange mix of different architectural styles; a startling mishmash, composed of frescos, columns, cantilevers, arches, and steel struts. Sharp lines and graceful, arcing curves lived side by side. It was as if the architect had decided to use all of his tools and themes in one building—his opus to chaos.

Wide granite steps led up to the entrance, and the circular doors were braced by a pair of eccentric statues—wireframe dancers caught frozen in the midst of motion. It was a strange thing to see though—not just a sculpture. The promise of movement, the inevitability of the next step in their dances was a promise rather than merely the setting. One dancer had a hand extended upwards gracefully, wrist cocked in the middle of a flourish, while the other arm arced around her midsection, but not touching. One foot was raised up to rest on the inside of the other knee.

The other dancer looked as if she had just finished a Fred Astaire move, one leg extended out to the side, foot nearly touching the floor. The other leg was bent outward, her knee pointing the opposite direction. Her arms were splayed out and in one hand a cane and the other what looked vaguely like a top hat. Everything about the dancers made them look as if they hadn't been sculpted as much as frozen in joy and concentration.

Overall Sidney couldn't decide if the building was fascinating and thought provoking or just plain ugly. Maybe that had been the architect's intention.

A huge glass dome was planted in the middle of the roof of the main structure and the sun struck the beveled edges of the panes of glass. On those edges many tiny prisms had been attached to refract and shoot shards of colored light all around. Sidney had read about it a few years ago after their first visit. It was truly magnificent to see in person. Colors and sparkles radiated from the dome as if a shining halo had been placed on top of it. The three of them stood and stared at it in openmouthed wonder.

"Wow," Penny said. "This looks just like something from the Dreamside. This could be one place where the waking world is stranger than the dream."

Colin chuckled.

"I used to think it was an eyesore. But over the years it's really kind of grown on me. And the exhibits are really wonderful. If you go for modern art, of course."

"Well, let's go!" Penny grabbed one of Colin's and Sidney's hands, bringing Sidney out of her reverie and began to drag them up the steps.

※

Sidney still wasn't a fan of modern art; that much hadn't changed since she was last in the museum. Some of it was really great, but the bulk of it seemed kind of silly. As soon as they'd gone in and Dad had purchased their tickets, they'd started walking through the various rooms. In one room there was an exhibit of old photographs of execution devices—hanging ropes, gallows, guillotines, electric chairs. The whole shebang. They'd moved through that one fairly quickly, and Sidney had asked Dad what made the exhibit art. He'd shrugged and given her the standard speech about beauty being in the eye of the beholder, speaking in pretentious tones.

He finished with "Life is art and art is life." Penny had giggled loudly, and of course, that had forced both Sidney and Dad to stifle laughs and they quickly moved on to the next room.

They'd also seen an exhibit on the toilets of the new world. Over 500 years of crappers, as Dad said. Sidney had led the flight from that room, none of them daring to speak for fear that they'd laugh uproariously. They got stern glances from not only one of the docents but other patrons as well which of course just brought them closer to laughter.

The room devoted to various paint splatters was one she remembered from her previous visit, and now several years later, she still didn't get it. She wasn't sure what made it art. Penny dragged them to a halt in front of a particularly messy canvas that stretched nearly thirty feet up and was another twenty feet across. All it had on it were pain splatters.

"Oh, can you sense the pathos?" Penny clasped her hands together. She spun to face Sidney and Dad. "Isn't it tragic?"

"Is that what you call it?" Sidney snorted.

"Oh, yes, tragic," Dad chimed in. "It speaks to me of the inadequacy of the machinery of man. The failure of technology to address the despair inherent in the human condition."

"More like the failure of the artist to paint," Sidney muttered but she was glad to see her father kidding around. It was something she hadn't seen in a while. A short shriek of laughter burst from Penny, and she immediately stifled it with her hand and blushed. They received more glares as they moved on.

"This is great fun, but we probably should be looking for..." Penny glanced at Dad.

"Yes, exactly. For what?"

"Well, I don't know, but I'm fairly certain we weren't sent here for a photograph of a noose or a toilet seat." Sidney grumbled. "Maybe we should look for a painting or sculpture of a crow?"

"That's an interesting idea, Sid," Dad said.

"Why couldn't we have our quest in the zoo, or the aquarium?" Sidney knew she sounded whiney and stopped.

"Or at the ballpark." Dad snorted and made his voice sound imposing. "You must save the world. Go to the ballpark, eat several hotdogs and drink a few beers and your quest will be complete! Do not fail!"

"Somehow I don't think quests are supposed to be fun," Penny looked thoughtful. "Although I'm having a good time."

"Somehow, Penny," Sidney said. "I don't think I can imagine you not having fun."

"Oh, sometimes I don't have fun. I just try to avoid those times if I can."

"All right, ladies, shall we go see what's in store for us?"

They moved on into a section of the museum with art that she could wrap her head around, and appreciate for its beauty and form. Of course she was drawn to a number of paintings by Kandinsky. There was something about them that she could get lost in. They sat down on the benches in front of the paintings and she just stared at them.

Penny and Dad stood up and walked into the next room. Sidney followed but wandered away from them aimlessly and after a while came to a halt in front of a beautiful painting by Paul Klee called "Fragmente." She stared up at it raptly. With her eyes slightly unfocused the painting appeared brown but when she concentrated on the details the colors came out—subtle blues, pinks and hints of green and orange against the muddy background.

Over the colors was a series of lines and curves seemingly thrown together haphazardly. As she stared the lines and curves seemed to coalesce into something different. She was able to pick out the rough outline of a town or village. It felt like a small hidden world blossoming to reveal itself as she watched. The buildings seemed to be leaning this or that way—as if they'd been dropped randomly on the ground in order to fill the city. Just props to flesh things out. It was not a place she'd really like to visit—ramshackle and empty, as if some tragedy had driven all the people away. Somehow the overall effect was still hauntingly beautiful.

Positioned in the upper reaches of the top right corner was a bright red circle. Sidney thought that it looked like the sun at sunset through a haze of clouds. She found the work entrancing and remained in front of it while Dad and Penny wandered off. She stared at the lines of the painting, sinking into the colors, and calmness flowed through her. For all that it was just pigments on canvas, it seemed to have a life beyond that—almost magical.

Then the colors appeared to move, to swirl slightly, and the lines curved toward the center slightly. For a moment she felt as if she were slowly sinking into the painting, but she blinked and everything snapped back into place. Sidney started as if waking, rubbed her eyes. She wondered if she'd been staring so hard at it that her eyes had gotten tired and she'd just imagined the motion. She studied it but it remained still.

Like a painting is supposed to look, silly.

But immediately in the footsteps of that thought, it began to swirl again, this time maintaining the motion and the edges of the painting began to rotate slowly around the center almost as if slipping into a whirlpool to be dragged down into some unknown place. This time it didn't snap back right away, but she rubbed her eyes again and when she opened them the painting was still again. She glanced around to find Dad or Penny and found her friend first. They made eye contact and Penny must have seen something in Sidney's expression because she came to stand beside her.

"What's up, Sid?"

"This painting." Sidney wasn't really sure how to describe what she'd seen, or if it was even just a figment of her imagination. "It was...moving."

"Moving?"

"Yes, swirling. Like a whirlpool."

"Oh, I'd like to see that!" Penny turned toward Dad. "Colin!" He turned to look with a questioning look. "Come here. Sid says that this painting was moving."

"Moving?" Dad came over and stood beside them.

"Yes, swirling like a whirlpool." Sidney was beginning to feel silly. They stared at the painting but nothing happened. *I imagined the whole thing.* She hated to look foolish in front of them. "Maybe I just —" She cut off as the painting began to gently swirl again. "Do you see that?"

"Yes, I do!" Penny clapped her hands and bounced on her feet slightly. "That's wonderful."

"I see it too." Excitement crept into Dad's voice.

The swirling colors began to pick up speed, flowing toward the eye of the whirlpool. Rather than leaching all the color out of the painting, more color seemed to just appear at the edges. For a few moments they just stared at the painting as it became a churning current of colors.

"Hey, do you see that?" Colin pointed at the outside of the whirlpool. Sidney looked closely and Sidney realized suddenly that the frame itself was being pulled into the flow of colors, sending a ribbon of black spiraling toward the middle. The colors expanded out beyond the frame until the whirlpool was no longer a picture but was simply a section of the white wall that had been overtaken by swirling, flowing colors.

During all of this, the red circle in the top right corner had stood steady as if it were apart from the rest of the painting, unaffected by the strong current. But now it began to float slowly toward the center of the painting until it hovered over the eye of the whirlpool. They all stared raptly at the circle as it began to expand into a rough oval oriented vertically, and as it got larger, it floated downwards and finally stopped moving, but still expanded toward the floor. As it touched the floor the bottom spread out.

Sidney realized with a start that it looked like a doorway; rectangular at the bottom and arched at the top. It finally stopped expanding when it was tall enough for each of them to walk through it.

"It's a door." Dad echoed Sidney's thought.

"Yes," Penny whispered.

So far the change in the painting and surrounding wall had been a silent thing, but suddenly a background noise grew out of the quiet of the gallery. It was a soft hissing sound that pulsed rhythmically, growing slightly louder with each pulse.

"I think we're supposed to go through it." Sidney raised her voice to be heard over the noise of the swirling colors.

Dad and Penny both nodded, but no one moved. She looked past them and saw a guard was just entering the room, on his usual patrol to make sure no one was touching or defacing the art.

Or perhaps to make sure that no one was walking into one of the pieces that had turned into a swirling whirlpool of color?

Sidney had to fight the urge to laugh. She saw along the wall opposite the portal that there was a pair of women studying another painting. Both of the ladies and the guard as well seemed completely oblivious to the noise and motion of the portal. Finally Sidney steeled her mind and moved to stand between Dad and Penny, where she took their hands and glanced up at them.

"Ready?" she asked.

Dad nodded slowly, looking slightly unsure at the prospect, but Penny nodded firmly, a glint of excitement in her eyes. Sidney took a deep breath and began to walk forward, edging toward the red. As she neared the picture a gentle breeze began to blow, becoming stronger with each step until it was fanning her hair to the side and she got scared and froze. The idea of walking into this mess of colors suddenly terrified her and she gripped their hands tighter.

"Allow me," Penny nodded decisively, stepped past Sidney into the red and pulled her in behind her.

Sidney winced and shuddered as first her hand and then her arm vanished into the red. It felt like she'd put her hand into warm water. There was a slight resistance but not enough to slow her down. As she broke the surface of the doorway with her face, her awareness, her thinking self, suddenly inside the door itself, she discovered that the door itself was not a thin barrier, but was like some space the bounds of which were unknown. For all she knew she'd wandered into an entire universe of opaque redness.

She was also struck by an almost deafening silence and her eardrums rumbled once at the sudden change in volume. For a few moments the entirety of the world was just a red blur and she began to panic. But still Penny drew her forward, the motion of walking held off her panic. Her heart beat rapidly, the pounding in her ears the only thing she could still hear and they walked forward for a time that felt endless. Sidney began to wonder if this was all there was—interminable red that hid everything, even her body.

"Penny?" Sidney's voice sounded muffled and deadened. She heard no answer, but she still felt Penny's and Dad's hands in hers and she focused on that sensation, levering against the deadness around her. She gave Penny's a little squeeze and Penny squeezed in return. That squeeze was vastly reassuring—she was able to calm down a bit and the beating of her heart slowed. Her breath came more slowly and she felt the tension in her body ease a bit.

Then suddenly she stumbled out of the red and into a confusing bluster of light and noise. She blinked and looked around her while her mind tried to deal with the abrupt change. After a few moments she was able to piece together what she was seeing. It was a small town, the buildings strange and slightly off, but the entire scene was vaguely familiar. She studied them, trying to figure out what was wrong and where she might have seen them before. Some of the walls were strangely curved—there were few right angles or straight planes. The windows were irregular in shape—instead of being square or rectangular, they were trapezoidal or pentagonal. Some of the houses leaned slightly in one direction and some in another. It made no sense and left her struggling to find some pattern to the town.

With a start she recognized where she'd seen them. This was the set of buildings she'd imagined in the painting. They had life and detail beyond the black lines and curves that defined the buildings in the painting, but they were unmistakably the same. She looked more closely and saw that each one had moss and tiny flowers growing on the walls, giving off faint hints of green, orange and blue. The entire view coalesced into clarity and she gave a little gasp.

"It's the painting."

Dad squinted at the buildings and then nodded slowly.

"I think you're right. Although it looks different somehow."

"I think it's how Sid sees the painting," Penny said. "What her mind interprets when she looks at it."

"That's freaky," Dad said.

"Not really," Penny said. "After all, we walked into the painting. What else would it look like from the inside? It didn't look like this to me, though. It was just random lines and curves and colors." She gave a little shrug. "Beautiful in a sad and lonely manner."

"Is this the Dreamside? We're in someone's dream?"

"I think so. We're certainly not in the waking world. Look at the sun." Penny pointed up at the red, perfect circle hanging in the sky, casting a faintly pink glow down on the landscape. "Definitely not the sun of the waking world."

Dad nodded.

"I guess I just didn't really believe the whole thing. I mean, I believed it, but my mind didn't really accept it. It is just too big of a thought to wrap my head around."

"I understand," Penny replied. "I had a similar reaction to the waking world. Such a slow changing place. So well defined and rigorous in its shape. Rules, rules and more rules."

Sidney watched Penny as she spoke animatedly. The girl used her whole body to communicate, hands moving, eyes shining as her voice rose and fell. Sidney felt a rush of affection—though they'd only known each other a few days, Penny already felt like a long lost sister to Sidney.

And of course that thought made Sidney feel guilty as if she'd somehow betrayed the memory of Emma. All the pain of losing her sister and mother reared up again, as if it had never receded and she felt stricken. As if reading her mind Penny glanced over at her and cocked her head.

"What's wrong, Sid?"

"Nothing." Sidney marshaled her face into neutrality again. Penny wasn't fooled and she stepped closer and wrapped her arms around her, pulling her into a hug. Sidney put her head on Penny's shoulder—they were about the same height—and the girl smoothed Sidney's hair soothingly.

"Hey, it's okay. Whatever it is, it's okay. Really."

Dad reached out and put a hand on Sidney's shoulder.

"What's up, honey?"

"I just miss them, Dad." Sidney felt annoyed at the tiny hitch in her voice.

"I miss them too, Sid. Every day I miss them."

"You two!" Penny said in affectionate exasperation. "You're supposed to miss them. They are your family. It's impossible not to miss them. There would be something wrong if you didn't miss them. But you should get strength from their memory. Joy. They're with you every day in your thoughts and dreams." She glanced away and then exclaimed. "See?"

Sidney pulled away enough to look where Penny faced. There, standing a short distance from them was Emma.

Setback

Sidney turned to face her sister and soaked in the sight of her, letting her younger sister buoy her spirits. Emma was dressed just as she had been the last time they'd swung together. She stood shyly with her hands clasped behind her back, looking at them out of the corner of her eyes.

"Emma?" The hitch in Dad's voice made Sidney wince. He stood frozen as he stared at the little girl before them.

"Daddy," Emma sounded nervous and Sidney had no idea what she had to feel nervous about.

Dad slipped down to his knees and his hands fell to his sides. Tears flowed freely down his face. "Emma," he repeated senselessly. He raised his arms toward her and she went to him, a quick skip and jump, and he pulled her into an embrace, squeezing tightly as if trying to draw her into him, make her a part of him. Sidney abruptly realized that this was the first time he'd met the dream Emma. She wondered if it would be a good thing—if he could handle this right now.

Emma giggled and gasped.

"Daddy, you're gonna squish me." She pushed against him. He immediately loosened his embrace but didn't let go. He held her at arm's length and stared at her as if trying to memorize everything about her.

"God, Emma, I've missed you so." His voice hitched and Sidney heard the threat of a sob.

"I know, Daddy. I've missed you, too." She gently wriggled out of his grasp and walked over to Sidney and hugged her. "Hiya, Sid!"

"Hi, Em." Sidney drew in the scent in her sister's hair. Emma pulled back and went up on her tiptoes to give Sidney a quick kiss on the cheek before turning to face Penny, who was standing with her arms crossed, weight on one foot and a small quirky smile playing at the corners of her mouth.

"You must be Penny." Emma studied her carefully.

"Yep, that's me!" Penny grinned. "And you're a sweet little dream. A healer. I can see you in them."

Emma nodded seriously.

"And them in me."

"Of course. Do they know?"

"No," Emma responded with a little shrug. "I didn't know until recently. She has been telling me a lot."

"It's unusual of her to get so involved with a dream."

Emma shrugged again and turned back to face Colin.

"Daddy, I'm not really Emma. I mean, I am, but I'm not. It's all so confusing. The shining lady said that I'm a dream—a reflection of how much you all loved the real Emma. Our family is strong in the dreaming." She turned to face Sidney. "When I first learned this, it hurt to find out. But now I think it doesn't matter. I love you and that's all that matters to me."

Sidney nodded.

"Emma." Dad's voice broke again. "I'm so glad to see you." Sidney wondered if he'd heard anything that Emma had said and she frowned in concern. Emma stepped toward him and gently raised her hands to his cheek. He put both of his own hands over hers and leaned into her touch.

"I'm glad to see you, too, Daddy, but I can't stay long. I have to give you a message. You need to find the Wall. Do you see that tower?" She pulled a hand free and pointed past them. Sidney turned to look. There was a tower looming over the center of town, leaning grotesquely, like a drunk trying to find a wall to prop up against. At first glance it made Sidney think of the leaning tower of Pisa, but on further inspection it was much different. The tower was bent to the side in two places: once near the base and again near the top, below the castle-like top. It leaned over so far that Sidney wondered how it stayed standing. "You can see the Wall from the top of the tower. Then you have to fix her."

"How will we fix it—her?" Sidney asked.

"She said you'd know what to do when the time came."

"She's very mysterious."

"Yes." Emma's mouth quirked in a flash of a grin. "After the Wall is repaired. You have to wake up and wait for another sign. There are several places where the Wall is weakening, and you have to get to them and repair them. But she also said that this is only buying time until you have the strength and knowledge to confront the Torment."

"Torment?" Sidney frowned.

"The worst type of nightmare," Penny answered for her. "This one seeks to tear down the Wall. It is a dark, dark dream."

"Where did it come from?" Sidney asked.

"It is made of the primal stuff of dreams—by a dreamer, of course," Penny's voice was matter of fact and Sidney understood how the girl could believe everything Sidney had told her.

Emma spoke up quickly, shooting Penny an odd look.

"My time is short. This is not my dream and something is pulling me out." She seemed to be fading slowly, her body becoming transparent. She looked at Sidney, but kept her hand on Dad's face. "Look for the sign, Sid."

"Will we see you again?" The panicky distress in his voice was heart rending to Sidney.

"Of course you will, Daddy." Emma's voice was faint as if from a distance. And then she was gone. He choked back a sob and covered his face with his hands.

※

Sidney was worried about Dad—after Emma had disappeared he'd withdrawn far into himself again. *No, worried isn't the right word really.* It was a mixture of disappointment and frustration. All the positive changes Sidney had seen in him over the last few days were completely undone. She glanced over and saw that Penny's brow was furrowed. They both snuck peeks at him as they walked through the town. Whenever Sidney stole a look at him, he was staring blankly ahead of them, not watching where he was putting his feet. She shared a quick glance with Penny, shrugged once.

"Hey, Col." Penny kept her voice soft and warm and Dad looked over at her in brief surprise as if just remembering she was there.

"Penny." His eyes were bleak, his voice was an emotionless monotone.

"So how do you think we repair the Wall?" She cocked her head thoughtfully. "I hope we don't have to use bricks and mortar. That might take a long time. Although, I've never done anything like that so it might be fun to try it." She maintained her grip on Dad's hand. Sidney walked over and took his other hand so that they bracketed him like bookends.

He looked over at Sidney for a moment, shrugged and immediately his eyes grew unfocused again. "I don't know."

They continued walking and he seemed to be lost—staring at nothing, eyes blank while he trudged on, unthinkingly putting one foot in front of the other. Penny and Sidney ended up having to guide him to keep him from walking into things. Seeing him like that made Sidney want to cry—or scream.

And so they walked, winding almost aimlessly through the maze of oddly shaped buildings. They saw no people, no animals—no cats, dogs or rats—nothing. The lifeless atmosphere of the town was spooky and began to wear on Sidney's nerves. With each house they passed the emptiness became oppressive and the silence of the town filled up the background and became a strangely oppressive white noise—a constant reminder that they were alone in this ghost town. Each step they took increased Sidney's feeling that someone or something was watching them.

The air itself began to feel heavy and thick, and there was a hint of malice that pressed against Sidney as they walked. They tried to keep the tower in front of them but it was as if the town had a mind of its own, and conspired against them. Broad avenues and narrow alleyways twisted and wound around the buildings, and Sidney could not tell if they were even getting closer to the tower. Her footsteps slowed and occasionally she staggered and lost her balance. She began to think something was purposely hindering them—trying to keep them away from the tower.

The Torment?

No one spoke, and both girls still held Colin's hands. Penny's brow was wrinkled in a delicate frown, the expression of discomfort looking out of place on her usually cheery face. They turned a corner that headed them toward the tower again, but the street ended in a dead end. Here the houses were butted right up against each other, allowing no path past them. Sidney glanced back and saw that behind them the road stretched in a straight path away from the tower, and there were no side streets visible. She frowned—the street they'd turned off of was no longer there.

"I think..." she began but paused. "I think the streets are moving and it feels like something is watching us."

"Yes," Penny's voice was wary. "There's something wrong here."

"I don't think it wants us to pass through. Something doesn't want us here." It sounded silly to Sidney but at the same time completely true.

"Emma..." Dad muttered softly under his breath, just loud enough for Sidney to hear. He stared at the ground a few yards in front of him, his face a blank mask.

"Oh, Dad." Sidney's heart ached and she squeezed his hand. He glanced at her in surprise and then his eyes lost their focus and he slid back inside himself. Sidney felt anger sweep through her body, but she shoved it down, carefully keeping it off her face.

"Let's rest a bit." Even as she spoke, Penny folded her legs up and settled on the ground in one flowing, graceful motion. For a moment Colin stood still and then he glanced around as if surprised at his surroundings, saw Penny sitting and sat heavily beside her. She put an arm around his shoulder and whispered something soothing to him. His eyes flickered some understanding briefly.

Sidney released his other hand and stalked over to the stoop of a building that led up to a misshapen doorway, and sat on the edge of the concrete, carefully not putting her back to the door. It was a relief to stop moving—the heaviness around her eased up and even the oppressive nature of the air seemed to fade. She took a deep breath and focused on putting her frustration aside—she didn't have time to be angry at her father.

Some of the houses looked like ugly, unfriendly faces: the doors and windows the eyes and mouth, the eaves of the roofs the hairline. She felt strongly that something hostile was watching them, waiting for them to wander too close to one of the houses. She shuddered, stood up and walked over to sit on the ground next to Penny.

"It feels like the houses are watching us." Sidney kept her voice low as if afraid something or someone would overhear her.

"Yeah, I noticed that, too." Penny leaned closer and kept her voice down.

Sidney looked up at the tower. Now that they'd stopped it appeared much closer. It dominated the view—like the town was taunting them with a view of the destination it had no intention of letting them reach. The two points where the tower canted over slightly reminded Sidney of knuckles—the stone jutting outward to create a bulge at each joint and making the whole tower a crooked finger gesturing them closer. Weather-worn banners hung from the walls, faded and tattered, each with a different symbol—none of which Sidney recognized. A disgusting yellow cloud hovered around the tower just below the top parapet. The cloud moved and churned slowly, with tendrils snaking out, testing the air before retreating and testing elsewhere and Sidney shivered involuntarily. It was almost as if the cloud was searching for something—as if it were a living thing. She was not sure if it was a part of the tower or had simply attached itself like a foul parasite. The mere sight of it made her skin crawl.

"That's...gross."

Penny just nodded and for a while they both continued to stare up at it.

"Well, let's get to it then," Penny said and then muttered, "I *really* don't want to go there."

"Me either. But Emma said we have to."

"Doesn't mean I have to like it." Penny pushed herself to her feet and pulled Dad to his feet, where he swayed in place, eyes staring sightlessly, cheeks wet. Sidney moved closer to him and reached up to dry away the tears.

"Mari?" he mumbled heavily.

"Dad." Sidney kept her voice low and soothing. "Dad, come back to us. We need you. I need you."

He looked up at her and his eyes cleared slightly as he focused on her. "I'm here, Sid." But as soon as he had spoken, his eyes clouded over and his chin dropped suddenly. "I'm here..." he muttered one last time. Sidney's breath hitched and she fought back a sob of despair. She'd begun to think she was getting him back—after four years of pain and suffering he'd finally began to break free and now it was as if he was back in the days just after the Accident.

It just isn't fair. The thought was bitter and then right away tried to shrug off the hurt and fear she felt.

She pursed her lips, took his other hand and they began to walk again, this time away from the tower. She felt like they'd been tricked. Lured in with that last turn toward the tower, and then immediately forced to go directly away from the tower. It wasn't enough to keep them away from the tower—Sidney felt like the town was trying to break her spirit as well.

The Tower

They pushed on doggedly against the psychological weight of whatever force wanted them to go away, and as they walked the streets shifted; the layout of the town changing behind their backs. Sometimes they reached a dead end and were forced to backtrack to a different path they'd passed by only to find that it was no longer there. At other times they would round a corner and a turn would appear before them where there had not been one moments ago. The shifts alternated between taking them closer and forcing them away from the tower as if there were two different tides at work here—one that wanted them to get to the tower and another that didn't.

Sidney never saw the actual shift. It always seemed to happen when she wasn't looking, or during the short moment while she blinked, or was distracted by something else. It was disorienting, often leaving her feeling dizzy and out of sorts. Her frustration grew into anger and she clenched up inside, tension consuming her. In some small corner of her mind she was surprised at the strength of her reaction—she rarely felt so angry.

Her father's fugue-like state hadn't improved at all, and that just contributed to her anger. Penny kept up a steady stream of chatter, trying to distract them all from their fight to reach the tower, but it wasn't working for Sidney. She began to feel resentful even toward Penny and wished for the first time that the girl would just shut up. She bit her lip several times to keep from shouting. Controlling her anger just frustrated her more. She knew that eventually she was going to explode, and she hoped that explosion wouldn't be directed at Penny or Dad. She decided to voice it before it came to that.

"Okay, this isn't working," she said angrily and stopped walking.

Penny looked at her in surprise, but then nodded in agreement.

"Yes, it's extremely annoying, but I don't see any other option than to keep trying."

"I still don't like it." Sidney ground out her words through gritted teeth. She held on tight to her anger, using it as fuel to keep her moving toward their destination despite the waves of oppression seeming to emanate from that direction. "I just feel so angry. I've never felt so angry in my life." She glanced over at Penny. The girl's eyes were unreadable, but she nodded solemnly back at Sidney.

"I feel it too." Penny cocked her head to the side slightly. "I think the town is doing this to us. We have to ignore it and keep going."

Sidney answered with a single nod. She knew Penny was right, and she tried to calm herself, but it was a lost cause. She felt her rage growing and growing into an irrational thing. For the first time in her life she felt a real capacity for violence—almost a desire for it. Her heart sang with an angry challenge, and she looked around, searching for a target for her anger. Deep inside, she was shocked at her emotions. She felt like she didn't belong in her own skin, but that only served to make her angrier. She stomped off again, and Penny followed behind her, guiding Dad carefully behind them.

Within moments they reached another turn that would take them toward the tower. Sidney's vision blurred with angry tears as she paused before it, not wanting to look around the corner. Another dead end was going to make her scream. She swore softly under her breath and felt, rather than saw Penny's surprise. After a moment Sidney squared her shoulders and moved forward with determination. When she went around the corner, she was shocked to see that the street widened and at the end of the street, not too far off, was a huge courtyard with the tower leaning in the center.

Without pausing, she stumbled forward and picked up the pace unconsciously. She was afraid to even blink for fear that the tower would move out of reach again, but when she finally entered the courtyard, the thickness of the air—the oppressive weight of it—eased and vanished. She staggered once as the force disappeared, feeling like a runner crossing the finish line of a long, tiring race. The suddenness of their arrival at the tower was shocking—it reminded Sidney of that moment when really loud music and gets turned off abruptly, leaving ears ringing, leaving behind an almost physical discomfort at the violent change in sound. Sidney lost her balance briefly, lurched to a halt and stared around her.

A short wall encircled the tower about forty yards out. It was maybe two feet tall and separated the area around the tower into an inner and outer courtyard. The ground was dusty and the limestone of the streets was cracked and fractured in places. Broken stone benches and garbage that might have been from a recent market littered the grounds. Shattered urns, dilapidated woven baskets and ripped and torn blankets, along with heaps of unidentifiable trash spotted the courtyard—artifacts of the human life the town lacked. Flies and other bugs swarmed around the piles as if the little mounds of broken, dusty things were urban centers in a vast world of insect life. Compared to the desolation of the rest of the town, the courtyard seemed to teem with life. The entire area reeked of urine, rot and sewage and a few small fires burned in small pits, expelling thick oily smoke that rose up into the air around the tower.

The smoke pressed against the yellow cloud that hung around the tower, but didn't seem to survive the encounter, leaving the yellow foulness dominant in the sky. As Sidney watched, sickly tendrils stretched and crawled down toward them, instinctively searching them out as if to see what they were and if they might taste good. Sidney shuddered at that thought; but pressed her lips together and faced the tower with her head held high.

"Okay, we're here." Sidney fought to keep the anger out of her voice but failed. "Now what?" She ended up shouting at the tower and her voice echoed around the courtyard, the sounds redoubling until there was nothing intelligible left of her words. The last few words returned as an inarticulate shriek of rage and Sidney was shocked by the sound. As the last echoes died, Penny gasped a tiny laugh.

"I'm sorry." Penny sought to contain the laughter, but she couldn't. "I'm not laughing at you, Sid. It just sounded so... monstrous. You're scary!"

Sidney tried to glare at Penny, but she couldn't pull it off. Despite her frustration she began to laugh as well, a first quick gasp and her anger began to bleed away. They both gave up trying to stop and their laughter echoed around the courtyard, and it sounded as if they were laughing with many others. The simple joy and pleasure that bounced off the walls returned to them magnified in the same way. The yellow cloud drew back sharply as if recoiling from the brief happiness in their laughter and then pressed toward them again. The tendrils still wound and snaked down toward the ground, they moved slowly as if tentative in their approach. She looked back at Penny, still laughing softly, and moved over to wrap her in a bear hug.

"Thanks, Penny, I needed that." She listened to the last of their laughter reverberating around them. Where her shout had become something monstrous, their laughter was a light musical sound that lingered in the air. She glanced over at Dad and saw that he stood motionless, still oblivious to his surroundings. He occasionally muttered under his breath and fresh tears tracked slowly down his cheeks. Sidney's unexpected joy faded but her anger didn't return. She squared her shoulders and took his hand.

"So do we go inside the tower?" She really didn't want to, but it was the logical next step.

"Why not!" Penny still sounded cheerful.

"Well, I can think of a lot of reasons."

Penny chuckled. "Me too. But there's no point in avoiding it. Let's do it." She started forward slowly and both girls pulled Dad forward by the hands. He staggered into motion and they made their way to the low wall. Stepping over the wall they moved into the inner courtyard. Once over the wall, the malevolence the cloud exuded increased with each step forward until they all stopped as if of one mind.

"That cloud hates us," Sidney said and Penny didn't laugh this time, but instead gave a short nod and frown.

"I'd say so."

The yellow fingers of the cloud had finally reached the ground, and rather than moving closer to the group, they dug into the rocky dirt where they touched and pulsed darkly. It looked to Sidney like some evil energy was being pumped into the ground. All over the inner courtyard tendrils of yellow smut dug down disappearing from view.

"What the heck," Sidney muttered.

Suddenly, while they stood there, roughly fifteen feet inside the short wall, there was a soft hissing noise all around them. The ground seemed to churn in the places where the yellowish smut penetrated the ground and girls backed up toward Colin until the three of them stood in a tight knot.

"What's that?" Sidney asked. Penny shook her head slowly and they just watched the places where the ground writhed and pushed up in tiny mountains, a miniature of millions of years of grinding tectonic plates and continental shift. Then like tiny volcanoes, the mounds started to burst and something unidentifiable slowly erupted from each. Sidney stared at the nearest one, trying to understand what she was seeing, but could not figure it out. It was as if her mind were protecting her from something horrific. Abruptly the visual image clicked into place in her head and she realized what it was.

It was a yellowed hand, rotting and vile, reaching blindly toward the sky—a scene right out of a horror movie. Once the elbow was free the hand flopped down to grasp the ground and lever up further. Another hand emerged from the rise of dirt and scrabbled at the ground and began pulling itself up. All around them hands and arms were coming up from the tiny mountains, and heads began to push free of the rubble and dirt, then torsos and faceless, humanoid creatures rose out of the ground and turned to face Sidney, Penny and Dad. The creatures' skin was the same rotten yellow color as the cloud above and tattered in places—rotten strips hanging away from bone as if trying to escape the wreckage of the body.

Sidney could do nothing but stare in shock as the figures continued to emerge from the ground around them. Once they were facing her, they stopped moving. Then a voice floated on the breeze, hissing and whispering from the direction of the tower.

"Sidney Pierce..." The 's' sounds were sibilant and serpentine, and the whisper had a hypnotic quality, lulling Sidney into a trancelike state. The nearest dust man raised its arms toward her but didn't move otherwise, as if offering her a comforting embrace. As she stared at the creature, its face began to change, features sliding slowly into place until it wore a mask of familiarity and empathic concern. The raised arms no longer looked repulsive and vile. Instead they looked warm and welcoming and against her volition she took a small step toward it. "Come to us, Sidney..."

All around them the dust men changed into human shapes, opening their arms toward her, and she heard a soft crooning. The sound was soothing and low—it made her want nothing more than to go into the safety of those arms, rest her weary body and accept the offered comfort. The idea of refusing was completely alien and unfathomable at that moment, and she took another small step forward. "Yes, come to us..."

Sidney continued forward until she was about three feet from the now handsome and affable man, and he leaned slightly toward her, fingers reaching forward and grasping at the air, trying to gather her in. She wanted to feel those arms around her and started to take that last step into their embrace.

Suddenly there was an inarticulate scream of rage and Colin barreled past Sidney and threw himself into the man, driving him back several yards and to the ground. At the moment of collision the man turned back into the ravaged zombie creature it had been and its body simply shattered into rubble, dirt and a thin swirl of dust. Sidney shook her head to clear the foggy feeling and looked down at the remains of the creature. Terror clawed at her mind as she realized how close she'd come before her father saved her. He leapt to his feet and turned to face another of the nearby dust men.

"No," he screamed. "You can't have her."

Loud malicious laughter rang out around them, voicing the promise of violence and death.

"She isn't yours any longer, Colin Pierce," the voice hissed loudly, and a wind buffeted Sidney from behind, making her stagger forwards another step. "You lost her a long time ago. You don't even want her. Admit it." Sidney wanted to scream her denial but her throat seized up, frozen by the horror of that voice. It was no longer soothing and persuasive, but instead was grinding and malicious; the sound of it painful to her ears.

"That's not true." Her father's voice was an angry snarl, all distance gone. He stood protectively in front of her, using his arms to reach back and corral her and she watched over his shoulder as the pile of detritus that had been the dust man began to swim and churn, gathering and slowly coalescing into the limbs and parts of the dust man. Within a few moments it rose from the ground and took an unsteady step back toward them. Colin lashed out again and this time the creature moved lightning fast to grasp his arm, and tugged him toward it. Colin used his momentum to pass the creature and pull it around him in a quick spin. The centrifugal force of the spin broke the creature's hold on Dad's arm and it spun away to smash into another one of the dust men, throwing them both to the ground and shattering them into the same bits of broken body parts as before. Immediately they began to reform.

Sidney had never seen her dad fight. The last thing she had expected was to see him kicking ass and taking names. He'd always taught her that violence was a last resort, but now she saw what he was capable of when pressed. He fought tenaciously and wildly, with a strength born of rage and desperation and drove the dust men back from the girls. It wasn't martial arts—more like what she thought of as brawling —wild swinging punches, kicks and pushes. Sloppy, but it was getting the job done. Watching him fight, Sidney realized that there was a lot about him that she didn't know.

One of the creatures managed to connect with a wild flailing swing and Colin fell back a few steps going to his knees but immediately pushed back to his feet, snarling loudly. He ducked under another haphazard attack, ran over to pick Sidney up and ran toward the tower. Penny flowed into motion and ran after them.

"Where are we going, Colin?"

"Inside. We didn't come all this way to turn around and leave."

"But inside?"

"Well, we're not having much luck outside."

"There is that," Penny said and shrugged.

Above them the yellow cloud was pouring downward rapidly, tendrils leading and searching, but before any of the cloud could touch them, they reached the door and Dad and used his shoulder to push the door, carefully shielding Sidney with his body. The door shuddered under the assault, but held. He stepped back, set himself in a balanced stance and drove his foot into the door, once, twice. With a shout of desperate rage, he kicked again and finally it smashed open and swung wildly back, hanging on a single hinge.

He stepped through the doorway and set Sidney down. Behind him, Penny was caught in the grasp of two of the dust men, struggling to get free grimly, but unable to shake them off.

"A little help here..." Penny's voice was grim and low.

"Dad!" Sidney cried out. "They've got Penny."

He jumped back out the door and drove himself into one of the dust men, and the momentum took all four of them to the ground, where the dust men shattered again, leaving both Dad and Penny lying in the debris. Already the stone and dirt was beginning to coalesce again and he pushed to his feet, pulled Penny up by her hand, and then they raced through the doorway. The remaining dust men and the few that had reformed enough to move all started awkwardly moving toward the doorway. Some shambled with a broken leg or ankle, dragging it behind them, lurching forward half a step at a time. Others appeared whole, but moved slowly as if unfamiliar with the use of their legs, advancing inexorably toward the doorway.

Sidney looked around the inside of the tower. It was completely empty apart from a rough hewn, railless, stone stairway wrapped around the inside of the tower, heading up toward the top. There was nowhere to go but up, and Sidney started up the steps, pushed against the wall and kept her eyes upwards.

"Let's go," she called over her shoulder. Dad and Penny followed her up. At first they made good progress, but as the floor receded Sidney began moving more slowly, each step more careful and deliberate. She wasn't good with heights to begin with—as a child she had fallen off a slide and broken her collar bone. But the shambling mass of dust men at the bottom of the stairs terrified her more. She didn't know if they were climbing behind them, but she didn't dare look back down the steadily increasing height to find out.

"Sidney Pierce..." She heard the whispering malevolent voice again and felt a soft breeze by her ears. The voice was alive—a physical thing—as if the sound had shape and form. She couldn't imagine what creature could make that sound but it was clearly not something human or familiar. "Wouldn't it be easier to just step off? Then you could rest and be done with this useless conflict. I'll catch you, Sidney, I promise..."

A part of her began to slip under the sway of the voice, but something had changed when Dad had broken the spell earlier.

She was able to resist the hypnotic, seductive whisper and it weakened. She growled under her breath, shook off the effects of the voice and continued climbing the stairs. As if sensing her new determination and resistance, the voice hissed angrily and then was silent again.

Colin's labored breathing drove her up the stairs, but there was no noise from Penny. Sidney's fear rose again and she risked a glance back and down, to see if Penny had made it onto the stairs. The young woman was there, not breathing any harder than normal with a small, determined smile on her face. She glanced up and met Sidney's eye and shot her a quick wink. Sidney returned the smile.

Then she made the mistake of looking past her and down. The bottom of the tower seemed to be dropping away, and the dust men milling about were as small as ants. She couldn't believe she'd come that far, and as she put one foot in front of the other, the floor of the tower seemed to move away at a rate that was disproportionate to how fast she was climbing the stairs. Dizziness overtook her and she pressed against the wall and halted. Dad caught up with her and took her shoulder.

"Hey, easy, Sid." Dad sounded strong and alert again and that soothed Sidney more than his words. The fight had snapped him out of his fugue-like state. "Don't look down, sweetie. Just look at the steps in front of you." She closed her eyes again and breathed regularly until she was able to banish her spasm of vertigo. Then she opened her eyes, carefully stared at the steps in front of her and took a slow, single step up the stairs, and then another.

The climb seemed to go on for hours. Before long, Sidney's legs ached and she felt the first sting of blisters on her feet. The air was musty and thick with the smells of age: rotting wood, sandstone dust and hints of the smoke outside. The stone of the wall was rough against her hands as she took step after step, fighting a painful battle against her fear, lurching stomach and spinning head. Relentlessly she pressed on, one foot after another and settled into a rhythm. After what felt like an age, she glanced up and caught a glimpse of the wooden ceiling above. She felt a moment of excitement and kept glancing up every so often, measuring her progress—it got closer much faster than she'd expected. With Dad and Penny whispering words of encouragement and the occasional reassuring touch of a hand on her shoulder or elbow, they finally reached the top of the stairs.

A ladder, roughly ten feet high, bridged the gap from the last step to a trap door, but the ladder didn't lead exactly to the trap door—the small opening was set about a foot away from the ladder's top rung, so that the edge of the hole was just barely in reach. Another perverse aspect of the bizarre tower, of the strange town of this dream. She'd have to climb to the top, reach out precariously and then grab the edge and pull herself up. For a brief moment she'd be hanging over empty space and one wrong move would send her plummeting to the bottom of the tower. All of this after she somehow managed to open the door, of course.

God, I hope it isn't locked. Her stomach flip-flopped and her palms became slick with sweat.

"I can't..." She stopped and licked her dry lips once. "I can't do this."

"Sure you can, Sid." Dad's voice was low and calm. "I'll help you. Squeeze up against the wall so I can go by, okay?" She nodded her head silently and flattened herself tight against the wall, giving him room to pass. She watched as he gathered himself and eased past her. The stairway was so narrow that he had to go sideways, and as he slid by her, she saw determination in his eyes—not fear. She felt an unexpected rush of emotion and tears welled up in her eyes. Then he was past her and turned to put his back against the wall beside her. He looked over at her and smiled, letting his nervous relief fill his eyes.

"I hate heights, too, Sid. But we can't sit here and we can't go back." He took a deep breath, pulled himself up the ladder and pushed at the trap door above him. It opened upwards easily, clattering noisily on the landing above them, and he reached out one hand to grab the edge of the opening. She watched him as he tested his grip for a moment, then closed his eyes and visibly gathered his courage. Then he opened his eyes again and without any further hesitation, pushed off the ladder with his other hand and reached up to grab the edge so that both hands held him and his legs swung away. For the space of a few heartbeats he just dangled over open air and then he began pulling himself up, until he could throw one elbow over and then the other. He kicked his legs to build momentum and pulled up to disappear through the trap door. Sidney released a breath that she hadn't realized she'd been holding as he pulled his feet up and out of sight.

Leap of Faith

Sidney and Penny waited for him to reappear above them but a minute passed and he didn't show. Another minute. Sidney's relief that he'd made it up began to bleed into worry. She had no idea what to do next if he didn't come back for them—there was no way she could reproduce his feat.

"Dad?" she called out, trying to sound calm. "You okay up there?" After a moment his head appeared in the opening.

"Yeah, just catching my breath, Sid. Let me take a look around up here." He disappeared from view and reappeared a moment later, leaned out further and reached down toward her. "Looks good. Nothing up here but more stairs. Climb the ladder, Sid, and I'll pull you up."

"Go ahead, Sid," Penny's voice was low and soothing. "I've got you from down here." Sidney couldn't decide if her words were reassuring or just more frightening. Things would have to go oh so wrong for Penny to have to catch her. But the encouraging tone of Penny's voice calmed her and she slowly moved one foot to the next rung. Then the other. Before she knew it she was moving up the ladder. The ladder had looked no more than ten feet tall, but as Sidney climbed, it seemed to grow impossibly higher.

"You're doing fine, honey." Dad's words floated down as she reached the top of the ladder. Her hands were slick with sweat, and her fingers beginning to cramp. She gritted her teeth and just looked at the rungs in front of her. After what felt like an eternity, he spoke again. "Okay, great, Sid. Now just reach up and back. Hold on tight with your other hand, until I tell you to let go, Okay?"

Sidney nodded once and tried to let go of the ladder, but her body wouldn't respond. She frowned and tried again but the fear gripped her like an electrical current, locking her in place.

"It's fine, Sid." Dad said. "I won't let you fall. Just reach out with one hand. Go ahead and let go." His voice was calm and Sidney closed her eyes, clenched her teeth and forced herself to release her grip on the rung of the ladder. It went against every instinct she had to pull her hand away but she did it, and reached back and up, stretching slightly. Her heart pounded and a small whimper of fear escaped her.

"Just a little bit more." She gave one last stretch. She knew she had reached the limit of how far she could reach out. Her arms were long enough to extend out a bit further, but there was no way her panic riddled brain would let that happen. She started to feel that she was not going to make it and fought not to snatch her hand back and hug the ladder again. Just as she started to give up, she felt her father grasp her wrist. "Gotcha. Keep holding the ladder with your other hand, Sid." She heard him shifting his weight and then he wrapped his other hand around her wrist slightly lower on her arm. "Okay, hon. I'm ready. All you have to do is let go with your other hand and reach for me with it. I'll have you up before you know it."

She hung there frozen, and her fear threatened to consume her entirely. She heard herself whimper again and was embarrassed. She closed her eyes and her embarrassment turned to anger.

"Trust me, Sid. I won't let you fall, I promise." She took a deep breath and let it out slowly. She did trust him. Completely. She realized this and a certainty and calmness filled her. She fought to release her grip on the ladder—her hands were sweaty and cramped from squeezing so hard. As her hand came away, she swung out away from the ladder and a tiny shriek escaped. She reached up toward Dad and he caught her hand and in one smooth motion pulled her through the opening and into his arms. Just like that, it was over and he set her down on the floor next to him with a smile. She refused to let him go and he pulled her close and wrapped his arms around her.

"Good work, Sid. Not that bad, huh?"

She laughed, trying to sound confident, but the tremor in her voice ruined the effect. Her fear and anger were gone now, leaving her shaking and exhausted.

"Okay, let's get Penny up here." He gently disengaged himself. She quickly scooted away from the opening, put her back against the wall and tried to catch her breath.

"Penny, your turn. Did you see what Sidney did there?" He started to slide out over the edge again but before he could get in position, Penny's hands appeared simultaneously gripping the edge. Sidney heard the woman's tinkling laughter come up through the opening and he reached down and pulled Penny up. He fell backwards as her momentum carried them to the floor beside Sidney.

"Holy crap, Penny." His face was a mask of shock. "You nearly gave me a heart attack." Sidney's eyes were wide with surprise as well.

"That was a great fun!" Penny said breathlessly and laughed again.

"You must be some kind of gymnast, Penny." The smile on Dad's face was forced.

"Or an adrenaline junkie," Sidney said through deep breaths.

"Just light on my feet." Penny scooted over next to Sidney and put a hand on her shoulder. "You okay, Sid?" Sidney pushed up into a sitting position and managed a smile.

"Yeah, I'm fine," she muttered. "Just peachy."

Penny snorted a laugh in response. Dad reached up and closed the trapdoor again. He slid a bolt in place, locking it firmly.

"We're lucky it wasn't locked from up here." Dad echoed Sidney's earlier thought. "I'm not sure how we'd have gotten up."

They sat on the floor for a while, catching their breath. Another set of stairs spiraled up along the inside of the tower wall, leading up to another wooden ceiling high above. There was a rough wooden railing on this set of stairs, and Sidney breathed a deep sigh. At the top of the stairway she could make out a small opening with light streaming through. She hoped there would be no gymnastics needed to get up through the opening—she wasn't sure she could handle it.

The floor she crouched on was at the point where the tower first canted slightly off center. Everything inside the tower looked correct—the steps were at the right angle to the wall and the floor, but Sidney's internal sense of balance didn't agree with what she saw. For the first time, she noticed a rushing, hissing sound that she couldn't identify.

"What's that sound?" Sidney looked at the others.

"Wind, maybe?" Penny cocked her head and listened.

"Yeah, that's what I was thinking." Dad pushed himself to his feet and dusted off his hands on his pants. "Okay, let's get going. The sooner we get this done the sooner we can...well, do whatever comes next." The sight of the lopsided grin on his face made Sidney breath deeply in relief.

Oh, thank God.

Sidney stood and started up the steps, leading the way again. Her footsteps reverberated up and down from the wooden floor and ceiling as if the top of the tower were a great drum. The climb to the top didn't take nearly as long this time, and as she'd hoped, the steps led straight up through the ceiling.

Into the Wind

Sidney pulled up through the small opening and out onto the roof. The top of the tower was open to the elements, offering little protection from the grasping, tearing wind howling loudly around her. Her hair was blown back from her face, her clothes tight against the front of her body and her eyes stung and watered. It wasn't cool or refreshing—it was a fierce blow that moved heat and humidity around roughly. With the addition of the wind, the heat seemed to increase significantly—not what Sidney would have expected.

She slid against a low wall that ran around the outer edge and when she felt the stone against her back she looked around while she waited for Colin and Penny. The tower was circular, and the top slanted wickedly, lower on the side directly opposite her. The large granite blocks held in place by chipped and partially eroded mortar looked old and worn down, the edges rounded by time and wind. A short wall ran the edge of the roof, crenellated, each jutting block separated by a gap roughly two feet wide.

The floor itself was wooden and the surface was slick—ground to a shiny smoothness by the elements. In the center of the floor was a large wide stone bowl that was about a foot and a half tall. From where she sat, Sidney could see that the inside of it was blackened and charred but otherwise empty.

A pile of junk had accumulated in a small pocket of protection at the base of the wall on the far side, shielded from the violence of the wind. Bits of charred wood, scraps of metal and some pottery all heaped together—a small pile of an unknown history. It wasn't long before Colin and Penny joined her, their own backs pressed against the wall.

"I think we're on the wrong side of the tower," Dad shouted over the wind. Sidney realized he was right—they were on the high side of the tilted platform and the wind cut into them unimpeded. Not only would the far wall offer them some relief from the wind, but she wanted to look over the rail and see what was out there across the landscape of the dream.

She scooted, crablike across the floor, moving slowly so as not to slip on the glassy wood surface. She caught herself on the fire pit and then moved past it until she had her feet against the wall on the other side. The sudden absence of the wind clawing at her hair and clothes was startling, yet wonderful. In the protection of the wall the wind was quieter—not much but it added to the sense of shelter a bit. However, she had to stand up into the wind again to see over the edge. She steeled herself and stood up behind one of the crenelations jutting off top of the wall, put an arm around it to anchor herself and slowly eased out to look down off the tower. Immediately the world spun slightly off axis as vertigo seized her. Her hands became sweaty and she gripped the wall tighter, closed her eyes and fought to regain her composure. But there was nothing for it—she was just going to have to deal with the dizzy sight of the yawning fall. She opened her eyes and kept them level with the horizon, trying her best to ignore the yawning fall below her, and after a few minutes her head stopped spinning. As she sat there getting her balance again, Dad and Penny slid down beside her at the adjacent openings.

"God, that wind sucks." He forced his voice to carry over the blasting, whistling sound.

"Stand behind one of the crenellations." Sidney's words were whipped away by the wind as they left her mouth so she repeated herself in a shout. He nodded and stood to look over the wall, and then pointed out over the landscape directly in front of them.

"Hey, I think that's what we're looking for." Dad was pointing out off the tower and Sidney glanced out and unintentionally looked down. The ground seemed to fall away at a frightening speed and the world swung into motion around her. Feeling dizzy she slumped back to the floor behind the wall. She had no idea how she was going to look over the edge again—the idea was enough to make her want to throw up.

Then she felt a hand under her arm and she looked back. Penny was smiling at her sympathetically as she gently pulled Sidney to her feet and took her hands.

"Here, Sid, close your eyes." Penny wasn't shouting but her words carried easily over the roar of the wind. "Let me help you. Let me take some of your fear away. We need you to see—you're our eyes." Her words were startling, but had the ring of truth, so Sidney obeyed and closed her eyes tightly. Penny slowly pulled her away from the wall and into a careful embrace. A wave of calmness and serenity swept through her and she sagged into Penny's arms as her rigid tension simply evaporated. "There, that's much better. Can you look at the wall for me? It's right in front of us."

Sidney opened her eyes and at first she couldn't see the wall. Then her mind began to piece together what she was seeing and she realized that the wall was taller than the tower. It stretched from horizon to horizon, blocking any sight of nearly half the world. It boggled her mind that she'd not even noticed it when she first emerged on the top of the tower, not to mention when they'd been walking through the town, making their way to the tower. It seemed impossible that this wall wouldn't dominate any view.

"That wasn't there before, was it?" She shouted as the wind surged around them.

"I didn't see it." Penny spoke close to Sidney's ear. "But that doesn't really mean anything—'being' is a nebulous thing on this side of the Wall. Maybe now that it's the focus of our attention it has become…more."

"So on the other side is the waking world? The museum? Tayport?"

Penny nodded but didn't speak and Sidney cast her glance out across the landscape to study the wall.

At first she couldn't gauge the scale of it—it could be a half mile away or a hundred miles—but then it snapped into perspective. It was miles away and that meant it was colossal. It was made up of huge dirty-yellow blocks of stone that looked weather-worn and bleak as if they had stood guard there for hundreds, maybe thousands of years. The topmost blocks were crenellated and hung out over the blocks below far enough that climbing them would be extremely difficult. Wooden spikes the size of redwood trees, and sharpened to polished points jutted out from the top of the wall, as if preparing to defend against a siege by huge giants. Sidney suddenly felt small, tiny like one of those people in Gulliver's Travels. She searched for the name for a moment. Lilliputians. That was it.

She cast her eyes along the wall, starting at the top and scanning the surface until she came upon a spot where it was visibly damaged. The expanses of stone were still in place, but the blocks themselves were fractured and little chunks had begun to fall away leaving shadowy crevices. The air around the stones was hazy with the same yellowish cloud that enveloped the midpoint of the tower.

"Okay, I see it. Now what?" Sidney shouted.

"Now we fix it." Penny smiled wryly. Sidney rolled her eyes but smiled back.

"How?"

"No idea." Penny shrugged and turned to Dad.

"Col? Any ideas?"

He didn't answer. His brow was furrowed in a frown and he stared across at the wall.

"Coilín?" Penny repeated. He looked startled as he turned to look at her.

"Sorry. What did you say?"

"Sidney and I wondered if you have any idea how to fix the wall?"

"No, not really. But I think we're going to have to come up with something fast." He pointed. "I think that cloud is coming our way." Sidney looked back to the wall and saw a churning mass of dirty mustard colored mist, similar to the one below the tower, floating toward them across the gulf from the wall. Filthy, grimy tendrils of yellow smut stretched, reaching and questing toward them.

Repairing the Wall

Sidney had a hard time gauging how far the cloud was from the tower. She knew the wall was colossal and distant, but there was really nothing to measure the scale against. No frame of reference. However far it really was, the yellow cloud was stretching across that gap fairly quickly. She figured they had ten or fifteen minutes before the yellow cloud reached them.

"That's disgusting." Sidney's stomach roiled at the sight.

"Yeah." Penny seemed to speak effortlessly over the wind.

"I guess we'll have to go back down and head that direction." Unlike Penny, who seemed to speak effortlessly over the wind, Dad was shouting to be heard. "Although that just gets us there. I have no idea how to fix it."

"Yes, but it's a good first step." Excitement filled Penny's eyes as she warmed to the conversation. "That cloud was put there or is controlled by someone who doesn't want the wall repaired. Probably our Torment."

Dad nodded.

Sidney let their voices fade into the background noise of the wind, and turned the problem over in her mind. She kept coming back to the idea that this was a dream—that they were in the Dreamside. She wondered offhandedly whose dream it was. Then with a start she realized that was exactly the point. Whose dream?

"Okay, but we're right back at how. Maybe we should just go there and cross that bridge when we get to it," Dad was saying and then Penny and he lapsed into thoughtful silence.

"It's just a dream..." Sidney murmured into the wind.

"What did you say, Sid?" Dad frowned.

"Whose dream..." Sidney began but then she slid back into thoughtful silence. In her mind's eye she saw herself standing before the painting the museum in Tayport, remembered how it had started to swirl as she watched it and something clicked. She took a deep breath as excitement filled her.

"What?" Dad struggled to catch her words, but they were already gone, ripped away into the wind.

Sidney didn't answer, but instead focused on the wind that rushed around them. She closed her eyes and concentrated on the sound and the feel, the small granules of dust that peppered her skin, the dryness of her eyes. She drew in the smell of the air, the way her body felt as the wind tried to rock her off her feet again. She felt the wildness of the powerful gusts. The wind was a living thing. She reached out with her senses and embraced the sense of the violent buffeting and insistent grasping—instead of fighting it unconsciously she just let it move through her. In a sudden rush, she felt the world expand beyond the chaotic space her body occupied. It was as if the world opened up, a flower blooming and revealing itself. Joy rushed through her—wildfire consuming the fear and desperation she'd been fighting, leaving her peaceful and elated.

Sidney pushed her awareness out along those currents and for a moment the wind fought to shove her back, but she steeled herself and moved forward anyway. The wind seemed to stretch a moment, and then give up, and Sidney's thoughts moved gracefully into the sky. She reached out and took hold of the wind, gently pulling it close, and as she held onto the rough currents of air, they seemed to slow and relax into something gentler. She concentrated on the wind, slowing it at the same time that she bled the heat out of it.

As easily as that, the wind dissolved into a cool, gentle breeze that soothed her face, delicately caressing and whispering. The sudden calm almost overwhelmed her, and glancing over at the others, she saw they were startled as well. She broke into a smile and gently pulled out of Penny's embrace, moving closer to the edge, her fear of heights completely forgotten.

"Hey, the wind is gone," Dad said. His voice seemed unnaturally loud and then he grinned. "That whole windy tower-top thing was seriously annoying."

"Thank you, Captain Obvious," Sidney murmured but smiled to take the edge off the words. He laughed easily, the light sound hanging in the air around them.

She closed her eyes and felt the floor under her feet, the slant of the wood. She could feel Dad and Penny standing nearby, their presence a tangible thing despite the space between them. For a moment she reveled in the soothing feel of them beside her and then she cast her mind along the top of the tower, focused on the sheer wrongness of the angle of gravity. She pushed her mind—her dream sense as she already thought of it—down through the wood and rough stone, on further into the ground of the inner courtyard that surrounded the tower. The ground was firm and cool, the mass of the tower plunging down to anchor the structure. Deep at the roots of the tower there was no sign of the foulness that swam around the base of the decrepit building. It was a firm bastion radiating strength and something else. History was what it felt like to Sidney. It felt as if the deep core of the tower held the stories and tales that the town was built upon. She sunk her awareness into the stone and dirt, focused on the rightness of it and then she changed the rest of the tower to share that rightness. As simple as that, she decided that the tower was straight and whole again.

It didn't move so much as suddenly become what Sidney wanted. She laughed—a joyful sound—as she and Dad lost their balance and sat down clumsily. Penny staggered a step but quickly steadied.

Dad's mouth dropped open and he turned to stare at Sidney. Penny stood back and clapped her hands, grinning widely.

"Of course," she said. "Why didn't I think of that?"

"What did you do, Sid?" Dad asked. "How did you do that?"

"It's a dream, Dad," Sidney said. "It's my dream. I was staring at the painting when the portal opened. Somehow we're in my dream. Once I realized that, I knew that I was the one in control. The Torment was only able to take charge of my dream because I didn't realize it was mine. So I just decided that it wasn't windy and the tower wasn't leaning." She laughed, pleased.

"Wow," he replied. "So you can just fix the wall, right? I mean, make it strong and whole again?"

"I think so," she answered, then glanced at Penny questioningly.

"Try it," the young woman replied, shifting from one foot to the other, seeming smaller and younger in that moment. Sidney smiled reflexively at her friend—so childlike in her excitement. Then she turned to study the wall, and the first thing that caught her eye was the yellow cloud that was getting closer with every moment. It flowed across the gap faster now, desperately, as if it sensed its own doom approaching.

"Let's get rid of that ugly yellow cloud," she said with a curl of her lip. She closed her eyes and sent her mind outward to meet the cloud. As the two forces met she felt the wrongness of the haze. It was a violation of the world around it—a malicious, filthy thing invading her dream. It assaulted her senses and made her stomach turn, but that feeling seemed distant and she took hold of the foulness. Where she held it, the cloud pulled back in on itself, seeking to escape her grasp. She didn't let it go, instead sent her thoughts to pursue it as it slunk away trying to escape her. She gathered the obscene smut into a dense thickness, slowly compressing it into a small black point of malignant darkness. Then with a soft pop, it was gone. In the wake of its disappearance they all heard a distant, soft howl of rage. Sidney glanced down over the side of the tower and got rid of the yellow cloud there as well, and again as the cloud shrunk to nothing there was another scream.

"There," she said distractedly.

Then she focused on the broken parts of the Wall and sent her dream sense outward to bridge the distance separating her from the towering bulwark. It took a mere fraction of a second for her awareness to reach the huge stone monolith. There was no sense of being out of her body—it was just that she had expanded to take in more of the dream around her. She let her mind crawl over the surface of the blocks, her thoughts as fingers examining the Wall. She explored some of the solid, healthy blocks of stone, and memorized how they felt, and then she moved on to the first of the broken ones. She slowly inspected the cracks, missing chunks of rock and the places where the other side of the wall could be seen. Up close the damage was much more extensive. She started making the blocks whole and strong again, one at a time, moving down the wall, shoring it up.

She moved slowly at first, learning the way to repair each huge block but with each that she fixed she gained confidence, skill and then speed. Then she was moving so fast that the reconstruction of the wall was like a wave flowing across the surface of the stone. The wall quickly became a shining, white beacon of strength, radiating a sense of rightness and Sidney felt exultant. She felt a wave of something from the wall. Some emotion as if the wall was a sentient thing and she realized that it was—it was the Wall. The woman that had sent them here. The emotion that flowed across her was gratitude—that was as near as Sidney could name it. And love.

That task finished, she extended her dream sense down to the base of the wall. As fast as thought she was there, and saw a multitude of creatures along the bottom of the wall, tearing at the blocks, using huge siege machines to shatter and fracture the stone and then pulling away the bits and pieces. She moved in close to them and stared in horror. No two were the same. Some were foul, disgusting creatures: tentacles, fangs, tusks writhing on half-made flesh, and oozing sores. Others were dark and shadowy. Wolves with foot long fangs and drool roping from their mouths, giant centipedes with hairy tusks protruding from their gaping maws, vampires, werewolves, zombies. Every possible thing that could be imagined as evil and dark walked the plain at the base of the wall. She felt the urge to vomit but managed to keep the contents of her stomach down.

But it was not only monsters. Sidney saw very normal people as well, but they had a dark glint of madness and malice in their eyes that she found more frightening than the most gruesome of the nightmares. She stared at the churning mass of creatures with a mixture of dread and revulsion, and she knew logically that she shouldn't feel so afraid—this was her dream after all. She took her fear firmly in hand as she realized what they were. These were nightmares dreamed over the ages by sleepers and now serving the Torment, trying to break down the wall so that they could escape into the waking world. The sheer evil of the nightmares was like a heavy weight on her soul. She had to unmake them—the wall wouldn't be safe until they were gone.

She took hold of herself and pushed the fear and panic down enough to concentrate on what she had to do. She forced her dream sense down among the nightmares—every instinct screaming to flee—and picked one out to unmake. She fixed it in her mind—it was a blind, mewling thing; eight legs, furry and a round mouth with short needle-like fangs all pointing inward radially. Each leg ended in a huge hand with dirty broken claws. Its body was long and ribbed; its skin was thick with green slime. Fluids seeped from between the ribbing, yellow pus-like scum. Sidney's mind shrank away in pure revulsion and the thing turned to face her, blindly sensing her. Its mouth pulsed open and a horrible shrieking sound blasted around her. All around it, other nightmares looked up from their various dances of destruction and saw her.

"Shit." Sidney was vaguely aware of Dad's soft snort of disapproval, but she put that out of her mind and concentrated on her first victim. She pursed her lips and decided it didn't exist. Nothing happened. She tried to push her dream sense into it, to understand the fiber of its being. She felt that if she could understand it she could unmake it, but for some reason, she was unable to get inside the beast. It was as if there was something blocking her—some shell or ward that kept her out. Nausea continued to rise and she found it harder to concentrate.

It occurred to her that maybe she couldn't unmake the nightmares—they were invaders that came outside of her dream—brought in by the Torment to work his evil against her dream. If she couldn't destroy them, perhaps she could force them to leave. She fixed her dream sense on the one she wanted to banish and muttered under her breath.

"You are not welcome here." She decided that it was no longer in her dream and it disappeared. A thrill of triumph flooded through her and she began to send the rest of the nightmares away as well. At first she attacked them one at a time, but after a few of them she realized that she might be here for days getting rid of them in this fashion. Already some of the nightmares had broken off from the wall and were scurrying and running pell-mell toward the tower. She concentrated on a group of the nightmares and banished them, then she tried a larger group and finally, with one sweep of her awareness, she sent all the remaining nightmares away. A glorious silence fell on the plain.

But she was not done. With a gentle push of her awareness she sent wildflowers sweeping across the plains, colors erupting from the ground in a rolling wave from the tower toward the wall, creepers of ivy and flowers settling at the base of the wall, already reaching green fronds up into the stone protectively.

Then she drew herself back to her body, opened her eyes and glanced around, slightly dazed and disoriented. Then she fixed her eyes on Dad and Penny, and broke into a huge smile.

"Done!" Sidney sounded triumphant.

"Done?" Dad asked.

"Done."

"Great work, Sid!" Penny threw her arms around Sidney. Dad peered over the balustrade and stared at the wall.

"Yep, great job, Sid." He shielded his eyes from the sun that had just emerged from the banks of brownish clouds in the sky. The clouds were quickly being swept toward the horizons and fluffy white ones flowed to take their place. A soft gentle breeze picked up, touching their hair and faces lovingly, and carrying the scent of the wild flowers to them. "Are you doing that, Sid?"

She nodded, and then turned to face the town. As she stared out at it the broken, canted buildings began to be replaced with clean, straight ones, and as her eyes swept across the city the process accelerated until the town below was beautiful, clean and inviting.

Penny clapped happily. "Oh, people! It needs people!" Sidney laughed and people began to appear in the streets, and the noises of the town began to rise up on the breeze. The newly created townsfolk walked the street as if they'd been there all along, picking up lives that hadn't existed moments earlier.

"There. I think that's much better. Boy, I really wish I could do this in the real world!" Dad had moved to stand beside her and he gently ruffled her hair. She shot him a smile and took his hand. "Okay. Now what?"

"I think we need to wake up," Penny said. "We've got a meeting with a crow."

"Okay," Sidney agreed but she already felt regret at the prospect of leaving this place she had created but she knew Penny was right so she waved a hand carelessly and a swirling, red vortex appeared in the air beside her.

For a moment she allowed her reluctance to leave hold her in place. The power she had over the world she'd created was intoxicating. Empowering. Even though she liked the way it made her feel and didn't want to let it go, she knew there were still things to do—the Wall needed to be repaired in other places. Maybe those places would be in another of her dreams and she'd be able to repair the Wall again.

Finally she pushed aside her reluctance, turned and grinned at Penny and Dad. "Right this way." Then she gathered her resolve, stepped into the portal and disappeared.

Part 3: The Underground

Subway

Colin felt nothing but awe at the way Sidney had fixed the wall and changed the town. He looked at her and instead of just seeing his little girl he saw the beginnings of a young woman. Strong, independent and smart. He realized that she'd been this person for a while but he'd just missed it, so mired in his own pain, so emotionally absent. And now watching her face her fears with determination and rise to the challenge made him so proud. At the same time, he also felt a wash of pain for Emma, for what could have been. He pushed that aside quickly—seeing her in the dream had been wonderful, but at the same time it had also been like ripping off a scab that was just starting to heal. The pain of the loss had come back in full force, as if the years of slow, painstaking healing had never occurred.

So he watched Sidney confidently step through the portal she'd conjured up and followed her. It wasn't like the first time; they didn't have to wade through the seemingly endless redness. The step he took in was the same step that took him out on the other side exactly where he'd been in front of the painting. He was only a few inches from the painting and while the wall had returned to its normal state, the painting was still swirling inward slowly. He watched curiously, wondering if it would be the same painting when it stopped. Already it was becoming difficult to imagine that it had been a swirling, churning carmine doorway into the Dreamside. The idea was just too large in the calm, quiet museum.

He looked away from the painting before it had stopped swirling, and took in the room. Everything in the museum was just as they'd left it. The guard was still stepping through the large doorway, and the two women were still studying the painting on the opposite wall. It was as if no time had passed at all. Between one heartbeat and the next they'd traveled to another world, nearly died, and repaired the Wall.

The guard looked in their direction with surprise on his face, and the surprise quickly became suspicion. He walked over toward Colin.

"Excuse me, sir," the guard asked as he approached. "Is there a problem?"

"Everything's fine." Colin kept his voice low so as not to break the calm quiet of the gallery. The guard seemed to evaluate him instantly and then his eyes moved past Colin to the girls.

"Could you all step back from the painting a little bit? We ask our patrons to stay at least three feet from the displays."

"Oh, sure, sorry." Colin moved back obediently.

"Thank you, sir."

Penny and Sid both stepped away from the painting as well and stood beside Colin, shoulder to shoulder as he faced the guard. Colin was careful to keep his stance non-threatening. The guard looked at the girls again. "You ladies all right?"

Colin glanced back and saw Penny give the guard a blinding smile.

"Oh, yes, sir!" She spoke enthusiastically, bouncing slightly on the balls of her feet. "We were just looking at this amazing painting." She turned and pointed at the Klee again and Colin realized that it was back to normal. Completely unchanged. Whatever magic Sidney had wrought upon the dream world that had sprung from it had not affected the painting in any permanent way. For some reason this made Colin sad. There had been something thrilling and amazing to the work she'd done to the colors and shapes on the canvas. She had improved upon it, made it into something grand and wonderful. Seeing the painting reverted to its original state was disappointing.

Nothing but a dream.

On the other hand, the way she'd seen the painting was indelibly etched in his mind—he never would have seen the hints of some bizarre village before she had imagined and dreamed it that way. Now he felt a personal connection to the piece that went deep into his own imagination. So not all was lost.

"I think this is my friend's favorite and she was just telling us what she sees in it," Penny gushed, stepping to the guard and putting her arm through his. Any hint of suspicion had evaporated as she had smiled and touched him. He allowed her to lead him toward the painting. "Go ahead, Sid, tell…" she glanced surreptitiously at the man's name tag without missing a beat. "…Earl what you see in this one." She lifted up a bit onto her toes to speak specifically to Earl. "She's got a really great eye for these things." She settled back onto her feet, raised an eyebrow and gave Sidney a playfully challenging smile.

Sidney stepped forward slightly and started in without any pause.

"This one is really cool. Not for what it shows, but for what it hints at—what was and what could be. Notice the way the lines seem to draw out buildings. Do you see these lines here?" She gestured at the painting. "They seem to describe a taller building, a tower possibly. But it is leaning and bent. The entire town seems bent and twisted just like the tower. If we just use our imagination we can see the town as it was, or as it could be." She went on describing the town as it could be, and Earl listened raptly. Colin found himself caught in her words as well.

Earl was nodding and staring at the painting as if seeing it for the first time. For all Colin knew it might have been the first time the man had stopped to look at the painting—really look at it and he was seeing it clearly through Sidney's dream. She finally stopped talking and Penny pulled Earl closer to the painting, both girls looked at the man expectantly.

"Well, I've never really looked at it like that before." The words came slowly as he studied the painting. "The way you describe it makes it look...beautiful. Never been partial to it myself. But it's kinda interesting, isn't it?"

"I know just what you mean, Earl." Penny winked at Colin while the guard wasn't looking. Colin hid a smile. She was so infectious—so full of life and energy. "I had exactly the same reaction, myself."

A while later, after they said goodbye to Earl, they sat at the bottom of the granite steps outside the museum. Colin glanced over at Sidney and saw her watching traffic blankly, drawn into herself tiredly. And he was tired too, he realized. He wondered how that worked—they'd only been away from the waking world for a moment or two. The whole thing was confusing as hell.

"Well, that was fun." Penny sounded unusually subdued. "So what's next?"

"Another sign," Colin spoke. "But let's rest here a bit first. What do you think, Sidney?"

"Yeah. Maybe the next sign can just meet us here." She grinned. "Probably doesn't work that way, huh?"

Colin reached over and ruffled her hair gently again. "Probably not."

Penny laughed softly and then they all lapsed into silence. Colin marveled at how vibrant and refreshing the city was after the lifelessness of the tower village. There was something soothing about sitting right near all the rush and noise yet still apart from it, an observer. A thousand little things to look at, a thousand stories passing by. He leaned back on his hands with his legs stretched out down the steps in front of them. For a time the three just let the city flow past them.

"Hey, guys," Sidney broke through Colin's thoughts. "Look over there." She pointed and he followed her hand. The museum was situated in the heart of an upscale shopping district and across the street a line of expensive boutiques, art galleries and various restaurants continued, interrupted only by intersections. The people walking along were wealthy— easy to see from their expensive jackets, designer shoes and jewelry. Even the subway entrance was upscale. The walls that lined the steps were made of marbled granite and there was a graceful red metal arch across the top of the stairs. The entire area struck Colin as almost surreal—as if someone had come along and painted a fine gloss over the natural character of the city.

It wasn't a neighborhood where people lived—the people who looked so natural and at ease on this street lived nowhere near here. It was a place where outsiders were suddenly insiders and the people who lived nearby only came to work. Colin found the whole scene strange and the writer in him reveled in it.

"What are we looking at?" Colin followed Sidney's finger.

"On the arch above the subway entrance."

Colin looked closer and for a moment couldn't see what she was pointing at, but then it leapt out of the surrounding scenery. A large crow was perched on the top of the metal arch.

"Could it really be that easy?" Sidney asked wryly.

"Let's go see!" Penny stood up, suddenly as energetic as usual and helped pull both of them to their feet. "Another train! This is great!" Colin shook his head with a smile and followed her as she headed toward the intersection.

✵

It turned out that the upscale shine ended on the other side of the arch—a portal from the wealthy shopping district to the dingy, noisy world of the subway. It wasn't a gradual change, but rather a sudden shift, punctuated by old, dried gum and cigarette butts scattered across the ground. The smell of thousands of daily passengers permeated the air—stale cigarette smoke and sweat dominated, but Colin caught the occasional whiff of some food or perfume that had been brought down into the darkness. It was like a whole different world. Colin found it strangely refreshing after the oppressive affluence of the street above.

"So are we going to ride?" Penny led them at a brisk walk—almost a trot and glanced back at Colin. "Or can we do some panhandling?" She shot him a playful grin and he smiled back.

"Panhandling, if you want to eat anything."

She stuck her tongue out at him and Penny laughed.

"Don't worry, Sid," Penny's voice was light and playful. "I've got you covered."

"Thanks, Penny. It's good to know someone cares."

"Tickets," Colin veered off toward a machine that sold subway passes. "We're going to need tickets."

"Yes, but what tickets?" Sidney asked with the slightest hint of exasperated petulance.

"I don't think it matters. You just buy a ticket to get into the station then you go where you want."

"So we don't have to decide yet." There wasn't even a hint of sarcasm in Penny's voice. Sidney rolled her eyes and smiled.

Colin used a credit card to get passes out of the machine; they all stopped to look at a schedule on the wall behind stained and pockmarked Plexiglass.

"It looks like the next train arrives right about now." He quickly found scanned the schedule. "Let's hurry and see if we can get on it."

"Okay," Penny immediately trotted off toward the turnstiles. The lines were short and they passed through quickly and hurried toward the platform. "Hurry," Penny called back and started running. Colin and Sidney followed and they made it with only moments to spare. The train screeched to a halt in front of them and the doors slid open.

Once the steady flow of exiting passengers slowed, Colin took Sidney's hand and pulled her onto the train. Penny followed and they walked down the aisle looking for a seat. Even though it was shortly after lunch, the train was crowded with commuters, and Colin only found a single bench open. He stood aside, gestured Penny and Sidney into the seat while he reached up and grabbed the hold bar above his head. The train lurched into motion as they took their seats, Colin standing beside them. The clickety-clack of the train moving over rough separations in the rails provided a rhythmic counterpoint to the creaks, groans and clashes the car made, moving slightly out of sync with the ones ahead and behind.

As they reached full speed the motion of the train settled into a slight, yet rhythmic sway and tug. For a while Colin just relaxed, soothed by the motion. He looked down at the girls and Penny's expression caught his attention. She didn't have her usual cheerful expression; instead, her brow was knitted in concentration and she looked around warily. Something about her posture made him feel tense and he pursed his lips and watched her face closely. As if she felt the weight of his stare, she looked up and met his eyes.

"Something is wrong here." She pitched her voice just loud enough for him to hear her. "I don't know what, but something is wrong."

Colin looked around at the other people in the car. Penny was right; something in their car made his skin crawl slightly, but he couldn't tell what it might be. It was as if something was different about the train; something was changing around them. Colin felt the indistinct edges of change—not touching him, or even happening while he watched—but leaving a sullen feeling behind. One row up and across the aisle, a small girl was looking back at him and when their eyes met, she gave him a shy smile. She was wearing a white dress with pink and blue polka dots, and her long blonde hair was pulled back into pony tail. She couldn't be more than four or five, Colin guessed.

He returned her smile and she ducked her head behind the seat playfully. After a moment she peeked back up and smiled again. He winked at her, and she giggled. Noticing the girl's movement, her mother looked at her and then followed her eyes to Colin. She gave him a slight frown and pulled the little girl closer and made her face forward. Colin sighed, but understood completely. Not only was he a stranger, but she was probably feeling the threatening atmosphere of the train car.

Colin looked beyond them, his eyes moving quickly over a few empty seats but no one else made eye contact with him. Many of the passengers were staring off into space blankly as if they were just heading in to work, still groggy and gearing up for the day—lost in the last peaceful moments before another busy day. But it was after lunch. Food coma? Late shift? He had no idea.

"You feel it, too." Penny spoke softly again—just enough volume to be heard over the rhythm and churn of the train. He glanced over and nodded at her. She and Sidney were holding hands, scrunched together in the seat. Sidney had a frown on her face and was staring toward the front of the car.

He shrugged slightly to let Penny know he didn't know what was going on, and then began studying the other passengers again hoping for some clue of what was making him and Penny feel so unsettled. Something was wrong. It was almost as if something were missing.

Then it hit him. He glanced across the aisle where the little girl and her mother were sitting and they were both gone. The seats were empty. He realized that though there hadn't been any empty seats when they'd boarded the train, the car was roughly half full. As he watched, a business man who was flipping through his newspaper began to fade away until yet another seat was empty.

"They're disappearing. The train was nearly full when we got on."

Penny nodded and was about to speak when abruptly her eyes widened and she gripped his arm tightly. He followed her line of sight and saw that the end of the car was beginning to swirl and shift, glowing in red hues. The colors and light began to swirl and churn until the entire end of the train was a frightening, chaotic maelstrom. The colors and light began to shift into a noticeable pattern, rotating wildly around the center, and as it began to solidify, a rising dull roar assaulted their ears. At first it was like white noise—pervasive and dense, but almost in the background. As the vortex spun faster and faster the sound rose to a screaming blast of noise, painfully loud. The violent eddy of power solidified into an exact duplicate of the portal at the art museum. Once it had solidified it began to float down the train, slowly at first then picking up speed.

"Uh, hold on to something," Colin shouted to be heard over the deafening roar of the portal, but his words were ripped away. "I don't think we're going to have to walk through this one." As the red cyclone of energy moved toward them, its edges appeared to eat at the metal of the train, consuming it as it moved. It accelerated slowly toward him and he gripped the back of the seat in front of him tightly. This was much more violent than the portal in the museum—he was sure it would hurt to go through it. But as the swirling red radiance pass through him, the sound and violence abruptly vanished, leaving him alone in the quiet blanket of redness. The world had no discernible shape—just the all-consuming red light.

After what felt like a lifetime in the red world, he emerged from the portal on the other side, and the red was gone, leaving him staring at a world tinged green. It jarred him to lose all sensation of their passage so suddenly, and Colin staggered, only managing to remain standing by his grasp of the hold bar above him. The train was coasting to a halt, the metronome clacking of the wheels slowly losing time until with a final shudder the car came to a halt. Without warning the lights went off, and after a moment emergency lighting came up, casting a dull yellow glow throughout the train.

"Jesus." Colin pushed himself back up to crouch on his feet. "I don't know whose dream this is but maybe next time we could have a door instead of one of these portals? Damn things are going to make my hair go gray."

"Colin." Penny still clutched his arm and he glanced down at her.

"What?"

"The ones who are left. Look at them. Look at their eyes."

Colin glanced up the aisle and focused on a commuter staring blankly into space, totally oblivious to anything. He studied the man's face carefully. The skin was smooth, with a slightly yellow cast and his features were plain: standard nose, mouth, ears—nothing out of the ordinary—but his eyes were black entirely, with no white surrounding his pupils. Colin began looking at the other passengers and all of them had the same eyes. He made a quick count; there were only twelve other passengers left on the train.

"Dad," Sidney leaned across Penny. "They're all empty."

"Empty?"

"Yes. It's like they aren't really people anymore. Zombies."

"I wonder if they eat brains." Penny's voice held a hint of humor, but when Sidney blanched, Penny put a hand on her knee. "Kidding, sorry,"

"Not funny."

As if they had heard her, all the commuters turned their heads slowly, moving in complete synchronicity, and stared at them. Their faces began to deteriorate quickly as if they were being shot in stop action photography, in some places bone was exposed and skin peeled away to hang in strips. In other places the flesh turned a horrible greenish color and began to drip pus down onto their clothing. One particularly gruesome transformation exposed the teeth and jaw bone on half of the mouth and a long strip of skin, including the entire nose dangled nearly down to its chin. As Colin watched some muscles disappeared and the jaw flopped down to hang open in a silent leer. The transformations began to slow and finally halted, leaving stereotypical, Hollywood zombies behind.

"Oh, gross." When Sidney spoke Colin saw fear on her face, heard it in her voice and he stood up beside Penny, with his back to her and pushed Sidney behind him.

"Yeah, definitely gross," Colin muttered. One of the zombies stood and turned to face him. One took a small shuffling step forward, and then the rest began to follow suit, slowly yet steadily moving down the aisle toward Colin and the girls.

"We have to move. Leave this train," Penny whispered urgently.

Colin nodded. There were two doors on the left that opened out onto the platform—when one was nearby. Colin and the girls couldn't reach either of those doors without trying to pass most of the zombies on the train, but the door that led to the next car was clear. When Colin glanced back he saw only a single zombie and it seemed to be stuck behind a seat, not smart enough to simply turn and walk into the aisle.

Unexpectedly grim images assaulted his mind—the memory of sitting on the dream plane beside his wife and girls as it plummeted toward the ground. He remembered the feelings of helplessness and despair coursing through him, but in the here and now he felt a wave of angry determination come over him.

Not this time.

"Okay, out the back. We'll see if the next car is clear." He started down the aisle, toward the sole zombie. "I'll go first and slow them down."

"Dad?" Sidney's voice hitched. "Don't—"

"Sid, go," He didn't let her finish the statement. "I'll be right behind you, I promise." He glanced back and nodded toward the back of the car. "Penny? Get going."

Penny nodded and stood, taking Sidney's hand and pulling her out into the aisle behind her. Colin stepped forward quickly until the zombie was in reach and gave it a hard shove, sending it off balance. The rotting and foul creature tottered for a moment, knees locked, and hands grasping futilely at Colin it fell heavily back into the seat.

"Go," he repeated.

The girls moved past him and up to the sliding metal door at the end of the car. Colin began to turn away from the zombie and it finally recovered its balance enough to shove up to its feet again. When it had its balance it lunged with startling quickness and grabbed Colin, digging its fingers into his arm painfully. Colin spun back and gave it another powerful shove but it held on tightly using Colin's own weight to keep its balance. The creature made a loud growling sound as it yanked Colin closer. "Shit," he said as it pulled him close enough to lower its gaping mouth to his shoulder and sink its teeth in. It didn't break the cloth, but Colin felt a flash of pain as its teeth crushed the cloth into his flesh. He gritted his teeth against the pain and struggled to push the zombie away, but the creature clung tenaciously, and ground its teeth back and forth, trying to break through the cloth. Blood soaked through, and the zombie seemed to become stronger and frenzied. It started to swing its head back and forth, like a dog with a bone in its mouth and the growl became a vicious snarl. In the back of his mind he wondered if this meant he was going to turn into a zombie, too, like in the movies.

"Dad!" Sidney gave a panicked shriek. Without looking, he spoke through gritted teeth.

"Get that door open, now. Hurry."

"Working on it." Her voice was shaky. "The others are getting closer..."

The only upside was that the zombie tearing at his shoulder was blocking the aisle, holding the other monsters back.

My own zombie shield.

Colin grunted and fought to break the hold the zombie had on him. Colin felt the pain rising in his shoulder and used it to draw desperate strength.

He reached up, the pain in his shoulder doubling, and grabbed the zombie by the head and started pulling as hard as he could. The zombie's head stopped whipping back and forth, but it kept grinding its teeth into his flesh. He kept pulling and started twisting the zombie's head, forcing the neck bones against the normal range of motion. There was a loud crack of the neck bones breaking and the tendons and muscles of the neck suddenly gave out as the force of Colin's pressure was no longer buffered by the spinal connection. Immediately the zombie lost its grip on him and slumped down, until it was held up by its teeth and the skin and remaining tendon in its neck. The snarling sound ceased, its jaw relaxed and then it fell away from Colin, leaving his shoulder a bloody mess. The pain was a shooting spike up and down his arm, but he ignored it, shoved the monster back into the others and turned to follow the girls.

Sidney was staring past him with horror on her face and Colin didn't even bother to look back.

Behind Sidney, Penny finally got the door open, yanking it and sliding it into the housing. She reached back without looking and took Sidney's hand and stepped through the door. To Colin's surprise they both disappeared downward from view, but less than a second later he realized what had happened—there was no car attached. The door opened directly outside.

He stepped up to the doorway, and went through, carefully staying on the edge of the small platform. He turned and started pulling the door shut again and barely got it as rotting hands slammed against the window, leaving pus and tiny bits of skin and flesh on the glass. For a moment he stared in revulsion but then he turned and dropped to the ground outside the car. The jar of landing sent a fresh wave of agony through his shoulder.

"Ah, crap." He spun around to look at the door which had slid shut behind him. There were thuds and crashing sounds and rotting, desiccated faces and arms pressed against the window, but the door itself seemed to hold. "Well, I don't think they're going to be able to get out and follow us, anyway."

"Let's put some distance between us and them," Penny said.

Colin nodded and glanced around at the tunnel. A few yards from the car in the direction they'd come from, the ceiling had collapsed; rubble and large chunks of cement with exposed rebar completely blocked the way.

"I guess we're going further in," he said. Behind them the sound of the zombies scrabbling and bashing the door was unnerving.

"Yep." Penny started walking around the train, heading deeper into the tunnel. As they walked by the train, the zombies inside tracked along, always facing them, but one by one they each got stuck in the seats, having shambled to a window to try to get to them. "Not too bright, thank goodness. We'd have been in real trouble if they knew how to turn or walk around obstacles."

Sidney tried to stifle a short giggle, the sharp edge of hysteria evident in the sound. "Or climb over the seats."

"Or open doors," Colin laughed and flinched at the pain it caused. "What I want to know is which of you two has this obsession with zombies."

"It's not mine. I already tried to change it. Must be Penny." Sidney mock glared at the girl.

"Not mine either." Penny put her hands up defensively. "Let's get moving. We need to take a look at your shoulder, but not here." They began to walk. The tunnel beyond the train was dark, but not without light. A pale glow seemed to emanate from the very walls, and moisture dripped down in places, making an odd plopping sound that echoed loudly, amplified by the strange acoustics of the tunnel. Every so often they passed by rusting, heavy metal doors.

Penny led the way and Colin struggled along behind her, with Sidney walking next to him, ready to grab his good arm if he started to fall. His breathing was getting labored and he felt slightly dizzy, but he managed to stumble on. After about ten minutes Penny halted and turned around.

"Penny," Sidney's voice was filled with worry. "I think we've got to take care of Dad."

"Okay, this will do. Sid, keep an eye on the tunnel." Penny strode over to Colin. "You get injured more than any three people I've met. Let me see that." She reached up and inspected his shoulder delicately, touching his shirt lightly but not moving anything. Blood had soaked through down to his elbow. "At least it's a different arm this time. Can you get your shirt off?"

"Yeah." He reached to undo the buttons on his shirt, sending a stab of pain through his arm. He hissed and lowered his injured arm, and tried to undo the button with one hand.

"Let me do that." Penny pushed his hand out off the way and started undoing his buttons. "I don't get to undress a guy every day." She grinned up at him and he gave her a weak smile in return. Once it was unbuttoned she peeled it back gingerly, starting with his uninjured side first. She glanced at his face for a moment, he nodded once and she started pulling the sleeve off slowly. "Easy. Tell me if this hurts and we'll stop."

"No," he lied through gritted teeth. "It's fine."

"Liar."

He shrugged. "Just do it."

When his arm was free, Penny held the shirt up—it was still stuck to him where he'd been bitten. "This is going to hurt. The shirt is actually jammed down into the teeth marks—that probably slowed the bleeding. That and your mutant healing factor." She grinned briefly but didn't take her attention off his shoulder. "It might start again when I pull it off the rest of the way. How do you want this? Slow peel or quick jerk?

"Quick."

"Are you ready?"

He nodded shortly and braced himself for more pain.

"Okay, on three. One..." Then she yanked and the shirt came away in a blinding shock of pain.

"Oh, fuck." His vision swam and he felt Sidney and Penny holding him up. "Damn, that hurt. What happened to two and three?"

"Surprise seemed like a good idea." Penny looked apologetic. After a few moments the pain receded slightly and he was able to stand on his own while she inspected the wound. "It's not as bad as it looks."

"Dad," Sidney said. "Can you do the thing where you heal yourself?"

"I can try. I don't know how I do it though. I mean, how it works." He closed his eyes and tried to imagine the pain receding, but after a moment he opened his eyes when the pain didn't change. "Nothing. Maybe I have to be awake for it to work?"

"Well, we'll take care of it the old fashioned way. I wish we had some water to clean this with. Wishes in one hand, shit in the other." The word sounded strange coming from Penny.

"See which one fills up first," Colin finished.

Penny grinned, never taking her eyes from his shoulder then sobered. "I'm going to have to rip up your shirt. You'll have to go without one, I guess.

"I'll just pretend we're at the beach."

"Good, good." There was a ripping sound and Penny started reducing his shirt to a series of long thin strips. Colin watched her hands move with a fluid economy of motion, graceful and efficient. They were small and for a brief moment he was struck with a strong feeling of familiarity. The sense fled, quickly buried under the pain as she finished tearing four strips, put them over her shoulder and ripped the rest of the shirt in half. As if she sensed his gaze, she glanced up and the concentration on her face briefly melted into a cheerful smile before she looked back at his wound.

"Wow, you're stronger than you look, Penny," Sidney looked impressed. "Can you rip phonebooks in half?"

"Thin ones!" She smiled brightly. "You know. For towns of twenty or so people."

Colin laughed and winced at the resulting jolt of pain. "Enough kidding around. You're gonna kill me."

"Okay, brace yourself, Col." Penny ignored him and leaned closer. "I'm going to clean the area around the bite." He nodded shortly. She reached up and began wiping blood away in soft short strokes. The pain wasn't as bad as he'd expected and he was able to relax slightly while she worked. She got closer to the bite marks and glanced up at him questioningly. "Still okay?"

"Yes. It doesn't hurt nearly as bad as it did a few minutes ago?"

"Good." She cocked her head. "I wonder if you'll end up with a scar in the waking world?"

"Scars are manly," Sidney said and Penny nodded in somber agreement.

"You're right, Sid. Maybe we should leave him a scar or two. He can use it to impress the ladies. That Kate perhaps." The mention of Kate jarred him and he allowed himself a brief moment to remember her face. He had no trouble picturing her face clearly—the freckles across the bridge of her nose, the laugh lines around her mouth and eyes. Her beautiful eyes. Immediately he felt guilty—it seemed like a small betrayal of Marianne. He pushed that aside and forced a smile.

"I don't need any scars to impress the ladies." He forced as much bravado into his voice as he could.

Sidney grinned and Penny kept working on his shoulder, her tongue poking out of the corner of her mouth in concentration, until at last she stepped back. She was frowning and her lips were pursed, and she met Colin's gaze, looking clearly worried.

"What's wrong?"

"Well, I don't know. There's something...not right about this." She put a finger up and pressed the skin around the wound. "Does that hurt?"

He realized with surprise that it didn't hurt at all. He shook his head. "No, it doesn't. That's weird." He could see that the bite didn't look any better—just cleaner. "It doesn't hurt at all."

"Not at all?" Her frown deepened. "I want to try something. Tell me right away if this hurts and I'll stop, okay?"

"Sure."

She reached up and gently put her finger against the wound itself. Colin frowned slightly.

"That hurts?" She was watching his face.

"No. I don't feel anything at all when you do that. It's numb." She poked his should a bit harder and looked up at him questioningly. He shook his head again. "Nothing." His entire arm was beginning to feel like dead weight—as if someone had given him a huge shot of Novocain.

Penny drew back and folded her arms across her chest, staring at the wound and biting her lip softly in consternation.

"What's wrong?" Sidney asked.

"I don't know, and that's what bothers me." Penny bit her lip softly and frowned. "I'll wrap it up and you'll have to be careful of it. Baby it even if it doesn't hurt, okay?"

Colin nodded.

She pointed to a large stone behind him. "Sit." He sat and she began to bind the wound with the strips of cloth over her shoulder. She fell back into her calm efficiency but the worry was still obvious on her face and that only made him more nervous. There was nothing he could do about it now, so he tried to put it aside and put his mind to figuring out what they were going to do next.

※

"Well, honestly I don't see any option besides just going forward. This tunnel has to lead somewhere, right?" Sidney spoke quietly.

"Yeah." Colin knew she was right. "We can't just sit here." He lifted his arm slowly, testing to see if there was any feeling. Nothing. Penny had bandaged the wound snugly but not too tight, and then used the rest of his shirt to make a loose sling. He could raise his arm up, but when he let it down, it was suspended in the sling comfortably. The worst part was that it felt useless. He hated that feeling—it only accentuated how out of control everything felt. "Let's get to it."

He stood up and surveyed the tunnel. It was dank and wet, lined by a tall yet narrow walkway on each side and thick, murky darkness. That was the worst part—the dark. There were small pools of yellow light spaced evenly along the walkway, placed over doors that were heavy, rusty and looked as if they hadn't been opened in decades. Ahead the tunnel curved out of sight as it disappeared into the dark gloom. Colin shivered.

He glanced at the tracks and saw that there was a third rail about six inches away from one of the other tracks on the outside.

"Watch that outer rail—it's probably carrying a heavy charge." He knelt and picked up a rock and walked over toward the rail. He carefully dropped it on the rail, but there was no reaction, so he dug into his pocket for a coin and repeated the process. Nothing. He wasn't entirely sure if his little tests meant the rail was dead or not. "Honestly, I can't tell if it's live or not, so let's just stay away from it." He glanced over at the girls and they both nodded as they came to stand with him.

Penny started walking and Sidney hurried to catch up and walk by her side. Colin fell in behind them and almost immediately tripped over a bit of garbage on the ground. As he fell toward the third rail, time seemed to slow and he fought to turn his body aside, but all he managed to do was twist so he was falling sideways instead of onto his face. He didn't have a chance to feel fear—only a moment to realize that if the rail was live he was a dead man. But when he landed heavily across the rail there was no surge of electricity through him, frying his insides and melting his brain. He heard the girls gasp behind him and the sound of his heart pounding at a gallop, threatening to burst from his chest. For a moment he just stayed prone as the sheer horror of what could have happened overwhelmed him. Relief followed quickly on it's heels.

"Colin!" Penny bent to help him to his feet. "Oh God, you're going to give me a heart attack."

"Well, now we know it's not live, at any rate." He spent a moment trying to rein in his frantically pounding heart.

"Yeah, not exactly the best way to find out, Dad." Sidney tried to inject some humor into her voice. Colin sat down on walkway at the edge of the tunnel and rested a minute before they continued walking. The tunnel was wide enough for a pair of trains to travel, so there was more than enough room for them to travel next to each other now that the third rail was no longer an issue. Periodically Colin would glance back, making sure nothing was shambling after them. After they had walked a while the tunnel broke off to the left in a gentle curve. They walked slowly, in no hurry and conserving energy but moving steadily forward. Apart from the echoing sound of dripping water, the tunnels were silent. At regular intervals they passed doors, but none of them were unlocked, and they were all too heavy to batter down.

They walked so long that Colin lost all sense of time passing. It wasn't that he was tired as much as simply numb from the monotony of the tunnel, and the endless repetition of one foot in front of the other. Finally he could stand it no more and he stopped.

"How long have we been walking, anyway?" he asked. The girls looked back and came to a halt. They looked as dazed as he felt.

"Feels like forever," Sidney muttered tiredly. "My feet are starting to hurt."

"I don't know. Time is strange in the Dreamside." Penny started walking again. As Colin moved to follow her, he thought he heard a sound beyond the usual dripping and the echoes of their footsteps.

"Hey, hold on a sec," he said and Penny stopped on a dime. "Do you hear that?" They all listened for a short time, but the sound didn't return.

"I don't hear anything," Penny said. "What was it?"

"I'm not really sure—a clicking sound. It was faint and I heard it just as you started to walk again."

"Well, let's sit down here and take a brief rest. We can see if you hear it again." She walked over and placed her hands on the walkway, and pulled herself up, spun and sat all in one smooth motion, then wiped her hands on her thighs and smiled. Sidney climbed up and sat beside her, then leaned over, put her head on Penny's shoulder and closed her eyes. Penny slipped an arm around her shoulders and pulled her closer.

Colin stood stock still and they all strained to hear any sound coming out of the darkness. As he listened, he watched the girls sitting together, taking comfort from one another. He realized again that they were like bookends—both were young, engaging and energetic. Both with good spirits and something else—not innocence—something clean and pure. He couldn't think of a way to describe it. When they were around he felt a strong sense of completeness—like something missing had been returned to him. He knew that Sidney had always had this effect on him, but with both of them together, so at ease with one another, the feeling was magnified many times over.

Each was bright like a small sun in her own right, but together they shined on him with an intensity that was as daunting as it was soothing. The surge of emotion—positive emotion—that flowed through him surprised him with its strength. He hadn't felt this in such a long time. The entire thing confused him at a certain level. He understood fully why Sidney affected him this way, but he'd only known Penny a few days, yet already it was as if she had always been in his life.

Colin's musing was abruptly interrupted by the clear sound of a rapid set of clicks. As suddenly as the sound had started it was gone again.

"There. That's what I heard."

Penny raised a hand, the smile gone from her face, her brow pinched in concentration. Colin heard the clicking again. This time it lasted a few moments longer before stopping. Then out of the dark they heard a low growling sound, and the clicking started again, slowly this time, but didn't stop.

"What is that?" Sidney asked. Colin looked over at Penny and her eyes were wide.

"Oh, god." Penny's eyes were wide and her face white.

"What?" Sidney repeated.

"Run! Now!" In one fluid motion Penny jumped down from the walkway and yanked Sidney after her. Sidney landed awkwardly but Penny steadied her and they started running back the way they'd come. Colin followed, careful to stay behind them.

"What are we running from?" he asked.

"Murkshifter."

"Shit." All the horror and revulsion he'd felt when he'd last seen the monster rose in his gut. He'd run from this beast once before without much success. Only waking up had saved him that time. He began to run, carefully staying behind the girls protectively. "Not this thing again."

"Yeah." Penny sounded grim.

"What's a murkshifter?" Sidney asked.

"A nightmare. Violent and powerful." Penny picked up speed. "It's what hurt Colin the other night. Now shush, Sid, and just run."

Colin listened as they ran, trying to hear beyond the loud pounding of their feet and the occasional splashing when they ran through puddles. He thought he could hear the scrabbling of claws on concrete and then there was a deafening roar that reverberated through the tunnel, surrounding him and making his skin prickle. The scraping, scratching sound of claws abruptly changed to hoof beats that clattered rhythmically behind them, slowly getting louder as the murkshifter closed the gap.

The tunnel unexpectedly straightened out, the train car bled out of the gloom into sight. Colin felt disoriented—they had walked for hours and hours away from the train and now only in a few moments of sprinting they were right back where they started. There was no way they should be back here so soon, but there it was—only a few hundred feet away. Colin slowed slightly, allowing the girls to pull ahead of him. He wouldn't let them be injured by the murkshifter without putting up a fight. But he knew it was hopeless, so he concentrated on simply buying them some time. Once he'd made the decision he came to a halt.

Before he was fully stopped the floor suddenly opened underneath him and his feet dropped out from under him. He didn't have time to make a sound as he tried to reach for the edge. His hand struck the lip but immediately bounced off and his momentum carried him into the wall. As he passed below the opening, his head struck the edge hard with a loud crack and the world went dark.

Separated

The sudden roar of the murkshifter froze the blood in Sidney's veins. She fought the urge to look back, but instead concentrated on running as fast as she could. She'd released Penny's hand so that they could both move faster, arms pumping, legs stretching out to eat up the ground. Sidney had always been a fast runner—tall and thin, with long legs and an abundance of energy—but she could tell that Penny was holding back to let her keep up with her. Sidney gritted her teeth and put everything she had into it. Between her labored breathing, the pounding of her heartbeat in her ears and the rhythmic sound of their feet hammering the ground, she could no longer hear the murkshifter.

Suddenly she could see the train directly ahead. She was shocked to see it so soon; they'd been so far away that at first she thought it was a different train car. In some ways it was easier to believe the dream had put another train in front of them than it was to reconcile the hours of walking they'd done with the few moments of running that brought them back where they started. It shouldn't be possible, but it was the same train—she could see the cave-in just behind it.

"What the heck." Sidney forced the words out between heavy breaths. Penny glanced back, eyes wide in surprise, and Sidney began to search for some escape from the dead end. They needed somewhere to go—obviously not the train. She could make out the forms of the zombies moving slowly and aimlessly inside the train. There was no safety there. She searched for a way out of the tunnel and was surprised to see a bright red metal door all the wall near the train. She hadn't noticed it when they'd fled the train, and the garish coloring was not easy to miss.

"Oh, that's subtle," Sidney muttered. The door was the only thing in the tunnel that didn't look worn and dingy. While the frame of the doorway was decrepit and dirty as the rest of the tunnel, the red metal of the door itself was pristine and seemed to pulse with energy.

Penny laughed and angled toward the door. As they closed on the train, Sidney could see the zombies inside more clearly, clamoring ineffectually against the windows still. Despite her terror, she had the urge to laugh dementedly at the creatures as they walked into the walls and windows, backed up a step and did it again. Over and over again.

"Wait," Sidney gasped but didn't stop running toward the door. "Doesn't red mean danger?"

"I think this is more of an open-me red." Penny skidded to a halt in front of the door and before she could grab the knob Sidney put a hand on her arm.

"Are you sure this is a good idea?"

"Well, the way I see it, we have exactly three choices and going through this door is the only one that might not end with us being killed." She gently pulled her arm away from Sidney, grasped the brushed nickel handle and pulled. The frame around it gave a creaking sound and flakes of rust fell away but the door didn't budge. Without speaking, she put all her scant weight behind it and yanked again with no result. She tried jerking the door back and forth but only managed to jar more flakes of rust and dirt free of the frame.

While Penny struggled with the door Sidney looked back up the tunnel. The murkshifter was not in sight yet. She felt like a knife had twisted in her heart as she realized that Colin was nowhere to be seen.

"Where's Dad?" Fear rose higher in her gut. She hadn't thought she could be more scared.

"Oh no." Penny stopped yanking on the door and stared back up the tunnel. "I imagine he's playing hero again."

"Hero?"

"Yes, that's how he got hurt before. He stopped to delay the murkshifter so that I could escape."

"No." Sidney shuddered at the thought.

Then she saw the murkshifter gallop out of the darkness. The sheer size of the beast was shocking—it towered over them even as it ran on all its feet. It radiated malice and violence that she could almost feel as a tangible thing against her skin. She shuddered as the beast came close enough for her to begin to make out details. It ran on six legs—not four—each ending in a large metal shod hoof. Its motion was disturbingly fluid—like nothing Sidney had seen before. She didn't even bother trying to see how it ran on six feet.

Sparks flew where the hooves struck the ground. Its head was a mass of tentacles and its body was huge, long and jet black. It was hard to make out any details as its skin was a sheet of blackness so profoundly dark that it seemed to drink in the light around the beast.

"Penny, it's here and it's ugly."

Penny didn't answer but grunted with strain as she began working on the door again. Sidney kept staring at the nightmare, unable to look away as it charged down the tunnel, now only a hundred yards or so from them. She had a hard time wrapping her mind around its impossible shape and as it approached, the blackness of it began to resolve into details more gruesome than she had imagined when she couldn't see it well. She knew she would carry this sight with her for the rest of her life. It would trouble her dreams until the day she died. She felt a hysterical laugh bubble up as she realized that she was not only in a dream, but it seemed likely this would be the day she'd die.

Her stomach rebelled when she saw its skin flow and churn chaotically, seeming to melt and shift, its form unstable. At first she thought it was some disturbance in the air, her mind frantically trying to explain away the liquid surface of the beast. Heat waves? Penny yanked on the door behind her and the sound was muffled as if at a distance. Sidney's fear began to bleed into despair, almost lassitude, as the murkshifter closed on them.

Abruptly, about fifteen yards from them the beast pulled up and slowed to a walk. It pushed its bulk up into the air with its front middle feet, to stand on its rear hoofs. When it stood, the front feet changed into arms and the hooves were replaced with long powerful hands with sharp talons on each finger. The middle legs melted back into its torso and disappeared. At the same time the hoofs on the back legs changed into large padded feet that gripped the floor easily. The tentacles on its head came together and merged into a single round shape and slowly coalesced into a head and its body settled into a more humanoid shape. It was bald and its skin glistened wetly. Where its face should have been there was only featureless, flat skin—a shiny black mask of nothingness. Sidney thought she might throw up.

Then the skin in the middle of its face split horizontally, a short line at first, but quickly spreading and opening up into a mouth with jagged yellowed teeth. When the mouth was fully formed it spoke. "Trapped," it hissed sibilantly. "Easy prey. Do not worry little girls. Over soon. Use your bones to clean my teeth of your flesh. Do you great honor." Sidney fought to keep the contents of her stomach down as the stench of the thing flowed ahead of it, surrounding her—a dank, musty odor full of rot and death. The murkshifter had slowed to a crawl and licked its lips with a long tongue. "Where is man? Dreamer?"

Sidney felt a rush of relief break through her lassitude— Dad had escaped the beast—but immediately that sense of relief warred with the fear. Eventually the fear won out. She backed up until she was crowding Penny, who had stopped yanking on the door, and instead was standing calmly in front of it, murmuring under her breath. Sidney couldn't make out what she was saying, but she started to push around her to begin pulling on the door herself. Penny put an arm up and held Sidney back but kept murmuring.

"Door will not work, little dreams. Dark father fixed it. You are in his dream now."

Well, now we know whose dream this is.

Sidney turned back to face the beast and it had halted ten yards away and grinned hungrily at them. She dropped into a crouch, ready to dodge and run again, knowing it was hopeless. She wondered where her dad had gone; why he had abandoned her. No—she knew he would never intentionally abandon her. Something had to have happened to him. She only hoped he was all right wherever he was. She held that thought close as she waited for the beast to attack. She hoped it would bring her some peace at the end.

"Little dreams are funny," it said and followed with a gravelly, grating cackle. "Fear makes you taste better. Keep struggling. Better meal." It took a slow step forward and cocked its head as if listening—without any ears, it was a strange gesture. "What do you say?" The murkshifter jerked to face Penny and snarled in rage. "No words of power, little dream." Then it broke into motion, charging toward them, its body already flowing into some other gruesome shape. At the same time Penny shouted a short word that Sidney didn't recognize. There was a flash of light and then a slow loud creaking sound. The murkshifter roared its fury, quickly closing the gap and Penny grabbed Sidney by the collar and yanked her back. They stumbled across the threshold of the now empty doorway and plunged downward into thick, inky darkness. Sidney shrieked as they fell away into the black.

※

They fell for a long time. Sidney couldn't resist looking down, fully expecting to see the ground rushing up at them, but below them complete darkness masked the bottom of the pit below them. With each passing moment she waited to hit the bottom of the hole and die, but time stretched on without that happening. They were falling so fast that the stagnant, heavy air around them became a rushing wind that buffeted her from side to side. The moment she had begun her fall her fear turned into complete, blind panic—adrenaline laced terror. Her heart pounded and the tidal wave of emotion became so crippling that her mind began to shut down, the terror slowly fading into something closer to a resigned lethargy, until after an interminable time she simply fell, lax and blank.

During the entire time that she hurtled downward into the inky blackness below, Sidney never thought to look for Penny, but suddenly she felt the other girl's hand in hers and the warmth, softness and strength of where their hands met soothed Sidney enough that she was able to begin rational thoughts again. To her mind it felt like power moved outward from that point of connection, revitalizing her. Penny pulled them together and they clung to each other, neither speaking as the air rushed by, buffeting them from side to side.

There was no real sense of time, and Sidney's mind tried to impose some temporal order again, but it wasn't working. The seconds bled into minutes, minutes into hours, hours into days and days into years. This senseless passage of now into then brought calmness to her eventually, until it almost seemed someone else was falling and Sidney merely watching. This time it wasn't lassitude that followed, but a sense of acceptance. And strangely, out of her fear she became impatient—she wanted the fall over one way or another.

"It's always something in this place." Sidney forced humor into her voice, putting her mouth close to Penny's ear to be heard over the wind.

"Yes, always something." Sidney could tell Penny was smiling. As close as they were to each other's ear, it was easy to talk over the wind.

"You're always so happy and upbeat, Penny. How do you do it?"

"Well, there doesn't seem much point in being morose or sad."

They both fell silent for a few moments before Sidney spoke again.

"We've been falling for a long time. Any idea on how long we have...?"

"Till we hit the bottom?" Penny replied lightly. "Nope, no idea. But I'll tell you this, Sid—if we're gonna splat on the ground, I can't think of anyone I'd rather splat with."

Sidney laughed loudly, and was amazed that she still was able to laugh.

"Well, don't take this the wrong way, Penny, but I'd really prefer not to splat on the ground with anyone."

"Aw, Sid, I'm hurt that you don't want to splat with me."

Sidney couldn't contain a short gasp of laughter and they both fell silent and the sound of the air rushing by was the only thing to be heard. Sidney found that looking down wasn't any different from looking anywhere else—there was murky darkness and nothing else beyond their feet. Now that she and Penny clutched one another, she had to crane her neck and look down over Penny's shoulder to see underneath them, but still she peered down often, scared yet anticipating the final sight of the ground rushing up. Suddenly there was a reddish glow far underneath them—a tiny circle of dim light that grew slightly bigger as they fell. With this unexpected visual proof that they were really falling, Sidney's sense of time returned to her jarringly—her sensory deprivation replaced by the sure knowledge that whatever was down there, they were approaching it fast. But sight of the red circle changed her lingering resignation and fear into a stabbing burst of hope. It was another portal.

"Penny, look down."

Penny craned over Sidney's shoulder and then pulled back slightly from Sidney, locking their hands but creating space between their bodies so that they could both look down more easily.

"I see it."

"Maybe we won't splat after all, Penny!"

"Well, at least not until we come out the other side of the portal. Kind of anticlimactic, isn't it? All this build up and no splat?" Penny managed to actually sound disappointed and Sidney giggled again. Even the possibility that they were going to crash into something on the other side of the portal wasn't enough to dent the flood of relief she felt. Something different was happening finally. The glowing red disk was rushing up at them faster now, growing outward until it appeared to be several times larger than the previous portals they'd come across.

"It's huge."

Penny nodded.

"Here we go!" Penny pulled Sidney close again into a tight hug. "See you on the other side, Sid!"

There was a bright flash of red and they disappeared into the portal.

Ahanu

Somewhere far away—or perhaps nearby, given the anatomy of the Dreamside—Ahanu was dreaming. It was a good dream—Amara was standing close by his side, holding his hand as they gazed out across the rugged plains that flowed and undulated to meet the horizon. The land around him was a vast sea of dusty green grass punctuated by small stands of trees here and there. He watched the sun travel across the sky, silently staring out into an endless future. In his mind, almost as if they stood right in front of him, Ahanu saw the children they would make and raise together. He saw himself growing old with Amara, always bound by a love that completed them both. The possibilities stretched out before them.

Yes, it was a good dream.

But it was only a dream. In the waking world, Amara had no eyes for him. Instead she was taken with Ebru—the bravest, most skilled warrior in the clan. Everyone was taken with the warrior. Ahanu was small, even for his people, and in a society where strength and cunning ruled, being small was not an attractive trait. His best characteristics—kindness and intelligence—were not in high demand in the harsh environment of the veldt. Sometimes he wondered if she even knew he existed, and there was emptiness in his heart which he looked away from constantly for fear of sinking into it and losing himself forever. Another man might be driven to darkness by these feelings.

Ahanu loved Amara so completely that under any other circumstances he would wish her well in the life she would make without him, taking pleasure in the simple fact that she was happy. But Ebru was a bad choice for her. This was not envy speaking, though when he was honest with himself he had to admit he did feel jealous. The fact was that Ebru was conceited, self absorbed and not given to caring for the needs of others. His strength and cunning were centered on a small-minded meanness. They had grown up together and not once had Ahanu seen the other boy make a single decision or do anything selfless. Generosity was a calculated thing when he exhibited it.

The large, well-muscled warrior helped provide food to the clan not because without it they would go hungry, but so that he could claim the role of the best hunter, the strongest male warrior among them. When they had been much younger boys, Ebru was given to bullying and hurting the other children, and while he seemed to have lost that behavior as he matured, Ahanu suspected that the warrior had simply learned to hide it away—it still lurked beneath the surface. Perhaps the most damning thing was that Ahanu would not want Ebru at his back in a fight.

Ahanu was often surprised and dismayed that no one else seemed to see the spite in Ebru's eyes. He feared that Amara would suffer for it when she tied her life to Ebru. The thought of her fate sent sadness roiling through him even in his dream and the dream Amara turned to him and spoke.

"Something bothers you, my husband," she said, concern in her eyes. But Ahanu was slowly surfacing out of the dream and he knew her concern for the falseness it was. The sadness in his heart became piercing. "My love," she continued and placed her hand on his cheek. "Tell me what is wrong." Even though he knew this was nothing more than a dream—fancies brought on by his sleeping mind—he took her in his arms and kissed her as if his life depended upon it.

Then she faded away until she was no longer in his arms. The shock of her disappearance made a hitching sob escape his chest, but immediately he berated himself.

"Crying over a dream." He berated himself aloud. "This dream is a dream even awake." The scorn in his voice was strong and bitter. He glanced around and saw that he was not awake as he'd thought. The world around him was foggy and dim—he could see nothing in the featureless void around him. Then he heard a voice behind him.

"Hey there, what's your name?"

Ahanu spun and saw a man emerge from the fog and come to stand only a dozen paces away. Ahanu stepped back a half step before catching himself. He would show no fear—one of the first lessons young warriors of his tribe learned was that showing fear in your eyes or your behavior was a sure way to make the beast charge. He wasn't sure if this man was a beast, but he was taking no chances. It was said that spirits could visit dreams and do good or evil there that lasted into the waking world.

Ahanu stood straight up but with his knees still slightly bent and brought his spear before him, placing the butt of it on the ground solidly and inspected the man before him.

The man's skin was pale like a ghost and at first Ahanu thought he was indeed a spirit. As he studied the man, he realized he was real, but nothing like any man he'd ever seen. The man was tall—taller than any warrior in the clan—but there was softness about him. His clothes were strange and covered most of his body and he had no visible weapons and Ahanu immediately felt more relaxed. He straightened and put the point of his spear on the ground before him, using it almost as a walking stick—removing any obvious threat.

"My name is Ahanu." He tried to fill his voice with confidence. Never show weakness.

"Hello, Ahanu." The man's smile was frank and friendly—nothing concealed behind his expression.

"What is your name?" Ahanu thought it was strange that the man had not offered his own name. It was tradition to exchange names to establish peace, and he wondered if he had found an enemy. The man smiled and then gave a little shrug.

"You can call me Dreamer if you wish, Ahanu"

"You are not from my world." Ahanu hid a frown. It was clear this man did not wish to give a name. "At least I've never seen any people like you."

Dreamer nodded once. "I am not of your world." Then he eyed Ahanu critically as if trying to see if the warrior measured up. "I need your help, Ahanu. I know this will sound strange, but yours was the first dream I found. I wouldn't ask if it weren't important."

Ahanu nodded his head once. He could see the need and worry etched on the man's face and behind that kindness and intelligence. He found that it made him feel closer to this man, vastly eased the tension of the failed exchange of names. He resolved in that moment that he would help him. Before he had a chance to really consider the idea, he spoke.

"Ask, Dreamer." The words shocked him as soon as they were out.

"There are a pair of dreams—young girls—that have found their way into danger." The Dreamer glanced off into the mist that still surrounded them. "They must be protected at any cost." He looked back at Ahanu with a slight frown. "They can probably take care of themselves just fine, but I can't take that risk."

"And you cannot go to them yourself?" Ahanu asked.

"No, I am only the smallest part of the man I am in the waking world." He smiled wryly. "It is unlikely I will remember this moment. Still, I am enough to at least ask you to help them."

"I will aid you, Dreamer," he blurted and immediately felt chagrined. They had not discussed a price, but now the bargain was struck. Ahanu sighed; what was done was done and Ahanu took his word seriously. *More seriously than Ebru does of his own word.* "If I can find them I will do everything I can to protect them," Ahanu told the man resolutely. He was surprised at how completely sure he was that this was the right thing to do. This was something he had been born to do. "If it can be done, I will do it. And I will not fail and live." He raised his spear so that his fist touched his chest over his heart and thrust it away slightly. "My pledge."

Immediately Dreamer looked relieved.

"Thank you, Ahanu." He paused before continuing. "One more thing—please don't tell them I sent you."

"Why not?"

"Because there is a nightmare hunting them, and I do not know how much it sees into their dreams. I can't risk revealing this part of me to him yet. Not until the rest of me is ready." The man's face reflected his need and he raised his hands in a half-shrug. "I know how confusing this all seems, but please trust me in this."

"I have already agreed to help you, Dreamer."

"Thank you, Ahanu," The pale man's face was flooded with gratitude and relief. "Sleep now, Ahanu and when you wake you will be near enough to them to find them easily. Keep them safe. Please."

Ahanu felt the mist closing in and his eyes became heavy and as he slipped back into a deep sleep, he heard the disembodied voice of Dreamer one last time.

"Keep them safe."

The Beach

Sidney dropped out of the air and plunged into water. Her momentum carried her deep, the shock of cold and wet causing her to sputter and flail. Then she forced herself to calmness and looked around, searching for the surface. She was disoriented and had heard stories of people getting turned around and swimming down instead of up, and the thought was horrifying. But the water above was crystalline and blue, and the sky clearly visible, sunshine sparkling off the small waves like a beacon calling her to safety, and she used her arms to pull herself up. As her head broke the surface she took gulps of fresh, clean air and looked around. The water was deep—it faded quickly into a dark, bottomless blue. Deep yet gentle waves lifted and lowered her in the water rhythmically. Overhead the sun shone down blindingly bright after the darkness of the tunnel and the timeless plunge to the portal.

She treaded water skillfully—years of summer swim camp paying off—and spun herself around to look for Penny or some sign of land. Because of the waves she could see only a short distance but she found that if she waited until the crest of one lifted her up, she could see much farther.

"Penny! Dad!" she called out. Despite the turbulence of the water, there was little noise and she listened for an answer but heard nothing but the rhythmic lap of the waves. "Penny!" A chill of fear swept through her. Trapped alone in deep water was not one of her favorite ideas.

If I can do heights, I can do this, she told herself firmly, but it was a losing battle, and she was already beginning to feel panicky. She imagined things under the surface, circling and cautiously drawing nearer to her. Extending her legs to tread water became a frightening thing.

Just as she was about to call out again, Penny dropped out of the sky and plunged into the water a few feet away, throwing up a great splash. Relief made Sidney giddy and she smiled deliriously as Penny surfaced and gave her a lopsided grin.

"Wow! That was great fun! So much for splatting!" She treaded closer to Sidney and peered at her closely. "Hey! You're all wet, Sid!" Penny shot her a grin and Sidney knew she was trying to calm her. Despite knowing this, it worked. Sidney stuck out her tongue and smiled back at her. "Okay, let's get out of this water before we catch a chill."

Penny watched the waves around her, timed it carefully and ducked down when the water was at its lowest point and then kicked and pushed up out of the water a bit just as the wave crested. When she had come back down and resurfaced, she grinned again. "Land ho!" She pointed. "Let's go!" She stretched out and began to stroke for shore, and Sidney followed along as they moved slowly, conserving energy.

After a few minutes Sidney began to get glimpses of tree tops over the waves and then the bottom of the ocean came into view, the sparkling white sand turning the blue water glassy and colorless like a tall glass of spring water. The slight undertow tugged at her as they got closer to land, but wasn't enough to slow her down. Within a few minutes she was able to stand up and walk up to the beach. Her clothes were waterlogged and she shook with the cold. She hugged herself and tried to get warm, but shivers wracked her body.

The pristine beach stretched along the coast as far as the eye could see, and was bordered on the inland side by thick, lush jungle. The sand was snowy white, finely grained and beyond the edge of the water, where it was dry, it was also warm. Sidney saw no rocks, shells or driftwood anywhere— the sand was smooth and undulated gently. The sound of the waves hitting the beach and then sliding back out was soothing, and the trees in the jungle waved slightly in the cool breeze that blew in off the ocean. The leaves seemed to whisper and murmur in soft waves as the wind caressed them.

"Do you think Dad is here?" Sidney's teeth chattered; the breeze had a slightly different effect on her than it did on the trees, almost seeming to drive tiny nails of cold into her skin. Cold as she was, worry for her father was the only thing on her mind. She looked around frantically, searching for him, hoping against hope to see him striding up the beach, or out of the jungle.

"I don't know." Penny sounded worried. "I'm sure wherever he is, he's all right. We can go search for him, but first we need to dry off and warm up. Let's get these wet clothes off—we can find a rock or something to dry them on."

Sidney knew Penny was right.

"You first. Give me your clothes, Sid" Sidney hesitated slightly and Penny snickered. "Oh, you can leave your undies on, Sid. Just the heavy bits come off. So modest!"

Sidney grinned back, her face coloring slightly, and began shucking off her clothes. The fact was she felt little modesty—she felt so comfortable around Penny that the idea of undressing in front of her didn't bother her. As the clothes came off she felt colder, shaking like a leaf as her shivering became more intense—body wracking shakes that she could not control. But the sand was hot and she could already feel warmth coming up through the soles of her feet.

"Now we walk," Penny said once she was undressed as well, and started walking down the beach parallel to the water. Neither girl spoke while they waited for the sun to warm them up. It didn't take long—within a few minutes she felt a lot warmer.

As they walked she looked around, hoping to see her father nearby, but as far as she could see they were alone.

"So where are we, Penny? Any idea?" The last of her shakes had subsided and the sun felt amazing on her shoulders and back.

"On a beach. An exotic, beautiful beach. Beyond that I have no idea."

Sidney rolled her eyes and smiled.

"Well, at least that murkshifter isn't chasing us still." Immediately she regretted the words and looked around nervously to make sure it was true. She was relieved there sign of life at all besides the trees.

"Well, murkshifters don't like water for some reason. So if it followed us here, we could just get back in the water."

"Yeah, what a choice—torn to shreds by a horrible monster or freeze and drown." Sidney gave a sarcastic huff, but smiled slightly to take the edge off her words.

"I've heard that freezing to death is quite easy after a certain point."

"I imagine being torn limb from limb is quite easy after a certain point as well."

"Good point," Penny responded soberly. "It's the getting to that point that sucks."

"In both cases," Sidney added.

They walked in silence for a while until in the distance they could make out dark rocks that cut off the beach and trailed out into the water a ways. The rocks, jagged and porous emerged from the jungle and poured down into the water, almost as if an ancient flow of lava had run that path, to sizzle, steam and finally cool in the waters. When they reached the rocks she touched them. The edges were rough and hot to the touch.

"Ah, perfect," Penny began to lay her clothes out to dry. Sidney followed suit, and then gingerly sat on the edge of the rock. The rough, sharp surface was not comfortable to sit on but the heat flowing up into her made it more than bearable.

"Oh, God, that feels wonderful, Penny." Sidney sighed with pleasure and Penny sat beside her and echoed the sound. They sat quietly for a while and just soaked in the sunlight. "Okay, so what do we do when our clothes are dry?"

"Put them back on?" Penny arched an eyebrow at her.

"Very funny." Sidney rolled her eyes. "After we put our dry clothes back on? Then what are we doing?"

"Look for Colin, I think."

"Where do we start? The beach looks empty. I saw no sign of people. No footprints in the sand." She frowned and thought for a second. "In fact, I didn't see any sign of life. No birds, no bugs, no animal tracks in the sand—nothing."

"I noticed that, too, Sid. I think we have three choices: stay on the beach, go inland or swim back out into the water."

"Why would we swim back out?"

"Well, that's where the portal dropped us. Maybe there's another portal nearby. Since the last one was at the bottom of a deepest pit I've ever fallen in, it wouldn't surprise me terribly if the way out was deep in the water." Penny gave a little shrug.

"I really hope that's not the case. If we swim out there and find out it's not there...well, that seems suicidal."

"Yeah, I agree. That's a last resort. If nothing else works."

Sidney thought back to her dream of the tower. Was this too her dream? She tried to reach out with her dream sense but was met by blankness. So, it wasn't her dream then.

"So that leaves waiting or searching." She bit her lip thoughtfully before continuing. "It might be smarter to wait. They always say to stay where you are if you get lost. And we're definitely lost. Of course, generally that's when you think someone is coming to find you."

"Waiting might be smarter, but can you really see us just sitting here until someone comes to help us? What if no one comes? Or if something comes that would rather eat us?"

Sidney sighed and shook her head slightly.

"Nope, I'd rather not wait."

"Me neither. Besides," Penny continued. "We still have to find the wall and repair it. If we can. It might be that we find Colin while we do that."

They both fell silent for a while before Sidney spoke up again.

"So we go inland once our clothes are dry. Just a *little* waiting first. Who knows, maybe we'll get lucky. We can draw a message for Dad in the sand, too."

"Great idea." After a brief pause Penny spoke again. "Sid, what was he like before the accident?"

"Upbeat. Positive. And he had a great imagination. Well, he still has a great imagination, but he doesn't seem to use it as much as he did." She paused. "He never yelled at me or Emma. Oh, he got stern with us, but I don't remember him ever raising his voice. I remember when I was seven I decided I wanted to be a beautician so I gave Emma a haircut, did her nails and put makeup on her. I absolutely ruined her hair, got fingernail polish all over everything but her actual nails and well, she looked more like a clown than anything else. I was so proud of myself. When Mom and Dad came upstairs and found me putting the finishing touches on her, Mom pitched a fit, but Dad laughed. He laughed so hard that Mom ended up yelling at him instead of us. Finally he had to leave the room and as he went he told me he was sorry, but I was on my own. After he left, Mom stopped being mad and I helped her repair the damage. She gave me a stern lecture and I nodded at all the right places."

Penny snickered.

"I was sent to my room for the afternoon, and eventually Dad came up and sat down in my room with me and we played games together for a while until Mom relented." She fell silent for a moment and tears filled her eyes. She sniffed once and wiped her eyes. "He was so patient with us. I think that patience was one of the things that Mom loved so much about him. He got away with many things other people might not have because he was so patient with all of us. Mom was much more...goal oriented and driven—he was a great balancing influence." She lapsed into thoughtful silence.

"Well, apart from the whole kicking-zombie-ass thing, he doesn't sound too terribly different now," Penny said. "Is he impatient with you now?"

Sidney shook her head.

"No, not at all. It's just that for so long now he's only been a shell of a person. Like he's going through the motions, but not really there. It's not so much that he ignores me, but he doesn't seem to have the capacity to focus on me as much as he used to." She gave a tiny smile. "He's getting a lot better in the last week or so. Ever since you showed up. You've got some kind of magic, Penny."

"Thanks, Sid, but I bet he was ready to come out of it already. He just needed a shove. And do you know why he was ready?" She looked at Sidney meaningfully. "Because you have been working on him for so long. It would have happened eventually. You saved him, Sid. So don't give me all the credit. I just swooped in to take all the glory!" She grinned and Sidney smiled back. "It was your magic, Sid. Not mine."

Sidney felt her face flush. "Well, whatever the reason it happened when you showed up, and I will always link the two things in my mind."

"I'm glad that you associate me with good things." Penny leaned over and gave her a quick hug. "I just hope that when this is all over you don't associate me with zombies. We seem to be spending plenty of time running from them." They shared a smile and then lapsed into quiet, listening to the surf pounding the beach.

※

Once their clothes had dried off they dressed and headed inland. It wasn't what Sidney had expected in a jungle.

The air on the beach was hot and thick with salty humidity, but as they passed over some invisible threshold, the air became wetter and cooler, though not uncomfortable. Sidney stopped and looked around, inspecting their surroundings carefully. She'd never been in a real jungle and was not surprised at how different it was from the versions she'd seen on television and in movies. The trees were dripping with water, and the bases of their trunks were covered by moss and lichen. There wasn't much undergrowth, and what little there was seemed smaller and sparser than the humidity of the climate led her to expect. Looking up, she saw that the trees were extremely tall, towering far above her and their crowns spread into each other, creating a thick, vibrant canopy. Very little sunlight got past the dense covering of leaves and branches, and the entire jungle was draped in shadowy half-dark. The noises of small animals, insects and other creatures all combined to create an almost melodious sound. Sidney was struck with how strange it was that the beach had been so devoid of life and the forest was teeming with it.

A lush carpet of moss, ground-cover plants and exposed roots spread between the gigantic trees. Sidney took a deep breath, pulling in the wet earthy smells of the jungle. Before them a path stretched away into the gloom, weaving around trees haphazardly as far as the eye could see.

"Well, this is so not how I expected a jungle to look, Penny. I mean, where's Tarzan, the gorillas and lions? The rubber trees and vines?"

"It's not a jungle really. It's a rainforest."

"Really. What's the difference?"

"Well, see how tall the trees are, and how the canopy is so dense that very little light comes through? A jungle has a much sparser canopy, and because more light gets through, the plants on the ground are much taller and thicker. That's what makes it so hard to travel through a jungle. A rainforest is much easier to traverse. See how there is a path here? You won't find many paths in a jungle." Penny paused and glanced over at Sidney. "I think the rainforest is much prettier."

"Wow. Where did you learn so much about jungles and rain forests?"

"There are many different landscapes on the Dreamside," Penny intoned mysteriously. Then her face broke into a wide grin. "That and National Geographic."

Sidney snorted a quick laugh.

"So what now? Follow the path?"

"I think that's the best idea, Sid. We might as well get going while it's still light. It will be very dark in here at night."

"And scary," Sidney muttered under her breath, but Penny heard her.

"And scary. But don't fret, Sid, I'll protect you."

"Yeah? Who's going to protect you?"

"I was hoping you would, Sid!" Penny smiled brightly and patted her on the shoulder before starting off down the path.

Sidney shook her head slightly and followed Penny deeper into the rainforest.

※

They walked for hours and because she could not see the sky, Sidney lost track of time, and there was nothing but the path, the trees and an endless sea of colors. Constant motion, no measure of progress. The leaves on the underside of the canopy were a dark bluish green, wide and graceful, and the moss, vines and lichen that draped around the tall trunks of the trees ranged from bottle green to a light yellow. It was peaceful and calm, but after a while she began to feel a slight tickling on the back of her neck. It came and went sporadically and she frequently glanced back down the trail as they walked. The creeping sensation was uncomfortable and disconcerting. She began to harbor the suspicion they were being watched.

She didn't say anything to Penny—it was probably just paranoia and fear of the unknown that was creating the feeling. God, but she was getting tired of feeling afraid. Plus, she was worried that if she said anything, it would feel silly and childish. The impression of being watched didn't go away. Instead, as the day wore on it became a constant, oppressive feeling.

They'd been walking a while—Sidney couldn't guess how long—when Penny stopped and reached down and picked through the undergrowth at her feet. She pulled up some kind of fruit that Sidney had never seen before. It was a long yellow thing that looked like an oversized banana. Penny pulled back the peel on one side and sniffed at the fruit then shrugged slightly and took a small bite before handing it over to Sidney.

"Here, try this."

Sidney took it and when she bit into it tart, sticky juices gushed out. She decided it tasted significantly better than a banana and ate it quickly.

Over the course of the day they stopped frequently and Penny discovered some other strange fruit. None of them were things Sidney recognized. One tasted just like an apple, but was blue in color and soft to bite. There was one that was shaped like two pears placed end to end and when Sidney took a bite it reminded her of anise—bitter and dry. She spit that right out, and was more cautious about tasting before she ate.

"Is this the normal rain forest type of fruit?"

"Not like any I've ever seen. Tasty though."

"For the most part." Sidney snorted.

"For the most part."

Eventually the gloom faded into darkness and walking became more difficult. In the dark the feeling of being watched was much stronger. It was worse because looking around did nothing to ease her worry—anything could be hiding in the shadows that blanketed the forest. She began to expect to see the worst: glowing eyes burning out of shadows, some dark form easing up behind her.

Zombies.

She stumbled several times over roots that snaked back and forth across the path like ribbons that had been curled with the edge of scissors. Penny didn't seem to be having the same difficulty, but after Sidney hit the dirt once, she stopped and helped her to her feet.

"It's getting too dark to continue. Let's find a place to rest until morning, Sid."

"A hotel maybe?"

Penny chuckled. "There's nothing around to start a fire, so we're going to just have to sit in the dark…"

"Okay." Sidney decided that the thought of just sitting staring out into the dark wasn't a pleasant one. She stretched her legs and fought not to peer out into the surrounding trees, and with each moment the weight of the stare of whatever was out there became harder to ignore. Finally she had to speak.

"Penny...I've had this strange sensation ever since we left the beach. It's almost as if someone is watching us."

"I've been feeling it as well. It's unsettling."

"You are the queen of understatement."

Penny laughed again but the forest seemed to absorb the merry sound, sucking the life out of it. "What's more worrisome is that I think we've been going in circles. A few of the trees have looked so alike that I started watching for them and we seem to keep passing by the same ones."

"Ugh," Sidney said. "That must make it easy to follow us." Another thing occurred to her. "Do you think we're stuck here? I mean, more than just lost. Like in the village?"

"I don't know. Maybe. I think we've just got to keep moving and hope something changes. It's not like we're going anywhere in particular, and there's plenty of fruit to eat. But we're both tired. Let's find somewhere to sit down." They walked up the path a bit further until she found a large log that was butted up against a still living tree. It created a makeshift seat that, while damp, wasn't as soggy as the ground. "I was hoping to find somewhere dry, but it is the rainforest after all." She shrugged.

Sidney sat down gingerly and sighed resignedly as moisture immediately made the seat of her pants cool. She hadn't realized how tired her feet were until she was actually off them, and having a wet bottom seemed like a fairly reasonable trade off. Penny plopped down beside her gracefully and slipped her shoes off. "Pardon the smell." She grinned and began massaging the ball of her foot. "Ah, that feels good..."

Sidney followed suit and it did feel amazingly good—she was surprised how the small things meant so much more out in the wild. Now that she was seated her mind turned immediately to her dad. Her breath hitched once and she hugged her knees.

She couldn't remember exactly when he'd disappeared. He'd been right behind her, bringing up the rear to protect her and Penny—typical Dad behavior—then he was gone. She hoped he wasn't trapped in the subway with the murkshifter. The beast had unwittingly revealed that it hadn't caught up with her dad at that point, but that didn't stop Sidney from imagining the worst. Graphic images kept flitting by in her mind, serving to heighten her fears for him. A small sound escaped her—something between a whimper and a groan.

"You're worried about Colin," Penny spoke quietly.

"Yes."

"Me, too. I'm sure he's fine, Sid. We have to hold onto that thought. He's fine."

Sidney nodded. "I know. I just can't stop thinking of all the dreadful things might be happening to him."

"Think about something else."

"Hah," Sidney snorted. "Easier said than done."

Penny gave a short laugh and reached over and took Sidney's hand. They sat in the cool darkness of the rainforest, backs to the huge tree that towered above them, stretching up to join the rest of the trees in the canopy. "I keep thinking that he needs us. That somehow that nightmare separated us from him on purpose. We've got to find him, Penny."

"Yes, but I don't know how to go to him. Other than to just keep walking until we find a way out of this dream."

Sidney leaned into Penny a bit for comfort and warmth and the other girl put an arm around her. "I guess we should take turns sleeping, huh? I can take the first watch if you'd like."

"No, that's okay," Penny replied. "I don't really feel all that tired. You rest and I'll keep an eye out."

"Fine, but wake me up in a while and I'll take a turn."

"Sure."

Sidney sat up straight and shifted to get comfortable against the tree. Eventually she just gave up on that idea and closed her eyes. As she started to nod off something occurred to her, dragging her back from the edge of sleep.

"Penny? Will I dream? I mean, here, in the Dreamside?"

"I always do. That brings up another interesting question— where do we go when we dream on the Dreamside? Dream worlds within dream worlds infinitely repeating perhaps?"

They fell silent, considering the idea until eventually Penny spoke again. "Well, that made my head hurt." Sidney heard the smile in her voice and it was a comfort. Sidney listened to the sounds of the night around them. Where the beach had seemed devoid of life, the rainforest teemed with it—the noises of small animals and insects created a wall of noise that was almost musical. The gentle rustle of leaves far over their heads was soothing as well, and before too long, she drifted off into sleep.

Guide

Sidney struggled up slowly from the depths of sleep as if hands were holding her down, and when she finally breached the surface, she was lying on the wet ground beside the log, with a hand over her mouth. After a moment she realized it wasn't her hand and that there was another hand on her shoulder, holding her down. Her first instinct was to struggle to rise and get away but before she could start moving, she opened her eyes and looked up into Penny's face. She realized that she had her head in the other girl's lap. She reached up and tried to pull Penny's hand away from her mouth but Penny made a soft shushing sound at her and leaned in closer.

"Quiet, Sid, something is out there." She released Sidney and pointed her eyes out toward the darkness that surrounded them quickly and then back. "Sit up slowly."

Sidney was instantly completely awake and alert—her heartbeat galloping off into a racing rhythm. She slowly sat up and put her back to the tree again. Penny leaned closer until her mouth was nearly touching Sidney's ear.

"I don't know who or what it is," she whispered softly. "But it's been watching us for a while now. I am going to talk to it, but we both need to be ready." There was a quick pause while Penny looked around, and then Sidney felt her breath on her ear again. "When I stand up, you stand up too, and keep your back against the tree. Keep your eyes open."

Sidney nodded slowly. Penny reached over and gave Sidney's hand a quick squeeze and then stood up.

"Hello," she called into the dark. "I know you're out there. Maybe you could step out where we can see you. Please." Her voice was pleasant and cheerful, but firm as well, and it hung in the air. Instantly the sounds of the night disappeared as if someone had pressed a huge mute button, but there was no response from the darkness. "Come on out. We won't hurt you. It's not polite to just follow us around and spy on us." She stopped speaking and took a step forward, so that she was in front of Sidney and dropped into a half-crouch. She froze in place and Sidney watched the darkness for some hint of what was out there. After a few moments of quiet, the sounds of insects and small creatures started up again, tentatively at first, but then more confidently when Penny didn't speak again.

Then a voice carried out from the trees, silencing the sounds again.

"Are you spirits?" It was a male voice, thick with an accent that Sidney did not recognize.

"Spirits?" Amusement rang in Penny's voice. "No, we're just people."

"You look like spirits to my eyes."

"We look like spirits?" Penny repeated his words again. She grinned out into the darkness. "I've never heard that one before." She stood up straight again and raised her hands in a placating gesture. "We are most definitely not spirits. We are dreams and we are lost." A shadow separated from a tree trunk half shrouded in the blackness of night, and a young, short black man stepped out of the shadows and halted a handful of yards away. He wore pants made of a strange material that fell slightly past his knees, leather shoes and had metal bands about each bicep but was otherwise bare from the waist up. He stood in a stance of readiness, relaxed hands away from his body. She was shocked at how close he had been—no more than fifteen feet from where they sat. He stood still and studied them quietly with a mix of apprehension and something else Sidney could not identify—it was almost like hope or expectation.

Sidney returned his frank appraisal and was surprised at how young he looked—her age or perhaps a year older at the most. His wiry hair was cut close to the scalp and his face was long and thin with wide cheekbones. Despite his cautious expression, his brown expressive eyes were bright and the hint of smile lines around his mouth reassured her. There were no signs of cruelty or meanness in his face. Something about it made her want to see him smile.

His eyes were wide—the whites almost glowed in the blackness of the night. He muttered something under his breath that she couldn't make out. Then he appeared to gather himself to speak.

"You are dreams?"

"Yes, dreams. Why else would you find us in the Dreamside?" She shot Sidney a glance.

"Spirits visit us in our dreams sometimes. And you both look like..." He clamped his mouth forcibly and glanced away quickly.

"We look like what?" Sidney spoke up. She felt like he was hiding something, but she had no idea what it might be. He looked back at her.

"I was going to say that you look strange to my eyes. Not bad—no, not bad at all." He didn't sound embarrassed. "I have never met any people with pale skin and such strange garb. Our elders speak of meeting with them occasionally." He looked at Sidney before continuing. "I could imagine your pale skin, though it is more pleasing to see than I had expected. But your clothing I could never have imagined. So, I feel that you must be...real." He shrugged slightly. "If you are real, it is hard to imagine you must be spirits visiting me in my dream."

Sidney liked the singsong quality of his voice. Something about him inspired trust.

"Well, we're not spirits, but if you want to think of us that way, we don't mind." Sidney frowned slightly and looked out into the darkness thoughtfully. "Unless, of course, you don't like spirits, in which case I'd prefer you just think of us as people. That's what we are after all."

"You said you were dreams," he repeated with a slight frown of confusion.

"Yes. Dreams are people too, you know." Sidney put the slightest trace of sternness in her voice and he ducked his head in a quick, apologetic nod. She liked that Penny had included her in the assertion.

Sidney's eyes were drawn to his upper body. There were several scars on his arms—they appeared to be decorative rather than the result of wounds—and some tattoos on his arms and across his shoulders. They were not the sort of tattoos that Sidney was used to seeing. They were small images and symbols that seemed to go together, as if to tell some story. She pulled her eyes away from the scars and tattoos and saw a long, wickedly curved knife under his belt, and diagonally across his back a spear was strapped in place. She knew at once that he was a warrior or hunter, but the kindness on his face made him seem less threatening.

After he had faced them for a long moment, his face broke into the slow smile that Sidney had been waiting for, and she was not disappointed. He smiled in the same way that Penny did—with every part of his face.

"Well, as long as you are not evil spirits, then I suppose it does not matter." He dropped gracefully down to the ground, into a cross legged position. "I am not here to harm you. I am sorry if I frightened you."

Penny sank down to sit across from him in the same manner, and she glanced back at Sidney and patted the ground next to her. Sidney sat down beside her and wrapped her arms around her knees, holding them tight to her chest.

"I am Penelope, and this is Sidney."

"I am Ahanu." He nodded his head once. His eyes sparkled cheerfully still. "I am glad that you are not spirits. I am a simple man—a hunter, not a wise man—and I have no skill with spirits." He carefully put his hands on his knees with palms turned up. "I am gladdened to meet you. It is a weary road I travel and it is good to be able to speak to others. Perhaps we might share camp tonight and in the morning, if our roads go in the same direction, we could walk together?"

Penny glanced at Sidney who gave a little shrug.

"We would be glad to share our camp with you, Ahanu. As to the other, we'll see." It was strange that when Penny was cautious it came off as something more negative—Sidney wondered if that was just because the girl was so effusively friendly normally. But Ahanu didn't seem to take any notice and Penny continued. "What brings you into the Dreamside?"

"I was dreaming. Sleeping beside the cook fires in the village of my people and I woke up here." A puzzled frown cleared the remnants of the smile from his face.

"You aren't awake, Ahanu. The Dreamside is the world that you come to when you dream."

"I am still dreaming? I thought that was the case, but it is strange to wake from one dream into another. I do not know what it means." Apprehension crossed his features slowly.

"Well, that's how most people get here," Penny said.

"Most?"

"Well, some are born here." Sidney added.

"So that is what you meant when you said you were dreams. You were born in this place?"

"Penny was." Sidney gave up the fiction finally and a small part of her wished that she too had been born here—had that in common with Penny. But more than that she wanted to tell Ahanu the truth more than she could bring herself to distrust him. "I wasn't. I was born out in the real world."

"The waking world," Penny corrected. "To those of us born here, this is plenty real." She shot Sidney a little quirk of a smile.

"Sorry, Penny."

"S'okay." Penny reached over and put her hand on Sidney's shoulder. She became thoughtful and glanced out into the darkness. "Funny thing about being born—we really have no idea where we were born—not factually anyway. We've all been told where we were each born, and we all accept it as truth because our parents told us when we were very young, and it became truth to us. So I suppose it's possible I wasn't born on the Dreamside, I guess. But that's what I was told, and that's what I choose to believe." She turned back and grinned at Ahanu who returned her smile.

"I was born in my mother's tent during the rainy season. That is all I can tell you. My people do not stay long in one place. We follow the herds." He shrugged slightly and Sidney smiled.

"I was born in Tayport." They all lapsed into quiet for a few moments, and Sidney stared at his torso again, trying to make out the various images. Some of them were clear, but others were unknown to her. They almost seemed like words—like Egyptian hieroglyphics in a way.

"So you never said where you are going to or coming from, Ahanu." Penny broke the silence.

"Ah, yes." The young man looked slightly discomfited. "I am on my First Hunt." He was blushing slightly now. "It is very embarrassing to admit that I am lost, but I do not know these lands. I have never seen their like before. I would not have dreamed that trees could be so tall."

"What is a first hunt?" Sidney asked.

"In my tribe, when a young man comes of age, he fashions his first real spear and knife, and hunts with the men of the tribe. They hunt until he kills his first animal and then there is a celebration to welcome the young man into adulthood, and to give thanks to the spirit of the animal that was killed. It was the night of that celebration after I went to sleep that I woke and found myself alone..." He shrugged briefly and looked away into the darkness.

"And you have become lost here in the Dreamside." Penny looked thoughtful. "Well, the good news, Ahanu, is that you are likely asleep somewhere, probably with your people."

"When will I wake up?" He spoke slowly and quietly. Sidney could hear the worry in his voice. "Will I wake up?"

"Oh, yes. After your body is well rested." Penny grinned. "That's when people usually wake up." Ahanu did not return her grin, but instead looked worried.

"I have already travelled these lands for seven full days and nights. I don't know that I feel any more rested than when I fell asleep."

Penny looked surprised.

"Seven days?"

"Yes. Is this a bad thing?"

"Oh, not necessarily. Time is different in the Dreamside. I wouldn't worry too much."

He gave a slow nod. Then he took his knife and spear out and set them down to his side, bending out to put them barely in reach.

"My weapons, my trust," he intoned. "I had forgotten. My mother would be sorely disappointed. I am afraid I am not the best example of my people right now." He looked embarrassed again.

"Well, I don't have any weapons to put aside." Penny held up her hands, palms upward. "But you have my trust, Ahanu."

"And mine," Sidney chimed in.

He nodded slowly to each of them in turn. Moving slowly he reached behind himself and pulled off a small pack that had been concealed low on his back. He rummaged around in it for a few minutes before pulling a small bundle out.

"Are you hungry?" He asked. "I caught and cooked a hare last night, and saved a few pieces of meat. I have already thanked it for its life." There was a slight glint of pride in his eyes. "I have eaten much fruit since arriving in these lands, and having meat sometimes is nice." He held out a small bit of meat to Penny and she took it from him and without hesitation took a bite of it.

"Oh, that is wonderful! Thank you."

Ahanu turned and offered a piece to Sidney and she tasted it gingerly. It was savory and chewy, and she ate the whole thing quickly.

"Thank you, Ahanu."

"You are most welcome, Sidney," he struggled over her name slightly, but spoke solemnly.

"How is it that you speak English?" Sidney asked.

"English? I do not know what that language is, but we speak the tongue of my ancestors—the First Men."

Sidney glanced at Penny questioningly and the young woman shrugged back.

"I imagine that in the dream the language becomes... irrelevant."

Ahanu began to ask her questions but Sidney quickly lost the thread of the conversation. Around them the sounds of the night slowly resurfaced, breaking up the silence around them as the creatures of the rain forest became comfortable with the alien noises of the conversation. Sidney tried to focus in on any one sound, but they blended into a swirling mélange. The harder she tried to pick out individual sounds the less discernible they became, and after a while even the sound of Penny and Ahanu speaking softly faded into the wall of white noise.

Eventually she gave up trying and just let the sounds flow around her. Her eyes grew heavier and she swayed slightly as sleep began to reclaim her. She felt herself move past her center of balance and begin to tip over and she startled awake. Both Penny and Ahanu looked at her and then Penny broke into a warm smile.

"Come here, Sid." She pulled her closer. "Put your head in my lap and sleep. I will watch over you."

"We both will guard your sleep," Ahanu added.

Sidney sank down against Penny and put her head into the girl's lap. As she snuggled in, she glanced up at Penny tiredly and gave her a brief smile.

"Thanks, Penny," she said around a huge yawn and before she even finished she drifted into sleep.

✸

When Sidney woke, it was to a chorus of birdsong, the chattering calls filling the growing light of early morning, sometimes a disorienting cacophony and others something amazingly musical. Yet again she was not where she'd been when she'd fallen asleep—this time she was sleeping in the crook of Penny's arm and shoulder, and the girl had Sidney snugged in tight against her side. Sidney glanced up and saw that Penny's eyes were closed and her chest moved slowly. She looked around until she found Ahanu sitting with his back to them. What she saw made her jaw drop—across his entire upper back was a huge tattoo of a black bird, wings spread and beak open, legs extended forward as if reaching for a branch to land on. The detail and colors were amazing. The wings were glossy and blue-black; the tiny eyes were beady and bright, and the beak was a sharp orange color. She was surprised at how beautiful it looked. She didn't know a whole lot about tattoos but she could tell that this was art—not just muddy ink under the skin, greenish black and already fading. It almost looked like someone had painted the bird on his back—if she reached out and touched it the paint would smear. She had the strongest urge to find out.

As if he felt her watching, Ahanu swung to look at her and broke into a smile.

"Good morning, Sidney." His voice was just above a whisper. "I hope you slept well and were not troubled by dark spirits in your dreams."

Sidney returned his smile shyly and nodded, not speaking for fear of waking Penny. Gently she started to sit up and pull away from the girl, being careful not to jostle her awake. When she was sitting up, still beside Penny, she whispered back. "Good morning, Ahanu. I slept well and I'm a bit sore, but I feel good. Did you sleep at all?"

While she'd maneuvered herself into a sitting position, Ahanu had turned himself around entirely to face her. "Yes, I slept for a time while Penny watched over us. I took a turn while she slept."

"Why didn't you wake me up to take a turn?"

"It was a short wait for morning. Neither Penny nor I stood watch for very long." He smiled. "If the night had been longer, I would have woken you, Sidney. I trust you to guard my sleep."

A warm feeling rose in her chest. She enjoyed it for a few moments and then whispered again. "Ahanu, can I ask you a question?"

"Of course, Sidney."

"It's about the bird on your back."

"Ah, yes, the black bird." He nodded once and furrowed his brow slightly.

"It's gorgeous."

"Is it? I have not yet gotten a good look at it. I managed to see it in the water of a small stream a few nights ago, but mostly I can't see it."

"You haven't seen it?" She found that puzzling. "How can that be? Surely when it was put on they showed it to you."

"Well, that's the strange thing. I woke up three nights ago and it was there. I have no idea how it got there." He frowned again. "I have gotten tattoos before from the elders, but they always hurt and take a while to heal. This just appeared on my back. No wound, no pain. Nothing."

"That's odd." They were both quiet for a few moments before Sidney spoke up again. "Does the crow mean anything special to your people?"

"No, I have never seen a bird like this before. Hunters in my tribe have spoken of seeing black birds, but they are rare in our lands."

Beside her, Sidney felt Penny stir. She glanced back and as the girl's eyes opened slowly, squinting against the daylight.

"Good morning, sleepyhead," she said to Penny with a smile. "Thanks for letting me sprawl all over you." Penny stretched and smiled through a yawn.

"G'morning, Sid. It was no problem. You are very warm, so it was pleasant." She sat up suddenly in one fluid motion, shook herself once and shot a grin at Sidney. "You're welcome to sleep on my lap or shoulder anytime, my little furnace." She turned to face Ahanu.

"Good morning, Ahanu. Thank you for watching over us."

"Thank you for your trust, Penelope." He was solemn and he returned her gaze.

"It was good to rest a while. So were you two talking about crows? Or did I dream that?"

"Sidney asked me about how my people view crows." He glanced over to Sidney.

"Penny, have you seen the bird on his back?"

"No," Penny looked confused, and glanced over at Ahanu searchingly. "I see no bird."

"No, it's a tattoo of some sort. You should look at it."

Ahanu rose gracefully and turned his back to them and raised his arms until they extended away from him parallel to the ground at shoulder height. The effect was that the wings of the crow seemed to stretch outward, as if preparing for a powerful down stroke. Sidney stared at it again, unable to look away right away, but she heard Penny inhale sharply.

"Oh, that's beautiful. Who gave you that?"

"I do not know. It just appeared the other morning. It wasn't there when I went to sleep, and in the morning it was there."

Sidney glanced over and met Penny's eyes.

"I think we found our guide," Sidney said.

Penny nodded with bright eyes.

"Exactly."

"Wait," Ahanu broke in. "I am your guide? As much as I am loath to admit it, I am lost and far from home. How could I guide you anywhere?" He looked confused.

"That's a good point."

"Just like we followed you in the city, Sid." Penny turned to look at Ahanu. "Just follow your heart, Ahanu. We will follow where you lead."

"I don't even know where you want to go."

"Neither do we." Penny shot Sidney a quick grin.

"What if I lead you into some danger? Or away from where you need to go?"

"We are as lost as you," Penny said. "We don't know where we're supposed to go. We only know that we have to find Sidney's father. We lost him." Ahanu looked off into the trees, his eyes turned inward as he considered her words. Sidney watched his face as it danced through a series of emotions—doubt, worry, resignation and finally determination. She liked the way his face looked at that last. He squared his shoulders and his face relaxed into a neutral expression. Then he broke into a wide smile which softened all the lines of his face and made him look even younger. Sidney felt slightly dazzled.

"Well, I would be glad to travel with you. But I can't promise that if you follow me I'll take you anywhere that you want to go. I am willing to try though."

"Good!" Penny clapped her hands together once before pushing to her feet. She offered Sidney a hand up. "Sid?"

"Sounds good. Better than just wandering around on our own." She stood and beat at her pants to clear the leaves and dirt that had accumulated on them. Ahanu rose to his feet, and picked up his spear and knife, tucking them back where they belonged.

"Well, what better time than now?" His eyes glinting in the early morning light. "Which way shall we go?" He glanced around thoughtfully. When neither of the girls answered he looked back at them questioningly.

"You're the guide, Ahanu." Sidney smiled. "You lead, we follow."

Ahanu's laughter echoed through the trees loudly.

"That is a heavy responsibility for a newly made hunter. But I have my honor and I know my duty." He lifted the spear to his chest in salute briefly before slinging it back over his shoulders. Then he turned to face the direction that they'd all been heading last night and strode off. "Let's go this way, then!" Penny reached over and patted Sidney on the shoulder once and they both followed after him.

Soul Eaters

Following Ahanu's lead, they rapidly left their campsite behind, but they didn't move with any sense of urgency. Ahanu was adept at finding quick passage through the foliage, sometimes sticking to the paths, but frequently pushing off a cleared trail to pass through hip deep foliage. To Sidney he seemed to have some idea where he was heading, and for her part she didn't really care to know. It was enough that she was following the crow on his back. She was filled with certainty that this was the right thing to do and so she relaxed and concentrated on putting her feet where they would serve her best—one in front of the other.

Every now and then Ahanu would stop so that they could all sit and rest for a few minutes before moving on. Around midmorning they passed a stream and drank. The cold water was clear and tasted sharp and clean. Sidney was sure it was the best thing she'd ever drunk in her entire life. She hadn't realized how thirsty she was until the water hit the back of her throat.

They sat by the stream for a while, resting, and Sidney watched the birds that flitted around high up in the canopy of leaves and branches. The trunks of the trees were round and relatively thin here; different from the huge redwood sized monsters they'd walked past when they'd first left the beach. Despite being thinner, they still reached far up into the sky before spreading their crown to join in with the canopy.

"Is it just me or does the forest seem to be changing as we walk?" she asked the others.

"Yes," Ahanu said. "I noticed that as well. The trees are slimmer and the sunlight is finding its way through the leaves in places." Sidney nodded—the quality of the light in the forest was definitely much better now. After a moment Penny stood and brushed her hands off on her thighs.

"Okay." Penny's voice was bright and confident. "I'm ready. Maybe we'll see the end of this forest today." Sidney stood slowly, stretching to ease the cramps from her legs and back. She wasn't used to walking as far as they'd come since landing in the water. Ahanu rose fluidly to his feet and began picking his way efficiently through the forest, and Sidney and Penny followed behind him. "What do you think will come after this forest?"

"With our luck, one big huge zombie-filled graveyard," Sidney said and Penny snickered.

"I'm going to vote for a beautiful spring meadow with wild flowers and soft grass to sit on. Or maybe a shopping mall."

Sidney glanced at her in surprise. "You like to shop, Penny?"

"Oh, I love going shopping. I don't really care about buying stuff; I just love to see all the people absorbed in what they're doing. So many strange and interesting people pass through the mall. I like to get a coffee and find a bench and watch them all go by. Sometimes I'll buy a book and pretend to read it so that I don't make anyone nervous."

"Somehow I can't see you making anyone nervous."

Before Penny could respond there was the sudden sound of a small animal crashing through the undergrowth away from them. The noise startled Sidney and she tried to spot the animal. All she managed to see was a slight movement of the bushes off to the left of the trail they were currently walking on.

She felt as if someone were spying on them and she glanced around. She caught Ahanu watching her with a small, shy, smile. Any trepidation she'd felt faded away and she smiled back at him.

"So Ahanu," she said. "Tell us about yourself."

"There is not much to tell." It didn't sound like an evasion to Sidney. He had turned back to the trail. "I am a young hunter of my tribe. Nothing has really happened to me yet." He glanced back and grinned with a small shrug. "Ask me again in a few years."

"Oh, come on, Ahanu," Penny chimed in. "There must be something you can tell us. What animal did you kill on your hunt? Do you have a sweetie?"

"Well, I took a water buffalo—nothing particularly exciting. Slow and stupid—as long as you can stay out of their way, they are not hard to get a spear into. The hardest part was finishing it off. It was strong and clung to life for a long time." There was a look of chagrin on his face. "I fear it suffered in the death I gave it. I will learn to do better."

"Okay, a water buffalo," Penny replied. "What about your sweetie? Do you have a girlfriend? A wife? A special someone in your life?"

His expression closed slightly and he hesitated before answering. "I do not have any one."

"Oh, come on. Surely you don't expect us to believe that a handsome man like you hasn't attracted hordes of women?"

He grinned. "You are a kind person, Penelope, but no, I do not have hordes of women following me around. Truly, there is no one." He shrugged slightly.

"Okay. But surely there is someone that you are attracted to?"

Ahanu looked mildly embarrassed and hid his face by concentrating on the trail ahead of them.

"Well," he said. "There is someone that I...care for. Her name is Amara. She is kind and beautiful, and strong willed and self-assured—all qualities that are admirable among my people. But I fear she has no eyes for me. I do not think she even sees me when she looks at me." He sounded sad yet resigned.

"Okay," Penny said. "Rest stop now. I want to hear all about this girl of yours."

While Penny peppered him with questions, slowly teasing the story from him, Sidney listened quietly and studied him. His eyes were so bright and quick to smile.

And he has a very nice body.

She almost laughed aloud at the direction of her thoughts, but she did not look away. His muscles were well defined but not bulky or out of proportion—a wiry strength.

"Well, this Amara is foolish if she doesn't notice you." The words burst from Sidney without volition. She immediately blushed and Penny grinned. Ahanu smiled also.

"You are kind to say so, Sidney."

"Well, it's just the truth." She worked to conceal how flustered she felt. She looked up and saw a small animal gliding out of the canopy above them and behind Ahanu. It didn't have wings, but instead there were flaps of skin between its legs that it spread wide while gliding through the air. "Look at that!" She pointed—grateful for the distraction—and Penny smiled at her knowingly.

As they travelled along at their easy pace, they managed to draw Ahanu into the conversation. Eventually the light of day began to fade into the gloom of early evening and then into deep darkness and Ahanu came to a halt. He turned back to them and arched an eyebrow.

"Okay, we have arrived." Ahanu's voice was serious but after a beat his face broke into a wide smile. Sidney snorted a laugh and Penny joined in, her voice chiming through the darkness. The clear bright sound almost seemed to make the night a little less dark. Ahanu gestured to the ground. "We can camp here tonight. The forest isn't as wet here. I think I can find some wood and we can have a fire to warm ourselves by. And fruit! More fruit."

Penny laughed.

"At least it's tasty," Sidney said, though in truth she was beginning to tire of it herself. "I mean we could be eating grubs and roots instead."

"Well, that orange one was not so tasty," Ahanu said as he strode around the small clearing they'd stopped in. "It tasted like the leather of my shoes."

"And how would you know how your shoes taste?" Penny asked archly as she cleared away an area for them to sit. Sidney went over and helped.

"You have not known the true depths of hunger until you have tried to eat your shoes." He threw the words back at them over his shoulder as he disappeared into the dark. "I will be just over here getting wood. So do not talk about my shoes—I will hear your words."

"I think he's got nice shoes," Penny stage whispered to Sidney.

"My shoes and I thank you for your kindness, Penelope." His voice floated back muted by the trees and distance.

Penny and Sidney looked at each other and then burst into laughter. For a brief moment, everything felt normal—just friends sharing a joke—and Sidney tried to hang onto that feeling as long as she could, but it faded away leaving only the distant memory of the flavor of that moment.

In the middle of the area they'd chosen, Penny and Sidney dug away the ground cover, exposing the cool dirt of the forest floor. Penny used the end of a fallen branch to dig a hole in the dirt and Sidney helped by pulling dirt out. Then they searched the area for rocks to line their fire pit with. There weren't many to find, but they did the best they could. Sidney could hear Ahanu moving through the underbrush, circling their little camp area just out of sight.

Penny slid closer and spoke quietly. There was a glint of devilish amusement in her eyes.

"Sidney likes Ahanu."

"Stop that." Sidney elbowed her softly. "I do not like him. I just think he's...nice."

"Nice? Just nice?"

"No, not just nice," Sidney said with exasperation. "More than nice. Very nice."

"Oh, more than nice." Penny snorted. "Well, I think he's wonderful. A woman could do a lot worse than a man like him. It's just too bad we're in someone else's dream or we could take him home with us." She grinned and bumped her shoulder against Sidney's.

"Is he a dream, too? I mean, Emma didn't even know she was a dream at first. Could it be that he just doesn't know?"

Penny shrugged. "I suppose that could be true. Why? Do you want to dream of him again?"

"Penny, stop it." Sidney rolled her eyes.

"Okay, okay." Penny held up her hands in surrender.

"Anyway, I think I like this whole guide thing, Penny. We get a fire tonight, and Ahanu seems to know what he's doing out here."

"Yes, I agree. Although I keep wishing I had my futon and coffee maker."

"I know what you mean." After a pause, Sidney continued, "I'm worried about Dad."

"Me too. But we have to trust in the crow to lead us where we need to be. At any rate, I'll be right back." She turned and strolled lightly into the darkness and was quickly gone from sight. Sidney was left alone in the dark with only her thoughts.

Moments later Ahanu strode quietly into view with an armload of wood. He unceremoniously dumped it all in a pile and spotted the little fire pit they'd made.

"Ah, very nice. We will have a good fire soon." He glanced around quickly and looked slightly worried. "Where did Penelope go?"

"I don't know." Sidney frowned. "She didn't say. Just sauntered off."

"Well, let's get this fire bright and hot so she can easily find her way back." He went to work arranging the wood in the pit, carefully stacking and adjusting the wood until he seemed satisfied. Then he opened up his pouch and rummaged inside of it. He brought out a tiny box, and a smaller pouch. Setting down the box and the larger pouch, he opened the smaller one.

"Whatcha got in there?"

"Wood shavings. A true hunter must always be prepared." He shook out a handful of the wood shavings and placed them in the center of his wood construct. He opened the box and pulled out a pair of small stones. He glanced up at Sidney again. "Flint. To create the spark. To burn the shavings. To start the fire. To warm us and drive back the darkness."

"Sounds good to me."

Within a few minutes he had a cheerful fire crackling in the pit. He sat down a few feet away from Sidney, and they leaned into the warmth of the fire. The night air was again brisk and between the warmth and light of the fire Sidney felt good.

"So you haven't told me about yourself, Sidney." Sidney sensed a touch of nervousness in Ahanu's voice.

"Well, what do you want to know?"

"What is it like where you come from?"

She considered for a few moments and then answered honestly.

"Busy. Big. Chaotic." She tried to describe life in her world and knew the picture she was painting wasn't clear, but Ahanu listened raptly, asking occasional questions. Eventually he changed the subject.

"So Penny is a dream?"

"Yep."

"And you are not?"

"Nope." She searched his face, trying to understand his reaction. From out of the dark a voice interrupted them.

"Don't let her fool you, Ahanu," Penny said as she emerged from the darkness carrying an armload of fruit. "She's completely dreamy."

Sidney blushed slightly and rolled her eyes at Penny, but the girl wasn't looking her way.

"I found some dinner. I couldn't find any pizza or steaks, but this fruit should do."

"I do not know what pizza is, but I still have some meat strips left," Ahanu shared out a couple of strips of the meat. It had become slightly dry but still looked safe to eat.

"Thank you, Ahanu." Penny nodded her head in a slight bow.

"Yeah, thanks, Ahanu," Sidney echoed as she chewed on a strip.

"You are welcome, of course." His smile revealed teeth bright in the half dark and his eyes were almost merry.

"I've never eaten rabbit before. It's better than I expected." Sidney took another healthy bite and chewed slowly.

"Well, truthfully, it wasn't really a rabbit, I don't think." Ahanu smiled wryly. "But a rabbit is the closest thing to it that I've seen. It had a long tail and rather sharp teeth." Sidney looked up at him, trying to gauge if he was pulling her leg, but his face remained serious. "It was the floppy ears that made me think rabbit."

They sat in silence, eating their meat and fruit as the fire crackled and popped. Some of the wood was slightly damp and hissed as the fire dried it out and began to consume it hungrily. Eventually Penny clapped her hands on her knees and sighed contentedly.

"Much better. We should get some sleep. We will have another long day of walking tomorrow."

"Okay," Sidney said. "I get the first watch."

Ahanu nodded solemnly. "As you wish, Sidney. I will take the second watch. Wake me if I sleep too long."

"I'm not entirely sure how I'll know how long is too long."

"Just wake me when you begin to have trouble keeping your eyes open, or after adding five logs to the fire—whichever comes first."

He and Penny arranged themselves around the fire, putting their backs to the fire and Sidney sat on the other side and began her watch.

She was careful to keep the fire alive and well fed while the other two slept, which kept the ring of light large. But the shadows at the edge were creepy and she found herself imagining that she saw things. Part of her wanted to wake Penny but the larger part wanted to do her watch, so she carefully put down her fears and kept her eyes moving around them.

Penny and Ahanu had been asleep for roughly an hour, when the sounds of the forest slowly faded into silence and she felt a tingle run up her neck and goose bumps rise on her arms. The fire had died down a bit and she quickly put some more wood in it. The new wood hissed and popped for a moment and then caught fire and the flames rose again. She looked around the edges of their camp, but saw nothing. If it weren't for the complete lack of woodland noises she would have put the fear out of her mind, but she knew that the insects and other animals wouldn't have gone quiet unless they perceived a threat. Perhaps some kind of bear or wolf or something. She had no idea what types of predators lived in a place like this. Her imagination began to run away with itself steadily picking up speed and she took a deep breath and fought to rein it in.

Then she heard the strangest noise off in the darkness. It was a whispering, hissing chatter. It wasn't a human sound, but even though she couldn't pick out any words, she knew it was some form of speech. Her heart began to pound loudly in her ears and she decided it was time to wake up Ahanu and Penny. She glanced over at Ahanu; his eyes were open, the whites shining in the firelight. He slowly raised a finger to his mouth, signaling her to keep quiet. Sidney stayed completely still, listening as the noise stopped. There was a faint rustling sound not far out in the darkness and she wanted to go sit by Penny.

Ahanu motioned ever so slightly at the fire. For a second Sidney wasn't sure what he wanted, and then he mimed putting food in his mouth and pointed at the fire.

Feed the fire.

She slowly began to put more wood on the fire and almost immediately the flames leapt higher, hungrily hissing and crackling as they began to devour the new fuel. The darkness pulled back from their little camp and Sidney heard a hiss of frustration followed by a loud gibbering sound and then the rustling noises seemed to melt into the night and a restless quiet fell over the small camp, leaving only the sound of the fire.

Both Sidney and Ahanu remained still until the hum of nocturnal insects started again. With the return of the sounds of the forest, the darkness drew back even further and became less opaque and inky. Sidney sighed heavily in relief.

"What was that?" She whispered. Ahanu shrugged and sat up.

"Whatever it was, it seems that it has gone." His expression was determined and he reached out and pulled a log from the fire, carefully holding it by the unburned end. He stood slowly and raised his makeshift torch over his head. "I will take the next shift. I am going to investigate for a few moments and when I return you should try to get some sleep."

"Are you sure that's a wise idea?" Sidney desperately didn't want him to go out into the darkness; she wasn't sure she'd sleep again. Adrenaline still coursed through her veins, leaving her shaky and her stomach slightly unsettled. "Whatever was out there...was scary."

"I agree." He moved toward the edge of the lit area, the torch creating a small pool of light. "I will remain close, but I think we need to know what was out there. It is gone and I will look for some sign." He stopped and looked over his shoulder at her. "This is the job of a hunter." As he turned and continued to head out into the darkness, Sidney had the urge to call him back.

"I've got a bad feeling about this," she muttered quietly to herself as she watched him walk away until all that was visible was the soft red glow of the torch.

She looked over at Penny, who was sleeping soundly, her chest rising and falling slowly at a tranquil pace. Sidney longed to wake her up—she was such a calming, comforting presence, but she resolved not to give in to that impulse and instead sat back on her rump, pulled her knees up to her chest and hugged them tightly, already wishing Ahanu would come back. She had no idea what she'd do if he didn't return.

A while later he still hadn't returned and there was no sign of the light of his torch. Sidney had begun fretting over what to do shortly after he'd left, and it had seemed to be a self-fulfilling prophecy. Finally she stood up and wiped her hands on her jeans, removing the thin layer of sweat that had accumulated there. She steadied herself and called out softly into the darkness.

"Ahanu?" There was no response and Sidney's stomach fell, doubling the sick sensation there. "Ahanu? Where are you?" Her call was restrained yet urgent and when there was again no response, she decided it was time to do something. She stood quietly and padded over to where Penny slept, knelt down and gently shook her shoulder.

"Penny," she whispered and immediately the girl's eyes fluttered open. For a brief second Penny looked confused but then she sat up and glanced around, alertness flooding into her eyes.

"It's my turn?" Penny sounded muzzy with sleep.

"No, Ahanu is gone."

"What?" Penny immediately sounded completely awake.

Sidney related the tale, starting with the sounds and ending with Ahanu's failure to return to their camp. "I don't know what to do." Penny grimaced and nodded her understanding.

"Well, I guess I'd better go look for him." She began to push herself up. "Wait here, Sid."

"Uh uh, no way. You're not leaving me alone here. What if you don't come back either?"

Penny nodded right away.

"Okay, let's go together." She tossed another log onto the fire to keep it bright, reached down to offer Sidney a hand and helped her to her feet. "So which direction did he go?" Sidney pointed and Penny started off in that direction, walking carefully through the underbrush and natural debris on the forest floor.

"Should we take a torch?" Sidney asked.

"No, I think that will just make it harder to see, I think."

At that moment Ahanu emerged from the surrounding dark, holding the now dead brand down at his side. "Penny, what are you doing up? I have the next watch."

"Sidney woke me when you didn't return. We were just going to look for you. I'm glad you're back. Did you find anything?"

"Some tracks about thirty feet out in that direction." He pointed. "I followed them a ways out, but they just kept going in a straight line away from us. I turned back once I was about ten minutes out. It was hard to find the fire." He grinned sheepishly. "At least until my log finally went out. Then I was able to see the light of it in the distance."

"What sort of tracks?" Penny asked.

"Very small. Nothing I've ever seen before. They looked like people's feet, but the size of a small child. I counted nine different sets of tracks." He looked thoughtfully into the dark, and then broke into a brief grin. "Unless they have more than two feet."

Sidney smiled quickly, walked over to him and gave him a quick hug. "I'm glad you're back—you had me worried." He had a surprised look on his face and then smiled crookedly before returning the hug carefully.

"You two should go get some sleep," he said after Sidney had broken away from him. "It's my watch." They both nodded and returned to where Penny had been sleeping.

"Bah, all that warmth gone already," Penny grumbled and then looked at Sidney, pretending to be irritated. "You're going to have to sleep next to me so I can steal some of your heat, Furnace Girl."

Sidney smiled but was relieved. They nestled close in a small hollow while Ahanu walked the perimeter of their camp and within moments Sidney was asleep despite her lingering fear.

✺

Morning came early, not with the glare of sunlight, but rather with the loud, cheerful sound of birds and the slow rising glow of daylight filtering through the trees, casting a soft light on everything around them. Penny's insistent tugging on Sidney's shoulder woke her up well before she was ready, but confronted by the spectacular beauty around her, she didn't mind.

"Time to get up, sleepyhead. I made breakfast. Fruit!"

"Okay, okay, I'm awake," She grumbled at Penny. Her friend leaned over her smiling brightly. "Have you ever had a bad day?"

Instantly Penny's face fell and she looked away.

"Yes, once." Her voice fell to a whisper. "The day I was born was terrible." Sidney was completely shocked at her reaction and she pushed herself into a sitting position.

"Hey, I'm sorry, Penny." She reached out to take her hand. "I didn't mean anything by it."

Penny took a deep breath and then put her smile back on and turned to Sidney. "It's fine, Sid. Someday I'll tell you about it."

"Okay."

Penny leaned in and gave her a quick hug and then jumped to her feet. Across the dead ashes of their campfire, Ahanu was packing up his various pouches and weapons. Sidney studied him for a quick moment. In his own way he was very like Penny. Guileless and cheerful. But where Penny seemed wild and impish, he was sturdy and duty bound. As if he felt her eyes on him, he looked up and smiled warmly, if a bit shyly.

"Good morning, Sidney. I hope you slept well. Especially after our visitors."

"I slept great. Speaking of our visitors, did they come back?"

"No. No sign of them." He stared out into the depths of the forest. "But my heart tells me we haven't seen the last of them." Abruptly he stood and hefted his spear. "Rub the sleep from your eyes and have some fruit. It is time we started to March again." He grinned at them.

"Walking will be good, Sid," Penny said. "You'll wake up all the way soon enough with some brisk exercise."

Sidney nodded and stood, stretched and grabbed a couple fruits off the ground where they were stacked. "Do you think we should carry the rest of these? In case we don't see any more food?"

Penny nodded.

"Eat those two. We can carry the rest. I'm sure Ahanu will wait long enough for you to eat." She arched an eyebrow at the man and he nodded graciously.

"Of course, Penelope. I was only joking. Though I'd prefer to leave sooner rather than later."

A short time later they were on the move again and Ahanu led them to a trail he'd found. The sun peeked through the canopy every now and again, casting its yellow shine on the forest floor. The streams of light cutting through the gloom were beautiful; Sidney watched for them, scanning the surrounding forest. She came to think of the golden pillars of sunshine as milestones, not measuring distance so much as the flow of her thoughts. Penny kept a running monologue going—every so often she asked questions to draw them in, but for the most part just providing a backdrop of sound and entertaining them all as they travelled. Sidney listened to the melodic rise and fall of her voice more than the actual words and took comfort in the sound.

They walked at a reasonable pace, not too fast and not too slow, winding through the forest, Ahanu leading them along surely as if he had a concrete destination in mind, sometimes down paths and other times across the rough terrain. As the morning coolness faded into humid warmth Sidney stopped and rolled up her sleeves. Penny found a large plate of bark and used it to fan herself as they walked, and lapsed into quiet, letting the thread of her monologue drop.

They came to a narrow stream and the cold water felt like heaven against Sidney's hot skin. She drank some, and dumped more over her head, soaking her shirt.

After she was cooled off and soaked, Sidney found a large rock on the bank to sit on, stripped off her shoes and socks and dangled her feet in the water.

"Well, this is far enough for me," she said. "Whatever is supposed to happen will just have to happen here."

Penny laughed and Ahanu smiled.

"Let's have something to eat while we're here. I could hunt for some meat if you'd like."

"No, it's okay." Sidney thought of her father out there alone somewhere in the Dreamside and suddenly felt desperate to resume looking for him. "We should get moving again soon, I suppose. Fruit will be fine."

"Try these." Penny doled out some sort of tubers she'd found as they'd walked. The thin fibrous roots were surprisingly tasty. They had a slightly salty taste with a slight oniony flavor—a pleasant break from the sweet, juicy fruit that they had been eating since entering the rain forest.

As they ate, Penny and Sidney dangled their feet in the water

"God, this feels wonderful." Penny sighed contentedly.

Ahanu watched for a moment, and then squatted on the ground nearby.

"You should try this, Ahanu." Sidney offered him a piece but he shook his head.

"I am fine." He pitched his voice low and his brow was furrowed in concentration as he listened. Sidney felt a prickle on her neck and cocked her head to listen to the forest around them as well.

"Something is wrong," Penny broke the quiet.

"I feel it, too," Ahanu said.

They listened mutely, each trying to figure out what was bothering them. Suddenly Sidney sat up straight on the rock and pulled her feet out of the water.

"It's too quiet. No sounds of nature. Only the leaves in the breeze."

"Yes." Ahanu's frown deepened. "Something has frightened the forest."

"This is what it sounded like last night before those creatures appeared," Sidney dropped her voice to a whisper. She reached down and pulled her socks on and started tying her shoes. Her feet were still slightly damp but her socks easily absorbed the moisture without getting too wet to wear.

"I think perhaps we should be on our way." Penny stood and Sidney saw the apprehension settled on her face.

"Yes," Ahanu said with a quick nod. He rose to his feet fluidly and stood in a state of readiness, arms bent slightly up, knees unlocked and his eyes moving constantly. He held his spear in his right hand—Sidney had not even seen him pull it out of the strap across his back that he had worn it in while they traveled. His left hand strayed to where his knife was pushed into the waist of his pants. When Penny had finished putting her shoes on, the girls stood up and Ahanu led them away from the stream, continuing in the direction they'd been going. Sidney thought she heard a rustling in the underbrush as they moved out of sight of the water, but when she glanced back she saw nothing besides the wind gently blowing the leaves and blades of the bushes to and fro. She picked up her pace until she was close behind Penny.

Over the next hour, the rustling sound came and went and at one point she thought she heard the rasping whispers behind them. When she looked back there was never anything to see. Eventually Ahanu noticed her and looked at her questioningly.

"Do you see something, Sidney?" Ahanu didn't break his stride.

"No, But I could swear I keep hearing noises behind us."

Ahanu glanced back again, this time past her, inspecting the forest behind them and he had a grim expression on his face.

"We must move faster." He picked up the pace slightly and Sidney and Penny followed.

Abruptly Ahanu stopped and Penny pulled to the side to avoid crashing into him. Sidney was not so lucky and tripped and sprawled to her knees at his side.

"You!" he gasped. "I remain true to my word—I have my honor. I know my duty." He said the last words in a ritualistic tone as if they were words of great importance. Sidney started to push herself to her feet.

"Colin?" Sidney heard the shock in Penny's voice and she rose and stared past Ahanu into the forest ahead of them. About twenty yards down the trail was her father, kneeling on the ground.

"Dad?" she stood frozen for a heartbeat—a tidal wave of elation washing over her—and then began to run toward him.

"Sidney!" Penny shouted behind her. "Stop!" Sidney came to a halt and looked closer at her father. He was slightly translucent—in places actually transparent, and his hands were bound before him. He seemed to be floating about three inches over the ground and when he looked up his face was bruised and his lip bloodied.

"Sid?" he rasped. "Is that really you?"

"Dad!" she cried out and reached for him, but her hand passed right through him.

"Sid." His voice was rough and pain was evident in his expression. "You have to run, honey. Run as fast as you can. They are coming and they are getting closer."

"Who?" She found she was unable to process what he was saying. "Who is coming?"

"No questions, Sid. Run!" He looked past her at Penny. "Penny, run! Now! Do not look back." As he spoke the words, he began to fade away, but before he was completely gone Sidney saw him look past her shoulder and an expression of utter horror crossed his features.

Then he was gone. Sidney froze, the shock of his disappearance rendering her unable to move. Penny grabbed her arm and started dragging her into a run. Ahanu sprinted past and cut off through the brush.

"This way," he yelled over his shoulder. "Stay close."

As Sidney broke into a run, she heard something crashing through the bushes behind her and the forest was filled with piercing shrieks and growls. She didn't dare look back, but concentrated on putting her feet in safe places so as not to trip. Immediately ahead of her Penny ran full out, gracefully loping through the brush. The noises behind her were getting closer, and Penny slowed enough for Sidney to catch up.

"Hurry, Sid." Penny's breath was coming short and fast. Sidney put on a burst of speed, but she knew she couldn't manage to keep this pace for long. She was running full speed, just hoping that her feet would find solid ground and keep her up.

But it was not to be. Almost simultaneously Penny and Sidney tripped over a log that hid under the brush, and they sprawled through the growth, rolling and sliding to a halt. Penny scrambled to her feet and reached to pull Sidney up, but before she did, a flood of small forms emerged from the trees and spread out around them, encircling them and cutting off escape. Penny pulled Sidney to her feet and faced the creatures that had them surrounded.

The forest was silent again as the creatures watched them excitedly. Sidney got her first look at them. They were tiny people—the tallest was roughly three feet tall. Their bodies were well proportioned and they were strong and wiry. They had the palest white skin and their hair was dirty blonde, long and hanging lankly down the sides of faces that were round and full of bestial malevolence—small beady eyes, wide long mouths, and most disturbing, their teeth. Each small mouth was opened to expose sharp triangular teeth, pointed on the ends and serrated on the sides almost like a shark's teeth. They carried tiny spears and feather-adorned breastplates that appeared to be made of rows of bones tied with leather strips —they almost looked like tiny washboards. Other than the armor, they wore only loincloths.

"What are they?" Sidney asked, panting heavily.

"Soul eaters," Penny said with a shudder. "Nasty little things. I have seen them in other parts of the Dreamside. They aren't something that we created—someone put them here."

"What's so nasty about them? I mean, aside from all that ugly?"

"They eat people."

"Eat people?" Sidney grimaced.

"Eat people. And not the flesh. They eat souls. You don't die—you are simply ripped out of the fabric of the world as if you'd never even existed."

"That's...awful." Sidney slowly turned, trying to keep her eyes on all of them at once.

Then one waved a spear, jabbing it at them and spoke to the others. Its voice was rasping and croaking, and Sidney didn't recognize the language it spoke. Several other creatures snarled and jabbed their spears as well, and took a slow step forward. The one that had spoken first stood up straight and faced the girls. It spoke in its gravelly voice and gestured with its spear again.

Sidney glanced over at Penny and saw that the girl had dropped into a defensive crouch. She shrugged back at Sidney without taking her eyes away from the creatures, panning around to scan all around them.

"What did it say?" Sidney whispered. "Where is Ahanu?"

"I don't know. He probably didn't see or hear us fall."

"God, I hope he comes back."

Before Penny could speak again, the speaker shrieked and spoke again in that rasping, guttural language. It raised the spear over its head and pointed at Sidney with the other hand. Sidney raised her hands slowly palms facing out.

The speaker waited for something, and Sidney realized it was waiting for her to answer whatever question it had asked. She shook her head slowly.

"I do not understand." Sidney enunciated each syllable carefully. Behind her Penny giggled shortly.

"Sorry, Sid. You just reminded me of the person who talks louder to a deaf person. Like volume is going to make them able to hear unexpectedly."

In any other circumstances Sidney would have laughed back, but at the moment she was terrified. A part of her wished the little thing had spoken to Penny instead—Penny always seemed to know what to do. Sidney had no idea.

The creature rasped at her again and strode forward with its spear leveled at her. It jabbed the sharp point at her and mimed putting its hands together. Sidney realized it wanted her to put her hands together so she did, wrist to wrist. The creature gestured angrily to the others and immediately three stepped forward and strode toward her. She saw that they held rope in their hands and she took a panicked step backwards.

"No way." Sidney's fear turned to anger in the space of a heartbeat. "You're not tying me up, you little monsters."

The three that were advancing stopped and glanced at the speaker. He gestured furiously at Sidney and shrieked something. All around the circle the rest of the creatures began to slowly advance, their spears leveled at the girls. The three that bore rope stood ready but waiting for Sidney to put out her hands again.

"This is so not going to happen, Penny." She gritted her teeth, her body tensed.

"Okay. Perhaps we should play football then."

"Football?"

"Punt the little beasties."

A nervous burst of laughter bubbled out of Sidney, humor combining with her growing rage. She could still feel the fear in the background but now it didn't rule her.

"On three, let's charge the loud one." Penny sounded grim yet determined and Sidney took strength from her.

"One, two..." Before Penny reached three, there was a loud shout and several high pitched shrieks. Sidney spun around and saw Ahanu yanking his spear out of the body of one of the little men. Their guide bared his teeth in a feral snarl and the rest of the creatures stared at him in shock. As he turned to stab at another one, Sidney saw that there were already two on the ground; one was dragging itself painfully away and the other was lying still in a pool of blood. Ahanu roared his rage again and drove his spear at another creature. The thing skipped back out of range and hissed at him. The rest of them all turned their weapons toward Ahanu and began to stalk forward.

Ahanu sank into a defensive stance and turned to point his spear at the closest, driving them back slightly, while others advanced. Sidney didn't think he would be able to hold them all off. He muttered to himself and this time she caught his words: "I have my honor. I know my duty. My word is given." Then he shouted over his shoulder. "Run! I will delay them. Go to the path and turn right, and do not look back. Run, now!" He slashed his spear at another of the closest creatures and it stepped back, hissing at him.

Sidney and Penny both broke into a sprint, passing out of reach of the closest of the little men and crashing through the underbrush. Sidney didn't look back, and searched wildly for a path, but she could see nothing ahead of them. She could hear the snarls and shrieks of the soul eaters as they attacked Ahanu. Her heart sank as she ran. She couldn't imagine that he was going to survive—he'd given his life for them to escape. Then against all odds she heard his voice behind them but not close.

"Veer right, Sidney. Right!" Ahanu's voice was commanding and she immediately obeyed and within a few strides burst through some particularly thick foliage and found herself on a path. She didn't slow down but turned down the path. She heard the sound of bodies crashing through the same growth and then the pounding of feet on the path behind her. She risked a quick glance back and saw that Penny was right behind her and Ahanu farther back. Before she turned her eyes back to the path, she caught a glimpse of the soul eaters flooding onto the path. They weren't falling behind, she realized, and the panic began to return. She had no idea how they managed to keep pace with them, with shorter legs.

"Sid," Penny said. "Eyes on the path. Run hard."

Sidney obeyed and put on a burst of speed. Ahead of her the forest seemed to grow brighter and a few strides later she saw the glare of sunlight through the trees. Then she burst out of the trees and into a vast ocean of sand. The abrupt change from packed dirt ground to loose, shifting sand made her to lose her balance and her feet slid out from under her. She put a hand down to catch herself and managed to come to a halt in a three point stance like a human tripod. She spun and looked back and saw that Penny was also floundering in the sand.

"Don't stop, Sid," Penny sounded frustrated. Sidney looked beyond her and saw Ahanu burst through the trees. He had one of the soul eaters on his back, hanging tenaciously from his neck, its shark teeth buried in his shoulder. Ahanu's face was a mask of pain as he shot out into the sand and rolled toward her. The little creature flipped off his shoulder and landed in the sand a few feet away and immediately started writhing and shrieking. Its skin began to smoke and hiss and while Sidney watched it melted away, flowing into a red and black pile of gore and bubbling in the sand.

She stared at the little mess it had left behind, and then back at the forest's edge. The rest of the soul eaters had run past the trees, but were carefully staying in shadow. Penny had turned when Ahanu crashed into the sand and now stood with her mouth hanging open in surprise.

"The sun," Sidney gasped. "They burn up in the sunlight."

"They still have their spears." Ahanu pushed himself up. No sooner had he spoken then the small spears—each one closer in size to a javelin—began to land around them in the sand. Sidney turned and ran further into the sand, moving out of range. She turned and put her hands on her knees and waited for Penny and Ahanu to catch up. Penny had an arm around him and was supporting him as they struggled toward her. Sidney strode forward and helped him on the other side and then they all slumped to the ground to catch their breath.

Sidney sat facing the edge of the forest, and saw the small creatures jumping and shrieking at them, but carefully staying out of the sun.

"Little bastards." She rasped and tried to catch her breaths. Then she turned to Ahanu. Penny was inspecting his shoulder. "How bad is it?"

"Not terrible. As long as it doesn't get infected, it will be fine." Penny grinned at Ahanu quickly. "I bet it hurts like hell, though." Ahanu grimaced and gave a short nod.

"It is not pleasant."

Penny sat back and pulled her shirt off over her head quickly, exposing her bra. Ahanu's eyes widened and for a brief moment he stared. When he realized he was staring he quickly looked away. Penny shot Sidney a grin and then started tearing off a strip of cloth from the bottom of her shirt. Once she had it, she pulled her shirt back on.

"Okay, Ahanu, you can turn back around." He did so and stared at her as she began to wrap his shoulder with the cloth.

"Penelope. You should warn me when you are going to remove your clothes so that I might marshal my stare."

"Didn't like what you saw, Ahanu?" She teased while concentrating on the wound.

"It is not that. You are indeed well formed and...attractive."

"Thanks." She grinned at him. "I've never had anyone say I was well formed."

Sidney snickered and Ahanu's blush deepened.

"Forgive me. I am not skilled at speaking to women of their beauty. You are both beautiful women; my tongue just doesn't know how to say it correctly."

"Actually that was quite nice," Penny said. Her brow had furrowed in concentration and then she muttered under her breath. "I probably should show them to you again right now..."

"Why?" His discomfort was obvious and Sidney was fairly certain that the wound wasn't what was making him uncomfortable and she had to grin.

"To distract you..."

"Distract me from what?" He wore his confusion on his face.

"This," she said and pulled the makeshift bandage tight. His face tightened in pain and he gave a slight gasp. Then he got himself under control and his face went blank. He looked at the ground in front of him until the pain faded and then he looked up at Penny.

"Ow."

Penny and Sidney both burst into laughter, and Penny leaned forward and gave him a quick kiss on the cheek.

At the forest's edge, the soul eaters had finally ceased their noise and began to turn back and disappear into the trees. The leader was the last to go and it raised its spear toward the three travelers and growled angrily in its harsh language and then vanished.

Part 4: A Meeting of the Mind

Salient and Argot

Colin woke abruptly, driven violently into consciousness by waves of pain and nausea. He gasped at the sudden shock of the transition from silent nothingness to crippling agony that spread from his left eye to his temple. For a while, how long he couldn't say, he simply lay on the ground, eyes shut, hoping that the pain would recede. Even behind his eyelids the world was brightly lit and his strong desire to see his surroundings warred with the sure knowledge that the brightness was going to hurt like hell. For the time being, the threat of more pain won out.

Finally he thought that the waves of pain were ebbing—though it was possible that he was just getting used to it.

At least it's not getting worse.

He hated this. He felt vulnerable being prone on the ground with his eyes closed, no hint of what or who might be nearby—and that finally drove him to crack his eyelids. That was a mistake—the searing bright light twisted the pain in his head up and his stomach roiled, his mouth began to water and the first jerking gags seized him. He rolled over onto his side just as the contents of his stomach came up, riding cramping waves of peristalsis up and out onto the ground beside him, in the cool, dark green grass.

While his stomach emptied itself convulsively, the pain in Colin's head faded slightly into the background—his body focusing on the more immediate sensations. He heaved over and over, his body curling into a tight knot with each wave. Finally, after his stomach was empty and he'd dry heaved a few times the nausea fled, leaving him cold and shaking. He had the most exquisite moment of pure relief, but that was rudely shattered as the pain in his head rose again to a fever pitch.

He pushed himself away from half digested remains of his last meal—pizza, he thought dimly—rolled gingerly onto his back again, and folded his arms across his head to hide his eyes from the light. But he kept them open and waited until they had adjusted enough that he could slowly look around.

He lay in the middle of a huge field. The grass was short cut, lush and dark green. At any other time he would have a strong urge to take off his shoes and socks and wiggle his toes in the grass. As it was, it was just another intrusive color that assaulted his mind. Off to his left there were a few well-tended flower gardens, and a path meandered across the field nearby. Everything was well tended and manicured—there was no hint of true wildness here—a park.

For a while he just stayed on the ground, waiting to see if he was going to be sick again, and if the headache was going to recede any time soon. The nausea didn't return—the throbbing pain in his head had his full attention, and it seemed to be getting worse, if such a thing were even possible. Colin had always believed that there was some sort of ceiling on pain—a maximum level that pain could register—but now he wasn't convinced. Every time he thought he'd finally reached that plateau, another sharp spike drove the pain higher. He knew he was going to pass out soon. Or die.

That thought struck fear into him—not because he didn't want to die, so much as that he'd be leaving Sidney alone. As she came into his thoughts, the memory of where he'd been before here flooded back to him: the subway, the zombies and most graphically, the murkshifter pursuing them down the rails. He had the sudden memory of the ground disappearing and then nothing more until he woke to this pain. It was hard to hold onto these things though—the pain was all consuming —but he concentrated on Sidney and Penny. There was a thought that drove right through the pain. They might still be in trouble. Or, God forbid, dead. He thought back to the Wall telling him that when you were fully in the Dreamside whatever happened to you there stayed with you into the waking world. Death included.

At that thought, terror and panic overwhelmed him, racing through his mind and down into his body, on a flood of adrenaline and endorphins. He gasped at the violent transition—the pain was shoved back by the chemicals his brain had released, leaving him with burning, twisting fear. He couldn't catch his breath, and his pulse raced out of control. He wondered if the girls had escaped the murkshifter, but there was no way of knowing and his subconscious mind flashed horrible images and fears at him. He forced his thoughts back onto a safer path—he had to believe they were all right, that they'd gotten away and were safe. If the worst had happened then he was already dead—just waiting for it to catch up with him. He had to think they were safe. Anything else was madness.

Probably wondering where I've gone. As distressing as that line of thought was, it helped him begin to get hold of himself.

He decided that while the pain was in the background he should make some attempt to move—to find help or the girls or well, who knew what else he might find. He realized dimly that he could feel his arm again—the numbness from the tunnel had faded away completely. That was one good thing, he supposed. He rolled over slowly until he was on his stomach, pushed his hands underneath his torso and used them to lever up onto his hands and knees. The world tilted madly and he froze until it settled enough for him to sit up on his knees and look around.

The field was surrounded by woods—tall trees and heavy undergrowth butted right up against the edge of its well-groomed border. The division created a startling contrast, as if wild and tame met at a hard, well-defined line, and the path meandered artfully across the field to disappear into the woods. He looked above and beyond the trees and in every direction he saw large skyscrapers reaching to touch the sky.

He had an urgent feeling something was missing. He listened carefully as the soft, cool breeze ruffled the grass around him. It was quiet. Far too quiet. There were none of the sounds he expected in an urban park: traffic faint beyond the boundaries of the park, people, dogs barking—nothing. He looked around and saw that there were no people. He was completely alone in this urban oasis. It was deeply creepy in a post-apocalyptic way. He almost expected to see tumbleweeds rolling across the park.

He wondered if this were another dream with no people, like Sidney's village. On the heels of that thought, a pair of figures emerged from the woods along the path, heading toward him at a slow jog.

A pair of young women all decked out in standard running gear: mid-thigh tight fitting running pants, sports bra—one bright green and the other blue—and flashy running shoes. He felt irrational relief as he watched their progress in his direction along the path.

He still wasn't ready to move so he sat still and waited for them. He concentrated on breathing slowly and pushing the pain in his head away. He didn't have much luck with his head, although the pain did seem to ease slightly. Even that tiny bit of relief felt wonderful and he began to feel hopeful about the injury. With any luck, and given his track record with dream injuries, perhaps he was already healing.

The runners were closing on him quickly now, talking to one another loudly and concentrating on the path. For a brief moment it looked as though they wouldn't even notice him— would just run right by. He took a breath to call out but before he uttered a sound, one of the women glanced his way, saw him and startled to the side, almost colliding with her partner. She gestured toward Colin, speaking in a low voice to the other woman, and both slowed to a walk, stepped off the sidewalk and walked toward him.

As they approached, he was able to see them more clearly; they looked young, healthy and energetic. Attractive as well. The one who had noticed him first had long strawberry blonde hair pulled back tidily in a pony tail. Her skin was fair and dotted with light freckles over the bridge of her nose. Her mouth was kind, and her eyes were friendly and Colin didn't feel threatened by her at all. There was a touch of something that made him think of Penny. Just a hint of the same friendly nature.

The other woman had brown hair that was cut short in a practical yet fashionable style. Colin couldn't put a name to it, but it framed her face nicely. Full lips with a natural pout didn't detract from her large grey eyes. They were light grey and startling against her darker complexion. She studied him with a suspicious expression and stood back with her arms crossed.

The freckled one smiled at him tentatively and spoke.

"Bath tub millionaire, speedboat index." Her voice was low and soothing.

Colin frowned slightly in confusion. He tried to push himself to his feet, but his head throbbed painfully and his vision spotted so he settled back, down and gave them a quick wave.

"Shampoo creature." It took a moment before he realized those weren't the words he was trying to say. He tried again. "Shampoo festival violins." Frustrated, he shook his head, sending further waves of pain through him, and his vision spun. When it cleared he was lying on his back, and the two women had moved closer.

The dark-skinned woman no longer looked suspicious as she knelt beside him. Instead she wore an expression of intense, clinical interest mixed with the concern a health care worker might express to a patient. It was clear that she was a doctor or a nurse or something. He knew he was in good hands.

She was careful not to touch him and still maintained a little space, but the other woman knelt on the other side of him, much closer.

"Bigger cell phone adjustment have book?" she asked and Colin just stared at her helplessly.

"Bigger house." He felt the same sinking feeling. "Lofty ideals granulated sugar steps." Both women looked alarmed and the one kneeling near him held both hands out in a placating gesture.

"Lofty ideals granulated sugar steps." He stopped and put his head down into his hands and a quick sob escaped him. "Lofty ideals. Football."

Colin felt a tentative hand on his shoulder. The touch surprised him and he dropped his hands and looked up into the face of the pale skinned one. She had scooted in close enough to touch him comfortingly. As their eyes met he shrugged helplessly and she smiled reassuringly. She settled back onto her bottom, folded her legs in front of her and pointed at her chest.

"Salient." Then she turned and pointed at the other woman. "Argot." She cocked her head at him slightly, waiting to see if he understood her and he shook his head slowly at her.

I don't know.

"Salient!" He wondered what it meant but when he said the words the woman smiled again and nodded with a quick shrug. "Argot." His voice dropped to a mutter, but she grinned even wider. He felt like a parrot repeating sounds back mindlessly. Her friend said something and both women laughed loudly, but she turned back to him and patted his shoulder again.

Names, he realized. Those were their names, as incomprehensible as all the other words they were saying. He wasn't going to know their names so Salient she would be. A laugh escaped him but there was a slightly hysterical edge to it. Both women smiled and laughed with him.

Humor the madman, he thought wryly. He pointed at his own chest and tried to say his name very slowly.

"Corn fed." He sighed and shook his head.

"Reverberate." *Salient pointed at Colin. He laughed softly and the sound contained a hint of mania as humor warred with panic, coming to an uneasy stalemate.*

This is like a really twisted game of telephone.

She stood up and took a small step back, then gestured for him to stand as well. He slowly pushed to his feet, carefully stopping a few times to let his head clear. The throbbing pain was making his vision swim again and he staggered once, but Salient stepped closer, grabbed one of his arms and helped him stay standing.

"Retro sand burn?"

"Foaming sand monster." He gritted his teeth in frustration. He closed his eyes for a moment to regain some composure and when he opened them he pointed to his head and didn't speak this time.

"Tempestuous." Salient pointed at her own head.

Yes, decidedly tempestuous.

Behind her, Argot approached slowly and stood next to her. She pointed at her own chest. "Argot."

He shrugged and shook his head slightly.

She nodded as if she'd expected it. She was suddenly businesslike as she stepped close to him, and held a finger in front of his face about a foot away. She gestured at him and moved her finger back and forth. Then she looked at him to see if he understood. He nodded.

I'm not stupid; I just can't understand your words.

He carefully schooled his face not to show his frustration.

Argot moved her finger back and forth and he followed it easily. Then she moved in closer and started to reach for his face, and then stopped abruptly and studied his face.

"Hamster flow." Her voice had become quiet and almost absent. Clinical. She frowned slightly and then pointed at Salient, and took her by the arm and pulled her close. "Circumspect." She demonstrated pulling back one of Salient's eyelids and looked closely at her exposed eye. Salient gave a short snicker, and Argot turned to see if he understood. He nodded and gestured to his own eyes, opened them wide and leaned toward her slightly. She gently put a thumb on his top eyelid and pulled it up, all the while talking in soft soothing tones. She studied his eyes one at a time and leaned in close. He could smell her breath, minty and fresh, she was so close. Then she pursed her lips and backed away slightly.

This time she put her hands on her own temples and rubbed in small slow circles. Then she arched an eyebrow at him questioningly and he nodded. She slowly put a hand on each of his temples. She closed her eyes and he immediately felt a coolness flow through the front of his head, and the pain eased back to a more manageable level. After a minute or so she removed her hands and glanced down at them. She looked surprised but pointed at his head and cocked her own slightly to the side.

Colin slowly moved his head from side to side, up and down through the full range of motion that his neck allowed. While it still hurt, there was no additional pain when he moved and the heavy throb had turned into an annoying headache. In contrast with the pain he was more than glad to deal with the little headache. He nodded gratefully. She smiled and pointed at his mouth, then mimed talking.

"Retrograde flatulence." Colin grimaced as the words came out.

Argot didn't look especially surprised and nodded resignedly. Then Salient turned slightly and pointed at the path and mimed walking with her fingers. Colin couldn't think of any reason not to go with them so he shrugged and nodded. She led the way to the path, and they set off the way the women had been going.

The path led them across the wide field and into another stretch of woodland. It was dark and gloomy, but the coolness was soothing, and he sensed nothing threatening. As they walked, Argot and Salient spoke constantly, at first trying to include him, but after a few attempts settled into conversing with each other. For his part, Colin made no effort to listen to their words, and his frustration gave way to a despondent resignation. He couldn't handle losing his ability to communicate; language was the tool of his trade—he was supposed to be good with words and ideas. Expressing himself. It scared him more than the thought of losing his hearing. Or a limb.

Periodically Salient would reach over to pat his shoulder and give him a reassuring smile, but she rarely spoke to him. She seemed to know instinctively that he was fighting off panic, and rather than poking at the wound repeatedly, she settled for using gestures, facial expressions and small touches to communicate with him. It was rudimentary, but he began to feel slightly less isolated and cut off. Every now and then he would forget and try to speak and his frustration would return.

Colin walked slightly behind them and wondered where they were going, and how far—how long it would take them to get there. Salient and Argot looked as if they were young professionals starting their day off with an early morning run. He suspected that Argot was a doctor or nurse. He imagined Salient as some sort of therapist. She seemed adept at gauging his mood and reactions.

To Colin, they seemed to walk the better part of the day without reaching an exit from the park back into the metropolitan area. They passed through copses, larger stretches of forest and well-groomed parklands, always sticking to the edged and trimmed path. They never seemed to get any closer to the tall buildings that pushed up above the trees all around the park. Colin was bothered by the fact that neither Argot nor Salient seemed to really even notice the strange quality of their journey. He tried to gauge how long they walked by watching the sun, but it never moved—always hanging just above the tree line, its light filtered through the skyscrapers. When he pointed to the sun and spoke pointlessly to the women, they both looked confused and regretful. He gave up and went back to the task of not dwelling on where Sidney and Penny might be. He could do nothing about that now.

I can't do much about anything.

Finally they emerged from a wooded stretch into a grassy open area that looked just like all the other ones they'd walked through and the women walked off the path slightly and sat down. Colin sat down as well and Salient shot him a friendly smile. Argot kept looking at him like he was going to jump up at any moment and start raving, and to be quite honest, he had to admit that he had moments where that seemed the right thing to do. His emotions swept back and forth between anger and despair like a metronome keeping time. For the most part, he managed to hide it from them—or so he hoped. From the quick, worried glances Salient shot him when she didn't think he was looking, he wasn't sure he was succeeding.

For a while no one spoke. After about fifteen minutes they stood up and Salient offered him a hand. When he took it, she helped pull him to his feet and pointed at his head questioningly. He realized with surprise that his headache had faded away at some point. He nodded and gave her the thumbs up. She smiled.

Colin turned to Argot and spoke.

"Retired postman." When he'd been a teenager he'd had a friend who was deaf, and while the girl could read lips she'd still taught him some rudimentary sign language. He'd forgotten most of it when they fell out of touch after high school, but he still remembered the sign for thank you. He gave the sign and Argot gave him a wide smile and nodded in return. Then the women turned and headed down the path they'd been on, Salient giving Colin a quick wave to follow them. So they moved back into the relative darkness of the woods and continued traveling.

By the time they rested again he was absolutely dying to ask them where they were going. It didn't seem to him that they were making any progress, and he was beginning to feel exhausted. Finally he stopped and spoke.

"Allied intervention airport." Colin stopped abruptly as his frustration ignite into fury. "God damn it this is maddening!" he yelled and both women turned to him quickly with shock on their faces.

Salient walked over, put a hand on his shoulder and spoke excitedly, but as before, the words she said made no sense to him.

"Grocery store apple cart." He sat down abruptly and stared at the grass in front of him, trying to figure out why he'd been able to say that sentence intelligibly for a change, and why he couldn't do it again.

Argot had stepped up near him and settled into a crouch, she spoke again and reached for his face slowly and felt his brow. Her hand was cool and soft on his forehead. There was something so comforting about her touch that he closed his eyes and calmed, his muscles one by one unwinding and relaxing. He hadn't realized how completely tense he was until he felt the tension flowing out of him. He wasn't sure how long he sat there with his eyes closed but eventually when he opened them he was lying on his back. He realized he'd fallen asleep. He heard the women whispering quietly nearby.

"How long have I been asleep?" He struggled to sit up. Both women looked around at him in shock.

"He did it again, Jill," Argot said. She turned herself around and scooted over toward him. "Can you understand me?"

Colin's heart flip flopped as he realized he could.

"Raindrops ergonomic recipe." Excitement and hope soured into frustration. He absolutely hated this. Argot spoke again and her words had retreated into a meaningless jumble. Colin's frustration quickly turned into anger and then into a seething rage.

I will not let this go on. He gritted his teeth and tried again.

"Flamingo based plastic...Flamingo based hate this... Flamingo I hate this," he closed his eyes and concentrated on the words. "God, I hate this."

"Wow, that's amazing," Argot said. "I've never seen anyone work through this sort of thing so fast before." She leaned in toward Colin again. "Can you understand us?"

"Oh, God. Yes, I can understand you. Oh, thank God."

"He speaks." Salient smiled warmly.

"How do you feel?" Argot asked, putting her hand on his forehead. "Hold still."

"I feel deeply relieved." He knew that his bark of laughter sounded manic. "That was utterly horrifying. You can't imagine how scary that was." Argot took his wrist and checked his pulse, and then she checked his eyes again. "What happened to me?"

"You suffered, very briefly, from a condition called aphasia. It is essentially the loss of language. In some cases the patient cannot understand other people but can speak fine. In other cases the patient can understand other people but cannot speak. You had a full blown case. You must have really banged your head. But I have to say I've never seen anyone recover so quickly and suddenly. How does your head feel now?"

"It feels much better." He felt giddy with relief and he smiled stupidly at her. "Thank you so much. I have no idea what you did back there, but thank you." For a moment she looked slightly confused but seemed to put it aside and focused on him.

"What's your name?" Salient asked.

"Colin. Colin Pierce."

"Well, I'm Jillian," she said with a friendly smile. "And the one with no bedside manner is Pamela." Colin felt a laugh bubbling up and when it burst forth he found that he couldn't stop laughing. He hugged his arms around his midsection and the laughter just came and came. Jillian looked surprised but then laughed with him. After a few moments Pamela gave a somewhat reluctant chuckle and then she too was laughing. Colin fell onto his side laughing so hard that his eyes were tearing and he was gasping for breath.

"Oh, shit," he said when he finally managed to catch his breath. "Shit."

"Okay, I love a good laugh as much as the next person." Salient—no, Jillian's laughter settled into an amused smile. "But what are we laughing at?"

"Your names." Another bubble of laughter escaped. Pamela arched an eyebrow.

"What wrong with our names?" She folded her arms across her chest.

"No, no. Nothing is wrong with them. They're lovely. Perfect." He took deep breaths to stifle the laughter that threatened to return. "But when you tried to tell me your names, you told me you were Salient and Argot"

"Oh yeah? Which was my name?"

"You're Salient."

"What's that mean?"

"Prominent."

"Important! Noticeable!" Jillian grinned.

"Striking," Colin added. She was really easy to talk to now that he understood her. "Pertinent."

"Obtrusive," Pamela said with a snort and they all laughed. "So what does argot mean?"

"No idea."

"Well, I'll just assume it means something really great until I can look it up. You must have taken quite a blow to the head. Did someone attack you? You were just lying there in the middle of the park by yourself."

"I fell."

"Yeah, I've heard that one before. Usually from abused women." There was a hint of sarcasm in her voice. "There wasn't anything out there hard enough for you injure your head that way. You were lying in the grass."

"No, really. I fell. It's hard to explain."

"Well, maybe you could try?" Jillian's voice was still friendly.

Colin took a deep breath and rubbed the bridge of his nose.

"This is going to sound so stupid." He looked up and met their eyes one at a time. "I fell out of the sky." They both just stared at him. "The last thing I remember I was running down the subway with Penny and Sidney—that's my daughter and our neighbor. Anyway, we were running down the subway tracks trying to get away from...well, we were running and I fell into a hole. I hit my head on the edge of the hole and when I woke up I was in the grass where you found me." He stopped and looked at Jillian. She just stared back at him, a hint of confusion on her face and her brow furrowed slightly.

"You fell in a hole and landed in the park." Pamela said in a flat voice. "Do you take us for idiots?" She pushed herself to her feet. "Listen, if you don't want to tell us, that's your business. But don't treat me like I'm a hayseed at the state fair."

"No, wait, listen to me." He stood as well, and half reached for her, stopping himself before touching her arm. "Haven't you noticed anything strange today?"

"Like what?" Jillian asked.

"Like where were we going?"

"We were taking you to the hospital." Pamela wasn't hiding her exasperation at all.

"Okay, so where is the hospital?" he asked.

Pamela started to respond but then she stopped and looked mildly confused. "It's just outside the park. We work there."

"How long do you think we were walking in the park after you found me?"

Neither of the women answered. Jillian was still frowning and Pamela had a shocked expression on her face. Both of them were starting to look like deer caught in headlights.

"I don't know what time it was when you found me, but we walked for a damned long time and from what I can tell we haven't gone anywhere. The sun has never moved in the sky." He turned and pointed to the sun, and they both looked.

"Fuck." Jillian whispered.

"And where are all the other people? I haven't seen anyone else all day."

Jillian met Colin's eyes. "What's going on?"

After a pause he answered her.

"You're dreaming."

"Dreaming?" Pamela sounded incredulous. "This can't be a dream. It's too real. We're on our morning run. We run through the park every day before we go in to work."

"I'd say you're going to be a bit late." Colin didn't blame her for not believing. He knew he wouldn't have believed—*hadn't* believed at first.

"Are you real?" Jillian was hesitant. "I mean, if I'm dreaming, then you two are just a part of my dream, right?"

"No, we're all real. You are both trapped in a dream." Colin had no idea how or why but they'd been drawn into the dream as completely as he was. One thing he did know was that it wasn't safe for them here.

"How can that be? That makes no sense." Pamela put her hands on her hips. "Dreams take place in our minds when we are sleeping. Electrical impulses." She frowned and leaned toward him with a hint of disbelieving belligerence. Colin put his hands up in front of him, to placate her.

"I know how crazy it sounds. I'm not sure I'd believe it either if I didn't already know."

"Well, I guess I believe that I'm dreaming. But I simply can't put any stock in the idea that we're all together in the same dream."

"If you believe you're dreaming that's enough for now. But you've got to be careful here, whether you believe me or not." He raised a single finger to forestall any interruption. "This is important. Very important. Dreams can be extremely dangerous if you are here in the flesh—if you are hurt in this dream, you will wake to the same injuries." Colin was struck by how odd it felt to be explaining what he didn't really understand himself.

Pam crossed her arms under her breasts and rolled her eyes.

"Why is that?" Jillian asked.

"Normally when we dream, our minds, or even just a small part of our minds travel to another place. It is known as the Dreamside. On very rare occasions people come into the dream fully—bodies and all. Back in the waking world your beds are empty." It struck him then how entirely he'd embraced what he was explaining now to them—only a day or so ago he'd been listening to the same explanations from the Wall.

"Wow."

"Yeah. So just be careful, okay?"

There was a moment's silence while Jillian mulled it over.

"Well, of course we'll be careful," Pamela said. "I'm not sure I can accept what you're saying. I mean, it's not that I don't want to...it's just really hard to wrap my head around."

"So just humor me." He tried for a reassuring smile but got wry instead. "I have a head injury, right? I'm probably suffering from some mental disorder. But whatever the case, please just be careful."

They both nodded.

"Humor the madman, gotcha." Pam smiled slightly. "I'm not a psychiatrist, but I can give you a referral if you'd like." She gestured at Jillian.

A therapist. I was right.

"Well, I must admit," Jillian said. "Normally this is where I'd be talking about the completeness of your delusion and discussing courses of treatment—maybe even a stay at a facility where we could work together more efficiently." She paused for a moment and looked at him carefully. "But for some reason...I don't think you're crazy. I don't know what to think about all this," she gestured vaguely around them. "For whatever reason it's hard to discount this as something in my mind."

Colin snorted a brief laugh. "It might be easier to pretend I'm insane." He was relieved that she at least was willing to believe what he said, at some level.

"So what next?" Jillian asked.

"Well, honestly, I don't know. We seem to be caught in some kind of...loop. I think we should start looking for a way out of the park. I don't know if there's anything out in the city, but deviating from the plan might snap us out of here." He looked them each in the eyes. "And you both should work on waking up."

"How do we do that?"

He shrugged. "I'm not sure. Just...try."

Jillian cocked her head for a second then pinched her arm. "Well, that didn't work."

"I think it's more an exercise of convincing yourself you're asleep and deciding to wake up. Just like you would in any dream. Usually when I dream normally, if I become aware that I am dreaming it becomes harder to hold onto the dream, and I wake up soon after. That might just be me, and I'm not sure that it even applies when you're here completely." He shrugged. "It's worth a shot."

"Okay," Pam said. "I'll try...but what about you?"

"I can't wake up."

"Why not?" Jillian asked.

"Because I'm not asleep. I came here while awake."

"How'd you do that?"

"Who knows." He grimaced. "It's something I can do, I guess. And even if I could leave, I wouldn't. My daughter and our friend are trapped in another dream somewhere and I've got to reach them."

"Are they in the dream fully, too?" Pam asked.

"Yes, we came together. We're on a quest, of sorts. Wow. That sounds really silly."

"A quest?" Jillian scooted closer. "What sort of quest?"

"I think I've gotten ahead of myself," he said after a moment's hesitation. "Let me start from the beginning. You both deserve to know everything I can tell you. We might as well sit and get comfortable. It's a fairly long story." They all sat down. Jillian wrapped her arms around her knees and leaned forward slightly, and Pamela sat cross legged.

"So I guess the story really starts when I was fifteen years old..." He spoke for a long time, relating his story and every now and then one of the women would interrupt to ask a question. Both of them concentrated on his story as he spoke. Finally when he was done he looked at them. Jillian appeared thoughtful, a slight furrow on her brow and her eyes turned inward. Pamela looked slightly skeptical, as he expected she would, but she too looked thoughtful.

"Well, I have to tell you, Colin. That is the craziest story I've ever heard."

He nodded but remained quiet.

"I can see why you're a writer." Jillian forestalled him by putting a hand up. "That's not to say I don't believe you—but you lead a very interesting life. I'm going to have to find and read one of your books when I wake up." She grinned at him and he smiled back.

"Look me up and I'll sign one for you."

"I might just do that. Even if it's just to see if this was real after all. I'll probably end up talking to you and you'll be like who is this crazy person?" They all laughed. "I still haven't decided if that would be worse than it all being true." He nodded in understanding.

"So bottom line—I've got to find my daughter and neighbor—"

"The dream," Pam said.

"Yes, the dream. If you'd like to come with me, you're more than welcome. If you'd rather stay here and wait it out, that's fine with me too. That's the smart choice. I think where I'm headed is dangerous, to say the least." He glanced up at Jillian. "It might be that when the dream ends one way or another, you two will just wake up. But that's just speculation."

They all fell silent for a while and Colin watched them considering all that they'd heard. Jillian had a bright, interested glint in her eyes. She was clearly intrigued by the entire situation. She made him feel slightly less insane, but he worried that she didn't understand or accept the danger she was in. Pam, on the other hand, didn't seem to want to believe any of it. He could see her wrestling with what she'd heard and seen, pitting it against her world view. He wondered if that focus on the known and understood made her a good doctor. He'd have to think that one through later.

Colin lay back on the grass, put his arms behind his head and looked up at the sky while the women thought things through.

"Colin," Pam said. "I think we're going to go talk a little bit, if you don't mind."

"I think that would be wise."

She smiled at him briefly and both women stood up.

"We'll be back in a few minutes," Jillian said, and Colin nodded with his eyes still on the sky. They walked away, leaving him to stare at the emerging stars. He'd never been a stargazer but was so completely out of his element he felt a deep reverence for the tiny glowing points in the sky. As the women talked he lost himself in the beauty of the sky. He found it soothing and for a few minutes he was able to put aside his worries and concerns. It left him with a strong feeling that things would be fine—everything would work out in the end. He carefully didn't examine that thought. He wasn't sure it would bear close scrutiny and right at that moment he needed to relax and think clearly.

Then suddenly he remembered that a few minutes ago it had been morning here. He shook his head and almost laughed at the sheer ridiculousness of the unnaturally swift change in the sky. He was adjusting to the Dreamside so quickly now that the bizarre didn't faze him.

Eventually his thoughts turned back to his predicament. He had absolutely no idea how to find Penny and Sidney. He knew he had to, but he couldn't even decide where to start. The only thing that came to mind was to keep moving, try to follow the dream to its edges or to its logical conclusion. Either way he imagined he'd reach the end of the dream and would end up in another dream. With a little luck, the one the girls were in. Maybe concentration would do the trick. If in that key moment when he changed dreams he was thinking about them strongly, concentrating on them in his mind, maybe he'd manage to end up with them.

Abruptly he saw Sidney's face in his mind and a sharp twinge of fear and pain rode through him, an ache in his bones. He knew that if he lost her he wouldn't survive. He couldn't handle that. One more person ripped from his world would push him right over the edge—especially Sidney. He would rather lose anything in the world before Sidney. He would die for her if he could to save her. If only he knew where she was. He sighed heavily and shook his head to clear his train of thought. It he dwelt on it any longer his mind might just shut down.

"Colin," Jillian said, surprising him. He pushed himself up into a sitting position. The two women had settled in the grass near him and were both looking at him. "We want to come with you. Whether this is all real isn't really even the issue."

She shrugged slightly. "It turns out that neither of us is the sort of person to just sit here and wait for something to happen to us." She grinned suddenly. "I've never been the sort to sit back and let life go by and I'm not going to start now." She shot Pam a questioning glance.

"Yeah, I'm in. I don't know when I'll next have a chance to watch a true paranoid schizophrenic in action." She smiled to take the sting out of the comment, but Colin suspected there was at least a grain of truth in there. He smiled back nonetheless. He knew he sounded crazy.

"Are you absolutely sure? Whether you believe it or not, you could get hurt here—even die."

"I'm sure," Pam said and Jillian nodded.

"Okay." He let out a deep sigh of relief.

"So what now?" Jillian asked.

Colin pushed himself to his feet and dusted his hands off on his pants.

"We walk. But this time, not on the path. This time we walk where we aren't supposed to go. We drive the dream instead of letting the dream drive us."

They both nodded and stood up. Colin stepped deliberately away from the path and headed toward the nearby woods, the women hurried to catch up and bracket him while they all walked quietly into the unknown.

※

They didn't have to walk long before the light woodland turned into a heavy, lush forest. The trees blocked out the sun, leaving them in gloomy shade. The air that ruffled Colin's hair was cool with the slightest hint of dank moisture. It wasn't entirely unpleasant, but it had lost the fresh taste the air had in the park. They worked their way through the increasingly heavy growth and their progress slowed to a crawl as they fought through heavy thorn bushes that tore at their clothes and scratched their skin, and around stands of tightly packed trees and tall bushes. Periodically they crossed paths that were clear, wide and inviting as if the dream was trying to coax them back to the park. Colin had this sneaking suspicion that if they took the path, they'd emerge in the park within a matter of moments, as if they'd gone nowhere at all.

"It's like the forest doesn't want us to go this way," Jillian broke the silence unexpectedly.

"Yeah." Colin realized she was right. "I think that means we're on the right track."

"I've never seen the woods so thick and overgrown in the park," Pam said.

"Come on, Pam." Jillian shot her friend a look. "We clearly aren't in the park anymore, if we ever were."

Pam nodded reluctantly. "Yeah. It sure seems that way." She shook her head slowly. "This is freaky." She looked at Colin. "So if this is a dream...am I going to remember this? I mean, I forget most of the dreams I have shortly after waking."

"I have no idea. To be honest I'm fairly new to all this. When you wake up, sit right up and write down what you remember." He grinned. "I hope you remember it. So you can call me and see that it was real." He sobered slightly. "But I bet you'll remember it all."

"I hope so. I don't want to forget any of this."

"You may change your mind about that," Colin muttered. He caught the question in Pamela's eyes and answered it with a weak smile.

They walked in silence for a while, concentrating on fighting through the nearly solid wall of plant life. And a battle it was. The branches grasped and dragged at them as they struggled through the ever thickening overgrowth. Bushes sharp with thorns seemed to appear in their path, trying to force Colin and the women aside, but they doggedly pushed on, a winding weaving path searching for passable places. On occasion they were forced to go through the thorns, moving slowly and gingerly but still unable to avoid the scratches and cuts that soon peppered their arms.

Finally it began to clear slightly. At first none of them really noticed it but before too long they were making better progress. Then abruptly they burst through a last wall of greenery, the branches dragging against them lightly as if making a last attempt to hold them back. Colin walked into a break in the forest. Ankle height grass was all that remained of the undergrowth and even the trees held back at the edges, allowing sunlight to spill around them, warm and inviting. The brightness of the sudden wash of light caused Colin's vision to haze for a few moments. He stood still and waited for it to clear up.

"Rest stop, Colin?" Jillian asked, but before he could answer Pam broke in.

"Uh, who is that?"

Colin put a hand above his eyes, shielding them from the sunlight, and peered across the clearing. As they finally adjusted to the change in light, he saw a man standing across the clearing, maybe fifty yards away. He had his hands on his hips and stood as if he'd been waiting for them for a long time.

"I don't know. But he looks familiar. Let's go." He raised a hand and waved in greeting as he started to walk toward the man. Pam and Jillian followed behind him. "Hello," he called out to the man, who nodded slightly in return. Something about the man troubled Colin, and he came to a halt, peered across the clearing, and tried to get a good look at the man's face.

"Colin," Jillian sounded uneasy.

"Yes?"

"That man." She paused. "He looks like you."

Torment

Colin's mind went blank; he stopped and stared at the man. Then the stranger dropped his hands to his sides and started toward them slowly. Colin realized that apart from the clothes he was looking at a mirror image of himself.

"Hello, Colin." A grin broke across the man's face. "I bet you weren't expecting this, were you?"

Colin shook his head slightly, trying to clear away the dazed feeling. "No."

His double came to a halt just a handful of yards away, laughed and folded his arms on his chest.

"Another brother?" Colin muttered to himself.

"The look on your face is priceless, Colin," he said. "Well worth the wait. Of course, I would have preferred to put this meeting off for a while yet, but what can you do? No matter how well you plan things out, something always goes wrong. The great generals throughout history have always been able to plan well yet still adapt to the unforeseen quickly and efficiently."

"Who are you?" Colin tried to pull himself out of the stunned confusion filling his brain.

"Oh, come on, Colin. Isn't it obvious? I'm you."

"Me?"

"Yes, you. I guess you could say I'm your better half."

Colin felt one of the women move closer to him and put a hand on his shoulder. "You didn't know you had a twin? This is like something out of a bad movie," she said. He knew she was trying to help him get past his shock. He was always trying to get past things, he realized, and that thought helped him pull himself together.

"No, not twins," the double said. "I am Colin. And he is me."

"That makes no sense..." Colin's voice dropped away as he tried to wrap his mind around what his double was saying.

"Colin, you should have figured out by now that making sense is simply not a requirement here."

"So what's your name, then?"

"My name? Colin, of course." Colin's double stopped and frowned thoughtfully. "I suppose we'll need different names or this could become even more confusing for everyone." He shrugged. "Torment. You can call me that if you need a name for me."

"So you're the Torment."

"Yes, I am the Torment." His voice was grim with a hint of anger.

"What's a Torment?" Pam asked.

"Not 'a' Torment. The Torment." Colin knew that this would be another thing she'd find hard to believe and it was critical to her safety that she do so. "He's a nightmare that someone dreamt up." He studied the Torment before speaking again. "This is your dream isn't it?"

"It is indeed my dream," the Torment said smugly.

Colin looked back at the nightmare. "Where are Sidney and Penny?"

"Don't worry about your girls. They're fine, for now. I've sent some friends along to play with them. If things go the way I plan nothing need happen to them." He grimaced slightly. "If you'd just stayed on the path I gave you, you would have been just fine as well."

The nightmare paused and studied Colin closely for a moment.

"You have been an interesting challenge, Colin. I had hoped your meeting with my murkshifter would shock and unsettle you enough to make you...shall we say, biddable. You have proven far more resilient than I'd expected." He gave a little shrug. "Who knows how things would have gone if your little dream hadn't interfered." He looked away thoughtfully for a moment and then turned back.

"But there's no point crying over spilt milk. As I said earlier—greatness lives in the ability to adapt to the unanticipated. And I am nothing if not great."

"All this and humble, too," Jillian said. The Torment glanced at her and smiled.

"Indeed, my dear Jillian." He fixed her with a stare and the friendly façade fell away, revealing a maliciousness that was frightening to behold and she took a half step back, and fell silent. The Torment looked back to Colin and he pulled the mask of friendliness and warm welcome up onto his face again effortlessly. "Where was I? Oh, yes, my plans changed and I thought to wear you down—to crush your spirit—by attacking the Dreamside here and there, sending little bits of evil into the various places. I knew that you would have to come to the rescue, and you did."

"That seemed to be working for a time. Especially when I allowed little Emma to slip into that dream. That was a nice touch, wasn't it? However, I admit I made a small miscalculation allowing the zombies to come so close to Sidney. And now you've managed to gather more allies to your side. You are an amazingly lucky shell of a man, Colin Pierce. You managed to escape my park before you were supposed to, and here you are." He spread his arms widely in a gesture of welcome. "Unfortunately, you force me to deal with you more...harshly." A malicious expression swept across his face. "Down on your knees, Colin Pierce."

"I don't think so." Colin was tired of this. Tired of being pushed and pulled around through someone else's dream. Tired of being hurt and attacked. He'd had enough.

"Oh, but I do think so." The Torment waved a hand almost negligently. A surge of force fell on Colin's shoulders and in seconds it doubled and doubled again until his legs buckled and he slumped down. As his knees hit the ground the force disappeared completely, leaving him kneeling before the Torment. "There, that's much better."

"Hey, I don't know what's going on here." Jillian's eyes were flashing anger. "But that was uncalled for."

"Oh, no." The Torment gestured at her. She fell to the ground behind Colin. "It was entirely called for. So much more will be necessary now that you have chosen this path." He gestured again and Pam fell to her knees as well.

"Bastard," Pam fumed and tried in vain to stand. The Torment studied the two women briefly before nodding to himself once.

"Now." He turned his attention to Colin again. "I believe you've met my friend." He gestured off to the side without looking and the murkshifter appeared and immediately began to lope toward them. Colin turned to watch it approach and remembered the searing terror he'd felt when he had run into the creature before.

It pulled up as it neared Colin and turned its ponderous head to look at the Torment, as if waiting for instruction. The creature's form was flowing slowly; different parts of its body changing, shifting, so that the entire effect was dizzying and loathsome at the same time. It sank back onto its haunches. Colin heard the women gasp behind him and then the sound of one of them retching. Colin understood what they were feeling—the creature defied anything that they could understand. It was a visceral attack on what they knew to be reality and in addition it was vile looking and radiated malice. The huge beast was hard to look at yet it was even harder to look away—it was no surprise that one of them threw up. The thing made his stomach roil as well.

"Oh, God, what is it?" Jillian whispered, disgust and horror in her voice.

"That is my murkshifter. It failed me a few times when I sent him after Colin and his family." He smirked conspiratorially. "Oh course, it was meant to fail. I am not entirely sure what I would have done had it managed to kill you, Colin." He appeared to consider that for a brief moment and then waved a hand negligently. "I'm sure I would have figured something out."

"So is this the place where you reveal your evil plans?" Colin asked sarcastically.

The Torment laughed. "No, there's really no need to tell you anything more than you already know. However, I am ready to start pulling a few pieces together." Then the benevolent smile dropped from his face, leaving an ugly snarl twisted his features. "Time for the pain."

"I think I'll take a pass on that."

"Good," the Torment responded. "I would have been disappointed if you had given in already." Then he spoke over his shoulder in a language that Colin could not identify—a chaotic jumble of rasping, coughing sounds that sounded vile. Immediately the murkshifter flowed into motion and raced toward Colin. In a flash it was on him. One of its huge paws shifted and transformed fluidly into a grasping hand, long fingers ending in sharp talons. It reached out and grabbed Colin by his neck. The creature lifted him off the ground and he was surprised at how gentle its grasp was. He felt a slight tingling under the pressure of its hand, that slowly started to burn and he could smell the odor of skin burning like meat overcooked mixed with a hint of hair incinerated in a flash— made all the worse by the knowledge that it was his own body. The gentleness of its grip on him quickly gave way to searing pain.

The creature held Colin several feet over the ground, its body stretching and becoming taller as it lifted him up. It turned its head nearly entirely around and looked blankly at the Torment. The nightmare nodded once, gestured and the murkshifter effortlessly threw Colin to the ground. He landed roughly and slid several yards before coming to a halt and the murkshifter was on him again. Its graceful and deadly hands shifted slightly to spread out wider and it swooped down to catch Colin's face in a heavy slap. The force of the blow lifted him up and threw him to the ground again violently, knocking the wind out of him and leaving him sprawled senselessly. His vision doubled and blurred, spots of black swimming before his eyes.

Through the waves of pain he heard Jillian. "Leave him alone!"

"You're going to kill him." Pam struggled to stand, reaching toward Colin. "He already had a head injury."

"You healed him of that injury, Pamela." The Torment's voice was almost kind as he easily fell back into the illusion of friendliness and beneficence. "Don't worry though—I don't want him dead, yet. Just softened up a bit. Tenderized, if you will." He gestured at them and Jillian fell back—whatever force had kept her kneeling was gone. She pushed up to her feet and ran to Colin.

"Bastard." Jillian knelt beside him and he saw her as if down a long tunnel. "God, that looks painful." She reached out gingerly toward his neck and then stopped short of touching him. Pam appeared at Jillian's shoulder, pushed around her friend and began to inspect the damage.

"Oh, it is," Colin groaned. He looked past her in time to see the murkshifter appear between the women and reach out to pluck him into the air by the arm, dangling him above the ground again. Another stinging blow and he flew through the air, and darkness claimed him briefly. The world swam back into focus and he saw that Jillian had placed herself between the murkshifter and Colin.

"Enough," she growled and her anger was a tangible thing in the air. "That's enough."

"Not quite yet, Jillian,"

The murkshifter gently reached out and pushed her aside. She stumbled and fell to the ground and the creature grabbed Colin by the leg and began to drag him back away from the women. Colin had a moment to wonder why it wasn't hurting the women before a huge sledge hammer fist crashed down on him and sent him into unconsciousness completely.

※

When he came to, he was on his knees, his hands tightly bound behind his back and a heavy stake driven down through the rope, pinning him down. His ankles were also bound and staked in a similar manner. He hurt everywhere and wondered how much more of a beating he'd taken while he was unconscious. He looked up and saw Jillian and Pam tied in the same way about fifteen feet from him. While Jillian looked defiant and angry, Pam was sobbing softly, her face wet with tears and her eyes red.

"Please let us go," she said between sobs.

"No, Pamela." The Torment stood a few yards from Colin with his back to the women and didn't look back as he spoke. "You had your chance to stay out of this. I don't know how you ended up in my dream but you should have stayed in my park." He shrugged and smirked. "So now your fate depends entirely upon Colin. I promise it won't be pleasant unless he cooperates with me. You'll cooperate, won't you, Colin?"

Before Colin could answer the world slowed and became foggy. He found that he could see through the Torment and the murkshifter crouching slightly behind him as everything became see-through and ghostlike. Around him trees and vines appeared, slowly fading into the same translucence like a double exposure photograph. It looked to him like some kind of jungle, wet and lush. He became aware of two things right away. First, he sensed a deep malevolence and could see what looked like pockets of heat waves rippling through the trees, and second, he saw Sidney and Penelope run toward him and come to a sliding halt. There was a man with them—he looked almost aboriginal, but he radiated a goodness that Colin could feel washing over his face gently, caressing him. There was something familiar about the small man. But immediately his eyes moved past the man and sought out Sidney. She knelt on the ground immediately behind the small man, and was looking over his shoulder at Colin, with wildness in her eyes.

"Sid?" Colin rasped. "Is that really you?"

"Dad!" Dismay and joy warred in her voice. He realized he must look a mess.

"Sid." He forced the word through the pain clutched his throat. The malevolence he felt grew stronger as the tiny dots of heat behind Sidney bounced and weaved, approaching quickly. He didn't know what the things were but the evil feel in the air made it obvious they weren't coming to say hello. He gritted his teeth and spoke impatiently. "You have to run, honey. Run as fast as you can. They are coming and they are getting closer."

"Dad." She looked bewildered—clearly unable to process what he was saying. "What is going on?"

"No questions, Sid." He forced desperate strength into his voice. "Run!" He looked past her at Penny. "Penny, run! Now! Do not look back." His words jarred them into action and they turned and began to run, Sidney moving away reluctantly, and her face was a mask of despair. He reached a hand out to her.

"I'm fine, Sid, just go." He knew she could hear the lie in his word.

No sooner were the words out than Sidney, Penelope and the stranger began to fade away again and the Torment and its dream slowly solidified again. As he watched Sidney begin to disappear, she turned and sprinted into the gloom of the jungle.

"What was that?" the Torment asked suspiciously. "Where did you go?" He strode forward and reached down to grasp Colin's hair roughly and pull up his head. "Tell me what you just did."

"None of your business, asshole." Colin tried to hide the fact that he had no idea. He knew that the Torment's rough grasp of his hair should hurt, but his body was unable to process it as pain—he wrestled with a dark despair at what Sidney faced. He couldn't help her and that knowledge hurt more than anything the Torment had done to his body.

The Torment snarled and flung Colin away and gestured carelessly. Flames burst out around Colin and his clothes ignited. As the fire took its first bites on his skin, the pain was intolerable and he began to scream. He hit the ground hard enough to knock the wind out of him and he tried to roll and put the flames out.

"Remember this, Colin? Remember a house on fire. Remember burning to death with those two girls. Shall we do it again?"

Then Colin's mind overloaded from the pain and the smell of charring skin and burning hair chased him back into the darkness once again.

Burn Again

Colin floated in profound darkness and quiet. It would have been complete sensory deprivation if not for the occasional light touches in various places as if gentle hands were exploring his body, taking stock of his injuries. He ignored them, and he ignored the distant muffled sound of voices. He knew he hurt all over but that had faded into the background—white noise lost in the blankness around him. He'd become accustomed to living with pain over the last few years. Granted, that had been emotional pain and this was purely physical, but after a certain point, pain was pain. Or so he thought.

Gradually the touches became more insistent and it took more of his will to ignore them and pretend they simply didn't exist. But when the touches became a gentle, yet firm shaking of his shoulders, he could no longer ignore it. He had the sense of floating upwards, as if slowly recovering the surface of the ocean by his natural buoyancy alone. Slowly drifting upwards, the first hints of distant light appearing above him, and a muffled low sound tickling his ears. Then he began to rise faster, no longer floating to the surface but instead rushing upward, gaining momentum and the light became brighter and the muffled sounds slowly becoming voices he recognized but could not place.

Then he burst through the surface of his unconsciousness and into the glaring, painful light of day. At first the light blinded him and the sounds confused him, but as his vision slowly returned he saw shapes above him resolve into the faces of Pam and Jillian.

"Colin?" Pam was shaking his shoulders lightly. Each shake sent shocks of pain through his body. With consciousness he lost his ability to compartmentalize the pain and it rushed to consume his entire being.

"Oh, fuck." The words escaped him through his gritted teeth, and he struggled to keep the sound from escalating into a moaning, tearing scream. "That hurts. Shit, everything hurts."

Pam stopped shaking him and sat back. Her face was a grim mask of horror as she looked at him.

"Of course it does." Over her shoulder Jillian looked at him with shocked revulsion and he immediately wondered what she saw that was so...repulsive.

"What's wrong with me?" Even talking hurt and he closed his eyes and tried to tied down and control the pain.

"He hurt you, Colin." Jillian's voice was hesitant and low. "He...he burned you. Badly."

"Where?" Neither of them answered. "Tell me. Where am I burned?"

"Everywhere," Pam said in a rough whisper. "I tried to heal you, but it didn't work this time for some reason."

"Oh, fuck. Why'd you wake me up? It wasn't this bad when I was out."

"Because we have to find a way out of here and we can't leave you here. But we don't know how to move you...without hurting you more."

Colin looked around and saw that they were sitting in the middle of a large bamboo cage. It was about ten feet square and another ten feet tall. Other than the three of them, it was entirely empty. The pain flared as he turned his head and his vision sparkled and starred. He closed his eyes and focused on the pain. It was the ocean he floated in, the red hot fire of it caressing him everywhere at once. He took a deep breath and the expansion of his chest sent more thrills of hurt rushing away from his torso to his extremities. He moaned softly and concentrated on the hurt. In his mind he dove down into it, seeking its white hot center. As he plunged downward the pain doubled and redoubled and he was vaguely aware of a ripping, rasping sound, but he kept moving into the core of the pain, searching for its origin. The noise increased in volume, each undulating rise and fall of it causing more spears of agony to rip into him. Dimly he realized it was his own screams he was hearing but he was powerless to stop them so he ignored them and pushed ever downward deeper into the pain. If he stopped or turned away now he was lost.

Finally he found the raging center of the fire and plunged into it. He felt as if he were already ash and charred bones. He even smelled smoke and the smell of burning flesh around him, and he felt the edges of his self curling and burning away. His screams turned into a roar of outrage and he focused on the white ball of pain, studying it and finding the definite outer shell of it he placed his hands around it and squeezed slowly. At first nothing happened, but after a few moments that seemed as long as lifetimes he felt the sphere begin to shrink. He kept pushing as hard as he could, and slowly the ball of pain shrunk and after an eon of struggling with it, the tiny ball sat in his palm, solid, diamond hard and bright like a miniature sun. He closed his hand around it and squeezed.

Then it was gone and with it a large portion of the pain disappeared, shocking his senses brutally. For a while he floated in the relief he felt. It still hurt but it had receded to manageable pain. Finally he opened his eyes and saw Pam and Jillian staring at him in shock.

"What did you do?" Pam asked in a whisper.

"I don't know." It didn't hurt to talk anymore. "It hurts less though."

"Your burns are almost gone. All you've got is what looks like a nasty sunburn all over, but that's significantly better than you had moments ago. How did you do that, Colin?"

"I'm not sure." He was unsure of how to explain it. "I looked inside myself and found the pain and...made it less." He reached out to her and she took his hands. "I have to sit up. Can you help me?" She pulled and he felt his skin stretching uncomfortably, but the small jolts of pain were almost pleasant compared to what he'd been feeling earlier. He sat up and realized for the first time that he was completely nude. He blushed and put his hands over his groin.

"I'm naked."

"Yes, we noticed," she said with a chuckle.

"Why am I naked?" He couldn't stop blushing.

"He burned away your clothes." Colin could tell Pam was trying to hide a grin. "Don't worry, Colin, I'm a doctor. I've seen it all before."

"Yeah, but not my doctor."

"Funny time to be modest," Jillian said. "You just healed yourself of horrible burns that covered one hundred percent of your body—hell, you grew back your hair—and you're worried about us seeing your unit?"

Pam broke out in a laugh finally at that and Colin rolled his eyes.

"What a bastard this guy is," he muttered. "What a complete bastard I am."

※

Colin spent a time propped against the side of the cage trying to pull himself together. He had to be focused. Find a way to defeat the Torment. The memory of the pain still seared through him, echoes of the ripping, tearing feeling of his skin burned and charred still filled his mind, making it hard to think straight. The only way to banish the physical memory of it was to pinch his arm and aggravate his sunburn. The slight slow burn of that contact was so much less than the pain he'd felt that for a few moments he felt like he didn't hurt at all.

"So how'd you get untied?" he asked.

"How does anything happen in here?" Pam answered with a resigned shrug. "One minute we're tied up watching you... smolder and the next we were in here with you." Her eyes flitted back and forth, her pupils tiny. He could tell she was right on the edge of panic, but he didn't know how to comfort her, so he just sat and concentrated on ignoring the last vestiges of the pain.

"Where did he go?"

"After playing campfire with you, he said something about still having use for us and then he disappeared." Jillian shrugged. "Poof."

"You seem to be handling this well."

She shrugged. "Either this is a dream, like you said, and we'll wake up, or it's not and we're screwed. I don't think there's a lot we can do about it." She gestured at herself and Pam. "We're just along for the ride. I think this is all your show." She glanced past Colin and her eyes went unfocused for a moment. When she looked back at him the corners of her mouth quirked in a small smile. "That's the worst part, to be honest."

"Yeah, I can understand that. Feeling out of control really bugs me too. But I think you're overestimating me. I don't think there's anything I can do here."

"Don't say that, Colin." Pam sounded urgent—almost desperate—and he realized how close she was to outright panic. "You've got to get us out of here. You are the only one who can, I think." She had moved to sit in one of the corners of the cage, the bars pressing up against her back. Jillian scooted over close and took her hand.

"Easy, Pam." Jillian crooned. "We'll get out of this. Just try to calm down." She glanced over at Colin. "He's stronger than he thinks." She shot him another brief smile, but couldn't hide a hint of desperation.

"I'll do what I can."

"I know."

The swirling pain was finally fading from his mind. The physical pain long gone, his mind was catching up at long last. He slipped down slightly and took in a large breath of air, slowly released and felt the relaxation radiate out from his chest, taking much of his tension with it.

"That's much better," he said and gave the women a quick smile. "That was the worst pain I've ever felt in my life."

"Well, you were missing most of your skin." Jillian sounded slightly dazed. Next to her Pam frowned again and her eyes focused on him.

"How did you do that, anyway?" She sounded slightly querulous. Colin shrugged. "Burns don't just heal like that. They just don't," she muttered.

"They do here." He didn't bother telling her that he had done it in the waking world too. "I just didn't know how it works. Perhaps it is triggered by need. I was starting to lose my mind."

"Pam," Jillian said. "We're in a dream. Anything is possible here. Remember how you healed him earlier?"

Pam refused to meet her eyes, and looked down.

"Yes. I guess I just don't...understand it. I hate not understanding." Then she glanced down with a puzzled expression, looking right at his groin area. He felt a moment of embarrassment. "Hey, look at that. I guess he decided to have mercy on you." She smiled wryly at him. He glanced down and saw he was wearing a pair of boxers now.

"Huh, that's unexpected." He realized he had to be careful in the Dreamside—thought became reality unbidden. That could be dangerous.

"Yeah," Jillian added. "It doesn't seem like something he'd do. Maybe he has a softer side and we just have to find a way to bring it out."

"I think I am his softer side." Something tickled at the back of his brain. Some idea that he couldn't get a handle on. Every time he felt like it was in reach, it slipped away. And it felt important.

They all lapsed into silence again and Colin's thoughts turned back to Sidney and Penny. He had no idea where to find them, or how to get to them if he could figure out where they were. He knew he wouldn't survive losing them. He'd only just begun to recover from losing the rest of his family. That had taken four years and an abundance of love and support from Sidney. He knew that if she died he wouldn't survive it. He wouldn't want to.

"Oh, don't be so melodramatic, Colin," a male voice rang out from behind him. Colin turned around quickly and saw his double standing a short ways away from the cage. He smirked. "If it comes to that, you won't outlive her by long. Who knows, if you're good I might do you first."

Deep in Colin's chest despair blossomed like a sick, corrupted flower on a thorny vine. It sent creepers questing for his heart as if to consume him from the inside. He knew this feeling well—it was like an unwelcome house guest that wouldn't leave. It was poison, a cancer in his soul and as it rose he slid slowly, helplessly into its embrace.

But then an image of Sidney in danger flashed through his mind. He remembered the blank resignation on her face outside the tower as the voice tried to seduce her to her death. He remembered his rage at that moment and it crystallized in the here and now, and he pulled it around him like a warm coat on a cold day. It was another sort of fire, crackling and spitting angrily deep inside him and he burned with it, his despair becoming rage and fury in a split moment—no gradual shift, just a lightning fast change. He bared his teeth and looked up at the Torment, met his eyes defiantly, furiously and at his sides his hands curled tightly into fists. He was so blindly angry that the brief look of surprise on the Torment's face barely registered. A small corner of his mind wondered at that microscopic expression, but that wondering was swept away by his anger.

"Now what?" he asked in a growl. "Come to finish what you started?"

The Torment walked closer and then cocked his head slightly, the beginnings of a frown on his face.

"What did you do? That's not how I left you."

"He healed himself, you fuck," Pam spat. The Torment glared at her briefly and then looked back at Colin, his expression flitted from suspicion to something that looked like fear and then finally to anger.

"Impossible. You did this." He turned to Pam and his voice was full of menace.

"No," Colin said. "I did it." His double turned back to him.

"How?"

"Does it matter?"

The Torment stared at him for a few moments and then carefully marshaled his expression into blankness and shrugged.

"No, I suppose not. Not really. It doesn't change anything. If I need to, I can easily return you to that state." Some emotion flew across his features and was gone before Colin could identify it. "But we won't have to go there if you're willing to cooperate with me."

"And do what?" But Colin had an idea.

"I want the wall torn down. And I want you to do it for me. Consider it payment for six lives spared, if that makes it easier."

"Why?"

"Because," the Torment's reasonable expression dissolved into rage. "I want to destroy it all. The waking world took everything from me. My children. My wife. My life. And everyone and everything is going to pay for that." He took a deep breath and closed his eyes and his expression faded back to something more neutral. Then he opened his eyes and smiled at Colin. "So what's it going to be, Col?"

"I can't do that," Colin answered quietly. "And you know it."

"Sure you can, Colin. You're probably the only person that can."

"So that's why you wanted us here…"

"Exactly. I need you to bring down the wall for me."

"And Sidney is leverage, I imagine."

"Motivation, should you refuse. And we both know you were going to refuse, don't we?"

Colin didn't respond to that. He thought for a moment before speaking again.

"Well, you don't have your leverage anymore."

"Sure I do, Colin." The nightmare turned and waved a hand and the air beside him began to ripple and churn, first looking like heat waves above asphalt, and then as the colors began to bleed into the swirling shape, it looked like a blurry kaleidoscope. The Torment gestured again and the colors coalesced into a blurry image. Slowly it came into focus and Colin realized he was looking at a picture of another place. He saw Penny and Sidney scurrying up a tree and the strange man they'd been with stood at the bottom, surrounded by some kind of lizard creatures.

"Sid..." Colin groaned.

"We can start with your two friends here, and if that is not enough motivation. We'll move on to your child and the dream." With a lazy wave he shrunk the portal to a point and it vanished. "But there's no need for all that, Colin." His voice returned to calm and friendly. "You know you want this as well. So much lost. Surely you want revenge upon the world that did this to you. To us."

"Who do we blame? God maybe? I have spent four years trying to get my shit together. Sidney has waited patiently. I refuse to destroy her. The life we have."

"You can bring her here to the Dreamside. You belong here anyway."

"The Dreamside can't exist without dreamers. It will be destroyed as surely as the waking world. Not that that even matters. I will not destroy the waking world for you. For anyone."

The Torment stared at Colin and then shrugged. "So be it. I guess we're back to threats and ugly conflict." The nightmare gestured carelessly again and they were all suddenly somewhere else.

Colin

Between one moment and the next the whole of reality shifted around them. One instant they were in the cage and the next Colin and the women stood shoulder to shoulder in the glade where Colin had first met the Wall. In the center of the grassy area the Wall was bound and gagged, facing toward them. Her eyes were bright and full of meaning as she looked at Colin. He saw that she was trying to tell him something and he had no idea what. Despite being hogtied on her side, she had lost none of her noble, graceful beauty. Colin started to walk toward her slowly.

"So where is the Wall?" Pam asked.

"Why, right in front of you, Argot." The Torment's voice was an audible sneer. He stepped past the women and stopped, watching Colin.

"The woman there? She's the Wall?"

"Yes." Colin continued to approach the woman. As before she shone brightly, her pure beauty almost a tangible thing pulsing all around them. "This is just one manifestation."

"I don't understand," Jillian said. "What exactly is the Wall?"

"She is the boundary between sleep and dream. What keeps them separate." The thought that had lurked in the back of his mind burst to the front and he blinked in surprise. "She is the Dreamside. Everything. She's the good, the evil, the beautiful, the ugly. All of it. But more than that, she is every one of us. The collective unconscious—the sleeping mind—of the human race. Maybe of all life."

"Ah, so that's why you want her destroyed. You want to burn everything down." Jillian's voice was distant and Colin saw that she couldn't look away from the Wall. She took a small step toward the glowing, beautiful woman and smiled tentatively. "You look so familiar." The woman managed a smile through her gag and nodded once. Jillian continued walking to her until she knelt down close. She started to reach for the gag, but stopped and glanced back at the Torment. "May I? Just the gag?"

The Torment considered with narrowed eyes and then shrugged. "Just the gag."

Jillian nodded and gingerly pulled the wad of cloth out of her mouth. The Wall immediately smiled up at her. Colin, standing slightly behind her felt the power of that smile as it warmed his heart. He felt a rush of hope. He had no idea how he was going to get out of this, but he still felt confidence flow through him.

"Hello, Jillian." The Wall's voice was melodic and soothing, rich with hope and promise. As Colin watched an almost blissful smile consumed Jillian's face.

"Hello, have we met before?"

"Yes, of course. Whenever you dream we meet." She favored Jillian with a last smile and then looked past her to Colin.

"Hello, Dreamer," she said. "I am glad to see you."

"I am glad to see you as well" Colin's smiled slipped. "I'm afraid I'm here to…He wants me to…"

"I know," she said while he searched the right words. "I understand."

"She understands," the Torment said with a desultory laugh. "That's priceless. Even in defeat she is the paragon of goodness and light."

Colin stepped forward, knelt down beside the Wall, brushed the hair out of her eyes and put a hand on her cheek. He skin was cool and soft, waves of soothing calm radiated outward through his fingers, up his arms and into his entire being. A tiny, sad sigh escaped him.

"I'm sorry. Truly sorry."

She smiled at him beatifically.

"Don't be sorry, Colin." Her voice dropped to a whisper, her words for him alone. "Just run. Run as hard as you can."

"What?" he said in shock. "But what about Pam and Jillian. And Penny and Sidney?"

"I will send you to your daughter. Your Torment blocks much of my power, but I still have enough to do this thing." She glanced at Jillian. "And I will distract him from these women." She looked back to Colin and cocked her head slightly to the side, inspecting his face carefully. What she was looking for, Colin couldn't guess. "You are coming into your own, Dreamer." She gave him the same smile. "Go to your dreams. Trust in yourself, Colin Pierce."

"What are you two talking about?" Suspicion replaced anger in the Torment's voice. Colin could hear the rustle of his footsteps through the grass as he approached. The nightmare reached into his pocket and pulled out a large curved blade. It looked too large to have fit and he flipped it casually in the air, catching it by the blade and holding it out toward Colin. "It's time to do your job, Colin. Bring down the wall now, or I will make these women pay first. Then your daughter and the dream. You must know I will do it."

Colin glanced back. "In a moment. You are asking me to do a horrible thing. At least have the decency to let me say goodbye to her properly." He turned to the Wall again and The Torment remained quiet. "He can still hurt you, can't he? He may not be able to bring you down entirely, but he was hurting you earlier in that village..."

"Oh, he can hurt me, it is true," she said with a wry quirk of a smile. "And I imagine that if he kept at it, in a few millennia he might actually succeed in bringing me down. But he lacks the patience to pursue that goal. So he will hurt me in anger or hatred once you are gone, but I can endure that. Sidney and Penelope need you desperately." Her brow furrowed slightly as she banished the cheer from her face. "It is time for you to take action, Dreamer. Time for you to take control of your dreams."

"How do I do that?"

"You are the Dreamer, Colin. You will figure it out. You must." She managed a small shrug though her bonds were tight.

"That is enough talking," the Torment said from behind Colin, his voice filled with hate and suspicion. Colin simply ignored him and kept his eyes on the Wall's face.

"But we're all dreamers," he said in a whisper.

"No, Colin. They are dreamers. Sleepers who have come to visit us. You are The Dreamer."

"I don't understand."

"Ask yourself this, Colin Pierce: who creates your dreams?" She stared into his eyes deeply and for a brief moment he felt like he was falling into them, dreams of worlds and possibilities surrounding him in the shining depth of them. "Now you must go before it is too late. Run, Dreamer," the Wall whispered to him again and closed her eyes.

The world flooded back around him and Colin turned to look at Pam and Jillian in time to see them begin to become immaterial and fade away. Both had surprised looks on their faces and Jillian reached out toward him, her mouth moving, and heard the sound as she said something to him, but the meaning flowed away from him. Then he took a deep breath and shot to his feet, quickly moving to a sprint. He had no idea what direction he was running, but he stretched his legs out and ate the ground up quickly. He pumped his arms and tucked his head down, trying to gather speed rather than worry about seeing where he was going. And with his head down, he never even saw the portal that slid into existence before him until he passed through it, chased into somewhere else by the Torment's inarticulate scream of rage.

Desert

Once the soul eaters disappeared back into the trees, Sidney stood and wiped her hands on her pants. Looking around she saw nothing but an endless sea of sand stretching away to the horizon, where the deep azure of the sky faded to a dusty blue. Heat waves rose off the ground, further blurring the line between sky and sand. Sidney found the view disconcerting—distances were hard to gauge and the sand looked like it rose up into the sky. She closed her eyes momentarily before turning back to the others, where Penny was helping Ahanu to his feet.

"Well, I think the forest is out of the question," Penny said as she surveyed the desert. "That means hot and sandy for us!" She shot Sidney a quick grin, and helped Ahanu get his balance—making sure he wasn't going to fall before letting go. He settled onto his feet, stood ready for a moment and then gave her a quick nod.

"Are you going to be able to walk, Ahanu?" Sidney asked.

"I am fine, Sidney." She knew his smile was meant to be reassuring, but she wasn't convinced.

"So…the desert." She glanced at Penny. "Sand, snakes and scorpions. Some of my favorite things." Sarcasm was better than fear, she decided.

Penny laughed. "Well, it's that or tiny men that want to eat our souls."

"Not good options." Sidney saw small beads of sweat on his upper lip. "But it is what it is."

They lapsed into silence. The breeze that blew in across the sand dunes was not cool or refreshing—it carried the oppressive heat of the desert as if it were exhaust from a furnace. Already Sidney felt sweat on her skin, making the back of her shirt damp. Finally she spoke.

"Well, I think whatever we do is your choice to make, Ahanu."

The small man grimaced slightly. "I was afraid you were going to say this, Sidney. I choose the desert."

Penny laughed again, a musical sound that floated away from them on the wings of a desert zephyr blowing across the sand. "Well, I'm glad that's settled. Which way, Ahanu?"

He turned, holding his shoulder gingerly and surveyed the horizon across the desert. He frowned slightly, closed his eyes and slowly turned in a circle several times. After a few revolutions he came to a stop, raised his arm and pointed out into the desert. He opened his eyes and gave a shrug. "This way." He led the way.

"Well, that was pretty random." Sidney chuckled as she fell in line behind Penny.

"I am following my heart. My head might get in the way."

"I can live with that," Penny said as they all trudged out into the desert, moving carefully, fighting the give and slide of the sand.

"I hope so," Sidney heard Ahanu mutter under his breath.

✺

Walking was hard; Sidney's feet shifted and slid in the loose sand. The sun beat down like a hammer striking an anvil again and again, and her mouth was dry and her tongue like sandpaper. Ahanu had berated himself for failing to fill his water skin—it was only half full when he first thought to check, and they were already an hour or so out into desert. So he was sharing out tiny sips, trying to stretch it out and make it last, but already the bag was nearly empty. Sidney resolved not to ask for water. She trusted Ahanu to know when to stop and give her some. Periodically she tried to find her dream sense, to create water, lessen the heat, but there was nothing here she could feel—it was not her dream.

Sidney spent her time carefully watching her feet, making sure to put them down solidly and not to slip and fall. They moved slowly to conserve strength. Finally after what seemed like an eon, Ahanu called for a halt and brought out the water skin.

"I'm so thirsty." The dry pastiness of Sidney's mouth made her words clumsy. The moment the words were out of her mouth she wished she could call them back.

"Don't remind me," Penny grumbled as Ahanu passed the water to them each in turn. Even warm and with a slight tang of leather from the skin the tiny sip Sidney took was the best thing she'd ever tasted.

"I am sorry." Sidney heard a hint of shame in Ahanu's voice. "I should have remembered the water. I am a fool."

"You are not a fool, Ahanu." Sidney spoke sharply. "None of us thought of the water."

"Sidney's right, Ahanu. Don't be so hard on yourself."

"Thank you, both, but I cannot help thinking that my heart has led us to our..." He paused a heartbeat before finishing "...to greater trouble." Sidney knew what he'd been going to say.

"Out of the frying pan and into the fire." Penny spoke under her breath but Sidney heard it clearly.

"Literally." They both laughed and it felt good.

Lapsing back into silence, Sidney listened to the rasp of the breeze blowing sand across the surface of the desert in gentle waves. She stared out over the rolling dunes and it looked like a huge brown ocean, waves frozen in place. On the upside they hadn't seen any snakes or scorpions yet. Probably at night they would see those creatures. She'd read somewhere that the desert got cold at night—there wasn't enough moisture in the air to hold the heat.

If there is a hell, this is what it looks like.

Finally Ahanu started walking again and the girls followed him. Sidney returned her focus to the ground in front of her and again time seemed to stretch out around them. After an interminable time, Ahanu stopped at the crest of one of the taller dunes and passed around the water skin. When it came to Sidney it was all but empty. Ahanu caught her eyes and arched an eyebrow.

"Drink it, Sidney."

"There's not much left. You need water, too."

Ahanu nodded. "I know. One sip for Penny and one for you. It will have to do. Now drink."

Reluctantly she did as he told her. She was able to get a small sip out of the skin by shaking it over her mouth. Not even a mouthful, but it was enough to wet her mouth and tongue. She swished it around for a few moments before swallowing, and when it was finally down her throat and gone, the enormity of their predicament hit her hard. No water in the desert meant dead. She passed the skin back to Ahanu and he reached out to take it. Penny approached and took Sidney's hand and gave it a quick squeeze.

"It will be okay, Sid. We did not come all this way to fail now."

She nodded but didn't believe it at all. Penny didn't let go of her hand as Ahanu turned to survey the horizon. Sidney stared at the sand in front of her unseeingly. She felt an intense urge to just sit down and rest. Give up. Then Ahanu broke the silence.

"What is that?" He pointed into the distance. Sidney peered in that direction and saw a dark blot on the horizon, as if something perched on the sand. Waves of heat rising off the desert obscured whatever it was, but Sidney still felt a burst of hope—maybe it was a town or an oasis—anything. She distanced herself from the thought—she didn't want to get her hopes up. It could also be a mirage conjured by the heat and their thirst.

"Is it trees?" Sidney could tell Penny was tempering her excitement.

"That is what it looks like." Excitement crept into Ahanu's voice. "Come on, let's head that way." He began walking down the dune, and he picked up speed. Sidney and Penny followed.

"Be careful, Ahanu," Penny cautioned. "If it's not trees, we're going to wear ourselves out for nothing."

"You are right, Penelope." He slowed his pace again, sounding chagrined.

They continued on, strung out like beads on a necklace; Ahanu leading, Penny behind him and Sidney bringing up the rear. They traveled carefully, and as they reached the top of each dune, Ahanu adjusted their course, pointing them back toward the spot on the horizon.

Eventually, the distant blur began to take on a greenish hue and Sidney found it difficult to contain her hopeful, yet subdued excitement. The closer they got and the more details resolved into view, the more convinced she became that they were indeed heading toward trees. And as her hopes rose, so did her fear of disappointment. When they walked down between dunes and the blur was lost to sight, she fretted and worried—would it still be there when they reached the top of the next dune? She was caught between the desire to run up and see if it was still there, and a creeping dread that it wasn't that slowed her feet.

But each time, the trees were still there, a little closer and a little clearer, and as the afternoon wore on the blurry green resolved further into what looked like a lush, vibrant oasis. Sidney knew that if there was no water there, they would be finished. If this were not a dream, the mere presence of the greenery would guarantee water, but this was a dream, and in dreams all things were possible—even an oasis without water.

What made it harder to face was that she knew if she died in this dream, she would be gone from the waking world—just as dead there as here. She held out hope that Ahanu would just wake up from the dream, but she was convinced that she and Penny were fighting for their lives now. The entire approach to the oasis began to feel like a huge roll of the dice—a toss of a coin.

At the top of the next dune, Sidney looked back the direction they'd come, tracing away from herself by following their tracks in the sand. She could see the tracks rising on the face of the dunes, weaving slightly back and forth as they'd made their way across the hot desert. As she stared she thought she saw dark specks in the extreme distance coming down one of the dunes they'd crossed. Before she could convince herself she was really seeing something they disappeared below the next dune. This time she decided not to wait and see—she'd learned her lesson.

"Guys," she called out. Penny and Ahanu both stopped and turned to face her.

"What's up, Sid?" Penny came to stand beside her.

"I think I saw something behind us."

"Pretty far away...they looked like dots. I saw them on top of one of the dunes and then they moved down and I lost sight of them." She glanced at Penny. "I might have imagined it."

Ahanu came up and stood on her other side and they all peered off into the distance.

"Better safe than sorry, Sid."

Ahanu shaded his eyes with his hand. "I don't see anything now, but the dunes might be hiding whatever you saw. Let's rest a few minutes and see if these dots reappear."

"Okay." Penny sat down in the sand. All three of them kept their eyes on the distant undulating dunes, waiting for something to show itself. Sidney wasn't even sure how far out she'd seen them anymore—the sameness of the landscape made it hard to gauge the distance. After a while, when the dots had not shown themselves again, she shrugged and sighed.

"I guess I imagined it. Sorry." Sidney felt both embarrassed and relieved at the same time.

"No problem, Sid," Penny said and stood up, dusted the sand off her rear end and patted Sidney affectionately on the shoulder again, and began to turn back toward the Oasis. Sidney began to follow, but Ahanu didn't move.

"Wait, Penelope." Ahanu pointed off at an angle to the direction they'd been looking. "Look there. I see your dots, Sidney." Both girls peered where he pointed and Sidney spotted the tiny dots. They seemed to be slightly closer, but were not moving toward them, but rather heading the same direction parallel to them.

"They don't seem to be following us," Sidney said. "That's a good thing."

Ahanu looked thoughtful with a tiny frown on his face as he stared. "I am not so sure of that."

"What do you mean?" Penny asked.

"They are moving pretty fast. Along our flank." He raised an eyebrow and looked at the girls. "What if they are trying to pass us so they can turn back on us? To get between us and the oasis?" It was a shocking thought, and Sidney was glad Ahanu was there to figure it out. She wasn't sure it would have occurred to her until they were cut off from the distant promise of water and shade.

"We have to move faster. We can't let them get there first." Sidney wondered if it was too late already.

"Exactly." Ahanu frowned. "They are still far behind us. If we speed up now we probably can get there ahead of them. But I cannot tell how far we are from the oasis."

"Well, let's get to it." Penny started off at a trot. "Hurry up, Ahanu. You're supposed to lead." She grinned over her shoulder at him. He returned her smile and loped until he passed her. Sidney brought up the rear and moved just fast enough to stay with them.

※

They trotted in silence through the oppressive heat that rose up from the sandy floor of the desert and Sidney couldn't tell who was going to reach the oasis first. She didn't glance over at their pursuers often, instead concentrating on where she put her feet. The flowing ocean of sand was featureless—nothing to trip over or fall into—but the soft surface was always shifting and sucking at her feet as if trying to unbalance her.

Ahanu led them along the ridges of the dunes where possible—going up and down the huge mounds of sand was too hard and time consuming. They were able to keep the oasis clearly in view, but in places the ridge was only a thin peak of sand, often falling away steeply into a valley between dunes. One wrong step and Sidney would go sliding down and have to waste valuable time and energy climbing out.

She still managed to peek every now and again when the ground seemed more predictable. The creatures were cutting toward them, angling to get in front of them now. Sidney could make out some details of the creatures. Her first thought was that they were some sort of lizard or dinosaur—maybe a large bird of some kind—loping gracefully on long legs. A shiver of fear ran up her spine so she tried to put the creatures out of her mind.

Ahead of her, Ahanu and Penny both moved across the sand gracefully and Penny seemed to leave only the slightest footprints as she flowed along on the surface of the sand. Sidney wondered how she did that but dismissed the question and concentrated on keeping her balance as they ran across the desert dunes.

Soon Sidney could make out individual palm trees rising into the sky above a carpet of greenery. Sidney hoped there was water there, and as the thought moved through her mind, she felt the rough dryness of her tongue again. She could easily see the oasis. It was a lush, green carpet of grasses and underbrush wrapped around trees—palms, creosote, palo verde—dry climate trees designed by nature to thrive in a desert environment. Strangely, there were also trees that looked startlingly out of place—a dappling of oaks and maples that were closer to the edge of a large, clear blue pool of water. Water, Sidney thought, her heart singing out in joy. Now we just have to survive the dinosaurs.

She focused on the promise of water, ignoring the burning in her muscles, the fire in her lungs—she just kept running. A glance off to the side and she saw the creatures cresting a dune only a few hundred yards away. Her first guess had been correct—dinosaurs of some sort, loping across the sand effortlessly like an ostrich, long legs scissoring in long strides.

The unfamiliar looking lizards were moving on a direct line towards them and getting closer quickly.

"Sidney," Penny yelled over her shoulder. "Hurry! We have to get up in a tree."

Sidney looked back toward the oasis and saw that Ahanu and Penny had really turned it on. The greenery was closer now than the creatures. She gave herself over to the desperate urge to sprint. No more worrying, just concentrating on pumping with her legs, stretching out her stride and for a quick moment she reveled in the speed, the ground flying out from under her so fast that it was a blur. Her breathing settled into a steady rhythm as she caught her second wind. She relished the flow of cooler air blowing her hair back, ruffling her shirt. The fear and desperation of their flight was momentarily forgotten to the pure joy of running as fast as she could.

Then suddenly she was on solid ground, the sand fading into the lush grasses of the oasis. She heard a loud screech behind her and abruptly all the fear rushed back and the burn in her lungs began to rise again. She didn't dare look back and instead aimed toward Penny and Ahanu. They had run up to the first tree they found. It was a tall palm that grew at a strange angle to the ground. Already Penny was scrambling up onto the trunk, with Ahanu helping push her up. She almost looked like a monkey, scampering up the thick trunk, using her hands and feet. Once she was on her way up Ahanu turned toward Sidney.

"Hurry, Sidney," he shouted. She closed the gap quickly and as she raced up to him, he grabbed her under the arms and lifted her up onto the tree trunk. For a moment she wasn't sure she was going to be able to climb, but once she had her feet planted, she realized that the tree was at such an angle that she could almost run up the trunk. She began easing up the tree as fast as she dared. She glanced back and saw Ahanu scrambling up behind her and on the ground the three dinosaurs approached the tree—all angry snarls and screeches as their prey moved up and out of reach.

Eventually Sidney reached Penny. The girl had settled back with her legs wrapped around the trunk and her hands in front of her. She helped Sidney sit down. Once she was sitting, Sidney glanced down and saw that they were only about ten feet above the ground. Her heart sank as she realized that it might not be enough to be out of reach of the snarling beasts below them. Sidney got her first up close look at the creatures. Their eyes were large and glassy, conveying no emotion and their mouths were open slits of hard flesh peeled back to expose rows of razor sharp teeth. On the tops of their heads each had a plume of blue and green iridescent feathers. The colors were startling and beautiful, belying their terrible destructive, murderous nature.

The creatures perched gracefully on their hind legs, balanced by their long sweeping tails. Their short arms were well muscled and equipped with razor sharp claws. With their heads carried low and forward as if reaching toward their prey, they looked positively alien to Sidney. She'd seen plenty of pictures of dinosaurs, just like any other kid, but confronted with one in the flesh she was surprised at how completely out of place they seemed. It wasn't that they seemed exotic—they were completely otherworldly. These weren't the intriguing and strange creatures that had walked the earth millions of years ago—these were beasts of muscle, sinew and bone. Their teeth were not fossils on a shelf somewhere. They were lodged in powerful jaws waiting to rend her limb from limb. She shuddered and tried to pull her legs up tighter to the trunk of the tree.

As she watched, one of the dinosaurs crouched down and hissed, gathered itself and then leapt straight up into the air. It led with its teeth and snapped the air near Sidney's exposed legs. She let out a quick shriek and pulled her legs back up onto the trunk entirely, gripping with her knees and hands.

"Sidney!" Penny said in a quick gasp. She pushed herself up onto her hands and knees and stretched out toward Sidney. "Hold on..." Sidney didn't bother answering and just concentrated on holding onto the trunk for dear life. She yelped again as snapping jaws struck the underside of the trunk. Sidney looked up in time to see Penny losing her balance. For a moment in time the girl appeared to be sliding off the trunk and Sidney's heart quailed in terror, but at the last moment, like a cat, Penny pulled herself back onto her hands and knees on the branch. She looked up at Sidney with wide eyes and then grinned weakly.

"Yikes." Penny settled onto the trunk in the same position as Sidney. "I think I'll just stay right here."

Sidney heard Ahanu mutter behind her.

"This will not do. I have my honor. I know my duty."

"Ahanu..." Sidney heard the suspicious note in Penny's voice. "What are you doing?"

Sidney looked back and saw him shimmying back down the trunk toward the ground. Then he leapt clear and landed on the ground beside the tree. The three dinosaurs swung their heads toward him and one hissed. They immediately began to ease in Ahanu's direction, one spreading out to each side to flank him. The middle creature took a few steps forward and snarled once, a rasping chucking sound, almost like a dog's bark.

"Ahanu, get back in the tree," Sidney yelled, but he ignored her and instead eased slowly away from the tree. He hefted his spear and knife and settled back into a defensive position—weight evenly distributed and his center of gravity low. The dinosaurs continued to move slowly until they were positioned at his flanks and the one in front of him hissed again and lowered its head and crept forward. Ahanu shook his spear and snarled at the creatures. The one in front stopped and lifted its head slightly to study the man. It cocked its head to the side slightly and blinked. It bared its teeth at Ahanu again and a low crawling growl sounded. The ones on the sides of Ahanu seemed to sink slightly, gathering themselves for the pounce. Sidney watched in abject horror as they prepared to attack and she screamed as loud as she could.

All three dinosaurs swung their long heads to study her, buying Ahanu a moments reprieve. She knew it wasn't going to be enough. She also knew she couldn't watch him—her friend —die, so she pushed up onto her knees and carefully turned around to face them.

"Get out of here," she snarled at the dinosaurs. The leader cocked its head and issued another barking snarl. All three turned back to Ahanu. "Leave him alone!" She slid down the trunk slightly, recapturing the attention of the dinosaurs.

"Sidney. Climb back up the tree. Now." Ahanu sounded calm and level. Accepting? Resigned? Sidney felt her anger grow into resolved and shimmied down toward the ground again.

"No."

"Sid." Penny's voice carried down. "What are you doing?"

The honest truth was she had no idea. She wasn't really thinking things through at the moment—just going on gut instinct. The dinosaurs were watching her come down the tree rather than attacking Ahanu, so she kept going.

"Sid!" Penny's voice became strident and desperate. "Honey, come back up here. What do you think will happen to Colin if you get eaten by those things?"

That stopped Sidney. She knew it would kill him as sure as if the dinosaurs had eaten him instead. But she couldn't let Ahanu face the dinosaurs alone.

"I'll tell you what," she said to Ahanu. "If you come back over here and start back up the tree, I won't come down."

"Sidney. It is too late. You are a brave warrior, but you must get back into the tree." There was a hint of frustration and anger in his voice that she'd not heard before. He didn't look at her and instead started to back away from the tree slowly. The dinosaurs swung their heads back to him and began to pace after him at the same careful speed. A low rumbling growl sounded from one of them and another one hissed slowly.

"Ahanu!" Sidney's voice was frantic, bordering on panicked. "Come back over here, please. Don't do this."

"Sid, come back up the tree, right now." Penny sounded angry and exasperated.

"Don't do this, Ahanu..." Sidney ignored Penny and pleaded with him.

"I thank you both for the journey, Sidney and Penelope." Ahanu's voice took on a formal timbre. "May you find what you seek." With that he turned and bolted away from the tree. Immediately the three dinosaurs burst into motion. Sidney could tell that in a matter of seconds they'd pull him to the ground. In her mind she screamed over and over, but her body was frozen. She knew she should look away but she couldn't pull her eyes away from the terrifying sight of Ahanu giving his life for them.

And then, out of nowhere, her father appeared between Ahanu and the raptors. They skidded to a halt and hissed, completely unnerved by his sudden appearance. They lowered their heads and stalked around him, Ahanu completely forgotten.

Sidney's jaw dropped in shock. Relief and elation at seeing him alive and well filled her in a rush—and that was followed by devastating fear as the dinosaurs closed in on him. Dad blinked twice as he took in his surroundings.

"Well, shit. She couldn't have put me in the tree?"

Rescued

Sidney watched in horror as the scene with Ahanu played out all over again, but this time her father was at the center of the raptors as they moved in slowly for the kill. He was standing loosely in the middle of them knees bent slightly, hands raised to his waist. He looked ready to fight, and that alone was enough to break through the shock Sidney was feeling.

"Dad!" she shouted. Her fear for Ahanu multiplied into mind numbing terror.

"Hi, Sid. Give me a moment, hon. I'm kind of in the middle of something here." For several moments no one moved. Sidney could hear the breeze playing through the grasses. Not even the dinosaurs moved. The leader cocked its head and then suddenly lowered it, thrust out and roared. The rasping, guttural sound was devastating to hear. Sidney thought for a moment how completely wrong the television shows and dinosaur documentaries had the sound. It was like nothing she'd ever heard before and it drove sharp stabs of panic through her. For a moment she was frozen by the sound, but then her fear took a new shape, changing from flight to fight in a heartbeat—she had to save her father. She had no idea how, but she had to save him.

She dropped out of the tree and started to run toward Dad. She was past rational thought, sure that he was about to die and wanting only to die with him. But before she'd taken two steps he did the strangest thing.

He stood up straight and turned to look at her, gave her a smile.

"Stop, Sid. Right now." The iron command in his voice froze Sidney and then as the first dinosaur leapt toward him, he reached out and touched the attacking dinosaur lightly. Sidney waited for the splash of blood as teeth met flesh, but instead the creature simply disappeared. The other two dinosaurs stopped in their tracks and studied her father as he walked forward. "Come here, big fella," he said in a soft croon and the nearest dinosaur cocked its head. He showed no fear as he walked slowly right up to it and touched it on the nose and it too was gone. The third one took a hesitant step toward him and was banished in the same way.

Dad turned around and faced Sidney. He opened up his arms and smiled at her crookedly.

"Okay, now you can come hug me."

Sidney lurched into motion and fled into his arms, burying her face in his shoulder. Suddenly all her exhaustion—the burning in her lungs, her painful thirst—all of it was simply gone. For a time she was unaware of anything but the feel of him, the smell of him. He smelled like home. A sob escaped her and she realized she was crying. He stroked her hair softly. "Shh, it's all right, Sid."

She laughed through her tears and hugged him harder. He laughed with her.

"God, I missed you, Dad." Sidney failed to contain a single hitching sob. She tried to get herself under control.

"I missed you too, Sid."

Behind her, Sidney heard a slight cough. She pulled her head away from his shoulder and looked back and saw Penny. The girl stood a few feet away and her eyes looked haunted.

"My turn?" she asked in a small voice.

Sidney made room but didn't let go as Dad pulled Penny into his arms. To her surprise the girl wrapped her arms around him and clung tightly. Sidney put her arms around her as well. "Thank you, thank you, thank you," Penny muttered over and over again. Sidney looked up at her father and saw that he looked just as surprised as she was. Neither of them had seen Penny look anything but thoroughly confident and self-assured. He just stroked Penny's hair the same as he had Sidney's and there was a slight hint of a smile at the corners of his mouth.

Ahanu came to stand next to Sidney, and her father looked up at him and nodded solemnly. The warrior returned the nod just as seriously but stayed quiet.

After a few moments Penny pushed back and looked up at him.

"You figured it out."

"I think so."

"I knew you would." She grinned. "Eventually." He smiled back at her calmly.

"Figured what out?" Sidney asked.

Dad didn't respond, instead keeping his eyes on Penny.

"You're my dream, aren't you? I dreamt you."

"Yes." Penny's eyes shone brightly, but her face was pulled down into a mask of seriousness, looking slightly vulnerable and nervous. "Dad. Can I call you that?"

"Of course you can. You don't even have to ask."

"Dad?" Sidney asked. She pushed back and looked at Penny. "You have another daughter?" She realized that it explained so much. Why the idea of Penny with Dad was so strange—almost wrong. And the way Penny felt like a sister sometimes. *Okay, all the time*, Sidney thought.

Dad laughed.

"In a manner of speaking. I dreamt her and made her real. I suspect it was after the dream of the house fire. Am I right?"

Penny nodded. "You infused me with what you knew of the twins. And in that creation, you gave a little of yourself as well."

"Yes. I can see a little of those girls in you. Or at least what I thought I knew of them. I was young at the time." He smiled apologetically.

"Oh, I like me just how you made me."

He frowned slightly. "So I dreamed you to look like this?"

Penny laughed musically.

"No, silly. I grew up to look like this."

"That makes sense." He nodded slowly, almost absently. Then he seemed to remember Ahanu stood nearby. "I am Colin Pierce. I saw you protecting my daughters. Thank you. I'm forever in your debt." He offered a hand while holding Penny with the other arm. For a moment Ahanu looked confused. As he reached out and took Dad's hand, he spoke slowly.

"I did what was promised, Dreamer. I have my honor. I know my duty."

Dad cocked his head at Ahanu and he too looked confused. Then something dawned in his eyes as if he were remembering a distant memory, long forgotten and pushed into the furthest corner of his mind.

"I know you." He spoke slowly. "Where have we met?"

"You do not remember?"

"I...I have this foggy memory of talking to you in a dream."

"Yes. You came to me in my dream and asked for my help. When you told me what you wanted, I could not refuse you. I made an oath to find and protect them as best I could."

"You met my father?" Sidney asked. "You knew who he was, and you didn't tell us?"

Ahanu looked embarrassed.

"I gave my word that I would not reveal any of this. I swore an oath."

Sidney wasn't sure how she felt about that.

"But you knew he was all right, the whole time?"

"No." Ahanu shook his head, holding up a hand to forestall her. "I didn't know anything about him—only that he wanted me to come protect you both. I am sorry to have withheld that from you, Sidney. And you too, Penelope." He shrugged apologetically. Then he turned back to Dad. "I must admit freely—they protected me as much as I did them." He glanced at Sidney and then Penny. "Your daughters are among the most courageous people I have ever met. Warriors in their own right." He focused on Sidney and she could see the unspoken question on his face. She gave him a small smile, which grew as she saw the relief blossom on his face.

Colin nodded and smiled. "A father never had better daughters." For a brief moment a dark thought raced across his face but then he smiled again and his expression cleared like a blue sky after inclement weather. "Now, would you like me to send you home?"

Ahanu pursed his lips and considered the offer. After a short time he looked up and shook his head. "I think I would finish this journey. I would not be able to live with myself if I abandoned your daughters at this point. A warrior does not shirk his—" he shot a quick smile at the girls. "Or her responsibilities. I will see it through."

"Ahanu." Sidney put her hands on her hips. "Don't be silly. You have brought us this far and you should go home to your people—your family."

"She is right," Penny added before he could object. "You have been a friend to us—willingly put yourself in the way of danger for us. Now it is time for you to go home. No more adventures for you." She grinned.

Ahanu grimaced and ducked his head. "I would indeed like to go home, but I am not sure it is the right thing to do."

"It's the right thing," Dad said. "You've already done enough—you've done your part and now you need to leave the rest to me. To us." He glanced at the girls briefly.

Ahanu sighed heavily and then finally nodded his head. "Promise me that you will come to me in my dream and tell me if everything ended well? I know that we come from different worlds, but I cannot help but feel I leave a part of me with you."

Dad met Ahanu's eyes and nodded gravely, but did not speak. After a moment Ahanu returned his nod and then turned back to face Sidney and Penelope.

"So be it. Penelope, Sidney. I will miss you both. In all my life I will never forget this journey we took." He stood straight and offered them a bow and then a quick salute. For a moment Sidney felt the urge to bow in return, but she glanced at Penny. The girl was looking at her too and they both broke into a laugh at the same moment. Then they pulled away from Dad gently, turned and as one pulled Ahanu into a hug. Briefly he struggled against the contact, but then relaxed, smiled and put his arms around them both gingerly; as if afraid to touch them for fear that he would break them.

"You thought you'd going to get away with a bow and a wave?" Penny asked in a voice laced with affection.

"Not going to happen, Ahanu." Sidney rose up on her tip toes and kissed him lightly on the cheek. Before he could react she smiled at him and placed another soft kiss on his lips. The shock on his face made Penelope laugh as Sidney gently pulled away from him. Sidney felt Penny slip her hand into hers and gave it a squeeze in return. Ahanu smiled at them both, reaching up to touch his lips softly.

"Goodbye, my friends," he said wistfully and then turned back to Dad, who had an eyebrow arched. Ahanu met his eye steadily, but Sidney could see the sparkle in both men's eyes. "I am ready."

Dad chuckled. "Be safe, Ahanu. Sleep and dream well." He reached out and touched the small warrior's brow lightly and Ahanu's eyes slowly slid closed and he faded away. Just like that Colin was alone with his daughters. "Well, that takes care of that."

Sidney could not help but feel a small emptiness in her heart, but she kept the memory of the feel of Ahanu's lips on hers, and held it close. "Now what? Home?"

Dad shook his head slowly.

"I think it's time to end this."

"Are you sure you can?" Sidney cocked her head at him, loving the sound of confidence in his voice. The strength.

"We'll see, I suppose. I've got to try, Sid." He paused and then smiled. "I'd send you both home but I think I'm going to need you."

"You're ready." Penny was still grinning.

"I hope so." He sounded wry but Sidney still heard the strength in his voice. "At any rate, we'd better go find the Torment."

"Do you know how to get there?" Sidney asked.

"Yep." Then his face fell into serious lines. "But you both need to brace yourself. The Torment is a little—surprising to see for the first time."

"Where is it? How do we get there?"

"Don't worry, Sid." He held out a hand to each girl. "I'll get us there."

Sidney reached out and took one of his hands and Penny took the other. The smile he gave them was calm and reassuring. Sidney couldn't remember the last time she'd seen him smile so completely.

"All ready?"

Both girls nodded.

"Okay, then, close your eyes." He closed his eyes. "Let's go." Sidney closed her eyes and waited for some sense of motion, some change, but there was nothing. "Okay, you can open them now."

She heard someone speak. The man's voice was familiar but at the same time completely alien. It sounded wrong. Angry. Hostile.

"Ah, you came back. And you brought our children. Wonderful!"

"My children." Dad voice was low, devoid of any emotion.

Sidney searched for the speaker. They were in some kind of glade—a large area of green grass and bright flowers that was carved out of the middle of a forest. It was beautiful beyond anything she'd ever seen before. As she looked around, her eyes passed over the beautiful woman from her dreams, bound and on her side on the ground. And then she saw him. Her mouth dropped open as she realized it was her father speaking. She still held his hand but impossibly he stood across the clearing as well.

"Dad?" Sidney felt the world crash down around her in a jolt of shock.

Her father—the other one across the clearing—laughed, a deep belly laugh, but with no hint of friendliness to it.

"Daughter. How good to finally meet you." He spread his arms wide. "How about a hug for your long-lost father."

A Dream Realized

Sidney stared at the man across the glade dumbfounded. It was not possible that her father stood there and also stood next to her. Yet it was undeniably true. She glanced to the version of her father that held her hand.

"I know." He was watching her with a slight quirk to his mouth. "It's unsettling, isn't it?"

"That's the Torment?" She still felt dazed.

"Yep," he replied. "I'm the Torment. And I'm not the Torment."

"Still haven't figured it out yet, have you, Colin." The malice in the other man's voice was daunting.

Dad shrugged but didn't reply.

"Well, despite your little jaunt nothing here has changed," the nightmare said, swaggering forward confidently. "You still have to bring down the Wall if you wish to keep your daughters. You just made it easier for me—now I won't have to go find them if you fail."

"I don't think so." Dad responded in a firm voice. "I think we're all done with your threats."

"Don't be foolish," Torment was scornful. "I don't want to hurt our daughters but I will if I must."

"And then you will be trapped here with no leverage to force me to do your dirty work."

"That won't matter. I can bring the wall down myself."

"No." Sidney heard the resolve in Dad's voice. "If that were true you would have done so long ago." He held up a hand to forestall the Torment. "I realize you can do it damage, and if allowed you could eventually bring it down on your own, but I imagine that would take a long time. Somehow I doubt you're patient enough for that." He arched an eyebrow and the corner of his mouth quirked in a half smile. "You need me."

Rage flowed across the Torment's face and Sidney knew her father had nailed it.

"Fine, you're right: I'm impatient," the Torment hissed. "That doesn't change the fact that I can kill the ones you love at my whim."

"You know. I think I've heard enough from you. Why don't you be quiet." Dad gestured and the Torment's mouth snapped shut. "And while we're at it, don't move." The nightmare's muscles became rigid and the rage on his face changed into an unseeing fury.

"So first things first." Dad turned and spoke to the Wall. Her bonds simply disappeared, allowing her to push herself to her feet. She wore a calm smile.

"I knew you'd figure it out, Dreamer."

"Figure what out?" Sidney knew she sounded querulous but didn't care. She felt like she was sliding into some strange nightmare. Dad glanced at her and gave her a reassuring smile.

"A moment, Sid." He looked back at the Wall. "Why didn't you just tell me?"

"To have any value, some knowledge must be earned."

"What does that mean?"

"You were like a child here—newborn and unused to the world around you. It's unlikely you would have believed me if I had just told you. You might have thought you believed me, but in your heart you would not have accepted the possibility. And that would have rendered you powerless." She began to walk toward him with an outstretched hand. "I couldn't take that risk. Our need was—is great."

"So what you're saying is that I'm a small child?"

The Wall's laugh was melodious and rich, but she didn't answer and that was answer enough for Sidney. Penny unsuccessfully tried to stifle a snicker and Sidney had to laugh as well. He glanced at them and then nodded wryly.

"Well, no big deal. Marianne always said I was like a third grader. So what about him?" He pointed his thumb over his shoulder toward the Torment. "Is he really me? How's that work?"

"He is a part of you. They all are. Parts of you were shucked off after your wife and daughters died in the plane wreck." He stared at her blankly.

"Daughters?" His voice was quiet but Sidney heard the slightest hint of panic. "Don't you mean daughter?" The Wall only returned his gaze seriously. "Oh God." Sidney heard the shock in his voice. "So that's why they thought she was on the plane."

"Yes. She was on the plane."

"What?" Sidney asked. Then it hit her and she felt the world shudder around her. "No. No way." The Wall looked over at her and smiled.

Again the woman didn't respond, simply staring into Sidney's eyes, waiting.

"That can't be" Sidney shook her head in denial. Suddenly she felt out of place—as if she were wearing someone else's clothes.

"It's okay, Sid." Penny's arm encircled Sidney, pulling her close in a hug. "It's not so terrible being a dream. It doesn't change anything. You still exist. You still feel and everything you feel is real. Our father made us, but we became more all by ourselves."

Sidney felt numb, but nodded. As she stared dumbly, her father walked over to her. He wrapped both girls in his arms and hugged them firmly.

"She's right, Sid. You are both my daughters. I may have lost my family, but I never lost you." He kissed the top of her head softly. "And we gained Penny. You two are my family— my whole world. Nothing will ever change that." They stood that way for a few minutes, and Sidney took comfort in his strong arms.

My father.

"But I'm not her. I'm not Sidney. I'm...I'm someone else." She pulled back slightly and looked at his face, searching for some hint of what he was feeling. She saw only warmth and love there.

"No, you're not her. You are you. Something of her lives in you, I guess. For four years you've been Sidney to everyone, including yourself. You have a choice—you can either remain Sidney, or you can choose another name and be someone else." He smiled at her. "Honestly, I don't care what you choose. I will love you either way." She buried her face in his chest again. "Of course, I have no idea what I'll tell your grandparents if you decide to be someone else."

Sidney's mind reeled at the possibilities.

Finally he disengaged from his daughters and gave them a quick smile before turning to face the Torment. The nightmare stood frozen and speechless where her father had left him.

"Well, now we deal with my worse half." He closed his eyes and concentrated for a while, but eventually opened his eyes frowning. "I can't seem to get rid of him."

Penny put a hand on his shoulder.

"You can't unmake him, Dad. He is a part of you. Even you cannot unmake yourself."

Dad stared past her distantly, his mind clearly far away. Then suddenly a light came into his eyes and he smiled. "I think I've got it."

Come Together

Colin was flying blind in uncharted territory that stretched the boundaries of his imagination. But he understood a fundamental fact that made everything possible. This was his dream. He was the Dreamer, and in a sense all dreams were his. He had no idea how this had happened—whether it was destined to be this way, or if it was something that was born during that first dream as a child. A change in him that was brought on by the sacrifice of the twins. He felt a twinge of sadness and regret. He knew he would trade all of this if the twins, his wife and his daughters could live again. Well, he wouldn't give up Penny and Sidney. He tried to imagine what he'd do with two different versions of her.

He'd love them both, of course.

As quickly as that he wrested control of the dream away from the Torment, gathering the reins of the Dreamside and smiled. He closed his eyes and concentrated on summoning all the parts of himself that he'd shed over the years in the dreams. He already had his darker side, frozen and straining angrily to break out of Colin's control. He just needed the rest.

"Come home to me." He felt the air around him change subtly, as if something had come to occupy the space nearby, displacing the air suddenly. He heard a soft gasp from behind him and he opened his eyes. He had suspected what would happen when he did this, but being confronted by the reality of it was shocking and he staggered back a step.

"Colin." He heard all the warmth of her love for him in the sound of her voice. "It is so good to see you again, love."

"Mari." He knew his voice was unsteady and filled with raw emotion. Beside her Emma stood and smiled up at him. "Emma." He reached out and took their hands carefully, as if worried that he would not be able to touch them—insubstantial ghosts of his past, memories that his subconscious, sleeping mind had created and then hidden away out of sight. But then their hands met and they were warm and soft in his. "I have missed you both so much."

"I know, Colin," Marianne said. "I have missed you as well, but it is long past time to move on. You have dwelt in the loss of us for too long. It is time to live your life."

"I know. I know you're right. It's just been so hard. I have such a hard time remembering things about...about us...about you."

Marianne chuckled. "Yes, you put those memories away. You can reclaim them if you wish." She gestured around. "All of this is yours. Is you. Make it what you will." She reached her free hand up to touch his face gently. "Oh, and one more thing, dear. Forgive yourself. It was not your fault that we died. It was not your fault that the twins died."

"I should have stopped you..." he began but she stopped him.

"No, it would have happened anyway."

As Colin nodded grudgingly, he realized that there were tears streaming down his face. She wiped one away and smiled at him again. "I love you, Colin Pierce. But it is time now to make this right." She looked past him at the Torment, and Colin looked back over his shoulder.

"Come here, Colin." He gestured and the Torment gasped and nearly fell on his face. The nightmare looked surprised that he called him by his name. "Come here." Colin allowed the nightmare's mouth to reform, giving that part of him voice.

"You can't do this," the Torment whispered, but almost against his will he walked slowly toward Colin.

"Sure I can. You belong to me. As you said—you are me and I am you. It's time for you to come home." Colin held out his hands, offering them to the nightmare version of himself and the Torment froze.

"No." The Torment was pale with fear. "I won't go."

"Come here, Colin," her father repeated. The Torment began to walk again; almost staggering as he tried to fight his legs and stop. Suddenly tears started streaming down his face. He sobbed softly and the sound tore at Sidney's heart. For the first time she recognized the nightmare as her father. She sensed something about this creature that was her father.

Colin allowed his darker half to come to a halt in front of him and he reached out and took his hand, a wry smile playing at the corner of his mouth.

"How many people get to say they held hands with themselves?" Behind him Penny laughed but everyone else was silent. The Torment was not looking at him though. He had turned to face Marianne.

"Mari?" His voice broke.

"Colin. It's good to see you as well. I always enjoyed your devilish side as well. Tempered, of course."

The Torment's breath hitched in a quick sob but he did not speak—he stared at her like a starving man staring at a seven course meal.

She reached out and took his other hand, so that they formed a triangle.

At the moment when their hands touched it was as if a circuit was formed, energy racing around and through them, and the nightmare's eyes opened wide in surprise. Slowly the terror on his face faded into wonder. The tears continued to course down his face but a tentative smile broke across his features.

"Oh."

Colin smiled back at himself and pulled him closer. Where their hands joined a light began to shine, pulsing with growing brightness until it was hard to look at them.

"Oh," the nightmare repeated and the smile changed into something radiant. "You're right. Oh God, you're right." Then the Torment strode forward directly into Colin and as their bodies merged, there was a blinding flash of light.

"Much better." He still held Marianne's hand and he turned to look at Emma. "Are you coming, sweetness?" he asked quietly. She smiled back at him.

"I don't think so, Daddy." He looked confused. "You didn't make me, Dad. Sidney made me. I am her dream, not yours." He nodded slowly.

"That makes sense, I think. I have never forgotten anything about you." He looked embarrassed briefly and glanced at Marianne guiltily.

She laughed and took his other hand. "Forgive yourself, Colin."

He turned back to Emma. "So will we see you again?"

"I think so. I am not the same kind of dream as Penny and Sidney. I am not as strong and I will always dwell in the Dreamside. But I think I will see you if you come visit." She smiled up at him and then slowly faded away.

Marianne reached out and put her hand on his chin, pulling his eyes back to her.

"It is time, Colin." She slowly stepped closer and leaned in to press her lips against his softly. As their lips met, a glowing light flashed and surrounded them. He felt a wave of warmth and love slide into his heart and all of a sudden he could remember everything. He remembered the first time they met. Their first kiss. The way she had looked in the exhausted afterglow of giving birth to their children. He could remember every detail about her—the lines on her face, the way her brow crinkled up when she smiled at him. The way her hands looked and felt. Then she was gone and all that remained were his memories of her returned.

For a long moment he stood with his eyes closed, tears streaming down his face and he smiled. Then he turned to his daughters and held open his arms and they walked over into his embrace. Sidney slid one of her arms around Penny so that the three of them were a gentle knot of warmth and affection.

"Is it over, then?" Sidney asked.

"Yes, it's over."

Penny

Penny stood still in the embrace of her sister and father. It felt so warm and comforting. It was a moment so perfect that it would be indelibly etched upon her mind—the sense of its wholeness so strong that she felt it physically. She had long ago come to the conclusion that life was a collection of such moments strung together like colorful beads on a necklace. The time between was important and could be good or bad, but it was those defining moments that made it all worthwhile. God, she loved being alive.

She noticed that everything was brighter, cleaner and more well defined when she was with these people. She had known the moment that she'd first met each of them that they were her home—her center. She smiled into the soft, slightly wrinkled linen of Colin's shirt. After a while she pulled back enough to look up at him.

"You know. Nothing really ends. It just changes into something different."

"I like that." His brow furrowed slightly as he considered the idea. "It feels so much more...hopeful."

Penny nodded sagely.

"Hope is good." She gave him a bright smile. When Penny smiled, she felt it throughout her whole self—a vibrant thrumming sensation that bubbled up from her middle out to every part of her body. Like a shout of light into the universe. This wasn't something that had always been true. She'd learned this as a result of growing up in the Dreamside. Life there was unpredictable, sometimes frightening and other times wondrous. She had developed the ability to take things as they came and see them in the best possible light. It was a skill that served her well—and helped her to survive.

"You know." He was smiling back at her—it was more tentative but carried genuine happiness. The first she'd seen on his face. It warmed her through. "You're going to have to show me how to smile like that. I think I've forgotten that somewhere along the way—if I ever knew."

"So that makes you my older sister." Sidney spoke. "I've never had an older sister before." Her face fell suddenly and Penny knew what she was thinking. This time she didn't let Sidney express it herself.

"Just as I have the essence of the twins in me, you have the essence of the original Sidney in you. You have her memories—and because Dad created you out of her, you are her. Remember what the Torment said—he was Colin." She wasn't sure if Sidney was soothed by her words, but she was hopeful that over time Sidney would come to realize that she was what she was, and nothing mattered beyond that fact. "And anyway, I love you as a sister, and Dad loves you as a daughter. What else matters?"

Sidney gave her a smile that started out tentative—almost grudging—but then it blossomed into something more real.

"Thanks, Penny."

"No problem, Sid. That's what sisters are for, right?"

"Right."

"So why did I create the Torment?" Colin asked, truly puzzled. "I mean, I understand why I created the two of you, but why such a negative creature?"

"You lost so much, so fast that you needed a way to compartmentalize the pain, rage and dismay that was dragging you down. Of course, you couldn't give all of it to him, but you did manage to give him the larger part in his making. I think you could not truly heal yourself of those things when you no longer had them. In essence, in the attempt to protect yourself, you created your own cage."

"So I had to take him back," he mused. "Well, I must admit that a part of me feels angry. Angrier than I ever felt before about the Accident." Penny watched as anger flitted into guilt and finally peaceful calm.

Movement beyond Colin caught Penny's attention and she saw the pair of women who'd been here already step forward. Both were attractive and young. The blonde one radiated bright strength and Penny instantly liked her. The other woman, raven haired and quiet was more withdrawn, with walls of her own erected to protect herself. Penny wondered what had happened to close her off so, but also recognized the fundamental goodness of the woman.

"Colin," the blonde one said. "Care to introduce us?" She had one eyebrow arched and her arms crossed over her chest.

Penny couldn't help but laugh.

"Introducing people is decidedly not one of his strengths." She stepped around her father and walked over to the woman and extended a hand. "I am Penelope. Call me Penny. This is Sidney—my sister."

"I'm Jillian, and this is Pam." The woman had a warm smile and her grip was strong as she took Penny's hand and the vibe that ran through their hands was good.

"You helped our father."

"Well, let's just say we helped each other." Jillian's smile changed into a grin. "We'd still be walking around that damned park and he'd be talking nonsense still if we'd not run into each other."

"Talking nonsense?" Sidney had stepped forward to stand beside Penny and now reached out to shake Jillian's hand.

"Long story," Colin said from behind her. "I'll explain everything later. Right now I need to get Jillian and Pam back home." He walked over, took Jillian's hand and pulled her back until he could take Pam's as well. "Salient. Argot. Thank you both for all your help. I don't think this would have ended quite so well without you two."

"It was our pleasure, Colin." Pam stepped forward and gave him a quick hug before stepping away but he didn't let her hand go. Jillian hugged him as well.

"Will we see you again?"

"Give me a call when you wake up. I'll be waiting."

Penny wondered if they would make that call. She couldn't tell how much of this dream they believed in. She hoped they would. "But now it's time for you to go home." He closed his eyes and concentrated and both women faded away, leaving Penny with her family. Family. She liked that word.

※

"One more thing to do, and then we can go." Colin turned to face the Wall. She stood apart from them, smiling benevolently at the three of them as if she were watching her children grown. There was something wistful hiding in that smile for Penny in particular. The Wall had been like a mother to her and had helped her to grow up into the dream—the woman—she had become. Even if she'd wanted, she couldn't resist returning that smile in spades. For the first time Penny noticed that the pure radiance of the Wall was dimmer than usual, and when Colin reached the Wall he stopped in front of her.

"I imagine you've taken quite a beating while you were waiting for me to come to my senses and figure this all out." It wasn't really a question, and Colin sounded almost apologetic.

"I've taken much wear and tear over the ages of mankind," the Wall responded in that startlingly musical voice.

"Well, let's see if I can't help you with that." He reached out both hands to her. She took them and he pulled her closer. Penny could tell he was being careful not to be overly familiar with her in a physical sense. Though the two of them stood close together they only touched at the hands. He closed his eyes and seemed to slip into a trance. The Wall closed her eyes as well and her face became expressionless. Her head sagged gently down to her chest and they stood that way for long moments.

Then Penny realized that Colin himself was beginning to glow softly. She hadn't noticed it at first as his glow was subsumed in that of the Wall. But as Penny watched his glow became brighter and brighter.

She felt Sidney take her hand, and she squeezed it in return. Colin's glow eventually surpassed the Wall's and then Penny lost sight of the two as the glow of each of them merged into a blindingly bright nimbus of light surrounding them both. Penny was forced to avert her eyes as the light became painful to look at.

Then the light disappeared and when Penny looked back Colin had lost his glow, leaving the Wall shining at her usual brightness.

"Thank you, Dreamer," the Wall whispered. She pulled Colin into a quick embrace, surprising him briefly. Again he felt the flow of calm peace move through him. Then she released him and stepped back. "You are everything I had hoped and more."

"Will we see you again?"

"Oh, every time you dream, I will be there and you can call me to you if you have a need." Her expression was warm and affectionate as she looked at him.

"Or if I just want to say hi?"

"Or if you just want to say hi." She turned to Sidney and Penny. "Make sure you two come to visit me often."

Penny nodded happily.

"All right then." Colin turned to his daughters again. "Ready to go home?"

Penny shook her head and walked to him.

"Not yet. We have one more thing to take care of before we can go."

Her father's expression turned puzzled.

"What's that?"

When she was close enough she reached up and put a hand on each of his cheeks and stared up into his eyes.

"You were not responsible for what happened in to the twins or to your family." Her voice was firm. She was repeating what the dream Marianne had told him because she knew he needed to hear it. She suspected that she and Sidney would be reminding him occasionally for a while still.

"I realize that, Penny.

She shook her head.

"You realize it up here," She touched him gently on the forehead. "But you must realize it *here*." She moved her hand and placed her palm over his heart. "You are not responsible for what you dreamt. I doubt you could have changed the course of those events. How could you know what you are, what you are capable of?"

This time he didn't speak, but a brief haunted glint passed through his eyes.

"Really." She caught his eyes in hers.

"I know. You two will have to help me learn that in my heart." He nodded at Sidney to include her.

"Maybe we can enlist a little outside help." Sidney had a mischievous glint in her eyes and Penny knew exactly what she meant.

"Yes, I think we can do that." Penny shared a knowing smile with her sister. God, she loved how that sounded.

"Meddlers." He rolled his eyes.

"Oh, yes," Sidney said behind Penny. "Definitely meddlers."

"Oh!" Something had just occurred to her. "We get to take the train!" Colin and Sidney both laughed. Penny stepped between them and hooked an arm through theirs and pulled them forward. "Take us home, Dad!"

So he did.

Epilogue

Ahanu woke slowly and opened his eyes to the brightness of midmorning. He lay on his bedroll near the fire. He sat up slowly and rubbed his eyes.

Home.

He looked around and everything looked familiar, yet at the same time different. Smaller. He smiled wryly to himself.

Maybe it is I who have become larger.

He cast his mind back, examining the fresh and strong memories of the time he'd spent with Sidney and Penelope, and he felt a pang in his heart. He would miss those girls. Penny, so resilient and strong—always able to see the best in the world around her, no matter how dark it was. And Sidney, shining like a star, yet completely unaware of her own strength.

And beauty.

Suddenly there was a commotion as people noticed he was awake again. Around him people abandoned what they were doing and came to him.

"Ahanu." His mother sat on the ground beside him. "Where have you been?"

He chuckled.

"I was walking with spirits and dreams."

She frowned as more of the people came and sat around them quietly, listening and watching.

"Spirits and dreams?" He heard her doubt.

"Yes." He was pleased with the feeling of self assurance—he rarely felt this way. These were his people—his clan—and he had always been the young child. He knew that his mother and father loved him, but it was not the practice of his people to openly dote on their children. The land they lived in was a dangerous and hard place and softness was a liability—so it was taught and trained out of the children. "Walking with spirits and dreams. One spirit and two dreams, to be exact."

"But you were not in your blankets when I woke. How could you walk with spirits and dreams if you did not sleep?"

"The spirit took me into the dream entirely—not just my sleeping mind." He spoke patiently. He wasn't sure he would be able to convince anyone, but that didn't bother him—he knew what had happened and that was enough. "The spirit charged me to protect his dream children, and I did so. I have my honor and I know my duty."

His mother watched his face and after a long moment she nodded decisively, and he saw pride in her eyes.

"It is good that you served the spirit well."

"So now he is a great spirit walker?" a scornful voice said from behind him. Ahanu would know that voice anywhere: Ebru.

"I would make no such claim, Ebru." Ahanu didn't bother turning to face the warrior.

"He probably wandered away from the fire to relieve himself in the night and got lost." Ebru's disdain was clear in his voice. "You are lucky to have found us again—I have seen you track. You are barely a hunter." The larger man placed his spear in front of himself, haft firmly on the ground, sharpened tip pointing skyward. This was as close to a challenge as a warrior could make without reciting the words themselves. It was a position intended to intimidate and belittle. For a moment, Ahanu was a young child again, facing Ebru's abuse with fear. His struggle had never been to win, but rather to hide his fear away. His mouth went dry as the memories of Ebru's unkindness flowed through him.

Like a shark scenting blood in the water, Ebru sensed Ahanu's fear and he sneered scornfully. "Would you have us believe you are a man now, little Ahanu?" It was a grave insult —one that would usually result in a duel but Ahanu felt no insult at the larger man's words. Ahanu was surprised at how little fear he felt as he faced the larger man.

A hush fell and the people made to move out of the way. A space was cleared between Ahanu and Ebru. Memories of his time on the Dreamside flooded through his mind. Penny and Sidney's faces floated before him in his mind, each smilingly her own special smile—Penny's face alight with cheerful happiness, and Sidney smiling at him with warmth and affection. He knew in that one moment that nothing Ebru could do here that would diminish what Ahanu had seen or done when he travelled with the young women. Somehow he had grown beyond Ebru.

Ahanu silently offered the dreams a prayer of thanks, and closed his eyes, holding their faces in his mind for a long moment. He would try to remember everything about them. He would miss them. He could almost hear their voices. Suddenly the memory of Sidney's kiss flowed through him—he could feel the softness of her lips on his—and he smiled before opening his eyes. He squared his shoulders, met Ebru's stare eye for eye, and pushed his chin in the air, offering no challenge, but no retreat either.

"I see you, Ebru." Ahanu picked up his spear and placed it haft down in front of himself. "You are the better hunter. I know where I stand among the People." Ahanu paused and glanced around. Then he hefted his spear lightly in his hand. Tension crackled in the air and around him he heard the People mutter and gasp. Ebru took a step back and raised his own spear, but before violence could erupt, Ahanu sank gracefully to the ground with his legs folded beneath him. He placed his spear and knife on the ground before him, his hands on his knees, palms up, and returned his eyes to Ebru. "I see you, Ebru. Can you see me?"

For a long moment, the silence remained, and he met Ebru's eyes with determination, and no hint of fear. He wasn't hiding fear—he didn't feel it. He knew that Ebru could offer him nothing that could diminish the things Ahanu had seen and done. He knew that while Ebru was the better hunter,

Ahanu was a tested warrior—blooded and victorious. He wouldn't point this out to Ebru, but it was true nonetheless.

Ebru watched Ahanu through narrowed eyes, and then suddenly huffed angrily, walked slowly across the dirt to stand in front of Ahanu. He looked down at him speculatively, with a tiny frown on his brow. Ahanu thought perhaps the larger man realized that a different kind of challenge had been issued— one in which there was no violence. He wasn't sure if the warrior would take the challenge or if he would reject it and lose face with the People.

Tension rose, but in the end, Ebru slowly sank to sit in front of Ahanu, and placed his spear and knife in front of himself, between them.

"I see you, Ahanu," he rumbled grudgingly. "I see you, little warrior." The People around them let out a collective sigh and began to crowd forward and sit around them. He glanced over Ebru's shoulder and standing a few yards away was Amara studying him as if seeing him for the first time. He offered her a smile—not too wide, or giving too much of his heart away— but friendly and warm. He realized that if she chose another man he would hope for her to have happiness, because that was what love meant—wanting someone else's happiness more than your own.

He was surprised to see the shy smile that bloomed across her features. She moved her lips and spoke silently across the crowd at him.

"I see you, Ahanu."

He nodded to her slowly and in his heart joy erupted. Against his volition, his smile widened and betrayed him, telling her everything. If anything her smile became warmer, just for him.

※

"So are we going to do this?" Jillian asked Pam. Her friend had an apprehensive look on her face, but then she shrugged in resignation.

"Sure, let's do it. What's the worst thing that can happen?" Jillian chuckled.

"Exactly. I have to know if..." she let her words trail off and Pam nodded once.

"I would like to know, as well."

Jillian picked up the phone and dialed the number quickly. They'd found the number on the internet and it had taken them several days to persuade themselves to make the call. She listened to the phone ring and with each ring she began to feel less sure of this course of action. Of course it had just been a dream. He would think they were insane—if he even spoke to them. She imagined they'd have to work their way through a few layers of people before they'd even get to speak to him.

The first thing they had done once they woke up was speak on the phone—confirming that they had indeed shared the dream. In the end that was why they finally were ready to make this call. Everything else could be explained away, but the fact that they both had exactly the same dream—that they could not explain, or even understand. It went against everything they thought they knew about the world.

She remembered that impossible moment when Colin returned and saved them all. She saw power in him that was bright and hard to look at. She saw his wife and his daughters and how they all came together like pieces of a puzzle that resolved into a beautiful landscape when they clicked together. She had seen Colin pull the Torment into himself and how that addition hadn't lessened his power and strength—it had only added another dimension to it. Brought him more alive. In those moments Colin had seemed more than a man.

When everything was done he turned to face her and Pam and smiled at them warmly. He thanked them and gave them each a hug, whispered his thanks. Told them he would wait for their phone call. Then he sent them home. Coming out of that dream had left her with a bittersweet feeling—the wonder and fear of the world they'd visited. The beauty of the Wall. That warm feeling of coming home when she was surrounded by Colin and his dreams.

It was hard to understand and accept that his daughters were dreams. The entire experience had been hard to understand and accept and so it had been no different—she just took it all on faith. It brightened her world.

All of that had led up to this moment.

Finally the phone was picked up.

"Fireside Literary Agency." A young woman answered. She didn't sound exactly bored so much as absent. Focused on other things besides the phone call.

"Hi," Jillian said after a brief pause. "I was hoping that I might speak to Darcy Stephens, please."

"May I ask who is calling?"

"Yes, of course. My name is Jillian Foster."

"Let me see if Darcy is available." Then the woman was gone, and soft, almost soothing music took her place. This was the first barrier—if they couldn't get through to speak to this woman, they were done before they'd really started. And then they'd never know. Jillian had to be honest—it was unlikely they'd get to speak to her. A literary agent based in New York? Everything about that combination spoke of busy. Then the music stopped and Jillian heard another voice.

"Jillian?" The woman's voice was soft and friendly. "I'm glad you called. Colin told me to expect you—he was hoping that you would call him. He asked me to give you his home number and tell you to call right away." Jillian was shocked—frozen and unable to respond. She looked at Pam and slowly nodded, and Pam's eyes lit up. "Jillian? Are you there?"

"Yes." Even though this was what she'd been hoping for Jillian couldn't believe it. "Yes, I'm here. He wants to talk to me?"

"Oh, yes, most definitely. He was extremely clear on that. Do you have pencil and paper?" Jillian took down the number and thanked the woman and they broke the connection.

She looked over at Pam.

"So?" Pam asked. "What did she say."

In answer, Jillian held up the paper with the phone number on it.

"He wants us to call him. At home." She smiled at Pam excitedly and her friend smiled back, the same excitement mirrored on her face.

※

Kate held her purse on her lap lightly and stared out the windows. It was nearly Christmas and the houses were aglow with bright and cheerful lights. She felt completely at peace with her world, and a small smile played around the corners of her mouth. Absently she reached up and tucked a loose wisp of hair behind her ear.

"Okay." Colin sat beside her in the driver's seat. "Why are you smiling like the cat that ate the canary?" She turned and her smile widened as she took him in, drank him thirstily with her eyes.

"I'm just happy."

He reached over and took her hand and gave it a squeeze. "Not nervous?"

"I suppose I should be nervous. Meeting the folks is a big step, I think." They had been dating for just over a month, and everything about the time they spent together was like coming home. A part of her was frantically warning her to slow down, take baby steps. But another part of her was impatient for him to take the next step. For some reason she had no doubt that he would eventually, and despite that hidden impatience, she would never push him.

"Yeah, especially my folks." There was a playful sparkle in his eyes as he looked back to the road.

"Great. Way to inspire confidence, Colin." She squeezed his hand again. Strangely she didn't feel nervous at all. Sidney and Penny had volunteered to watch the boys. Kate was still a bit confused at the whole Penny thing—Colin's long lost daughter? But it was undeniable. In addition to looking a bit like both Colin and Sidney, Penny fit right into the little family that they were all building like she truly belonged.

At any rate, Kate was looking forward to hearing that story. Colin had promised he'd share it with her eventually, but it was Penny's story, too. Kate had been surprised to discover that Penny and Sidney were like bookends. Along with their father, they were dreams come true, and Kate was thrilled to grow closer to them.

"You know..." Kate changed the subject. "I wasn't sure if you were ever going to ask me out."

"Have a little faith, Kate." He chuckled softly. The sound was easy and warm and sent a tiny thrill through her. "I mean, with Sidney pulling for you, I never had a chance."

It was her turn to laugh. It was true that Sidney had become the arch conspirator and manipulator. But it had taken too long for Kate's tastes, so she'd asked him to coffee. She wasn't sure how it had gone—he hadn't seemed completely ready yet, and the last thing Kate wanted was anything from him until he was ready. Then two days later he'd shown up on her doorstep with a little smile playing across his mouth. He'd looked ever so slightly nervous, and Kate found it endearing. Plus he was devastatingly handsome. Serious eye candy, she'd confided in Sidney recently. The fact that he had no idea was endearing.

"Hello, Kate," he had said.

"Colin." She'd felt slightly flustered. "Hi."

There had been a brief moment of uncomfortable nervousness, but then suddenly they shared a goofy smile and both laughed. She'd invited him in, and after a few minutes obviously working up her nerve he'd asked her to dinner. That night when he dropped her off, she let him kiss her, and murmured "About time, Colin," before going inside. She'd loved the look on his face as she left him there. He'd looked like a little boy with a new toy, and at the same time an expression of surprise that made his eyes widen. Remembering that look made her feel warm inside, and she smiled again.

Colin slowed and turned into his parents' driveway, pulled forward and turned off the car. For a moment they sat in the stillness of the night, listening to the soft ticking the engine made before going quiet. It was like a metronome losing the rhythm and staggering to a halt. Once it was completely silent, Colin angled himself to look at her, reached out and reclaimed her hand. She studied his face as if seeing it for the first time. The warmth in her body spread and she smiled at him helplessly.

"You sure you're up for this, Kate? It's not too late to run screaming. We can go get pizza and drink some beers."

"Are you kidding me? I've been waiting for this for a long time."

"Wow, so this is your secret agenda. You've only been going out with me to get invited to my parent's house. I feel so...used."

Kate leaned into him and kissed him softly on the lips; what started out as a soft touch quickly became more. She could sink right into that kiss; bask in the warmth of his breath and skin—live there forever. Eventually they broke for air. "Hmmm," she murmured. "Maybe we should just go back to my place." She looked up into his eyes and saw her need reflected in his eyes. She chuckled throatily. "We have to stop this. They're probably all watching us from the window."

Colin laughed and opened the door and pushed himself out into the night. He strode around to her side, but before he got there, she opened her own door and stood. He grinned at her. "Someday I'm going to get to open your door for you." She took his hand and they started toward the front door. As they reached the porch and started up the wooden steps, her heart fluttered and she felt butterflies in her stomach.

"Okay, now I'm nervous," she said under her breath, and he squeezed her hand once.

"Don't be. They'll love you. Hell, they already love you, Kate. And when they meet you, they'll love you even more." They stopped in front of the door and he turned to look into her eyes, his expression suddenly serious, tender. "I never thought I'd be able to feel happy again, Kate." He stopped speaking and stared at her. She stared back and loved him with all her heart. The tiny ripple of apprehension she always felt at these moments was smaller. Giving herself so completely to another person was hard now, but now warmth and need finally drove it away.

Finally he broke the spell by leaning forward and kissing her on the forehead. "So, are you ready for this?"

"I'm ready. Are *you* ready?" She eyed him with mock suspicion and he chuckled.

"I'm ready."

"About time." She reached out and rang the doorbell.

Made in the USA
Lexington, KY
04 November 2013